For Stan

Order this book online at www.trafford.com
or email orders@trafford.com

Most Trafford titles are also available at major online book retailers.

Note for Librarians: A cataloguing record for this book is available from Library
and Archives Canada at www.collectionscanada.ca/amicus/index-e.html

Printed in Victoria, BC, Canada.

ISBN: 978-1-4251-9183-2 (sc)
ISBN: 978-1-4269-2040-0 (hc)

*Our mission is to efficiently provide the world's finest, most comprehensive book publishing
service, enabling every author to experience success. To find out how to publish your
book, your way, and have it available worldwide, visit us online at www.trafford.com*

Trafford rev. 10/07/09

 www.trafford.com

North America & international
toll-free: 1 888 232 4444 (USA & Canada)
phone: 250 383 6864 ♦ fax: 812 355 4082

Acknowledgements

I would like to thank the following people.

Jason Pitt for his help in editing the original manuscript and for his invaluable insights.

Michelle Pitt for her amazing photography and for taking the time to help me out.

Russ Egler, Talia Cronk and Arthur and Kaleigh Lewis for their contributions to the story.

The people at Trafford Publishing for their hard work and dedication.

My family for your patience and understanding.

And my favorite fantasy author Terry Goodkind who inspired me to tell the stories of my imagination.

Thank you all for your support and enthusiasm.

The Lost Empire Series

Avenger Rise
Phoenix Rise *

* forthcoming

Avenger Rise

C.J. Night

Part I
Hope Lost

'Hope is that which all others cling to when there is no longer anything they can do for themselves. It is what can see us through the night.

We are the hope of our people, we must stand strong to give them strength and stand against all that would harm them to give them courage.'

Creed of the Egyptian Defense Force.

Chapter One

Taymen Orelle walked through the deck ten corridor of the Dark Avenger and climbed up the ladder to deck eleven. He continued up the corridor towards the bow of the ship tugging on the bottom of his black uniform jacket straightening it out.

Taymen wore a black tee shirt and his black pants were trimmed in white matching the jacket. His straight brown hair was cut short so as to keep it off his ears and collar. His eyes were an icy blue and there was a small scar that ran diagonally across the bridge of his nose, a constant reminder of past battles before he was the Captain of the Dark Avenger.

On his right ear was a small wireless communications device that tied into the ship's main communications system as well as acted as a short range radio when he was away from the ship. The right shoulder of his jacket displayed the ship's crest in a diamond shaped patch and his collar displayed the rank of Major, a rank he wore for almost a year now.

About twenty meters from the ladder the corridor came to a pressure hatch that was marked 'C.A.C.' which stood for 'Command and Control'.

Taymen swiped the implant on the top of his right hand across the lens next to the door and the hatch unlocked allowing him to open it. As he stepped through he heard someone yell. "Captain on deck!"

Everyone in the room snapped to attention and waited.

"Carry on." Taymen said a second later.

He moved passed the operations stations and down the six steps to the lower level of C.A.C. where the command console was located.

The console itself was a large table with a touch screen top that displayed an image of the Dark Avenger amongst a series of navigation and ranging lines that allowed Taymen to see what heading the ship was on as well as the range and location of any other sensor contacts in the area.

Centered above the command console was a group of four flat screens that mounted around a central beam in the ceiling. Each screen displayed the same sensor data as the command console so that it could be seen from anywhere in the room.

Sitting at the head of C.A.C. were the ship's three helmsmen. They were under the command of the helm officer Lieutenant-Commander Aurin Bahll. Two of the helmsmen performed conventional maneuvers, one controlling the ship's main drive thrusters while the other controlled the maneuvering thrusters. The third helmsman was in control of the protostream systems and the power distribution for the entire drive unit.

Behind the helm station and to the left was the ship's weapons control station, where four non commissioned officers under the command of Lieutenant-Commander Carrey Tarma sat.

Mounted on the wall ahead of the helm station were three large display screens that could be used to display just about anything Taymen wanted. Normally one showed the same data as the command console, allowing the helmsman to maneuver more effectively. One displayed the ship's status and the other showed a three dimensional image of the ship's arcs of fire.

Behind the command console was the C.A.C. flight controllers where the ship's flight deck launches and landings were coordinated from. The two flight control officers in C.A.C. relayed Taymen's orders to the flight control officers on the two flight decks.

The main damage control station was to the right of the flight control station and the ship's main operations and communications consoles were in the corner across from the flight control station to the right of the main sensor station.

The ship's third officer Lieutenant-Commander Titus Daverro was in command of the ship's operations stations. He was a young but very capable officer. His curly dark hair was slightly longer than Taymen's, but he still managed to keep it off his ears and collar. His brown eyes remained fixed on an electronic data pad in his hands as he read over the communications logs from the night watch.

Titus served with Taymen before he was given command of the Dark Avenger. Taymen knew him well enough to know he didn't have to check up on Titus. If there was something of significance he'd let Taymen know.

Taymen placed his right hand on one of the interface lenses on the main sensor console and used his nano-device interface to access his command system.

The NDI provided any information he needed directly to a processor implanted at the base of his skull which allowed him to directly access and control ship's systems. It was a way of keeping people without the proper implant from accessing sensitive systems.

Taymen and his crew had spent the last two weeks patrolling the inner defensive line of the Netara colony where Princess Releena resided. It wasn't an exciting assignment but it was a nice change of pace after seven months of combat.

It had only been a month since the government and the separatists called a ceasefire. It didn't really mean the war was over but Taymen figured that both sides were tired of fighting each other. His ship was part of the Egyptian Imperial Guard, which was made up of the most experienced crews of the fleet.

The Imperial Guard was the Princess' personal defense fleet, she had direct control over them with the guidance of her Council of Generals and her safety was their primary responsibility during wartime. They were formed almost seventy years ago by the current Princess' predecessor during the Egyptian civil war.

During the course of the war they proved themselves to be a devastating attack force and were fully integrated into the Egyptian Defense Force as a reserve unit for the main fleet.

The Dark Avenger was commissioned only two years ago and Taymen was her second Captain.

He was the youngest commanding officer in the history of the entire fleet. He earned his position during a battle with a separatist attack force while he was still a lieutenant. It was shortly after he was transferred to the weapons officer position aboard a light cruiser. He was forced to take command of the ship after the captain had been injured by an exploding bulkhead and the executive officer was killed. Taymen took command of the ship and managed to delay the separatists from advancing to a defenseless colony long enough for reinforcements to arrive. Not long after that he was transferred to the Imperial Guard and given command of the Dark Avenger after his command course at the academy.

The ship wasn't the largest in the fleet by any means but it was certainly one of the toughest. It was an avenger class battle cruiser, not nearly the size of a destroyer or even a light cruiser.

There were only fifteen avenger battle cruisers in service throughout the fleet but the Dark Avenger was a specially modified version of the standard service model. Over the last year eight of the remaining fifteen cruisers including the Dark Avenger were overhauled and updated but the Dark Avenger was sent to a civilian contractor for an extensive set of upgrades which set it apart from the others. Nobody could really tell Taymen why.

"Sir."

Taymen looked up at Ensign Sairon sitting at the communications station. She was a skinny young woman who couldn't have weighed more than a hundred pounds. Her long brown hair was kept in a tight bun on the back of her head and her eyes were a very dark brown.

"We're receiving a transmission from Imperial Command, priority one." She reported.

"Forward it to the command system." Taymen replied.

A few seconds later the file was uploaded from the ship's communications log to the command system. When Taymen opened the file he immediately recognized it as a mission briefing. It looked like his crew may finally have something to do after all. As he looked over the briefing he noted the target destination and the staging point for the mission before he went into the mission details.

"Helm take us out of the system, all ahead full." Taymen ordered.

"Aye Sir." Aurin replied.

As Taymen read over the mission details he began to put together a preliminary plan, making minor adjustments as he learned more about the situation. It appeared that the separatists have been moving more and more ships into the outer belt, which was a dense asteroid field that surrounded the Egyptian home system of Abydos.

It was as good a location as any to put together a strike force since it was almost impossible for long range sensors to distinguish ships from asteroids, so there was no telling how many of them there were. Not to mention the obvious problem with sending a battle group into the belt after them. Larger ships wouldn't be able to maneuver making them easy targets for smaller more maneuverable ships.

Taymen's mission was to get in and find out how many ships they were dealing with, and if possible find out what they were planning so an effective blockade could be established.

In principle it was a fairly simple mission to execute. They would plot a stream that would land them inside of the belt so they could use it as cover like the separatists were. From there they would launch a group of prowler class scout ships into the belt to search for the separatist ships since sensor drones weren't really effective in asteroid fields or planetary systems. They were only meant to extend the ship's sensor range in open space.

"Titus." Taymen said. "Plot a stream to take us into the outer belt and upload it to the helm."

"Yes Sir." Titus replied as he moved to the navigation console and accessed the navigational computer.

A stream to the outer belt from their current location would only take him a few minutes to plot, however actually getting there would take about two and a half hours in real time.

The protostream was the only way they could travel long distances through space, but the technology was still a little alien to them. It was discovered nearly a hundred years ago almost completely by accident. Scientists found that an ancient network of hubs was placed in subspace throughout the galaxy by a race they've come to know simply as the ancients.

These hubs were designed to change matter into energy and transmit the energy to the next hub and then change it back at a specified point in space. The hardest part was getting the ship into subspace close enough to a hub to be picked up converted to energy. That was what the protostream generators were for.

They forced open the fabric of space around the ship exposing it to the hub, and just before the hub converted the ship and everything in it into energy, the generators transmitted the target coordinates to the hub which then transmitted everything to the next hub in the series, and so on and so forth until the ship arrived at the hub closest to the target coordinates, then the last hub converted them back into matter. Time passed normally for everyone else but everyone on the ship would experience an instantaneous transfer.

The only problem was that the ship could not travel in the protostream for more than eight hours or the subspace radiation would accumulate on the hull when they transited back into normal space killing everyone onboard. So they have to bleed off excess radiation between jumps. It wasn't really the best way to travel long distances, just the only way.

Taymen closed off the mission briefing file and disconnected from the command system.

"Ex O, with me." He said as he left C.A.C. with Captain Avril Raquel close behind.

The corridors of the ship were just over two meters wide and three meters high with steel support frames every six meters or so. Between each set of support frames were armored plates that were designed to withstand armor piercing bullets and grenade shrapnel in the event they were boarded. There were eight rectangular plates on each side of the section running horizontally, two plates wide and four high.

At the top corners of the corridor were a series of lights mounted behind white panels which illuminated every corner of the deck. All the doors throughout the outer sections of the ship were heavy pressure hatches designed to prevent decompression of adjacent sections in the event of a hull breach.

Taymen led Avril to a ladder at the aft end of the deck and climbed down to deck ten.

"I want you to brief all the prowler pilots on the mission briefing we just received." Taymen said.

Avril hooked a few strands of her long dark hair that had escaped her braid behind her ear.

"Aye Sir." She replied.

Her brown eyes remained fixed in front of her as they passed a few crewmen who saluted as they passed by. She was a small woman; only about five feet tall but she had an average build for someone of her height.

She was Taymen's second executive officer since he took command of the Dark Avenger, his first retired just a few weeks ago. It was Avril's first Ex O position and she found herself a little intimidated by Taymen.

The fact that he was almost seven years younger than she was didn't bother her, it was his command style. He expected discipline, professionalism and loyalty from his crew just as she did, but he put more trust in them than she would in his position. He rarely asked for section reports and almost never questioned his section commanders' policies.

Still, it was Taymen's ship to run as he saw fit and there never were any issues with the crew so Avril was content to keep her concerns to herself.

Sometimes Taymen wasn't sure what to make of Avril. She was an excellent executive officer from what he has seen so far, though he has never seen her in an actual combat situation her record spoke for itself.

She served on a number of cruisers and frigates in command of operations and tactical stations. She also had a number of commendations from her commanding officers and one from the Egyptian Military Council, which was rarely awarded to anyone but the CO of a ship or station, but despite all that she seemed a little cold.

"I'll meet you in the pilot's briefing room after I've spoken with the Chief." Taymen said.

Avril nodded before turning down the corridor that would take her to the briefing room.

Dark Avenger, Pilot's Briefing Room
15:52 Abydos Standard Time
Day 12, Second Cycle, Egyptian Year 3201

Everyone snapped to attention when Taymen entered the briefing room.

"At ease." He said as he moved to the podium at the head of the room.

Taymen hit a series of controls and brought up a map of the outer belt and the surrounding area.

"We don't have much time so I'll get right to it." He started. "Sensor stations have detected an increased number of separatist ships moving into the outer belt, and as of six hours ago none of them have come out. Imperial Command wants us to find out how many there are and what they're up to so an effective defense can be mounted." Taymen hit a few more controls which caused the image to zoom out and a red icon representing the Dark Avenger appeared on the screen.

"This is our staging area." He said. "From there we will stream into the outer belt and go into stealth mode." He zoomed the image back into the belt. "Given the density of the field we can't use sensor drones reliably, so it's up to all of you to scout the area."

"In a field this dense prowlers will be vulnerable." One of the pilots pointed out.

"And sending sword breakers out would leave the ship in a vulnerable position if we're discovered." Taymen added.

"Can't we just stream out of the field if we run into trouble?" Another pilot asked.

Taymen recognized the young pilot. He was fresh out of flight training and had only been onboard for a few weeks.

"To do that you would need to keep your stream generators charged as you searched the area. It would increase the chances of you being detected." Avril said.

"The deck crews will mount a rocket pod on each prowler and load it with chaff rockets since your decoy drones won't be of any use in the asteroids. If you run into trouble the rockets will buy you the time you need to charge your stream generator and escape." Taymen explained. "You launch in two hours, good luck."

As he began to move to the pressure hatch Avril called the room back to attention until Taymen was gone.

Chapter Two

Taymen stood at the command console watching the display on top. They had been in the outer belt for almost three hours now and have identified at least a dozen ships scattered throughout the area. They've intercepted a number of transmissions, some of which were encrypted but most of them were just general chatter over open com. channels.

From what they heard so far it didn't seem to be an attack force at all, most of the ships were transport vessels but there was still no telling what they were up to.

"Sir." Titus said from the operations station. "We're receiving a transmission."

"Source?" Taymen asked.

"We're not sure Sir but it's definitely coming from within the outer belt."

"One of our prowlers?" Avril asked.

"No I don't think so Ma'am."

"Put it on speakers." Taymen ordered.

"This is General Eazak of the Demon's Light calling the Egyptian battleship in the outer belt." A voice said over the speakers. *"We know you're out there Major Orelle so you may as well respond."*

Taymen remained silent. General Eazak was formerly a battle group commander in the Egyptian Defense Force, but during the last few months of the war he joined the separatists taking over twenty ships with him, to this day nobody really knows why.

"We have no quarrel with you Major but I think we should speak face to face." Eazak continued.

After a few moments Taymen finally gave in to his curiosity.

"Open a channel." He said as he tapped the control on his earpiece. "This is Major Orelle of the Egyptian battle ship Dark Avenger, what is it you want General?"

"Exactly what I said Major, to talk." Eazak replied. *"I'm transmitting rendezvous coordinates to you now; meet me there in thirty minutes, Eazak out."*

The line went silent and Sairon closed the channel.

"We're receiving the coordinates Sir." She reported.

"Prep one of our remaining prowlers and recall the recon teams." Taymen ordered.

"Do you want me to prep a fighter escort as well Sir?" Avril asked.

"No, I don't think we'll need them." Taymen replied.

The coordinates led to one of the larger asteroids in the outer belt. The Demon's Light was using it for cover. When they landed in the Demon's Light's hangar there was a small group of unarmed civilians waiting for Taymen. They led him to the ship's briefing room where an older man, General Eazak waited for him.

Taymen knew Eazak when he was in command of the Abydos Battle Group. He felt a little strange standing there in front of him again now on opposite sides of the table.

"I must say this is truly an honor." Eazak started. "You've done very well for yourself since we last met Taymen…"

Taymen cut him off.

"Why don't we dispense with the pleasantries and you tell me what you're doing here General."

"Still so direct I see." Eazak said with a smile. "As I told you Major we have no interest in fighting you, we're simply here to evacuate."

Taymen wasn't sure if he believed him or not.

"Evacuate? why?" He asked.

"Because this galaxy is doomed." Eazak started. "Are you aware of all the ships that have been disappearing recently, not far outside of the system?" He asked.

Taymen said nothing.

"Of course not, your superiors in the government are trying to cover it up." Eazak continued. "One of our ships detected an unknown vessel advancing through Egyptian space, unlike anything we've ever seen before. They witnessed a battle between these aliens and a Defense Force heavy cruiser. The cruiser was clearly more powerful, but shortly after it engaged the alien vessel three more streamed into the system. The cruiser was quickly destroyed."

Taymen's expression changed to show a little interest.

"Recently more and more of these ships have been detected deeper and deeper in Egyptian territory; nobody knows who they are or what they want." Eazak explained.

Taymen was starting to understand why the separatists were running. If what Eazak said was true, then they were all in a lot of trouble. Neither the separatists nor the Egyptians were in any position to mount a major defensive on their own; they'd surely be outnumbered and outflanked with little hope for victory.

"In any case we feel that it's only a matter of time before you find yourselves dealing with a full scale invasion force." Eazak continued.

"So like rats on a ship you're simply going to run at the first sign of trouble." Taymen said.

"We've seen what these ships are capable of we'd be no match for their superior numbers." Eazak said in his defense. There was a long silence before he spoke again.

"We have sixty eight ships in the outer belt; we will be departing here within the next twenty-seven hours so you can tell your superiors they have nothing to worry about from us."

Suddenly there was a knock at the door and one of the pilots from the prowler walked in.

"Sir, we're receiving a message from the Dark Avenger requesting our immediate return."

"What's wrong?" Taymen asked, his eyes remaining fixed on Eazak.

"They say Abydos is under attack, all ships are ordered to return immediately." The pilot explained.

"It's already begun." Eazak said calmly.

"Prep for launch, we're leaving." Taymen ordered.

The pilot nodded and headed off to ready the prowler.

"You want my advice Major, get your princess and leave the system, get as far away as you can and don't look back." Eazak said.

Taymen shook his head.

"Victory isn't assured by numbers alone." He said.

Dark Avenger, C.A.C.
21:32 Abydos Standard Time
Day 12, Second Cycle, Egyptian Year 3201

"Report." Taymen said as he entered C.A.C.

"All stations report battle ready Sir." Avril reported.

"All sword breakers are ready for launch." One of the flight controllers said.

"We're ready to stream out." Aurin reported from the helm station.

"Last reports indicate over four hundred alien ships in the Abydos system." Avril reported as she handed Taymen a small data pad.

Taymen briefly read through the transmission.

"Helm, reset your course for Netara." He said.

Everyone in C.A.C. suddenly stopped what they were doing for a moment.

Abydos was the home system of the Egyptian Empire, its defense was paramount. If Taymen was refusing to commit the Dark Avenger to Abydos' defense, it could be considered treason.

Avril moved closer to Taymen and spoke just loud enough for him to hear her.

"Sir Abydos is under attack, we're needed there to defend the system." She said.

"If Abydos is requesting our help then it means they are well into a losing battle and this ship won't make much of a difference." Taymen started.

"Our primary concern is Princess Releena and she is on Netara. If we can get there first, we can evacuate her before our attackers advance through the system."

"But Sir, our orders..." Taymen cut her off.

"These orders are from the military council and mean very little to us, we report to Imperial Command, if the council doesn't like it they can take it up with Command but in the mean time we have a job to do."

"Sir..." Avril tried to object, but Taymen cut her off again.

"In addition Captain." He snapped. "On this ship you follow my orders and my orders are we stream to Netara, any problems you have with that you can take up with Imperial Command as well, understood?"

Avril straightened a little trying to hide her embarrassment.

"Understood Sir." She said quietly.

"Sir, course to Netara is plotted." Titus reported.

"Helm, stream us to Netara." Taymen ordered.

"Aye Sir." Aurin replied just before he ordered the protostream officer to begin to power up the ship's protostream generators.

After thirty seconds or so one of the helm consoles showed the protostream generators were powered up and ready to go. Titus transferred the stream coordinates from the navigational computer to the protostream control system and prepared to make the jump.

"Ready to stream in fifteen seconds Sir." The protostream officer reported.

Taymen accessed the ship's internal com. system through his earpiece.

"All hands prepare to stream out."

His voice echoed through the ship advising the crew they were about to transit out of normal space. If Taymen didn't announce it first, most of them wouldn't even notice the transit.

With five seconds remaining, the stream officer began to count down.

"Streaming in Five…four…three…two…one."

Taymen felt a slight tingling sensation throughout his body which lasted for only a second or so before it faded. Then there was a brief moment of darkness as if someone had turned off all the lights and then quickly turned them back on again before his head felt clouded for a moment. When his head cleared Taymen heard Titus report from the navigation station.

"Stream complete Sir, we've reached Netara."

"Any sign of unknown vessels in the system?" Avril asked.

There was a moment of silence as Titus checked the sensor display just above the navigation station.

"Nothing in sensor range." He reported.

"Aurin put us in a synchronous orbit with the Princess' residence." Taymen ordered.

"Sir." Sairon started. "We're receiving a transmission from the Daemon's Sun, General Bail is requesting a closed circuit with Dark Avenger Lead."

The request meant that the CO of the Daemon's Sun wanted to speak with the CO of the Dark Avenger on a private com. channel.

The Daemon's Sun was the Imperial Guard's flagship, so any orders from her CO usually came from Imperial Command.

"Patch her through." Taymen said as he tapped the button on his earpiece allowing Sairon to forward the signal.

"This is Dark Avenger Lead." Taymen said.

"This is Daemon's Sun Lead." A woman's voice replied. "Evacuation of Princess Releena is underway, her transport will be taking off within the next few minutes."

"Understood." Taymen said.

"We lost contact with Abydos almost an hour ago, Command has sent over half the battle group to re-enforce them but we haven't heard from them either." Bail continued.

Taymen remained silent.

"Taymen." She said. "Last reports indicted over twelve hundred enemy ships in the Abydos system alone. We have only seventy two ships in Netara and my ship is the only heavy cruiser, if they advance here…" She trailed off.

"I understand." Taymen replied before he tapped the button on his earpiece again to close the channel.

"Sir the Princess' ship has just cleared the atmosphere and we're receiving a transmission from the Daemon's Sun to stream to evacuation point alpha." Sairon reported a few minutes later.

"Very well, Titus plot a stream to the evacuation point." Taymen said.

"Sir, reading multiple sensor contacts entering the system." Avril reported.

Taymen looked at the main display.

"Identify." He ordered.

"Unknown, they're firing, missiles targeting the Princess' ship and the Daemon's Sun." Avril replied.

"Deploy armor! Helm move us between those missiles and the Princess!" Taymen snapped.

Within seconds the hull of the Dark Avenger was covered with a super dense resin that was held in place by a powerful electro-static field. The resin acted as a thick layer of armor that could absorb and disperse massive amounts of thermal and kinetic energy.

As the ship moved to intercept the incoming missiles three of them struck the Dark Avenger on her upper port side. Four more struck the Princess' ship while another eight struck the Daemon's Sun.

"Sir all ships are being ordered to cover the Princess." Sairon said.

As Taymen looked at the main display he could see the rest of the battle group was already moving to engage the enemy fleet.

"Launch six electronic countermeasure drones around the Princess' ship." Taymen ordered.

The drones would generate a group of false electronic signatures that would confuse the enemy's sensors making it more difficult for their missiles to lock onto the ship.

"Drones away Sir." The missile officer reported.

"Sir we're receiving a transmission from the Daemon's Sun." Titus said.

"On speakers."

The C.A.C. speakers crackled with static for a second before the General's voice broke through.

"Taymen." She shouted over the background noise. *"The Princess' ship has taken damage, they can't stream out of the system. We're evacuating her crew to the Daemon's Sun but it's going to be another ten minutes, I need you to stay in close proximity to us and form a defensive line with the Phoenix Flame to buy us some time. I'm sending the rest of the group to engage at close range."*

"Understood." Taymen replied before the channel closed.

"Helm move us out five light seconds from the Daemon's Sun and maneuver our port side to face the enemy fleet."

"Aye Sir." Aurin replied.

"Titus." Taymen said.

"Course to the evacuation point plotted Sir." Titus reported.

"Very well." Taymen replied. "Helm charge the protostream generators and prepare to stream us out as soon as the Daemon's Sun is clear."

"Aye Sir."

"Sir." Titus started.

"A group of enemy fighters has broken off from the main group and is making a run for the Daemon's Sun."

Taymen turned to the flight control station. "Launch sword breakers to intercept." He said.

"Sir another enemy ship just streamed into the system, it's launching fighters." Avril reported.

"What kind of ship?" Taymen asked.

"Looks like some sort of heavy cruiser Sir." Titus replied.

"Should we order the sword breakers to engage?" Avril asked.

"No have them engage the enemy fighters, we'll handle the cruiser." Taymen said.

"Carrey." Taymen started.

"Arm all valkerie cannons, order all port side cannons to target that cruiser's fighter bays with plasma rounds."

"Aye Sir." Carrey replied.

The Dark Avenger had sixteen turret mounted valkerie rail cannons along its hull capable of firing a variety of eighty-five millimeter shells. The master arm control for the cannons was in C.A.C. at the weapons control station, but each cannon was directly controlled from the remote fire stations throughout the ship.

A few seconds later the port side valkerie cannons opened fire, launching eighty-five millimeter plasma rounds at the enemy cruiser.

Each glowing blue round housed highly charged plasma that was released on impact burning through the target.

"Sir the enemy cruiser has painted the Daemon's Sun and is launching missiles." Titus reported.

"Move us in to intercept."

"It's too late Sir, the missiles are too far out and we're out of range for countermeasures."

Before Taymen could react the enemy missiles detonated against the hull of the Daemon's Sun.

"Port side missile tubes ready a salvo of saber anti-ship missiles and target the cruiser." Taymen ordered.

The saber missiles were used for short range engagements. They were fast and maneuverable with an artificial intelligence comparable to a drone which allowed them to avoid enemy countermeasures and seek out the most vulnerable points on a target.

"Missiles ready Sir." The missile officer replied.

"Fire!" Taymen snapped.

Each of the six missile tubes on the ship's port side launched a ninety millimeter saber missile at the enemy cruiser. A few seconds later they detonated against its hull tearing through the armor to the interior of the ship.

"We're receiving a message from the Daemon's Sun." Sairon reported. "Message reads… minor damage….evacuation complete…streaming to…. evacuation point alpha."

Taymen glanced at the main display.

"Continue firing, recall all but the alert fighters." Taymen said. "Send a confirmation signal to the Daemon's Sun."

Avril moved to the flight control console and made sure the alert fighter wing was ordered to continue to engage the enemy.

A few minutes after the order was given, the Daemon's Sun along with over half of the remaining ships had streamed out of the system.

"Sir the enemy ship has launched a missile, it's locked onto the Avenger." Titus said.

"Just one?" Taymen asked.

"Yes Sir." Titus replied.

Suddenly an alarm at the operations station went off.

"Radiological alert!" Sairon snapped. "Nuclear missile inbound, impact in twenty-five seconds." She said.

"Alert fighters combat landing now, helm stream us out as soon as their aboard!" Taymen ordered.

As soon as the remaining sword breakers received the landing order they accelerated towards the Dark Avenger at speeds that would kill a pilot, which was why they were unmanned drones.

Sword breakers were small and extremely maneuverable, no pilot would be able to withstand the forces they would be subjected to.

It would take the last sword breaker fifteen seconds at full throttle to land which only left them five seconds to safely stream out of the system. The first sword breakers hit the landing deck hard and skidded to a halt near the far end of the deck.

"Three sword breakers left Sir, fifteen seconds to missile impact." Sairon reported.

Taymen waited silently as he watched a timer on the main display. Avril stood at the command console next to Titus while everyone else remained at their posts nervously waiting for the order to stream out.

"One sword breaker remaining, landing in seven seconds."

Taymen watched nervously as the missile closed in on them.

"Last fighter's aboard Sir." Sairon said.

"Helm now!" Taymen snapped.

The helmsman engaged the protostream generator almost instantly and just as the generators engaged the missile detonated where the Dark Avenger had been only a half second ago.

Chapter Three

Taymen leaned over the command console as he tried to shake off the dizziness. He had completed hundreds of streams before and never felt like this. It was a strange sensation, as if he had been hit over the head with a steel pipe. He took a brief look around C.A.C. and noticed that most of the crew looked like they felt the same way as he did.

"We've streamed out of Netara Sir but we are not where we're supposed to be." Titus reported.

"Where are we?" Avril asked.

"It'll take some time to plot the coordinates." Titus replied.

"Get on it Commander." Taymen said.

"Damage report." Avril said.

"Minor damage to the armor plating, the lateral auxiliary heat exchanger has taken heavy damage, phase transition generator two is starting to overheat." The damage control officer said.

"Shut down PT generator two and retract the armor." Taymen ordered. "Switch the effected systems to back-up power supplies."

The ship's two phase transition generators used a microscopic singularity to provided power to all of the ship's systems. If one of them went off line almost half the ship's systems went with it so each system had its own independent power supply as a back-up, however the back-ups weren't nearly as efficient as the PT generators.

"What's the status of our fighters?" Taymen asked.

"We lost four sword breakers Sir, all the remaining fighters are safely aboard." One of the flight controllers answered.

Taymen sighed.

"Sir." Titus said.

"What is it?" Taymen asked.

"I can't plot our location." Titus replied.

"What?" Avril asked.

Titus hesitated for a moment.

"Our navigational sensors can't get a fix on our position with the local constellations, and they can't seem to detect any navigational markers." He

19

explained.

If they were too far out for the sensors to detect any navigation points and they couldn't identify any local constellations, then they were very far from home.

"Ship's clock also indicates that we streamed away from Netara four days ago." Sairon added.

"How is that possible?" Avril asked.

"It's not." Taymen replied. "Not for this ship under its own power."

"What if that missile had something to do with it?" Titus started. "If the warhead detonated as we were transiting the energy from the explosion could have overloaded the protostream hub. It could have caused it to send us much farther than it normally would."

"You can't be sure of that Commander." Avril snapped.

"And we can't be sure he's wrong either." Taymen said. "The fact of the matter is that weather he's right or wrong it doesn't really matter at this point. We need to figure out where we are first, then we'll figure out how we got here and how to get back."

Taymen took a moment as he considered the situation. Somehow the ship managed to stay in the protostream for four days without the lethal effects of the radiation. They were lost and alone and their people were under attack.

"Launch a wing of prowlers to scout the system, see if they can find any sign of life, hostile or otherwise." He ordered. "Titus, get down to the astronomy lab and see if they can get a fix on our position with the extreme range telescopes. Avril, have damage control teams begin repairs immediately and put all available sword breakers on standby, I have a feeling we haven't seen the last of our attackers."

Dark Avenger, Starboard Hangar Deck
17:50 Abydos Standard Time
Day 16, Second Cycle, Egyptian Year 3201

Taymen made his way down the ladder from the catwalk to the main level of the hangar deck and took a brief look around at the deck crews as they went on with their work. Everyone was doing something. Most were repairing the sword breakers that had been damaged in the last battle. Some were rearming the ones that were already repaired while a few others were preparing the prowlers for launch.

"Sir." The deck Chief said as she approached Taymen from one of the sword breakers.

"Chief." Taymen replied. "How are we doing?" He asked.

Kaile sighed as she pulled a small ribbon from her pocket and tied her brown hair into a ponytail.

"Prowlers will be ready to launch in an hour, three sword breakers are down until I can get parts and two more will be ready in a few hours. The rest are being fueled and armed now, they'll be ready in half an hour or so." She said.

"Why so long for the prowlers?" Taymen asked.

"We're still reconfiguring them for long range surveying." Kaile replied. "We stripped them down for the scouting mission in the outer belt so we had to reinstall all the long range sensor equipment and drones."

Taymen nodded.

"I'm afraid you're out of luck with those parts for a while Chief." He started. "Do what you can, cannibalize one of the downed sword breakers if you have to." He said.

Kaile nodded.

"Aye Sir." She said before turning back to her crew.

Taymen turned and made his way down the hangar deck towards the heavy pressure doors at the far end. It had been a while since he visited the hangar. He used to make his way down every now and then to see how the deck crews were doing. He liked talking with his crew and not just about work. He felt like he had gotten fairly close with some of them and they seemed to enjoy him coming down to talk for a while.

Taymen looked around at all the sword breakers tucked away in their bays on either side of the deck. The arming crews past by with carts loaded with light missiles and depleted uranium rounds.

'Sir." One of them said to Taymen as he passed by.

Taymen nodded in greeting as he carried on down the deck. He passed by the alert fighters which were lined up just outside of the launch bays ready to go at a moments' notice. If the order to launch came down, all the deck crews would have to do is arm the weapon systems, prime the thrusters and push them into the bays. The launch controller would signal the sword breaker to launch and the artificial intelligence of the drone would take over.

As he reached the heavy pressure doors at the end of the hangar, he took a quick look at the three prowlers sitting side by side waiting to be towed into the airlock and onto one of the lift pads so they could be taken up to the landing deck for launch since they were too big to fit into the launch bays.

"Did you need something Sir?" One of the deck crewmen asked.

"No." Taymen replied. "Just having a look around." He explained.

The crewman nodded and went on with his work.

Taymen looked over the outer hull of the light scout ship. It was similar in design to the Avenger itself, just much smaller and a little bulkier in proportion.

The prowlers could be configured for a wide range of missions, from combat to cargo transportation. Right now they were set up for long range space surveying. There were long range sensor pods mounted on the outer hull and a drone compartment installed on the underside that carried three small sensor drones.

"Excuse me Sir." A voice said.

Taymen turned around to see two pilots standing in front of him.

"Ready to go?" Taymen asked.

"Yes Sir." One of the pilots replied.

"Just need to start our preflight Sir." The other said.

"Of course." Taymen said as he backed away from the hatch on the side of the prowler.

"You're clear on you mission?" He asked.

"Yes Sir." One of the pilots replied.

"Not to worry Sir." The other started. "I'm sure we'll find something out there."

Taymen nodded.

"I'm sure you will." He said. "What you'll find is what worries me."

Cairo Satellite Control Station
22:28 Abydos Standard Time
Day 16, Second Cycle, Egyptian Year 3201

Elisha watched her monitor intently for a moment. She could have sworn she saw something appear in orbit for a second, but when she checked for a communications signal there was nothing.

She went into the data log and accessed the file to see if she could find the object in the system's memory file. It took her a moment and she almost missed it the second time around. It was a very small metallic signature that showed up in an extremely high orbit for about a half a second before it was gone again.

Elisha stood up so that she could look over her monitor at the older man sitting across from her with his feet up.

"Hey Frank." She said.

"Yeah." Frank groaned.

"Did your satellite register anything unusual around 13:17?" She asked.

Frank sighed as he accessed the data log from his satellite.

"What the hell?" He said as he put his feet down and leaned forward in his seat.

"What is it?" Elisha asked.

"There was a massive energy spike at 13:16." He explained. "The readings are off the charts. Protons, electrons, neutrons and some kind of radiation that isn't even on record." He continued.

"What does that mean?" Elisha asked.

"I don't know." Frank replied. "But whatever it is there was another one at 13:21. What time is it now?" He said.

"13:23." Elisha replied.

"Well it's gone now whatever it is." Frank said.

"So what do we do now?" Elisha asked.

Frank sighed.

"I'll email the program coordinator and see what he wants us to do, for now just keep quiet about it."

Dark Avenger, C.A.C.
26:45 Abydos Standard Time
Day 16, Second Cycle, Egyptian Year 3201

Titus moved up beside Avril who was standing at the command console.

"Ma'am." He said as he handed her a small data pad with one of the prowler's flight reports.

"The last prowler has just returned from its patrol, they report finding an inhabited system with an artificial satellite network around one of the planets."

Taymen moved closer to Avril to check the report.

"What kind of network?" He asked.

"We're not sure Sir, but the prowler crew reports that some of them look like they could be used for deep space observation." Titus replied.

"Any sign of aggression from the inhabitants?" Avril asked.

"None, but the report did indicate that the system's inhabitants showed no signs of advanced space fairing technology. The satellites didn't appear to detect the prowler, so it's possible that their sensors can't see through our stealth technology."

Taymen sighed. If the satellites were for deep space observation they may be able to see further than the deep space telescopes on the Avenger. On the other hand, if they couldn't detect their ship then how advanced could they be. Still it was worth a look.

"Plot a stream to the outer reaches of the system and put the ship into stealth mode." Taymen ordered.

"Aye Sir." Titus replied.

He began to move to the navigation station but paused for a moment.

"Sir." He started. "I should point out that without knowing the gravity fields from any of the singularities and stars in this galaxy, plotting a stream could be a little more risky than usual."

"Understood Commander." Taymen replied. "Stream us there as soon as you have the course."

Taymen checked the main display briefly. He knew Titus was right, if they didn't know the location of the gravity fields and anomalies in the area, they risked plotting a stream that would land them in the middle of a star or a black hole.

"I have it Sir." Titus said a few minutes later.

"That was fast." Avril said.

"I used the prowlers last stream coordinates to calculate our course. It should put us roughly in the same area the prowler streamed into. I just had to compensate for the mass difference."

"Nice work." Taymen said. "Aurin, take us out."

"Aye Sir." Aurin replied. "Stream system charging."

"Stream complete Sir." Aurin reported a few minutes later.

"Bring the ship to stealth mode Commander." Taymen said.

Titus tapped the button on his earpiece and accessed the internal com. system.

"All hands set the ship to stealth mode." He said.

"Any sign that we've been detected?" Avril asked.

"No Ma'am." Sairon replied.

"All stations report stealth mode Sir." Titus reported.

"I have a fix on the third planet of the system Sir." Aurin said.

"All ahead full, put us into a high orbit." Avril ordered.

"All ahead full, Aye." Aurin replied.

"Commander prepare a landing party to scout the planet for anything we can use to help expedite repairs but tell them to do it discreetly, I don't want the locals to know they're there." Taymen said.

"Yes Sir." Titus said.

"Time till we reach the planet?" Avril asked.

"Two hours, eighteen minutes." The helmsman said.

"Sairon." Taymen started. "Begin monitoring all communications in the system, get us an idea of what we're dealing with." Sairon nodded as she accessed the external com. receiver.

By the time they had arrived in orbit around the third planet, Sairon had monitored hours of communications from across the planet. There were no indications that the planet's inhabitants detected the Dark Avenger but they seemed to be divided into several factions.

There were several different languages, one of which was similar to their own with a few differences in certain expressions and some of the more common words.

"Prowlers away Sir, they're beginning their approach to the planet." Avril said.

"Sensor contact!" Titus said as he moved to the main sensor station.

"Identify." Avril ordered.

"Six enemy fighters on an intercept course." Titus said.

"Launch the alert fighters!" Taymen ordered. "Bring the ship to battle mode."

"Signal the prowlers, advise them that an enemy attack force is on route to the planet." Avril ordered.

"Yes Ma'am." Sairon said.

"Alert fighters away." One of the flight controllers said.

"They'll be in weapons' range in two minutes." Titus reported.

Avril accessed the internal com. system. "All hands bring the ship to battle mode." She said.

Taymen checked the main display. On the right side the display showed six red x's which indicated the enemy fighters. Under each was a target designation ranging from target one to target six. Advancing towards the enemy fighters was a group of ten blue x's representing the alert fighters, each sword breaker was identified by their serial numbers.

Suddenly the enemy fighters disappeared from the display.

"Sir the enemy fighters have streamed out." Titus reported.

"How do ships that small have protostream capability?" Avril snapped.

"It doesn't matter." Taymen said. "They've escaped, now it's only a matter of time before they return in full force."

"What are your orders Sir?" Titus asked.

"Continue with the operation planet side for now." Taymen said. "Get down to the astronomy lab and see if they can tap into one of those satellites remotely."

"Yes Sir." Titus replied.

"Sairon keep monitoring all communications throughout the system, I want to know the second someone shows up."

"Aye Sir." Sairon said.

"Aurin move us into a low orbit on the night side of the planet, keep us hidden for as long as you can."

"Aye Sir adjusting course." Aurin replied.

Taymen activated the internal com. channel.

"All hands stand down from battle mode, continue stealth mode operations." His voice echoed throughout the ship.

Almost four hours had passed since the enemy fighters had streamed out of the system, and there was no sign of any other enemy ships in the area. Taymen hadn't slept since they began the operation in the outer belt and his body was starting to remind him of how tired he was. The astronomers were still trying to plot their position and the first of the prowlers were beginning to return from their scouting missions. So far, they hadn't found anything.

"Sir." Avril said. "Chief Assurman reports all but three sword breakers are ready to go, but she had to cannibalize parts from those three so they'll take a few days to repair assuming she can rebuild the parts."

Taymen sighed. "Nice work, tell the Chief to do what it takes."

Avril nodded.

"Sir." Sairon said. "The master at arms is requesting you meet him in the brig."

"Did he say why?" Taymen asked.

"No Sir, he just said it was urgent." Sairon replied.

"Tell him I'm on my way."

"Yes Sir."

Taymen left C.A.C. and turned down the corridor towards the ladder that would take him down to deck four. He made his way to the aft end of the deck to the brig where Sergeant Geraan met him.

"Sir." Geraan said with a salute.

"What was so urgent Sergeant?" Taymen asked as he returned the salute.

"We have a situation Sir." Geraan replied as he gestured to one of the holding cells.

"What in the name of Anubis is this?" Taymen said.

Standing inside the cell were a young man and woman in civilian clothing. Neither one of them looked to be any older than twenty-five and both were clearly frightened.

The man was about as tall as Taymen but with a slimmer build. His blue eyes remained fixed on Taymen as though he were waiting for him to do something.

The girl's blue eyes were bloodshot and slightly swollen underneath. Several strands of her dirty blonde hair had come out of her ponytail and stuck to the tears that had run down her face. She was a fairly small girl, almost a full twelve inches shorter than Taymen but her build was average for her height.

"Lieutenant Paullin ordered them to be brought back Sir." Geraan replied.

"And where is the Lieutenant?" Taymen asked.

26

"I'm not sure Sir." Geraan said.

Taymen sighed as he tapped the control on his earpiece which put him through to Sairon in C.A.C.

"Sairon." He started. "Have the marines that just returned from the planet report to the briefing room immediately and ask Captain Mentz to join them."

"Right away Sir." Sairon replied before closing the channel.

Taymen had no idea what he was going to do with two civilians. He couldn't just let them go now, not after all they've seen and it didn't feel right to just leave them locked up.

"Open the door Sergeant." Taymen said.

"Sir?" Geraan said in confusion.

"You heard me, let them out."

Geraan used his implant and accessed the brig's security system to unlock the door.

"It's alright, you won't be harmed" Taymen said as he entered the cell.

"Who are you people?" The man asked.

"My name is Taymen."

"Where are we?" The woman asked quietly.

"You're aboard the battle ship Dark Avenger, I'm sorry that you were brought here but I'm afraid you're going to have to stay with us for awhile."

"Why, we didn't do anything?" The man asked.

"We can't risk being discovered by your people." Taymen replied.

"Our people?" The woman asked.

"Please, if you'll just come with me I promise that when we're ready to leave you'll be returned to the surface." Taymen said avoiding her question.

"What's your name?" He asked the young woman.

She looked at her companion briefly who simply stood silent.

"Elisha." She said in an unsteady voice.

"And you?" Taymen asked turning to the man.

"Russ." He replied quietly.

"Welcome aboard." Taymen said softly.

He led the two out of the brig and into the corridor. It took them a few minutes but they finally decided to trust Taymen, or at least to go with him.

"You must be tired from everything that's happened." Taymen started. "I'll have some quarters prepared for you, in the mean time I'd like you to stay with me for a little while."

Taymen continued down the corridor to the ladder near the aft end of the deck and climbed up two decks. By now Captain Mentz and his men should be waiting for him in the briefing room.

"Where are we going?" Elisha asked quietly.

Russ simply shrugged his shoulders.

"We're going to find out why you were brought here in the first place." Taymen replied.

He finally stopped at a pressure hatch and used his implant to unlock it. He opened the door allowing the two to step inside before stepping through himself.

"Sir." A man said as he snapped to attention.

"At ease Captain." Taymen said as he closed the hatch and directed Russ and Elisha to a couple of empty seats near the head of the long table in the center of the room.

"Now then." Taymen started as he sat down at the head of the table.

"Captain have you been made aware of this situation?" He asked.

"Yes Sir." Mentz replied. His fury was clearly indicated in his tone.

"I apologize Sir, I've already assigned extra duties to those responsible." He continued.

"I assume there was a good reason as to why two alien civilians were brought aboard my ship." Taymen said.

"Yes Sir." The team leader replied.

Taymen shifted in his seat as he gazed at the young officer to his right.

"Go ahead Lieutenant." He said.

"Well Sir, we had just finished our recon of what we thought was a satellite control station." The Lieutenant started. "We were heading back for the prowler when we were engaged by a local security force."

"You were engaged?" Taymen asked.

"They opened fire on them Sir." Mentz clarified.

"I see, go on." Taymen said.

"We pulled back laying down covering fire, I ordered my team to aim well above their heads to avoid casualties while we were falling back."

"Well you made a good decision there." Taymen commented.

"The last of our team was heading for the prowler when they bumped into these two." The Lieutenant continued.

"Bumped." Russ said. "They plowed through the both of us!" He snapped.

"Lieutenant." Taymen said, urging him to carry on.

"Yes Sir, they were running full out when they ran into them, they all hit the ground."

Taymen simply nodded as he continued to listen.

"A few of us ran out of the prowler to help them. When I realized what had just happened I ordered my team to grab the civilians and bring them along."

Mentz looked at Taymen, waiting for some sort of response.

"You ordered them to bring the civilians along?" Taymen repeated.

"Yes Sir." The Lieutenant replied. "It was a snap decision Sir, there was weapons fire directed at us and we had just been compromised, I didn't want my men getting hurt and I didn't want to cause any civilian casualties so I chose the lesser of two evils and got them out of harms' way."

Taymen thought it over for a moment. He understood the Lieutenant's reasoning for what he did. In fact Taymen probably would have done the same thing in his position.

The Lieutenant watched silently his expression showed his anxiety as Taymen sat pondering.

"Very well Lieutenant, you and your team are dismissed." He finally said.

"Yes Sir." The Lieutenant replied as he stood up and left the room with the rest of his team.

Taymen waited for the hatch to seal before turning to Captain Mentz.

"What do you think?" He asked with a sigh.

Mentz simply shook his head.

"I may have done the same thing in his place." He replied.

Taymen nodded.

"Me too." He said.

"Alright, I want all teams to return from the surface immediately for the time being." He said.

"Yes Sir." Mentz replied before leaving the room.

Taymen turned to Russ and Elisha.

"Well." He said. "I guess that just leaves the matter of what to do with you now."

Elisha turned to Russ who shifted in his seat a little.

"What do you mean?" He asked. "You said we'd be returned to the surface."

"I said you'd be returned to the surface when we are ready to leave, unfortunately that doesn't address the issue of what to do with you in the mean time." Taymen said.

He sat silent for a moment as he thought the situation over. He really had no reason to leave them in the brig and since he had no idea how long it would be before they could leave, it really wasn't a preferable option.

"I'm inclined for the time being to give you free access to the ship, but there are of course some limitations." Taymen started.

"Like what?" Elisha asked.

"For starters, weapons lockers and ranges would obviously be off limits as well as engineering sections and any areas containing sensitive information or systems." Taymen replied.

"Alright." Russ said hesitantly.

"You'll be allowed on the hangar deck only with escorts and C.A.C. only with my direct permission." Taymen added. "I'll assign a security detail to each of you to ensure you don't get lost and accidentally wander into an area that's restricted."

Elisha turned to Russ who kept his gaze on Taymen.

"Fine." He said.

"Good." Taymen replied as he stood up.

"Wait." Elisha started.

Taymen paused a moment.

"So you're just going to leave us with our escorts and send us on our way?" She asked.

"What else would you have me do?" Taymen asked.

"Well we have questions." Russ said.

"We want to know what's going on, who you people are and what you're doing here." Elisha added.

Taymen sighed.

"I guess you do deserve to know." He started.

Suddenly the room was filled with the harsh buzz of the internal com. system.

"All hands bring the ship to battle mode, Major Orelle to C.A.C." Avril's voice echoed throughout the ship.

"Come with me." Taymen said as he made his way to the hatch.

He led them through the corridors and up a few decks to C.A.C. He opened the hatch and let Elisha and Russ through before stepping through himself.

"Report." He said.

"Sensor contact, twelve enemy fighters are inbound." Titus reported.

"Launch the alert fighters." Taymen ordered.

Avril moved closer to Taymen as he stood at the command console.

"Sir?" She asked glancing at Russ and Elisha.

"One of our teams picked them up from the planet, I'm afraid they're stuck with us for a while."

Avril didn't say anything.

"Sir the enemy fighters are retreating." Titus reported.

"Sword breakers are requesting permission to pursue Sir." One of the flight controllers reported.

"Negative recall the fighters." Taymen ordered.

"Sir they have our position." Avril said.

"Something's not right." Taymen said. "They already had our position, why only send a dozen fighters?"

30

"Sir." Titus started. "The enemy fighters have turned around to pursue our sword breakers."

"Order our fighters to establish a perimeter two light seconds out, do not pursue past that mark." He ordered.

"Sensor contact, enemy light cruiser on an intercept course from the night side of the planet." Titus said.

"Here we go." Taymen said.

"Launch the remaining fighters." Avril ordered.

"They're baiting us." Taymen said.

"Sir?" Titus asked.

"The fighters were meant to draw our sword breakers away to leave us vulnerable." He said.

"They had to know we'd have more fighters in reserve." Avril said.

"That's what the cruiser's for. They're trying to force us to spread out our defenses."

"So what do we do, at this rate we'll be outnumbered in no time." Avril said.

"Which is why we spring their trap." Taymen replied. "Order the alert fighters to pursue and destroy the enemy fighters."

"Third sensor contact Sir, it's another light cruiser." Titus reported.

"Order the remaining sword breakers to engage the second cruiser, have all valkerie cannons target the first cruiser and fire at will, batteries four through eight lay down enemy suppression fire." Taymen ordered.

"Incoming ordnance!" Titus shouted.

"Deploy Armor!" Avril snapped.

Taymen quickly turned to Russ and Elisha who were standing near then end of the command console.

"Brace yourselves." He said.

Less than a second later the ship shuttered as two missiles impacted the outer hull.

"Fighters will be in weapons range in forty seconds." Titus reported.

"Launch a salvo of saber missiles at the second cruiser." Taymen said.

"Missiles away Sir." Carrey reported a few seconds later.

"Cruiser one has taken heavy damage, they've stopped firing." Titus reported.

"Launch a pair of javelins at cruiser one and shift valkerie cannons to cruiser two." Taymen ordered. "Batteries one through three switch to suppression fire."

A second later two javelin medium anti-ship missiles erupted out of two of the Avenger's starboard missile tubes and sped towards the disabled cruiser.

The javelins had the same intelligence as the saber missiles but with a higher explosive yield and a slightly longer range.

The two missiles flew parallel to each other as they approached their target splitting apart at the last second. The first missile circled around the port side of the cruiser and detonated against what it identified as a reactor vent while the other moved around the starboard side to the aft section hitting the main thruster assembly. Both hits caused a group of secondary explosions inside the cruiser that tore it apart.

"Cruiser one is down." Titus reported.

"Sensor contact, enemy heavy cruiser at extreme range." Avril said.

Taymen sighed as he glanced over to Russ and Elisha. He could see the panic in their eyes.

"Sir cruiser two just streamed out." Titus said.

"Order all gun stations to hold fire and have our sword breakers re-establish their perimeter." Taymen ordered.

"Another wave of enemy fighters has streamed into the system." Titus reported.

"Order all sword breakers to engage." Taymen ordered.

"Incoming ordnance!" Avril shouted just before the ship was hit by three heavy missiles.

Several crewmen were thrown from their feet with the impact. Elisha lost her footing and hit her head against the command console knocking her unconscious.

"She's hurt!" Russ shouted from her side.

Avril tapped her earpiece. "Medic to CAC." She said.

"Sir, multiple sensor contacts." Titus said.

"How many?" Avril asked.

"One hundred enemy fighters and they're right on top of us." Titus replied.

"We've really stirred up a hornet's nest." Avril said.

Taymen ignored her.

"That's it, all guns switch to enemy suppression fire, take out those fighters but watch for our sword breakers." He ordered.

"Aye Sir."

"Ready four electronic decoy missiles, set them to detonate three light seconds off the heavy cruiser's hull." Taymen continued.

"Sir?" Carrey asked.

"Just do it and ready three javelins." Taymen snapped.

"Missiles ready Sir." The weapons officer said a few seconds later.

"Launch decoys." Taymen ordered.

The four decoy missiles sped towards their target. When they reached the programmed range, instead of exploding they shed their outer casing leaving thousands of nano-transmitters in their wake. The transmitters gave off a signal that would block the enemy's sensors for a while leaving them with a blind spot.

"Decoys detonated."

"Launch javelins!" Taymen ordered.

The three missiles flew on almost the exact same path that the decoys did until they reached the field of transmitters where they broke off and slammed into the heavy cruiser in three different locations. The first missile hit the launch bays while second hit the underside of the hull and the third went for a maneuvering thruster.

"Direct hit." The weapons officer reported.

"Helm bring our bow to bear on the cruiser, all ahead full." Taymen ordered.

"Aye Sir." Aurin said.

"All gun batteries switch to direct fire on the heavy cruiser, have the sword breakers cover us." Taymen continued.

"Radiological alert, nuclear missiles inbound!" Titus shouted.

"Nuclear!" Russ said in a panic.

"Shift all batteries to suppression fire, take out those missiles!" Taymen ordered.

Avril checked the main display to see three missiles speeding towards the Avenger. Within a few seconds two of the missiles disappeared from the display.

"Two missiles down Sir, the third is still inbound impact in twenty seconds." Avril said.

"All sword breakers break off." Taymen said.

"Bring our bow up ninety degrees and rotate the ship a hundred and eighty degrees on the 'Y' axis." He continued.

The maneuvering officer pulled the bow of the ship up hard while firing the vertical maneuvering thrusters to rotate the ship so the upper hull was exposed to the missile since the armor was thickest there.

As the missile continued to close in the sword breakers broke off and accelerated away from the Avenger at full speed to avoid the shockwave. Just as they reached a safe distance the missile impacted the Avenger on the forward starboard side on the upper hull and detonated.

Taymen and most of the crew in C.A.C. were thrown to the deck as the entire ship shuttered violently. The lights flashed as sparks erupted from some of the consoles that overloaded while all the display screens turned to static for a few seconds. The shockwave expanded out from the Avenger destroying the enemy fighters that were still in range.

Taymen quickly recovered and got to his feet.

"Avril get on damage control." He ordered.

Avril slowly stood up and looked around briefly to get her bearings before moving to the damage control console.

"Report." He said.

"The heavy cruiser is bearing down on us and our sword breakers are holding just outside the blast range." Titus said.

"Recall the sword breakers to re-establish their perimeter." Taymen said.

"Helm bring our upper hull to bear on the cruiser. Carrey ready all tubes with saber missiles and light up that cruiser. Empty the clips Carrey and order all gun stations to keep firing." He ordered.

"Aye Sir." Carrey replied a few seconds later.

Each missile tube had a rotating clip assembly that housed six of each type of missile to facilitate continuous fire.

In only a few seconds all the clips containing saber missiles were empty and the twelve valkerie cannons that were still online began to fire plasma rounds at the target. The missiles tore apart the cruiser's outer armor and ripped through the outer deck just before the plasma rounds burned through the exposed sections of the ship.

Finally, a few rounds penetrated the aft section of the cruiser and burned through a fuel tank detonating its contents. The explosion enveloped the cruiser and anything nearby leaving nothing but charred debris in its wake.

"All enemy ships have been destroyed Sir." Titus reported.

Taymen checked the display and sighed, finally able to relax. He tapped his earpiece and accessed the internal com. system. "All hands stand down and return the ship to stealth mode. Good work people." He said.

"Avril damage report."

"Working on it Sir but it doesn't look good." Avril replied as she made her way back over to the command console.

"Most of the armor generators are going to need major repairs after that blast." She started. "Valkerie batteries five through eight are down, we've got hull breaches throughout several decks and we've had to expose several sections to vacuum to put out fires and now we can't re-pressurize them."

Taymen shook his head. "Is that all?" He asked.

"I wish." Avril said. "The upper heat exchanger is fried, several primary systems are already beginning to overheat and that's just what we know about right now."

Taymen sighed.

"Titus deploy damage control teams to seal those breaches and re-pressurize the sections exposed to vacuum." He said.

"Yes Sir." Titus replied.

There was a moment of silence before Avril spoke again.

"Sir, how did you know about the trap?" She asked.

Taymen smiled slightly.

"Because it was a very old tactic." He said

"I don't think I'm familiar with that particular tactic." Avril said.

"The idea is to engage your enemy in a rapidly changing battlefield so they make a stupid mistake like overextending their defenses or forgetting about a particular target which would leave your target vulnerable." Taymen explained. "It's used when you're attacking a larger force like an escort fleet to try and confuse them so that you can slip a ship in to destroy your primary target."

"So then why would they use that kind of tactic against a single ship?" Avril asked.

"I don't know." Taymen replied. "Maybe their Commander was inexperienced in combat, or maybe they consider us a superior threat. Either way it's not really important." Taymen answered. "We need to focus on repairs before they decide to try a different tactic."

"That could be easier said than done. We have a serious disadvantage right now, they know where to find us." Avril said quietly.

"Agreed." Taymen said. "We need to buy some time."

Chapter Four

Russ sat next to Elisha's bed as the Doctor checked her vital signs on the monitor. He had never seen equipment like this before in any hospital, it was unlike anything he had ever imagined and yet when he looked at it he recognized most of the characters on the screens.

The other thing that raced through his mind was how Taymen and his crew knew their language so well. There were some minor differences but the overall dialect was the same. Russ had grown up in Canada but moved to Egypt after graduating from university. He spent several years in the field recovering artifacts and studying pyramids before taking a full time position at the Cairo museum.

"How is she?" Russ asked.

The Doctor didn't look up from his data pad as he answered.

"She'll be fine." He said. "There's no evidence of brain swelling but she'll probably have a bit of a headache when she wakes up."

Russ sighed with relief.

He sat silent for a moment watching Elisha before looking up at the Doctor again.

"Doctor." He started. "Where are you from?" He asked.

"Originally I was born on Abydos." The Doctor replied. "But my father was in the Defense Force so we moved around a lot."

"Who's Defense Force?" Russ asked, trying to be discrete.

"If you have something you want to ask just come out and ask, don't try and hide it." The Doctor said.

"Sorry." Russ replied. "I guess I'm just trying to figure a few things out."

The Doctor finally looked up from his data pad.

"We call ourselves Egyptian." He said before walking away.

"Helm, prepare to land the ship." Taymen said.

Aurin paused for a moment before turning to face Taymen.

"Sir, I think I should tell you that I've never really landed a ship this size before."

Taymen smiled slightly.

"Neither have I." He said. "Just remember she's not a prowler and take her down easy."

Aurin chuckled slightly.

"Yes Sir." He replied.

Taymen accessed the com. system. "All hands, prepare for landing, secure all stations and standby." He ordered.

"All stations report ready Sir." Avril reported.

"Good." Taymen replied. "Helm rotate the ship, face our keel towards the planet's surface." He ordered. "Lock in the landing coordinates and take us in."

"Aye Sir." Aurin replied.

As the ship began to descend into the atmosphere Taymen moved closer to the command console.

"Alright Aurin, she's all yours." He said.

"Aye Sir, everybody hang on this is going to be a little rough." Aurin replied.

"Take the protostream system off line and re-route power to the main landing thrusters." He ordered.

"Bring the bow up thirty degrees and rotate the ship positive six degrees along the X axis." He continued.

"We're in position Sir." The maneuvering officer replied.

Shortly after it began to descend, the lower hull began to glow red hot as the ship accelerated further into the dense atmosphere until it passed through the thermosphere and the hull began to cool again.

"We've cleared the thermosphere Sir." The maneuvering officer reported.

"Adjust our heading to take us to our landing sight and prepare to set us down." Aurin said.

"Aye Sir half a light second to the landing sight, we're beginning our final descent."

Within minutes the ship began to decelerate.

"Cut forward thrust, full stop in ten thousand foot cubits." Aurin said.

"Full stop, aye Sir." The drive officer replied.

"Bring vertical thrusters to one quarter." Aurin continued.

"One quarter vertical." The maneuvering officer repeated.

"Extend the landing struts and reduce vertical thrust, take us down slowly Lieutenant."

"Aye Sir."

The ship slowly began to drop to the ground.

"Thirty-six hundred foot cubits to landing."

"One hundred and fifty foot cubits to port, eight hundred foot cubits aft." Aurin said.

"We're in position Sir." The maneuvering officer said after making the corrections.

Suddenly the ship shuttered as it touched down on the surface.

"We're down Sir." The drive officer reported after a deep breath.

He felt as though he had been holding his breath for the entire landing.

"Well done." Aurin said.

"Take the main drive units off line and vent the drive exhaust." He ordered as he turned to Taymen. "We're down Sir." He said.

"Good work Commander, Titus I want a repair schedule on my desk tomorrow morning." Taymen said.

"Yes Sir." Titus replied.

"Avril." Taymen continued. "Launch a couple of sensor drones to run combat patrols for a radius of a quarter light second, I want to know the instant something comes our way."

"Yes Sir." Avril said.

Taymen turned and moved towards the pressure hatch. "I'm going to get some rest now that we have a moment, Ex O you have command." He said.

"Aye Sir." Avril replied.

Dark Avenger in Antarctica
07:20 Abydos Standard Time
Day 17, Second Cycle, Egyptian Year 3201

Russ stared out the window at the endless desert of snow and ice. It was the complete opposite of what he was used to seeing when he looked out his window.

He spent the last day or so simply running the events of the past few days through his head again and again. He and Elisha were now considered Taymen's personal guests. They each had their own room, though they weren't extravagant they were comfortable.

The technology that surrounded them was just unbelievable to them both. Even something as simple as the windows, which Russ later learned were actually a one way transparent section of the hull. He could look outside, but if he were to try and look in all he would see is a section of the hull, indistinguishable from the rest.

Russ shook himself out of his thoughts when he heard his room buzzer. He walked across the room and opened the hatch to see Elisha standing there with her escort.

"Taymen wants to see us." She said.

They followed their escorts through the corridors to the briefing room. The ship was so immense Russ couldn't see himself ever finding his way around without an escort. When they entered the room Taymen was standing at the head of the table waiting for them.

"Come in, sit down." He said.

Elisha sat to Taymen's left and Russ took the seat next to her.

"Is something wrong?" She asked.

"Not at all." Taymen replied. "I simply remember you saying you had questions you wanted answered."

Elisha turned to Russ who simply shrugged.

"I thought that now would be a good time to try and answer those questions." Taymen added.

Elisha sighed.

"Well." She started. "Where to start?"

She thought it over for a moment. Russ recognized the look on her face, she was simply ecstatic.

Elisha was always a bit of a dreamer when it came to aliens and things like that, so her excitement really wasn't surprising to Russ given the situation.

"Well where you're from would be a good place to start." Elisha said.

"That's sort of hard to explain right now." Taymen started. "We're actually lost, we came here by accident and now we don't know how to get home."

"What?" Russ said in disbelief.

"We can safely say that we are not from any of the neighboring galaxies, our home seems to be beyond our telescopes range right now." Taymen explained.

"But your home planet is called Abydos?" Russ asked.

Taymen looked at Russ in surprise. Obviously he had been speaking with some of the crew.

"That's right." Taymen said.

"What else do you know?" He asked.

Russ sighed.

"Just that you call yourselves Egyptian." He said.

Elisha looked at Russ then back to Taymen.

"What!" She said.

Taymen looked at them both in confusion.

39

"Is something wrong?" He asked.

"The Egyptians were a race of people that pretty much disappeared from our planet over two thousand years ago." Russ explained.

"Two thousand years ago, are you sure?" Taymen asked.

"Yeah, we're still finding artifacts left behind by them." Russ said.

"What is it?" Elisha asked.

Taymen shook his head.

"It's not important right now." He said. "I'm sure you have more questions."

"What are you doing here?" Russ asked.

"As I said we arrived in your galaxy by accident, we were under attack. We're not entirely sure but we think that when we tried to stream away a nuclear detonation overloaded our stream system. The overload caused it to send us to your galaxy instead of our rendezvous point." Taymen explained.

"Stream system, what's that?" Elisha asked.

Taymen smiled a little. He was actually rather impressed at Elisha's curiosity.

"We employ a technology that allows us to travel great distances in space." He started. "It's a network of hubs in subspace that can transport a vessel between them minimizing travel time. We think the hub overloaded and sent us here by mistake."

"Can't you just stream home then?" Russ asked.

"Normally a ship can only spend eight hours at a time in the protostream before it begins to break down. The overload caused the hub to send us farther than is normally possible in that amount of time, we can start streaming home in eight hour increments, but we need to know which way to go first, not to mention the fact that not knowing the locations of gravity fields and anomalies in this galaxy makes plotting a stream more dangerous than usual." Taymen said.

"So what are you going to do?" Elisha asked.

"Right now we're trying to gain access to your planets satellite telescopes to see if they can locate our galaxy. If they can, then once repairs are complete we'll be on our way."

"What about the ones who attacked you?" Russ said. "How did they get here?"

Taymen sighed.

"I don't know." He said.

"It's possible they were too close when we streamed out and were pulled into the stream with us."

"What about this ship?" Elisha asked.

"What about it?" Taymen said, unsure of what she was referring to.

"Well what's it for? What's it called? How big is it? How big is your crew? Everything."

Taymen chuckled.

"Slow down." He said.

Elisha sank in her chair a little as she took a breath.

"The ship is called the Dark Avenger." Taymen started. "It's an avenger class battle cruiser about sixty-three thousand foot cubits long with a crew compliment of about twelve hundred."

Russ did the math quickly in his head. Sixty-three thousand foot cubits translated into about seven hundred meters.

"Originally it was designed as an escort vessel for high priority targets, but it's proven to be more than capable of operating in an offensive role."

"That's obvious." Russ muttered.

"Wait a second." Elisha started. "You said you were trying to access our satellites to try and find your way home?"

"That's right." Taymen said.

"I have access to a few deep space satellites." She said.

"What?" Taymen asked.

"I work at a satellite listening station, we use satellites for deep space observation and listening, we may already have your galaxy in our database." Elisha said with excitement.

"Can you remotely access one of your satellites from here?" Taymen asked.

"Probably not." Elisha said. "They require access codes that are changed weekly, I'd have to get them from my computer at work."

Taymen stood up.

"I'll have a prowler ready in twenty minutes to take you there." He said.

"Wait a second." Russ objected. "Do you know how much trouble she could be in if she's caught helping you? Our government has laws against this sort of thing."

"Your government has laws against helping alien races?" Taymen asked.

Russ sighed.

"Against providing just anyone with information like satellite codes." He said.

"Russ!" Elisha snapped. "They need our help."

"This is crazy." Russ said. "If we're caught we could be arrested."

"If we help you will you take us with you?" Elisha asked.

Taymen wasn't expecting that.

Russ just looked at Elisha nearly in shock.

"Excuse me?" Taymen said.

"When you leave here, would you consider taking us with you?" Elisha repeated.

Taymen shook his head.

"I'm afraid that's not an option." He replied. "This isn't a passenger ship it's a battle cruiser, it wouldn't be safe for you here."

Elisha sighed.

"But..."

Taymen cut her off.

"I'm sorry but it's not an option." He said as he made his way to the hatch. "I'll have a prowler and a team on the starboard hangar deck ready to leave in twenty minutes."

Taymen left the room and closed the hatch behind him.

"Go with them!" Russ snapped. "Are you crazy?"

Elisha ignored his tone.

"Well why not?" She replied.

"Why not?" Russ repeated.

"Did you hear a word the man said, they're from another galaxy." He continued.

"Exactly." Elisha said. "A whole other galaxy of planets and stars that nobody here has ever seen before. It's something I've dreamt about since I was a kid."

Russ sighed.

"You'd be alone in an alien galaxy." He said.

"How alien could it be?" Elisha argued. "They're humans Russ, Egyptians, real live Egyptians. Wouldn't you want to see how they live, how they've evolved first hand instead of studying artifacts and making theories that may never be proven?"

Russ had to admit the idea of seeing and interacting with living Egyptians was appealing to him, but he couldn't leave his family, his home in fact his whole life behind.

"It's too dangerous." He said. "You saw how bad that fight was yesterday, these people are in the middle of a war."

Elisha sighed. She knew Russ was right it was dangerous but she didn't really have anything to hold her back. Her parents died while she was still young and her adopted parents passed away a few years ago. She had no other family or any other ties aside from Russ keeping her from leaving.

Suddenly the hatch opened and one of their escorts walked in.

"If you'll come with us we'll take you to the hangar deck." He said.

Chapter Five

Taymen sat behind the desk in his quarters going over the damage assessments from the last battle when he heard the door buzzer.

"Come in." He said.

Avril opened the hatch and walked in.

"Sir, am I disturbing you?" She asked.

"No, please come in." Taymen said.

Avril closed the hatch and walked across the room to the front of the desk. Taymen gestured to the leather chair near a small round wooden table to the left of his desk. Avril moved to the chair and sat down as Taymen took a seat on the couch against the wall to her left.

"Repairs are on schedule, they should be complete by twenty-two hundred today." Avril started.

"Good." Taymen replied.

"Also two more sword breakers are down for repairs and we're going to need to get fuel from somewhere for both the sword breakers and the Avenger."

"Of course." Taymen said.

"We only need to refuel once every thirty days and it just happens to come up now." He said sarcastically.

"I don't suppose any options for fuel have presented themselves?" He asked.

"Actually one may have." Avril replied. "The fitters suggested we may be able to get what we need from the sun in this system." She explained as she handed Taymen a data pad.

Taymen looked over the report from the engine technicians.

"They want to try using the missile tubes to bring hydrogen and helium aboard." Avril explained.

Taymen nodded as he looked over the data. The fitters basically wanted to attach a large vacuum unit to the missile tubes to draw in the gasses from the sun. Then they would use a particle separator to filter out the hydrogen and rout it directly to the Avenger's fuel cells.

It wouldn't require any modifications to the missile tubes. They would simply empty out one of the missile clips and route the line through that to the missile tube, then they would simply have to seal it in place and open the outer doors to take in all that they needed.

"This would require us to be in a low orbit around the sun." Taymen said.

"Yes Sir." Avril replied. "They estimate that with armor deployed we would be able to hold our position near the sun's outer corona for about twelve hours before we would have to move away to bleed off the radiation."

Taymen checked over the rest of the data before handing the pad back to Avril.

"Tell them to get started on the modifications." He said.

"Yes Sir." Avril replied.

"Anything else?" Taymen asked.

"There was one other thing Sir." Avril started.

"It's about our guests, are you sure we can trust them to help us?" She asked.

Taymen sighed. "We really don't have much choice." He said. "They seem willing to help and I don't think they have much of a reason to betray us."

"I'm not sure I would be so trusting with them Sir." Avril said.

Taymen smiled a little.

"I've learned to trust my instincts." He said. "But I've also learned to be cautious, which is why I sent them with a detail of marines."

"Understood Sir." Avril said.

There was a brief silence and Taymen could tell that Avril had something else on her mind.

"Something else Captain?" He asked.

"Well Sir, I heard that they've asked to stay aboard."

Taymen sighed.

"Elisha has asked to stay aboard, but that's obviously out of the question." He said.

"Is it really Sir?" Avril asked.

Taymen looked at her waiting for an explanation.

"We've pretty much told them that everything they believe about the universe is wrong, is it right for us to just send them on their way now?"

Taymen hadn't really thought about that aspect of it, but what was the alternative? To take them along to a galaxy that they may not even make it to? To tear them from everything they have ever known and simply rip what's left of their reality apart, what right did he have to do that?

"If it were simply a matter of us going home then I would consider taking them, but we may not even reach home, and if we do we still have a war to fight."

Taymen paused for a moment.

"I won't take them from the safety of their own planet to bring them into a war that has nothing to do with them."

Avril couldn't argue with that and it was Taymen's decision.

Suddenly Titus' voice came over the internal com. system.

"Captain and Ex O to C.A.C." He said.

Taymen moved back to his desk and put on his uniform jacket which was hanging off the back of the chair.

When they arrived in C.A.C. Titus was standing at the command console watching the sensor display.

"What is it Commander?" Avril asked.

"Sensor contacts, three heavy cruisers have streamed into the system along with a full fighter escort numbering one hundred fighters. They're in a high orbit on the far side of the planet." Titus reported.

"Recall our sensor drones, prepare for emergency ascent." Taymen ordered.

"Aye Sir." Titus replied.

"Incoming ordnance!" Avril snapped.

Taymen checked the display.

"They're bombarding the planet." She said.

"Where?" Taymen asked.

"Missiles impacting all over the surface, the closest hit within a tenth of a light second from our location, the others are spread throughout each of the continents." She replied.

"What are they up to?" Titus asked.

"They're baiting us." Taymen replied.

"Their sensors can't pinpoint our position on the planet so they're trying to make us panic and lift off, giving away our position. They know we're on the surface and they know we can't attack them effectively from the atmosphere, but they can blow us out of the sky before we clear the thermosphere." He continued.

"Sir one of the cruisers is broadcasting a message on open channels." Sairon said from the communications station.

"Put it on speakers." Taymen said.

The speakers crackled for a second before they heard a deep voice.

"This message is for the Egyptian battleship hiding on the planet. We know you're there, give up your ship and you will not be harmed, if you refuse we will bombard the entire planet's surface destroying you and every living thing on it, you have twenty minutes to respond."

Sairon deactivated the speakers when the channel closed.

"The message just repeats itself after that Sir." She said.

"What's the status of our repairs?" Avril asked.

"The upper heat exchanger is back online but it's not operating at full capacity, if it takes another direct hit we probably won't be able to repair it." Titus replied.

"Tell all hands to prepare for takeoff." Avril ordered.

"Show me the damage to the planet, where did those missiles hit?" Taymen said.

The main display changed to an image of the planet's surface. Several areas were highlighted in red indicating the impact sites. There were over forty locations, entire cities were completely destroyed and several more though they survived were in shambles.

"What do you want to do Sir?" Avril asked.

"We're not leaving before Elisha and Russ are back aboard." Taymen said.

"We need to buy some time then." Avril replied.

Taymen turned to Carrie at the weapons control stations.

"Carrie, ready two nukes for launch."

Cairo Satellite Control Station
09:00 Abydos Standard Time
Day 17, Second Cycle, Egyptian Year 3201

Elisha logged into her computer and pulled up the satellite access codes. She took a moment to memorize the ones she needed and left the document open before switching screens.

Four marines and an astronomer from the Dark Avenger stood over her as she worked. The other four marines went with Russ to the museum.

She worked as fast as she could, entering the access codes to the long range telescope satellites. It took a few minutes before the system let her into the satellite controls.

"Got it." She said.

The astronomer handed her a data pad that contained a map of the constellations from their galaxy. Elisha took the pad and starred at him, unsure what to do with it.

"Can't your system search for those?" He asked.

"And how is my computer supposed to read this?" Elisha asked.

The astronomer sighed as he took the data pad and accessed the wireless interface.

"These computers have a wireless interface device right?" He asked.

Elisha nodded.

The astronomer didn't say anything as he searched for a wireless signal to tap into.

"There we go." He said a moment later when he found one. He uploaded the star maps directly to Elisha's computer and Elisha began a general search. It took a few minutes but the computer eventually found a match.

"That's it." The astronomer said.

"Where is it?" One of the marines asked.

"The satellite's projecting the coordinates now." Elisha said. "It'll just take a minute."

"That'll be enough Elisha."

Suddenly the marines spun around with their weapons at the ready.

"Frank?" Elisha said.

Frank stood in the door way with a group of six soldiers standing just behind him.

They entered the room slowly with rifles trained on the marines around Elisha.

"What's going on here?" Elisha asked.

"These men are here to take you and your friends into custody." Frank said.

"For what?" One of the marines asked.

"We have some questions for you." Frank replied.

"Frank, what's going on?" Elisha asked.

"That energy signature that you found, we've seen it before." Frank started.

"About ten years ago one was detected just like it, but it was gone before we could find anything. Ever since then a government observer has been stationed at this facility incase another one was ever detected."

"But why?" Elisha asked.

"They're aliens Elisha, just imagine what we could learn from them, the technology we could acquire."

"Please, they're just trying to get home." Elisha said.

"Sorry, but we can't let them go just yet." Frank started. "We've detected another group of those energy signatures in orbit about ten minutes ago, and the air force is closing in on their ship in the arctic, they're going to put a stop to this invasion before it goes any further."

"What are you talking about?" The astronomer asked.

"Your ships launched an attack against our planet!" Frank said. "Dozens of cities are in ruins because of you."

The astronomer turned to one of the marines.

"They found us." He said.

"We don't have time for this." The marine whispered.

"Put down your weapons and come with us." Frank ordered.

"Frank please don't do this." Elisha pleaded.

"Elisha think about what you're doing." Frank said. "You're helping our enemy, this is treason."

Elisha shook her head.

"They're not our enemy." She said.

"Alright, we don't have time for this." One of the marines said.

He tapped a control on the side of his rifle. An instant later the site on the top emitted a blinding white light at Frank and the soldiers. At the same time the rest of the marines dropped to the floor, one of them pulled Elisha down with them before they opened fire. Two of the soldiers dropped to the floor dead as the others back out of the room.

When the light cleared they still couldn't see anything. One of the marines grabbed the computer monitor and through it through the window shattering it.

"Let's go!" He said.

As they helped Elisha through the window a few rounds flew past missing them by mere inches. One returned fire as the others climbed through the window, and provided cover fire for him to climb through.

"What about Russ?" Elisha asked.

"We'll pick them up on the way." One of the marines replied as he led them to the prowler.

Elisha suddenly stopped in her tracks.

"Wait." She shouted. "The coordinates, we didn't get the coordinates."

The astronomer grabbed her by the arm and pulled her along.

"Relax." He said. "I downloaded the information onto the pad while your friend was busy talking."

Elisha sighed with relief.

When they were safely aboard the prowler took off and sped towards the other teams' locator beacon.

"Well I guess I can't go home now." Elisha said.

Chapter Six

"Sir I'm receiving a transmission from the away team." Sairon said. "They say they're on their way back, ETA ten minutes."

Taymen sighed.

"Sensor contact!" Titus said. "Unknown craft on an intercept course."

Taymen checked the sensor display.

"Identify." Avril said.

"Unknown, they don't match the enemy fighters we've encountered before." Titus said.

"Whatever they are they're closing in fast." Avril said.

"Launch sword breakers." Taymen ordered. "Let's see if we can scare them off."

"You think they could be local?" Avril asked.

Taymen nodded. "Maybe." He said.

"Sir one of the cruisers is entering the atmosphere, they'll be right on top of us in six minutes." Titus reported.

"Oh this should be interesting." Avril said. "Ever fight inside of an atmosphere?" She asked.

Taymen sighed.

"Once." He replied. "Didn't like it much. Aurin get us off the ground and set a course for that cruiser."

"Sir our sword breakers are receiving a transmission from the unknown aircraft." Sairon reported.

"Patch it through." Taymen said.

The speakers crackled for a second before the transmission came through.

"Unknown aircraft you are ordered to stand down and await further instructions. If you do not reply you will be fired upon."

Taymen turned to Sairon.

"Open a channel." He said

"Go ahead Sir." Sairon said.

"This message is for whoever is in charge." He started. "We have no fight with you, we are leaving the area however if you interfere with us we will destroy you." Taymen said.

There was a moment of silence as he watched the display screen. The aircraft were still closing in on them.

"Listen to me." Taymen started. "You are outnumbered and massively outgunned, even you can see you have no chance against us, turn back now or we will destroy you."

Again there was no response and the aircraft did not change their heading. Taymen closed the channel as he turned to the flight controllers.

"Recall the sword breakers, order them to form up off of our bow and prepare to engage any enemy fighters." He ordered.

"Sir the heavy cruiser has launched fighters and is closing in." Titus reported.

"Carrey, target the cruiser and launch nukes." Taymen ordered.

"Aye Sir, nukes away." Carrey replied.

"Deploy armor." Taymen said.

The two missiles sped towards their target detonating just a few meters off its outer hull. The blast wave incinerated most of the fighters and tore apart the ships outer armor.

"Direct hit." Carrey reported.

"Target is still closing with what's left of its fighters." Avril said.

"Sword breakers are in position Sir." One of the flight controllers reported.

"Valkerie batteries one through ten prepare for direct fire on the cruiser, remainder prepare for enemy suppression fire." Taymen ordered.

"All batteries report ready Sir." Carrey said.

"All starboard missile tubes ready a javelin missile and prepare for a broadside. Helm maneuver us to pass the cruiser on her starboard side." Taymen continued.

He watched the display as the cruiser and its fighters closed in until they were right on top of each other.

"Sword breakers break! All batteries fire at will!" Taymen ordered.

Instantly, the sword breakers broke formation and went after their closest targets while all of the Avenger's valkerie batteries opened fire. The air suddenly became a battlefield as it was filled with ordnance from both sides.

"Helm all ahead full, bring our starboard side to bear." Taymen said.

The Avenger charged forward as it slid slightly left to pass the heavy cruiser on its right side. When the two ships were parallel to each other six javelin missiles sped out of the Avenger's starboard missile tubes and impacted the heavy cruiser before they could react.

Two of the missiles struck one of the vertical thruster assemblies knocking it offline.

The Avenger continued to pull away as the heavy cruiser began to descend towards the ice. A few seconds later it crashed through the thick ice and into the freezing ocean beneath disappearing into the darkness.

"The cruiser just crashed into the ocean Sir." Titus reported.

"The remaining fighters are retreating." Avril added.

"Recall the sword breakers." Taymen ordered.

"Sir the local aircraft are still closing." Titus said.

"Incoming ordnance!" Avril said.

Taymen checked the display and saw twelve missiles speeding towards them. Before he could say anything they detonated against the Avenger's armor, but there was no shock from the impact.

Taymen looked at Avril who simply shrugged.

"Damage?" Taymen asked.

"Nothing from that salvo." The damage control officer said. "Enemy fire is ineffective."

Taymen smiled as he shook his head.

"Sir the aircraft are retreating." Titus said.

"Noted." Taymen replied.

"Sir the away team's prowler is requesting permission to land." Sairon said.

"Granted." Taymen said. "Aurin as soon as they're aboard take us up into a high orbit."

"Aye Sir." Aurin replied.

"We're not done yet." Taymen said.

A few minutes later the entire ship began to ascend through the atmosphere.

"We've cleared the thermosphere Sir." The drive officer reported.

"Set a course to intercept the enemy fleet."

"Enemy fighters inbound." Titus reported.

"Launch sword breakers." Taymen ordered.

"Enemy cruisers are moving in to intercept us."

"Sir the lead cruiser is transmitting a message." Sairon said. "Message is an order to surrender."

"Yeah, I'll surrender all right." Taymen replied. "Carrey launch all saber missiles at the lead cruiser."

"Missiles away Sir." Carrey reported.

Thirty-six missiles impacted the first cruiser's forward section exposing a large area of the inner hull.

"Incoming ordnance!" Avril snapped.

"All batteries to suppression fire!" Taymen ordered.

Almost instantly all the valkerie cannons opened fire detonating the incoming missiles before they impacted the hull.

"Sir a group of enemy fighters are on an attack run heading right for us."

"Order all batteries to redirect fire at those fighters and fire at will." Taymen said.

"Anybody else find this strange?" Avril asked.

"What is it?" Taymen asked.

"I don't know." Avril started. "It just feels like they're not putting up a serious fight."

Taymen had the same feeling but had just ignored it until now.

"You're right, something's wrong." He said. "We need to finish this off fast, have our sword breakers engage cruiser two." He ordered.

"Sensor contact, unknown enemy ship has just entered the system." Titus reported.

"Unknown?" Avril asked.

"It's larger than a heavy cruiser." Titus said.

"Sir the new ship is transmitting a message in real time." Sairon reported.

"Put it on speakers." Taymen said.

"This is General Assh of the Egyptian Empire, stand down and await further orders." A voice said over the C.A.C. speakers.

Taymen didn't say anything. He turned to Avril who looked at him in confusion.

General Assh was one of the Princess' military council members. He was one of four Generals who were in direct command of the Imperial Guard with the Princess. What he was doing here Taymen couldn't imagine.

"Sir." Titus started. "The enemy fighters have started to retreat to the cruisers."

"Recall our fighters and order all gun batteries to standby for direct fire." Taymen ordered.

"I repeat." The General said. *"This is General Assh of the Egyptian Empire, command code three three seven omega two alpha, respond."*

"Confirm that code." Avril ordered.

"Confirmed." Sairon said. "It's the General's command code."

Taymen hesitantly accessed the com. system.

"This is Major Orelle of the battleship Dark Avenger." He said.

"Major you are ordered to stand down and hold your position, we are sending over a boarding party."

"Negative General, any ship attempting to board the Avenger will be fired upon." He said.

"Stand down Major!" The General snapped. *"This is a direct order, Princess Releena and I will be arriving shortly with a Tray security detail."*

"Tray Sir?" Taymen asked.

"We'll explain everything when we get there, you have your orders, Assh out."

The channel closed and Taymen stood silent.

"Sir, I don't like this." Avril said.

"Neither do I Captain." Taymen replied. "I want two full marine sections on the hangar deck when that ship lands and escorts to the briefing room, keep all stations on standby and ready a nuke for launch, target the unknown ship and await my orders."

"Yes Sir." Avril replied.

Dark Avenger, Starboard Hangar Deck
10:55 Abydos Standard Time
Day 17, Second Cycle, Egyptian Year 3201

Taymen stood on the hangar deck along with sixteen heavily armed marines as the Tray shuttle was brought aboard.

When the hatch on the side of the shuttle opened, sixteen assault rifles were at the ready. A second later four armed guards poured out of the shuttle and took up positions on either side of the hatch. Taymen was ready to give the order to fire until he heard the General's voice come from inside the shuttle.

"Stand down Major." He ordered as he stepped out of the ship and onto the hangar deck.

"With all due respect Sir." Taymen started. "This is my ship and your friends have weapons trained on my men, tell them to stand down, then we'll talk."

Taymen could see he was trying the General's patience but he didn't care.

"Very well, let's talk in private Major." He said.

Taymen didn't move.

"I want them to stand down first." He replied.

"They're with me." A man said as he stepped onto the hangar deck.

Taymen immediately noticed a certain arrogance about him.

"And who are you?" Taymen asked.

53

"I am Fleet Marshal Ourik, of the Tray Alliance." The man replied.

"Ok then, why should I care?" Taymen said smugly.

"Because I am your new commanding officer." Ourik replied.

"Well Fleet Marshal you don't have permission to come aboard, so I'll say this one more time, either your men stand down or I give the order to fire."

Taymen wasn't bluffing and Assh knew it.

"Such hostility." Ourik said.

Again his arrogance was all too apparent to Taymen who had enough. He drew his side arm and fired. The ceramic round impacted the side of the shuttle missing Ourik's head by a few inches. Both the Tray guards and the marines tensed up but nobody fired yet.

"Last chance!" Taymen shouted.

"Major, that's enough!" Assh snapped.

"Sir, with all due respect, you're next." Taymen said turning his weapon on the General.

"Think about what you're doing Major." Assh said.

"Here's what I'm thinking Sir." Taymen started. "My ship was attacked without warning again and again.

"Now, one of my superiors is standing next to our attackers on my ship telling me to stand down while we're surrounded, tell me Sir what would you do in my place?"

Assh didn't respond.

"Very well Major." Ourik finally said. "Lower your weapons."

The Tray guards did as they were ordered without hesitation.

Taymen hesitated a moment before he replaced his sidearm.

"Alright then." He finally said.

"We have a lot to talk about." Assh said.

"Apparently." Taymen replied.

"Major Orelle." A voice said from inside the shuttle.

Taymen looked up to see Princess Releena step onto the hangar deck.

"Princess Releena." He said.

"We don't have much time Major so let's dispense with the pleasantries." She said.

"Very well." Taymen replied. "This way."

Taymen led them all off the hangar deck and through the corridors to the briefing room. When they entered the room the Princess sat at the head of the table, to her right sat General Assh and next to him was the Fleet Marshal. Taymen sat to the left of the Princess and his marines lined the wall behind him, the Tray guards stood behind the Fleet Marshal.

"Well, let's begin." Ourik started.

"Princess, what's going on here?" Taymen asked.

"You will address me Major." Ourik said in a calm but commanding tone.

"I will address who I choose, and on this ship you will not address me unless I speak to you first!" Taymen snapped.

Ourik looked insulted, as if he actually expected Taymen to bow down in front of him.

"Major what do you know about the current situation?" Assh asked. Taymen turned his attention back to the General and the Princess.

"Nothing Sir, we were attacked while evacuating the Princess from Netara. When we went to stream out of the system something happened and we ended up here." Taymen answered.

"Then listen closely, because you've missed quite a bit." Assh started. "Not long after the Princess was evacuated from Netara we found ourselves overwhelmed by Tray ships. We were vastly outnumbered and they captured the Princess rather quickly despite our efforts."

"What of the rest of the royal family?" Taymen asked.

The General simply shook his head before the Princess began to speak.

"I made an offer to the Tray, my co-operation for the lives of our people." She said.

This was sounding an awful lot like a surrender to Taymen.

"The Tray agreed and we formed an alliance, which began with the immediate demilitarization and integration of our people.

"We surrendered." Taymen said.

Releena sighed.

"You would have lost anyway." Ourik said. "It was just a matter of time."

"You don't know that!" Taymen snapped. "A war is not over until everyone agrees it is, and I don't think this war has even begun yet." He continued.

Ourik simply chuckled.

"Then we will simply destroy your ship, execute your crew and get on to more important matters."

Taymen stood from his seat.

"You're more than welcome to try, we've already proven to be more than you can handle."

"Enough Major." Assh said.

"Taymen sit down." Releena said softly.

Taymen was surprised to hear the Princess use his first name. He had never spoken with her directly before but he never imagined she would be so informal with him.

"Leave us for a moment Fleet Marshal." Releena said.

Ourik hesitated for a moment before he stood up from his seat.

"Very well." He said. "But only for a moment."

"General Assh please wait outside." Releena said.

"Clear the room." Taymen ordered.

When the room was clear and the hatch sealed Releena leaned in closer to Taymen.

"How is it that the Fleet Marshal feels he can leave you alone with me?" Taymen asked.

"Tray arrogance seems to have no boundaries." She replied.

"Listen closely." She started. "Things are very bad right now and you're the last free ship we have. Our people are practically slaves to the Tray, our fleet has been devastated, and the ships that weren't destroyed have been marshaled and left in locations that are classified. We think the Tray are trying to reverse engineer them."

"Why?" Taymen asked.

"They're technology is not as advanced as ours but they outnumber us greatly. They also use a form of NDI implants, it's not as advanced as ours so they can't use it with our technology." Releena explained.

"Now listen, this is important." She moved in even closer.

"When Ourik comes back in here I am going to give you an order but the order I am going to give you right now overrides it, understand?"

Taymen nodded.

"You are the last chance for our people. There are at least a dozen ships unaccounted for including yours, find them if you can and bring them home. Never surrender, understand?"

Taymen nodded again.

"Understood Princess." He said.

"Here."

Releena handed him a small data chip she had hidden in her shirt.

"What's this?" Taymen asked.

"When I heard the Tray located your ship I recorded a message for you and your crew, when you get out of here pass it on to them." She replied.

Taymen took the chip and put it in his jacket.

"General Assh has also included some tactical information that you may find useful." She said.

Releena looked at the hatch briefly.

"You'll most likely have to fight your way out of here but don't worry about us, they still have a use for me so they won't harm us."

Suddenly the hatch opened and Ourik walked back in with General Assh.

"All taken care of I trust." He said.

"Yes." Releena said as she straightened herself out.

"Now then." She continued as the others sat back down. "Major, as I explained to you the Tray are now considered allies of the Egyptian Empire, therefore you are ordered to return to Egyptian space under Tray escort. Upon your return, you and your crew will be offloaded and transported to the Netara colony where you will receive further orders."

Taymen nodded slowly.

"Very well." He replied with a sigh.

"Prior to us departing from this system." Ourik started. "Your ship will be disarmed and a full security detail will be brought onboard to ensure your full co-operation."

Taymen didn't say anything.

"Now, if that is all we really must be departing." Ourik said as he stood up again.

"Major." Assh said. "We'll see you at Netara."

Taymen nodded once before he moved to open the hatch. The marines and Tray guards were still out in the corridor waiting.

"Escort our guests back to their shuttle." Taymen said before turning to Ourik.

"I'll brief my crew and prepare to receive your security detail." He said.

Taymen waited until they were all out of sight before making his way back to C.A.C.

"Carrey retarget that nuke to detonate between the two cruisers and prepare a full salvo of saber missiles from every tube to finish them off." He ordered as he moved down to the command console.

"Sir what's going on?" Avril asked.

"No time to explain Captain just trust me."

"What about the other ship?" She asked.

"Let it go." Taymen said

"Sir?" She asked.

"Princess Releena is on that ship." Taymen explained. "We're letting it go she's safer with them for the time being, we need to clean up these bastards before we can do anything."

"Sir the Tray shuttle is requesting permission to launch." One of the flight controllers said.

"Get them off my ship Lieutenant." Taymen said.

"Order all batteries to prepare to fire and ready all sword breakers." Avril said.

Taymen accessed the internal com. system.

"All hands remain at your posts and prepare for battle, all marines report to the starboard flight deck and prepare to repel boarding parties." He said.

"Alright listen up." He started after closing the channel. "Here's what's going to happen. The main ship is going to stream out of the system taking General Assh and Princess Releena with it. The cruisers are going to send a full security detail to board us; they think we're going to surrender."

"We're going to fire everything we have at those two cruisers while our sword breakers mop up the fighters."

Taymen looked around to make sure everyone understood the plan.

"Patch me through to Captain Mentz." He ordered.

"You're live Sir." Sairon said a moment later.

"Captain listen to me, there will be a Tray security detail landing shortly when they do, kill the bastards." He ordered.

"Roger that Sir." Mentz replied.

"Sir, the main Tray ship has just streamed out of the system and I have two inbound shuttles requesting permission to land." Sairon reported.

"Here we go." Taymen said. "Permission granted."

Taymen watched the shuttles on the display as they made their landing approach. He was about to declare war on the Tray. The Fleet Marshal underestimated his people and Taymen's crew, it was a mistake Taymen would make sure he'd regret.

"Tray shuttles are aboard Sir." One of the flight controllers said.

"Carrey launch the nuke." Taymen ordered.

"Nuke away Sir."

A few seconds later the missile detonated between the two cruisers sending out a massive shockwave that devastated both ships.

"Heavy damage to targets one and two Sir." Avril reported.

"Tray fighters are closing." Titus added.

"Order all batteries to fire at will and launch sword breakers." Taymen said. "All missile tubes fire at will on targets one and two, finish them off."

"Aye Sir." Carrey replied.

Within seconds both Tray cruisers had taken several direct hits and were unable to maneuver. The shockwave from the nuke had disabled their propulsion and countermeasures so they were wide open for an attack.

After the first salvo of missiles hit the two cruisers drifted into each other and exploded.

The sword breakers quickly engaged the remaining Tray fighters inflicting massive losses. Those that escaped the sword breakers were destroyed by the Avenger's valkerie batteries.

"Remaining fighters have been destroyed, no other sensor contacts within range." Titus said a moment later almost in disbelief.

"Put the ship into stealth mode and recall the sword breakers Captain." Taymen said.

Avril accessed the internal com. system.

"All hands set the ship to stealth mode." She said.

"Damage assessment."

"A few dents in the armor plating but that's about it, we took the Tray completely by surprise." Titus said.

"Something we won't be able to do again." Taymen said quietly.

"Status on the hangar deck?" Avril asked.

"Captain Mentz reports boarding parties have been neutralized." Sairon said.

"Set course for the system's sun, tell the fitters to prepare for refueling." Taymen ordered.

He pulled the data chip the Princess gave him from his jacket and handed it to Sairon.

"Load this into the com. system, be ready to play it ship wide." He said as Sairon took the chip.

Taymen tapped the control on his earpiece and accessed the internal com. system.

"All hands this is Taymen, well done. The remaining enemy ships have retreated to deliver our message to their superiors. There are some things I think you should know however." He paused for a moment and looked around C.A.C.

"Our attackers, who call themselves the Tray have completely overrun our home. Princess Releena and her council have offered their co-operation to save the lives of our people but the rest of the royal family did not survive."

There was another brief silence.

"The Princess was aboard this ship with the Tray delegation, she gave me orders not to surrender to the Tray, and she asked me to pass on the following message to you all."

He gestured to Sairon to play the message.

"This is Princess Releena of the Egyptian royal family to the crew of the Dark Avenger, there isn't much time." The message started.

"I am safe for the time being, I have secured the lives of our people by offering the co-operation of myself and my council of Generals. We have been made aware of your situation and the battles you fought against the Tray forces sent to destroy you thus far.

"We are so very proud of you all. You represent the last hope for our people's freedom and I know you will fight as long and as hard as you can.

"There is very little I can do to help you but I will try to disrupt the Tray leadership for as long as I can. In the mean time there are at least twelve of our ships unaccounted for that need to be rallied and led home."

There was a brief pause.

"Therefore on my own authority I am granting Major Orelle a battlefield promotion to the rank of Colonel, and I'm granting him full battle group command authority. Any of our ships you encounter in your travels will fall under your command now Colonel."

Taymen looked around briefly.

"My heart is with you all, good luck."

Taymen waited a moment before accessing the com. again.

"I know what you're all thinking." He started. "We're one ship, one crew against a vast fleet and impossible odds. We're a long way from home with no support and limited supplies but we have a job to do.

"The Tray seem to have a more advanced understanding of the protostream allowing them to travel much further in less time and their fleet is vast, this puts us at a disadvantage but I'm not going to let that stop us.

"We are the last hope for the Empire, failure means the extermination of our people and that is not an option. We will not surrender. We will engage the Tray at every turn and they will see how grave a mistake they've made when they attacked Egyptians.

"Stand fast, stay strong and stay sharp."

Part II
Burden of Command

'The hardest job in the Defense Force is being in a command position. The hardest thing about being in command is giving the orders that will cost the lives of your crew.'

Defense Force Command Academy lesson 01.

Chapter Seven

As Taymen rounded the corner leading to his cabin he heard a young woman's voice behind him.

"You're up late." She said.

"I could say the same to you." Taymen replied as Elisha walked up behind him.

"I was on my way back to my cabin from sick bay." She said.

"I see." Taymen said as he opened the hatch to his cabin. "Come in."

Elisha followed Taymen inside and Taymen closed the hatch behind her.

The room was larger than the standard crew cabins. There was a small bunk built into the wall to the left of the hatch with a book shelf built into the head. Just ahead of the back wall was a large wood desk with a leather chair that faced the hatch. Against the wall to the right of the hatch were a small leather couch and a wood table as well as a small chair.

"Have a seat." Taymen said gesturing to the couch.

Elisha sat down and picked up a picture off of a small end table next to her. It was an image of a young woman in her late twenties, she had crimped brown hair down to her shoulders and green eyes.

"Girlfriend?" Elisha asked.

"Sister." Taymen answered as he sat down next to her. "She lived on a planet called Cairon last I heard." He continued.

"She looks like you, were you close?" Elisha asked as she placed the picture back on the table.

"Sort of." Taymen replied. "She was the only member of my family who would still speak to me after I joined the Defense Force." He continued. "My parents were against any military action against the separatists like a lot of people on our world. They held the government and the military responsible for the separatist's actions. Nobody wanted a civil war but it happened anyway. Some groups went so far as to call people like my parents traitors when they were nothing more than peace activists."

Taymen paused for a moment.

"I decided to join the military against my parents' wishes and when I told them my father refused to listen to my reasoning. He pretty much disowned me on the spot, he didn't care why I felt it was the right thing to do.

"My mother felt sorry for me, calling me a victim of government propaganda as if I had been brainwashed.

"My brother sided with my parents as always, he thought I was abandoning the family for my own selfish reasons.

"Torri was the only one who accepted my decision and supported me. I haven't spoken to her since I left for basic training."

There was a moment of silence.

"Do you know what happened to her?" Elisha asked.

"I checked in on her from time to time, sent her money to help her through some tight spots. Last I heard she got married last year to some archeology professor at a university on Cairon."

Elisha didn't say anything as she scratched at the top of her right hand.

"Implant still bothering you?" Taymen asked.

"A little." Elisha answered.

"You'll get used to it." Taymen said. "It'll take a few more weeks for the nanites to finish building the pathways to your processor."

Elisha still wasn't used to the idea of a bunch of microscopic robots floating around in her body.

When Taymen finally changed his mind about letting her stay aboard she was insistent on helping out in some way. She got the implant about a month ago so she could access the ship's systems.

It was relatively simple. The Doctor gave her an injection of nanites that built a microprocessor at the base of her skull under the skin. Then they built a group of pathways from the processor to the interface they built in her right hand.

It was a strange sensation feeling the nanites build the implant in her hand, it still itched and she swore she could still feel them moving around under her skin, though the doctor insisted it was all in her head.

"How are you finding communications?" He asked.

"Good." Elisha replied. "I think I've got the hang of most of the systems and procedures now." She continued.

"Good." Taymen replied. "I think we'll leave you there for a few more weeks so you can get a little more familiar with your implant before we rotate you through the other operations stations."

"Actually." Elisha started. "I was wondering what the chances were of me getting on as a flight controller?" She asked.

"I don't think it'll be a problem, I'll arrange for you to get some time at flight control to start your training." He said.

Suddenly the room was filled with the harsh buzz of the internal com. system, which meant Taymen's night was probably going to be a long one.

"All hands set the ship to stealth mode Colonel Orelle to C.A.C." Avril ordered over the com.

Taymen sighed.

"Well, if you'll excuse me." He said as he led Elisha to the hatch and out of the cabin.

Dark Avenger, C.A.C.
24:45 Abydos Standard Time
Day 10, Fifth Cycle, Egyptian Year 3201

"What is it Captain?" Taymen asked as he made his way to the command console.

"A Tray light cruiser has just streamed into the system at extreme range." Avril replied.

Taymen checked the main display to see the sensor contact near the edge of the Avenger's sensor range.

"Have they detected us?" He asked.

"Not yet." Avril replied as she hooked a few strands of her long dark hair behind her ear.

Taymen turned to Titus.

"How long until bleed off is complete?" He asked.

"We can stream out any time now Sir." Titus replied.

"Has Kaile and her crew finished examining the Tray shuttles?" Taymen asked.

"I believe so." Avril replied.

"Then let's send them back to the Tray." Taymen ordered.

"Sir?" Avril asked.

"Make sure they transmit distress signals on all bands so the Tray don't miss them."

"Aye Sir." Avril said after a moment.

"Stream us out as soon as the shuttles are clear." Taymen ordered before leaving C.A.C.

Releena sat at the desk in her room reading over the Tray report that Fleet Marshal Ourik had given her earlier that morning. It confirmed that the two shuttles recovered a few weeks ago were the ones sent to board the Dark Avenger before it opened fire on its escort ships. When the shuttles were recovered they found no sign of the security detail aboard.

Releena placed the report down on her desk when she heard a knock on the door.

"Come in." She said.

General Assh walked in and closed the door behind him.

"General." She said as she hooked a lock of her long dark hair behind her ear.

"I assume you've read that." Assh said referring to the report on Releena's desk.

"It seems Taymen is taking this war a little personally." She replied.

"He's sending a message to the Tray." Assh explained. "He wants to scare them, hoping they'll do something stupid like expose all of their forces at once in an attempt to destroy his ship. If they do that, he can stream out to a safe location and he'll have ten hours while the Tray ships bleed off radiation to set up a defensive line before the Tray can stream their ships back to Abydos."

"But the Tray ships can stream further than ours." Releena said.

"Yes but Taymen probably doesn't know that yet." Assh replied.

"Do you really think the Tray would expose their entire fleet like that?" Releena asked.

"No." Assh answered. "And I'm sure Taymen knows it, but at the very least it will make the Tray re-evaluate their tactics which should buy the Avenger some time."

Taymen woke up from a dreamless sleep to hear Titus' voice over the com. system in his cabin. He sat up and reached for his earpiece, placing it in his right ear before hitting the control to access the com. system.

"Go ahead Titus." He said.

"Sorry to disturb you Sir, but we're receiving an automated distress signal." Titus said.

"I'm on my way." Taymen replied.

When he got to C.A.C. Titus was watching a sensor contact on the command console. It was close to the ship but not quite in weapons range.

"Report Commander." Taymen said.

"We think it's some sort of escape pod programmed to broadcast an automated signal." Titus said.

"Any identification?" Taymen asked.

"No Sir, but the signal is being transmitted on the Egyptian emergency band."

Taymen didn't say anything. He expected to find survivors but not this far from home, it was impossible.

"Deploy a search and rescue prowler to recover the pod, have a team of marines on the hangar deck just in case." He ordered.

"Aye Sir." Titus replied.

"Deploy sensor drones to make sure there are no surprises around." Avril said.

As Taymen waited in C.A.C. he heard the call for a medical team to report to the hangar deck, shortly after he was called to sickbay. When he got there the first thing Taymen noticed was a little girl laying unconscious on one of the beds. She couldn't have been more than nine years old.

"She suffered from mild oxygen deprivation, another few minutes and there'd be permanent brain damage." The Doctor said as he walked up beside Taymen.

"Any identification on her?" Taymen asked.

"Just this." The Doctor replied as he handed Taymen a small card that was attached to a silver chain.

Taymen immediately recognized it as a citizens' ID.

The girls' name was Allia, she was apparently ten years old and she was from one of the outer colonies near the edge of the Egyptian territory.

"Is this legitimate?" Taymen asked.

"Well I doubt it's a forgery but we don't have access to the data network to confirm her identity. I don't think she's a threat though." The Doctor replied sarcastically.

Suddenly Allia woke up coughing.

"Easy now." The Doctor said as he sat her up.

"Please." Allia said between breaths.

"We need your help."

"It's okay." Taymen replied. "You're safe here."

67

"No." Allia said in a panic. "My family, the others they need your help. The Tray, they were chasing us." She continued.

"Where are they?" Taymen asked.

"I don't know." Allia whined. "I wasn't supposed to be near the pod, but when the attack started I hid inside it, I don't know what happened after that."

Taymen tapped the control on his earpiece to open a channel to the com. station in C.A.C.

"Put me through to Chief Assurman." He said.

A moment later Kaile was on the channel.

"Kaile I want you to go through that escape pod's computer, see if you can find out where it came from." Taymen said before closing the channel again.

"Please you have to hurry." Allia pleaded.

"Don't worry we'll get there as soon as we can." Taymen said reassuringly.

Titan at Abydos
08:00 Abydos Standard Time
Day 23, Fifth Cycle, Egyptian Year 3201

Releena stared out the window of her quarters as they passed by Abydos once more before leaving orbit.

Ourik had been called back to one of their field stations just outside of Egyptian space and he insisted she go with him. Releena was getting tired of being carted around like some trophy while her people suffered in work camps.

Abydos was completely occupied by Tray forces, though there were still some areas where they hadn't been able to establish a base.

It's believed that there are some small groups of Egyptian soldiers holding up in those areas but nothing has been confirmed yet, and Releena was doing everything she could to make sure it stayed that way.

General Assh had managed to sneak a few of his soldiers into minor positions in the Tray military, which gave them a few operatives to provide information back to Releena who uploaded it to a storage device in orbit which was programmed to transmit all its stored data to the Dark Avenger as soon as it was in range.

From what she learned so far, the Tray understanding of the protostream is no more advanced than the Egyptians' like they first thought. They simply discovered a more advanced version of the technology in their own galaxy. It seems that the type discovered by the Egyptians was a simple short range system while the one discovered by the Tray was an intergalactic system meant for extremely long ranges.

As Releena sat lost in her own thoughts the door to her quarters opened and Fleet Marshal Ourik let himself in.

"Come in." Releena said sarcastically.

"Enjoying the view?" He asked.

"I was enjoying the company." Releena replied.

Ourik ignored her remark and sat down in the chair across from her.

"What am I doing here?" Releena asked.

"Well it's a long trip to the outer field stations and I thought this would be a good time for us to get to know each other." Ourik replied.

Releena made no attempt to hide her disgust.

"And why would we want to do that, I can't see you staying here much longer." Releena replied.

Surprisingly Ourik picked up on her subtle implication.

"Now Princess do you really think that those twelve missing ships will make any difference against a fleet as vast as ours?" He asked.

There was that Tray arrogance Releena had come to expect.

"No, I don't Fleet Marshal." She replied. "I believe that one ship will make the difference, even against a fleet as vast as yours."

Ourik chuckled a little.

"Of course, the Dark Avenger." He replied. "I'm surprised that you would put your faith in such a small class of ship with such a young commander."

Releena smiled smugly.

"They've proven to be more than you can handle so far, how many times has it defeated your ships and escaped now, six?"

Ourik didn't say anything.

"Be careful Fleet Marshal, they say that those who hide behind numbers and boast about size are compensating for other...shortcomings."

Dark Avenger, Location Unknown
11:30 Abydos Standard Time
Day 23, Fifth Cycle, Egyptian Year 3201

"Stream complete Sir." Aurin said.

"We're running in stealth mode." Titus reported.

"Sensor contacts?" Avril asked.

Titus checked the sensor display and sorted through the readings.

"I have a single large contact dead ahead, it looks like it may be a station of some kind." He reported.

"It's broadcasting a general distress call on an encrypted Egyptian channel." Sairon said.

"Helm all ahead full put us into a standard orbit around the station." Taymen ordered.

"Should we contact them Sir?" Avril asked.

"Not yet." Taymen replied. "We don't know who else may be listening."

"Multiple sensor contacts." Titus reported. "Two Tray light cruisers, they're painting the station."

"Battle mode Titus." Taymen ordered.

"They've launched missiles at the station." Avril said.

"Deploy armor." Taymen snapped. "Carrey launch a salvo of counter measures."

As the Avenger sped towards the Tray cruisers and the station, eight decoy missiles closed in and detonated between the Tray missiles and the station.

"One of the cruisers is moving to intercept us; the other one is closing on the station." Titus reported.

"Bring all batteries to bear." Taymen ordered. "Batteries one through eight direct fire on target one remainder on target two." He continued.

"Incoming ordnance!" Avril shouted.

A few seconds later the ship shuttered with the impact of three missiles striking the ship's upper hull.

"Load missile tubes one through four, fire a half salvo of javelins at each target." Taymen ordered.

"Missiles away Sir." Carrey reported.

"The cruisers are launching fighters." Titus said.

"Launch sword breakers." Taymen ordered. "Batteries three through eight switch to enemy suppression fire."

"Sir a group of fighters are making a run at the station." Avril said.

Taymen checked the sensor console to see at least fifty enemy fighters head for the station.

"Helm get us between the station and those cruisers and bring our starboard side to bear."

"Aye Sir." Aurin replied.

The Avenger continued forward at full speed until it was blocking the cruisers line of fire to the station.

"All port side batteries switch to enemy suppression fire, take out those fighters." Taymen ordered.

Just as the Avenger turned its starboard side to face the Tray cruisers four missiles impacted her hull. Taymen and Avril were nearly thrown to the floor.

"Direct hit to the starboard control thrusters." The Damage control officer reported.

"We're in an uncontrolled lateral spin." Aurin added.

"Disengage the port control thrusters to compensate." Avril said.

"We can't." The maneuvering officer replied. "The fuel valves are locked open."

"Have a damage control team cut the fuel feeds to the port control thrusters." Taymen ordered.

"Sir." One of the damage control officers called.

"What is it Sergeant?" Taymen asked.

The deck shuttered with the impact of more ordnance before the Sergeant replied.

"Fires are spreading through decks twenty-three and twenty-four moving aft of frames thirty-seven and forty-two."

"Fire suppression systems?" Taymen asked.

"Off line Sir."

Taymen froze in place.

He had to do something quickly, both about the Tray and the fires. "Carrey, all missile tubes full salvos of saber missiles on both targets." He continued.

"Ready Sir."

"Fire at will, all batteries switch to direct fire on those cruisers, target their fighter bays and missile batteries!" Taymen said. "Sergeant, evacuate decks twenty-three and twenty-four."

"Already done Sir, but we have people trapped in several sections." The sergeant reported.

"Fires have spread aft of frame forty-seven on deck twenty four."

Taymen's mind was racing. If the fires reached frame fifty-three they would ignite the fuel cells and they would lose the ship. He had to get his people out of those sections or they would die.

The deck shuttered more and more as Taymen thought back to his training at the academy. This was what they called a damned order. The solution to the problem was simple enough, but giving the order was one of the hardest things he would ever have to do. Taymen had no choice, he had to act fast or his ship would be lost, and with it any hope for his people.

"Sergeant seal off those decks from frames thirty to fifty-four and decompress all sections." Taymen ordered.

Avril and Titus along with half the crew in C.A.C. stood frozen for a moment.

"Sir, we have people trapped in those sections, if we..."

Taymen cut him off.

"Now Sergeant."

"But Sir." The Sergeant pleaded.

"Seal off those sections and decompress them now or we'll lose the ship!" Taymen snapped.

Avril recognized the look in Taymen's eyes. She had seen it hundreds of times in other commanding officers. It was the cold heartless look of a ship commander when his instincts took over to give the orders they otherwise couldn't give in order to save their crew.

"Aye Sir." The Sergeant finally replied as he accessed the com. and gave the orders to seal the bulkheads so he could decompress the decks.

"As he turned away Taymen glanced at the sensor console and noticed one of the Tray cruisers was gone.

"Status on the Tray." Taymen said.

"Cruiser one has been destroyed along with eighty percent of their fighters, cruiser two has taken heavy damage and..." Avril paused for a moment as she checked the display.

"They just streamed out of the system along with their remaining fighters."

Taymen checked the display for a moment.

"Sergeant, status." He said.

"Decompression cycle complete Sir, the fires are out and we're pressurizing the decks."

Taymen nodded slowly.

Avril moved closer to Taymen and spoke softly.

"If they remember their training they'll be fine." She said coldly.

Taymen only nodded as he exhaled.

"Sir, we're receiving a hail from the station." Sairon said.

Taymen stood silent for a moment while Sairon waited for his response.

"Patch it through." Taymen finally replied.

The C.A.C. speakers crackled with static for a moment.

"This is Captain Alleron of the Egyptian Defense Force calling the Egyptian battleship, do you read me?"

"This is Colonel Taymen Orelle of the battleship Dark Avenger, what's your situation Captain?" Taymen asked.

"We're in pretty rough shape Sir but we have no casualties from the attack, request permission to come aboard."

"Negative Captain, we will be sending security and medical teams shortly, standby for our arrival."

There was a brief pause before Alleron answered again.

"Understood Sir, we'll be waiting for you." He said before closing the channel.

"Titus have three prowlers prepped for launch, I want medical and security personnel ready to go in ten minutes, secure the station." Taymen ordered.

"Aye Sir." Titus replied.

Taymen sat across from the hatch of the prowler as it glided across the void space towards the station. The security teams had secured the station almost ten minutes ago and when they reported back they said that Captain Alleron had requested to speak with Taymen personally.

Avril was of course against the idea of Taymen going over to the station at all, but he had some questions he wanted answered and he didn't want to risk a boarding party invading his ship.

Allia stood in the cockpit of the prowler watching the station as it got closer. She made no attempt to hide her excitement. She was obviously glad to be home and was no doubt worried about her family on the station.

"Stand-by for landing."

The pilot announced as the prowler approached an open landing bay on the station's upper section.

The forward breaking thrusters fired for a second bringing the ship to a gradual halt just before the dorsal thrusters fired driving the ship down into the landing bay. A few feet off the deck and the keel thrusters fired bringing the ship to float off the deck before the drive thrusters fired again moving the ship forward. The pilot maneuvered the ship through a small tunnel that led to a large bay where he set the ship down near a set of heavy pressure doors.

"We're down." The co-pilot said as they contacted the deck.

A second later a set of large pressure doors at the head of the bay had closed sealing them off from the tunnel and the landing bay was pressurized.

"Bay's pressurized Sir." The pilot reported a few minutes later.

"Open the hatch." Taymen said.

As the side hatch of the prowler opened, so did the heavy pressure doors to the bay.

As he stepped out of the ship with Allia close behind Taymen noticed four figures entering the bay.

As they got closer he recognized the Defense Force uniform on one of the figures in the middle. It was worn by a young man who couldn't have been more than twenty-five years old.

His head was shaved and his blue eyes remained fixed on Taymen. His collar displayed the rank of Captain and his shoulder flash displayed the crest of the Saber Blade, a small frigate that fought alongside the Dark Avenger during the separatist war.

As the party got closer Taymen saw the other three people with who he assumed to be Captain Alleron were civilians.

Alleron stopped a few paces from Taymen and saluted sharply. Taymen returned the salute and moved closer to the Captain.

"Captain Alleron." He said.

"Welcome aboard Sir." Alleron replied. "These are the station council members." He said.

"This is Seahla Vrohl." Alleron gestured to a small older woman to his left.

"This is her daughter Sharn Vrohl." A tall young woman to Alleron's right nodded once in greeting.

"And this is Jassen Pitt." He said gesturing to the man to Sharn's right.

The others seemed to be happy enough to see Taymen and his security teams, but something about the look on Jassen's face told Taymen that he didn't want them there.

He was a tall man in his mid thirties with a mess of brown hair. He wore several necklaces around his neck and a thin set of glasses over his green eyes which told Taymen one of two things. Either he was incapable of receiving nanite treatments to correct his vision or he was one of a group of people who rejected any technology used by the military as a form of protest against violence. Ironically enough it was that protesting against violence that started the separatist war in the first place.

The other feature about Jassen that leapt out at Taymen was his left arm. His forearm had been replaced by a crude cybernetic implant. It was a metallic gray color, darker in some spots where the alloy had begun to corrode.

Taymen had never seen an implant like Jassen's, most replacement limbs were made up to look like the real thing but it was clear that Jassen's was made with no effort to conceal it. It took a second glance but Taymen quickly recognized the two thirty caliber gun barrels mounted on the sides of the implant, a unique modification to say the least.

"If you'll come with us Colonel we can talk in the board room." Alleron said.

"Very well Captain, but first I think this one should be returned to her family." Taymen said referring to Allia who was standing just behind him near the hatch of the prowler.

"Allia." Sharn said in relief as she knelt in front of the little girl.

"Are you okay, what happened to you?" Sharn asked.

"We found her adrift in an escape pod." Taymen said.

"The pods were launched with automated distress beacons. They were programmed to transmit to Egyptian signatures and lead any friendly ships back here." Alleron explained.

"If you'll come with us we'll explain everything." He continued.

Taymen simply nodded.

Alleron and the others led Taymen and the marines to the main habitat section of the station after they took Allia to find her family. They were so grateful to have their daughter back, Taymen barely managed to pull her mother off of him.

Taymen looked around the habitat section and thought it looked more like a refugee camp than a space station.

Families huddled in shelters made of sheets and scrap metal that were built up against the bulkheads or under staircases. Portable heating units were spread throughout the habitat section along with CO_2 scrubbers to purify the air.

A deeper look at the station's interior indicated that it was clearly Egyptian design, though it was a much older style and Taymen had never heard of any outposts this far from Abydos.

"Are there no quarters on the station?" Taymen asked.

"There are." Alleron started. "But the life support systems aren't functioning in any of them yet. It's barely running in the main corridors, we've had to use scrubbers and mobile heaters to help take the strain off the station's systems." He explained.

Alleron turned down the corridor and led them into a small room just off the habitat section.

The marines took up positions against the walls while Sharn and Seahla took seats near the door. Jassen sat at the head of the table as Taymen took a seat to his right, noting the scowl on his face.

"So Colonel it would seem that we owe you a debt of gratitude." Seahla said in a raspy voice.

"I'll settle for an explanation." Taymen replied. "This station for starters, and how you got here."

There was a brief silence before Alleron answered.

"We were aboard the Saber Blade during a Tray attack on one of the outlying outposts." He started.

76

"We just evacuated the colony and were trying to stream out of the system when we were attacked.

"Our navigation computer was damaged and when we streamed out we ended up in void space, alone. Two months of streaming blind and we hit a strange stream hub. It sent us two stream distances from this station, we still don't know how."

"So you found this station and just decided to move in?" Taymen asked.

"Sort of." Alleron said. "When we got here it was abandoned."

"The station is Egyptian, we believe it was built by the ancestors." Seahla said.

"It was in rough shape when we got here." Alleron continued. "We managed to get limited life support up and running and offloaded the civilians. Somehow though the Tray managed to track us here. The Saber Blade destroyed a small patrol but they transmitted our location beforehand.

"We knew they would be back so we offloaded anything we could use from the ship and sent it out to lead the Tray away."

"What happened to them?" Taymen asked.

"We assume the ship was destroyed by the Tray." Jassen said.

"We haven't heard from them since they left. I stayed behind with a prowler and a few engineers and marines, nobody else made it." Alleron said.

"We've been trying to repair the station, we knew the Tray would come back for us so we sent the escape pods to see if we could find help, the rest you know."

Taymen sat silently for a moment.

"So what do you plan to do now?" He finally asked.

"That would depend on you young man." Seahla said.

"We are content to repair this station and live in piece out of the way under the protection of your ship."

"Sorry." Taymen cut her off. "We're not staying." He said. "We have to get back to Abydos, I have orders from Princess Releena."

"Do you really think you'll even make it home?" Jassen snapped.

"You have one small ship, what can you hope to accomplish?" Taymen ignored his tone.

"There are other ships that are missing, if we can find them we can marshal a fleet large enough to liberate the outer colonies and close in on the Tray."

Jassen gawked.

"You won't even make it to the outer colonies." He said.

"That's enough Jassen." Seahla said.

"We won't ask you to disobey your orders Colonel." She said. "But any help you can offer would be appreciated."

"We don't need their help." Jassen said.

"What do you need?" Taymen asked, ignoring Jassen.

"Engineers mostly." Alleron said. "Any food and medicine you can spare would be helpful as well Sir."

Taymen stood from his seat.

"I'll have engineering teams sent over in the morning along with any supplies we can spare." He said.

"Thank you Colonel." Alleron replied.

Ancient's Space Station
17:40 Abydos Standard Time
Day 23, Fifth Cycle, Egyptian Year 3201

Jassen stood on the upper level of the habitat section staring at a silver ring that was on a leather strap around his neck. The ring that once sat on his left ring finger, the one thing he still had that reminded him of his family.

He glanced down at the implant that now occupied where his left arm once was. He still had nightmares about the day he lost it but the memory of his lost arm didn't make him feel nearly as bad as everything else he lost that day.

The first Tray attack on his colony was a massive missile attack on the planet's surface. One missile struck the colony directly in the residential section causing a massive shockwave that practically leveled the entire area.

Jassen was in the transport district trying to arrange for passage off the colony for him and his family. His son attended an academy on Abydos, he still didn't know what happened to him.

His wife and two young daughters were in the residential section when the shockwave destroyed their home.

Jassen got back to what was left of his house before the rescue teams were even dispatched only to find his wife and older daughter dead outside.

His youngest daughter was partially buried under the rubble just out of his reach. He tried to dig her out but the debris was too heavy for him to move and what was left of the house structure was threatening to collapse on them both.

Jassen continued to try and get her out until the rescue teams arrived what seemed to be an eternity later. As they went to get something to cut through the debris Jassen continued to dig.

He was inches away when the rest of the house collapsed on him, knocking him unconscious. When he came to, he found himself on the Saber Blade in sick bay, his left arm was gone and his daughter was nowhere in sight. The collapse had buried her completely, by the time the rescue teams got to her she was dead.

Jassen's arm had been completely crushed and they had no choice but to replace it with the crude implant they managed to improvise onboard. Surprisingly his wedding ring was the only thing that was intact.

"Still beating yourself up I see." Seahla said as she came up behind Jassen, who didn't respond.

"It's not your fault you know, you did all you could." She continued.

"Wasn't enough." Jassen replied.

Seahla leaned over the railing and glanced down at the lower level.

"So, what do you think about Colonel Orelle?" She asked.

"I don't trust him." Jassen said coldly.

"You don't trust anyone who wears a uniform." Seahla replied.

"They've never given me a reason to." He said. "I don't think we need them, they haven't done us any good so far."

"Have you forgotten that it was the Colonel and his crew who fought off the Tray?" Seahla said.

"He's young, too young to be a Colonel." Jassen replied.

Seahla giggled.

"Perhaps he is, but I see wisdom and sincerity in his eyes, I believe we can trust his word."

"Even if we can trust him what's the point, he won't stay. He's a soldier, the only thing he knows how to do is wage war. Of course he's going to choose to leave us so he can go fight."

Seahla shook her head.

"I don't know what his reason for fighting is, perhaps you should ask him yourself." She said as she turned and walked away.

Jassen continued to look down at the lower level. He didn't want to know the Colonel's reasons. He was a soldier, they were all the same. Single minded violent killers who lived for nothing but destruction.

Dark Avenger, Captain's Cabin
14:00 Abydos Standard Time
Day 24, Fifth Cycle, Egyptian Year 3201

Taymen looked over the casualty report from the attack reading the names over and over again burning them into his memory.

Ninety-six of his crew were trapped on those decks when they were decompressed, only twelve walked out. Eighty-four of his crew were dead because of what he had done. Eighty-four sons and daughters and husbands and wives and parents are dead because of Taymen's decision.

He had lost friends in combat before and he always felt the loss but this was different. Since he had been in command of the Dark Avenger he had never lost anyone in combat, but now he was staring at the names of eighty-four people that he killed.

Many of them he knew very well, they had served aboard the Avenger before Taymen took command and now they were gone because of him.

Lieutenant Mentiel was only twenty-two years old. Taymen met his grandmother on Abydos during shore leave after the ceasefire, she couldn't stop talking about how proud she was of her brave grandson.

Sergeant Noria was an experienced veteran, one of the best armament technicians he had on board. His wife had invited Taymen to their home on Pria for dinner. Taymen couldn't believe how much Noria's son looked like him.

They were all close to him, they were his crew and he was responsible for them. He knew many of their families, they all trusted him to keep their loved ones safe and now, how was he ever going to face them again?

Suddenly the sound of the door buzzer filled the cabin.

"Come in." Taymen said as he placed the report on his desk.

Avril walked into the cabin and closed the hatch behind her.

"We've just launched the prowlers carrying the DC parties and supplies to the station Sir." She said as she walked up to the desk.

"Thank you Captain." Taymen said as he shuffled some data pads around, trying to conceal the report.

A few seconds later he noticed Avril still standing in front of him with no indication that she was about to leave.

"Something else?" He asked.

"It's not your fault." Avril said.

Taymen didn't respond, which made Avril feel a little awkward.

"You made a decision to save the ship and the crew, no one can blame you for that. We would all be dead now if you hadn't given the order to decompress the decks."

Taymen sighed.

"I know that." He answered. "I knew that when I gave the order to seal those decks and I knew what would happen to the people trapped in those sections, it doesn't make it any easier." He said.

Avril didn't know what else to say.

"Launch a pair of sword breakers for a combat patrol around the station and have them replaced every eight hours for maintenance." Taymen ordered. "Inform the crew that there will be a memorial service in cargo bay three at twenty-two hundred hours." He continued.

"Aye Sir." Avril said before she turned to leave.

Avril left the cabin and closed the hatch behind her before heading down the corridor. As she made her way to the ladder leading to the next deck, she couldn't help but think about the look in Taymen's eyes. It was the first time she found herself actually worrying about him.

Before, whenever she looked into his eyes she could see confidence in his command abilities and the certainty that he was doing the right thing with each decision, now however she could see fear and uncertainty, which was a very dangerous thing for the crew.

Chapter Nine

Taymen woke up in a cold sweat breathing heavily. He looked around to find he was still in his cabin, a glance at the clock on his desk showed it was twenty-one hundred hours.

As he stood up he heard the com. unit chime indicating there was a transmission coming into his earpiece. He placed the com. device in his ear and hit the control to open the channel.

"Go ahead." He said.

"Sorry to disturb you Sir." Sairon answered. *"There's a shuttle from the station requesting landing clearance, they say they're carrying the station council."*

"Very well Sairon let them land, I'll meet them on the hangar deck." He answered.

"Aye Sir."

Taymen put on his uniform and left his cabin making his way down to the port hangar deck. When he got there a prowler was being towed out of the airlock and onto the deck. The hatch opened and the deck crew helped Sharn and Seahla out while Jassen jumped out beside them. Sharn helped Seahla across the hangar deck and stopped in front of Taymen.

"Welcome aboard." He said.

"Thank you Colonel." Sharn said.

"We're sorry to arrive unannounced." Seahla added.

"Not at all." Taymen said. "Is everything alright?" He asked as he slowly led them towards the pressure hatch leading out to the corridor.

"I understand that several members of your crew perished in the battle with the Tray." Seahla said.

Taymen took a moment to respond.

"Yes." He answered. "Eighty-four crewmen were killed in the attack; we're holding a memorial service in just under an hour." He said.

"We've come to pay our respects; after all they died protecting us." Seahla replied.

Taymen glanced back at Jassen whose expression remained blank.

82

"Of course, we'd be honored to have you." Taymen replied as he opened the pressure hatch and led them off the hangar deck.

Taymen took Seahla and the others on a brief tour of the ship until the memorial started. By the time they got to the cargo bay most of crew with the exception of the on duty personnel was assembled along with the ship's priest.

"Captain on deck!" Someone yelled.

Everyone in the bay snapped to attention and waited silently.

"As you were." Taymen said as he made his way to the head of the bay where Titus, Avril and a few other members of his senior staff stood facing the back of the bay.

Behind them on a raised platform was the ship's priest. In front of Avril and the others were eighty-four closed munitions containers that served as caskets arranged in two even rows with a wide space in the middle for a walkway. The crew was arranged in eight even rows, four on either side of the walkway. Taymen and the others took up positions with the rest of the senior staff at the head of the bay. Shortly after they arrived the ceremony began.

The priest's prayers went on for only ten minutes or so and the following hour was crew members speaking about their lost friends. Finally it was Taymen's turn to speak as he was the commanding officer, it was expected that he say something about the lost crewmen.

He moved up to the podium on the platform and paused for a moment. He hated public speaking but it was the least he could do in this case.

Taymen looked across the room at the faces of his crew, each looking to him for strength. Before, Taymen had no reservations about being in command. The fact that his entire crew was relying on him never bothered him. Now however, when he looked at the faces staring up at him Taymen felt overwhelmed. He began to question every decision he made since he took command of the Avenger, it was as if he had suddenly realized that he never had the ability to lead.

"We find ourselves here." He started. "Looking for the answer to a question that I've been asking myself since we arrived here. Why them?" He paused for a moment to look across the room again.

"I don't know why, I don't know why they had to die so the rest of us could live but I know the look in all of your eyes. I know the question that plagues us all, the one we're too afraid to ask." Taymen paused again.

"Are they the lucky ones? I can't answer that and I don't want to answer that. It falls to us now to continue to fight for them, for their families and friends so that everything they've done in their life will be remembered.

"They've entrusted the future of their families and friends to us so I will continue to fight for them as long as I'm alive, and I ask that you all choose to do the same." Taymen's voice gradually got louder as he spoke.

"We're at war, it's a cold hard reality that friends die but it's a reality that we can't change. All we have is each other and it's times like this that we need each other the most.

"Draw strength from your colleagues, from your friends and from the memory of your families. We're not alone and we're not going to let them die for nothing because I will be damned if I'm going to let our people suffer at the hands of the Tray because we were too afraid of dying.

"This is bigger than me, it's bigger than any of us and it's our job to make sure that this is the last time any of us suffer a loss like this."

There was a long silence across the room as Taymen stepped down from the podium. He took up his original position and brought himself sharply to attention.

There he stood with his heels together and his arms tight into his sides for only a second.

"Attention on deck!" He shouted.

The bay echoed with the sound of everyone coming to attention simultaneously.

"General salute, present arms!" He called a second later.

Everyone's right arm shot up into a salute and remained there for a few minutes.

"Order, arms!" Taymen called before returning his arm to his side.

"Honor guard, dismissed!"

Everyone in the bay turned and moved out of their ranks in a relaxed manner.

Some left the bay while others stayed to speak with friends.

"I wonder if I could speak with you in private Colonel." Seahla asked.

Taymen nodded once before turning to Avril.

"Captain take Mr. Pitt and Miss. Vrohl to the officer's mess, we'll join you there shortly." He said.

"Yes Sir." Avril replied. "If you'll come with me." She said leading Sharn and Jassen out of the bay through the aft pressure hatch.

Taymen led Seahla back to his cabin so they could speak.

"I wonder Colonel, do you really believe you can return home?" She asked.

Taymen simply nodded. "I can't afford to think we can't, I owe it to them to at least try." He answered.

"You mean you're dead crew members." Seahla said.

Taymen nodded again.

"Why do you bear so much on your shoulders?"

Taymen simply sighed, but he didn't say anything.

"It's not just the death of your crew members that you blame yourself for is it?" Seahla continued. "You hold yourself responsible for the Tray occupation, for the capture of Princess Releena and for all the deaths at the hands of the Tray don't you?"

Taymen thought about how to respond.

"It's hard not to." He said. "When we got word of the initial attack, I ordered my ship to Netara instead of Abydos going against our orders." He paused for a moment.

Seahla recognized the look of sorrow in his eyes.

"I have to wonder if I should have done things differently. Eighty-four of my crew are dead because of an order I gave, because I was too frightened to wait another minute for them to get to safety, I ordered their deaths."

Seahla could see the pain in Taymen's eyes slowly fade and be replaced by anger.

"How can I not hold myself responsible for things that are so obviously my fault?"

Seahla sighed.

"I see." She said. "So you went to Netara because you didn't want to save Abydos?" She asked.

"Of course not." Taymen replied. "I didn't think one ship would have made any difference at Abydos by the time we got there, I went to save who I thought...I...could."

Taymen's voice trailed off slightly.

"And when you left Netara, you left the Princess behind to save your own ship?" She asked.

"No." Taymen said quietly.

"The Princess's ship was away, we were leaving to meet her at the evacuation point."

Taymen noticed a slight smile on Seahla's face.

"And had you not given the order that got those crew members killed, they would all be alive now?"

Taymen sighed.

"None of us would be here now if I hadn't given the order." He said.

Seahla nodded as her smile widened.

"Amazing how the small details manage to escape your memory when you're too busy blaming yourself for everything isn't it?" She said.

"You see Colonel some people are realists, seeing everything for what it is at face value. Others see only what they want to see to make them feel better about themselves and the mistakes they've made. For these people the ends always justify the means. Others however, like you Colonel see only the negative side of their decisions in hindsight, thinking they were all just a constant trail of mistakes leading to the worst possible outcome. People like this tend to think that unless everyone is happy, unless that everything went right and everything is perfect they made the wrong choice."

There was a brief silence before Seahla continued.

"We are not gods Taymen. We cannot see what will come of our actions and the universe is not perfect. I've never been a soldier but I've lived long enough to know that sometimes there is no right decision. In the end the only way someone like yourself can justify their decisions and accept the consequences of them is to accept the fact that the only thing you can truly control is your intentions."

Before Taymen could respond the internal alarm went off and he was called to C.A.C.

"Come with me." He said.

He led Seahla through the corridors to C.A.C. where Avril had brought Jassen and Sharn.

"Report." Taymen said as he approached the command console.

"Two shuttles from the station are on approach." Avril reported.

"They're not responding to hails and they're not changing course.

Taymen turned to Jassen and the others.

"Any idea what this is about?" He asked.

Jassen simply shook his head.

"Sairon open a channel to the lead shuttle, general broadcast." Taymen ordered as he tapped the control on his earpiece.

"Go ahead Sir." Sairon said.

"This is Colonel Taymen Orelle of the Dark Avenger, state your intention." He said.

A long moment passed with no response before Taymen closed the channel.

"Sir they're on approach for the starboard landing deck." Titus said.

"Bring all starboard batteries to bear." Taymen ordered.

"Colonel!" Jassen snapped. "You can't intend to destroy them." He said.

"Relax I only want to give them a reason to reconsider." Taymen replied.

"Battery eight fire a warning burst across their bow." He ordered.

There was a brief silence as Taymen watched the main sensor display.

"Battery eight reports they fired across their bow, still no change in course and no response to hails." Titus reported.

"Now what?" Avril asked.

"Seal the landing deck outer doors and have our patrol sword breakers paint the shuttles." Taymen said as he glanced over at Jassen.

"Doors sealed Sir." Titus said.

"Incoming ordnance!" Avril snapped.

Less than a second later four light missile impacted the starboard landing deck's outer door and the two shuttles sped into the bay.

"Shuttles have landed, we're being boarded Sir." Titus said.

"Evacuate the starboard hangar deck and seal it off, I want marines at every access point, order them to fire only if fired upon and avoid casualties." Taymen said.

"Aye Sir." Titus replied.

"How did civilian shuttles get missile launchers?" Avril asked.

Taymen turned to Jassen and the others while Avril pulled a side arm out from a hidden compartment under the command console.

"I would really like to know what's going on here." Taymen said.

Jassen looked at Sharn and Seahla who simply nodded once.

"He has a right to know Jassen." Seahla said.

"Know what?" Taymen asked, his patience clearly running thin.

Jassen sighed for a moment.

"There is a movement on the station, a small group who believes the military is responsible for our situation." He started.

Taymen didn't like where this was going.

"Since you arrived here several members of their group thought that we should take over your ship and keep it for our own defense here."

Taymen took a step towards Jassen.

"And how would you know about this group's intentions Jassen?" He asked.

"Because I'm one of those people."

Before Jassen could do anything Avril had her weapon trained on him with a targeting marker projected on his head, a few seconds later Titus and a few other members in C.A.C. had weapons trained on him as well.

Jassen made no attempt to move.

"Wait a minute." He said. "I don't think we should take over your ship, I was against that from the beginning. I thought you should've left as soon as possible to avoid this." He explained.

There was a long silence before Sairon interrupted.

"Sir." She said." Fire team two reports they've had to fall back, boarding parties have advanced beyond frame forty five."

There was another moment of silence.

"Alright, stand down." Taymen said.

"Sir." Avril protested.

"Stand down Captain!" Taymen repeated.

"Keep an eye on him for now." He said.

"Boarders are advancing beyond frame forty-eight." Sairon reported.

"Evacuate the entire deck and depressurize it." Taymen ordered.

"Aye Sir." Titus replied.

"I must apologize for this Colonel, I assure you that this attack is unsanctioned by the station council." Sharn said.

"Don't worry about it right now." Taymen replied as he turned to Seahla.

"You know this could result in casualties." He said quietly.

Seahla nodded slowly.

"Do what you need to Colonel." She replied.

"Have all fire teams secure that deck, order them to fire on sight but do not kill them if they can avoid it." Taymen ordered.

"Sir." Titus interrupted. "We've lost atmospheric control to deck thirty, we can't depressurize it." He said.

"They're cutting themselves off." Avril said.

"Digging in is more like it." Taymen said.

"Do we still have control of the internal defense system?" Avril asked.

Titus checked his console.

"Negative, automated defenses on deck thirty are off line." He reported.

"Sir." Sairon said. "There's an incoming transmission being routed through the internal com. system."

"It's them." Avril said.

"They're requesting to speak to you Colonel." Sairon continued.

"Put them on speakers." Taymen said.

A second later the C.A.C. speakers cracked with the sound of the channel opening.

"This is Colonel Orelle, who are you and what are you doing on my ship?" Taymen asked.

"Who I am is not important." A woman's voice replied over the speaker. *"By now I'm sure you realize that you've lost control of this deck."*

"What do you want?"

"We want your ship Colonel. You have one hour to evacuate your crew and release control of your ship to us or we will destroy it." Taymen could hear the uncertainty in the woman's voice.

Clearly she was in over her head and was just saying whatever she figured would sound intimidating.

Taymen along with most of the crew were well aware that there was no way they could destroy the ship from deck thirty. The Avenger was designed to prevent just that in the event that they were boarded through the hangars.

"You're hardly in a position to make threats Ma'am." Taymen said. "You may have cut off atmospheric controls to deck thirty, but we can depressurize every section surrounding that deck and seal you in. I doubt you'll last very long with no food or water."

There was a long silence before the woman spoke again.

"One hour Colonel, or we destroy your ship."

The channel closed before Taymen could say anything.

"Anyone you know?" Taymen asked Jassen who simply shook his head.

"Orders Sir?" Avril asked.

"She's in over her head, unless they have a nuke there's no way they can destroy the ship from deck thirty." Taymen replied.

"How can we regain control of that deck?" Titus asked.

"Evacuate the surrounding decks and depressurize them." Taymen ordered. "Have two prowlers prepped for launch in the port hangar deck and have two marine sections ready for departure. We'll come in through the landing deck and take them from behind." He said. "Order them to avoid casualties at all costs."

Dark Avenger, Starboard Hangar Deck
23:45 Abydos Standard Time
Day 24, Fifth Cycle, Egyptian Year 3201

Captain Arkeal Mentz held his position at the head of the hangar deck just inside of the airlock. It took him and his men almost fifteen minutes to repel down the maintenance shaft from the landing deck and get past the manual pressure seal.

He had two eight man sections with him, echo and delta teams. Arkeal took command of delta team and led them down to the main airlock at the head of the hangar deck. Echo team was using the crawlspaces to make their way to the far end so they could move in from both sides.

As he continued to hold his position, Arkeal noticed at least four different men patrolling the deck at random intervals.

As the next guard came into view Arkeal raised his rifle and aimed it at the man's shoulder. He had orders to avoid casualties if possible, so if he had to open fire he would take non-lethal shots if he could. Of course if his target should happen to shift a little or the round continues through his target's shoulder and into his chest, Arkeal wouldn't lose any sleep over it.

As the man made his way closer and closer to Arkeal he adjusted his aim and prepared to fire. A few seconds later he tapped the control on his earpiece to open a channel to his team.

"All teams move in now." He ordered just before he pulled the trigger.

A single round fired and buried itself in the flesh of his targets left shoulder. The man hit the deck in a fit of pain as Arkeal and his team moved in. Arkeal kicked the man's weapon away while one of his team bound his hands behind his back.

Within seconds the deck became a battlefield. Rounds flew through the air in all directions, most of them striking the bulkheads.

"Grenade!" Someone yelled as Arkeal noticed a small gray object land just past him.

He jumped behind cover just before it detonated. Luckily, it was only a flash grenade so the shockwave was worse than anything.

Two of his team were caught in the blast and thrown against a bulkhead before hitting the deck hard. Arkeal moved back towards them, firing a few rounds for cover.

"You guys okay?" He asked.

The two marines stumbled to their feet and moved back behind cover as the invaders continued to fire. Suddenly one of his team fell to the deck with a wound in his chest. Arkeal fired off a few more rounds before backing up.

"Sir, they've overrun our position, they've made their way off of this deck." Someone said over the com. channel.

"All teams." Arkeal said. "Withdraw to the next defensive line, I say again fallback to the next defensive line."

He picked up his injured team member and threw him over his shoulder while the rest of his team covered their escape.

Dark Avenger, C.A.C.
24:20 Abydos Standard Time
Day 24, Fifth Cycle, Egyptian Year 3201

"Sir." Titus said. "The intruders have overrun one of our defensive positions and have left deck thirty."

"What?" Taymen asked. "Weren't the surrounding decks depressurized?"

"Yes Sir, but the intruders seemed to be wearing pressure suits, depressurizing the decks simply slowed them down."

Taymen sighed. He had to stop the intruders from advancing, if they reached any of the critical sections they could take control of the ship.

"Titus." He said. "Is there any indication as to where they may be going, any critical systems in the area that they may be trying to reach?"

Titus brought up a schematic of decks thirty and twenty nine on the command console to see if there were any likely targets for the intruders. At first he didn't see anything. Most of the systems in the area wouldn't give them any major tactical advantage.

"Nothing on deck twenty-nine Sir." He reported as he moved on to deck twenty-eight, then to twenty-seven were he finally found something.

"Primary atmosphere valve is on deck twenty-seven, frame eighteen." He said.

"What exactly does that valve do?" Jassen asked.

"It's the main control valve for our internal atmosphere, if you wanted to you could depressurize half the ship from there." Taymen explained.

"Yes but the automated defenses in that section make it difficult to get to that frame, they wouldn't stand a chance." Avril said.

"They wouldn't need to, a couple of well placed grenades would be enough to rupture the conduits to the valve and all of the primary decks would be depressurized, including C.A.C." Titus explained.

"I want two fire teams guarding that valve, evacuate decks twenty-five through twenty-nine and bring the internal defense systems online. Make sure our people have their friend or foe identifiers on." Taymen said before turning to Seahla and Jassen.

"What are the chances of this ending peacefully?" He asked.

"Not good." Jassen replied. "To say these people hate the military would be an understatement. Remember, they think it's your fault we're in this situation in the first place, you being here gives them someone to take out their frustrations on."

"I'm afraid I have to agree Colonel." Seahla said. "They want you and your crew dead so they can take your ship for themselves, I'm afraid you may have no choice but to fight back."

Taymen checked the sensor display again. He knew it wouldn't show anything of any consequence, he did it more out of habit than anything. Whenever he was trying to evaluate the situation he checked the sensor display to get a clear view of their situation, now however it was practically useless.

"Sairon." He said. "Put me through to deck twenty-nine." He said as he tapped the control on his earpiece.

"Go ahead Sir." Sairon said a few seconds later.

"This is Colonel Orelle." He started. "This is your last chance to return to your shuttles and leave my ship."

There was no reply.

"If you insist on continuing on this course I suggest you consider this. You have maximum fifty people with you, I have a crew of over twelve hundred including over a hundred trained marines. The only reason you're still advancing is because they have orders not to kill you. So if you think you can fight us all off to take the ship or to even get to an area where you can destroy the ship then by all means, but make no mistake we won't hold back anymore, this is your final warning.

"I am instructing my marines to shoot to kill from here on out, you have five minutes to decide what you want to do." Taymen closed the channel.

"Are you really going to kill them?" Sharn asked.

"If they force me to." Taymen replied.

Five minutes went by and there was no indication that the intruders had left.

"Alright." Taymen said.

"Sairon contact Captain Mentz, instruct him that they are to fire on site at the intruders and instruct him to shoot to kill."

"Aye Sir." Sairon replied.

"Colonel." Jassen said. "I'd like to help."

Taymen stood surprised for a moment.

"How?" He asked.

"Let me talk to them face to face, I may be able to convince them to leave."

"And if you can't?" Taymen asked.

"Send me with a team of your marines, if they refuse to leave we'll force them out."

"Jassen!" Sharn said in shock.

Taymen stood silent for a moment considering the idea.

He could see clearly from Jassen's expression that he meant what he said.

"Why do this?" Taymen asked. "Why help us?"

Jassen sighed.

"You tried to solve this without hurting anyone to the point that it put your people at risk. I guess maybe you're not what I originally thought you were." He said.

"Alright." Taymen said. "We'll try it your way."

Dark Avenger, Deck Twenty-Nine
24:45 Abydos Standard Time
Day 24, Fifth Cycle, Egyptian Year 3201

Celia stood at the corner watching the pressure hatch at the end of deck twenty-nine. She knew all too well that there were at least four armed marines on the other side waiting for them to try and get through.

They had been waiting there for almost twenty minutes now since the Colonel's last message and some of her team were getting worried that something was going to happen.

At least they left the deck pressurized this time so she didn't have to wear her pressure suit. The smell inside the suit was almost unbearable, it was hot and the air in the tanks was stale. She'd almost rather risk holding her breath in vacuum than sit in that pressure suit much longer.

As she continued to stare at the hatch, Celia could feel the distinct presence of her second in command hovering over her.

"What is it Auress?" She asked.

"Are you sure we should stay here boss?" Auress asked. "I mean, we're hopelessly outnumbered and I don't know about you, but I'm starting to wonder how reliable those schematics we got are."

Celia remained silent. It's true that their intelligence about the layout of the ship has already proven to be wrong. Both the primary power relays and the main atmospheric valve were supposed to be on decks twenty-nine and thirty-two. They've looked all over deck twenty-nine and there was nothing.

Now, they were surrounded and the next time they came across any marines they wouldn't be so lucky. The only reason they got this far was because the marines were trying not to kill them.

"What do you want to do Auress!" She snapped. "Go back to the shuttles so they can shoot us down on our way back to the station."

Auress didn't say anything.

"We can't go back now, we need to finish this." Celia continued.

"But what if…" Suddenly the hatch at the end of the corridor began to unlock.

Celia and Auress readied their weapons and took aim as the hatch opened and four marines poured into the corridor with weapons firing.

As the bulkheads beside and behind Celia and Auress became riddled with ceramic rounds they began to fall back behind the corner to the next intersection in the corridor where six other members of their team were waiting.

Celia waited at the ready, her gaze remained fixed on the corridor ahead as she waited for the first marine to round the corner, they wouldn't get the best of her again.

As they sat and waited she could hear the sound of foot steps moving closer to them.

"Hold your fire!" A voice shouted from around the corner.

Celia didn't move.

The voice was that of a man and it sounded very familiar to her.

"I just want to talk to whoever's in charge here." The man continued.

Celia lowered the muzzle of her rifle a little as she glanced over at Auress who simply shrugged his shoulders.

"Who are you?" She asked.

"My name is Jassen." The man answered.

Celia paused for a moment. She suddenly realized why the voice was so familiar.

"Jassen." She said. "Jassen Pitt?" She asked.

"Yes, who am I talking to?" Jassen asked.

Celia hesitated a moment.

"Celia." She finally said.

"Alright Celia." Jassen said. "I'm coming out."

A few seconds later he rounded the corner with the marines and stopped when he saw Celia and her team.

Celia kept her rifle trained on Jassen as she spoke.

"What do you want?" She asked.

"Just to talk." Jassen answered.

"We're not leaving." Celia replied.

"This ship doesn't belong to you, you have no right to do this."

"No right!" Celia snapped.

"If it wasn't for the Defense Force we'd…"

Jassen cut her off.

"We'd all be dead." He said.

Celia didn't say anything.

"This ship is our last hope at regaining our homes and its crew are fighting to protect us, and for what. So you and your men can force your way aboard and try to take over. What right do you think you have?"

Celia lowered her rifle a little, just before the entire deck shuttered and Celia and Jassen were thrown from their feet.

"What was that?" Celia shouted as she struggled to regain her footing.

Dark Avenger, C.A.C.
25:25 Abydos Standard Time
Day 24, Fifth Cycle, Egyptian Year 3201

"Report!" Avril snapped.

"A Tray heavy cruiser just streamed into the system and opened fire, it's launching fighters." Titus reported.

"Battle mode!" Taymen ordered. "Deploy armor and launch the alert fighters, bring all gun batteries to bear and fire on the target when they're ready." Taymen checked the sensor display briefly.

"Helm move us to three light seconds from the station and bring our starboard side to bear on the cruiser all ahead full."

"Aye Sir." Aurin replied.

"Carrey load all missile tubes with saber missiles and prepare to fire on my mark."

"Incoming ordnance!" Titus snapped.

Taymen braced himself against the command console just before two missiles struck the Avenger on the starboard side.

"Sir." Titus started. "A section of the armor plating was damaged by the initial attack, starboard side hangar deck and adjacent decks are exposed." He reported.

"Damn." Avril snapped. "Our starboard side is to the cruiser." She said in a panic.

"Helm rotate the ship along the 'X' axis, bring our port side to bear on the cruiser." Taymen ordered.

"Fighters incoming." Titus reported.

"Batteries one through five switch to enemy suppression fire." Taymen ordered.

Dark Avenger, Deck Twenty-Nine
25:40 Abydos Standard Time
Day 24, Fifth Cycle, Egyptian Year 3201

"What about all the people who died because of the military, not just recently but during the separatist war?" Celia said as she stumbled to her feet.

Jassen could see the tears well up in Celia's eyes. He could see that she lost someone close to her in the war.

"Where was their last hope?" She continued.

"You can't blame the entire military for every individual death at the hands of the Tray or the separatists." Jassen said.

"They didn't start the war with either of them, they simply fought it to protect people like us. It wasn't their fault."

Tears ran down Celia's face as she brought the rifle back to bear.

"You're wrong, it's all their fault. They chose to fight, if they didn't fight nobody would have died. We could have surrendered and spared countless lives." She said.

"And we'd be living as slaves!" Jassen snapped.

The deck shuttered again just before the bulkhead near the end of the corridor exploded. Before anyone could react they were all thrown from their feet as the air began to violently rush out through the breach.

"We have to get out of here!" One of the marines shouted.

Jassen could barely here him over the sound of the rushing air.

Everyone struggled to get to their feet against the super vacuum that was dragging them towards the breach in the hull. They had less than a minute before all the air was gone from the section and they suffocated.

"Sir deck twenty nine's been hit, starboard side frame twelve." Titus reported.

"That's one of the exposed sections." Avril said.

"We're venting atmosphere." Titus continued.

"Seal off that frame before the entire deck decompresses." Taymen ordered.

Sairon accessed the maintenance com. channel and called for a damage control team to seal off frame twelve.

"All missile tubes target the cruiser's fighter bays." Taymen ordered.

"Target locked Sir." Carrey reported a second later.

"Tubes one through four fire three salvos!" Taymen said.

A second later twelve missiles sped towards the cruiser's fighter bays. Two detonated against a couple of Tray fighters while five others were shot down by the cruisers point defense system. Two of the remaining five struck the hull surrounding the fighter bays while the last three made their way inside the bays striking fuel lines and critical electrical components.

Within seconds the cruiser stopped firing and the defense system went off line as more of the Dark Avenger's plasma rounds burned through the outer hull decompressing the interior.

"Sir the cruiser has ceased firing." Titus reported.

"All batteries switch to suppression fire and take out the remaining fighters." Taymen ordered.

"Keep an eye on that cruiser Titus." Avril said.

"Aye Ma'am." Titus replied.

Jassen put all his weight against the hatch with two of the marines to try and force it open against the vacuum. As it slowly opened another marine began to push forcing the hatch open the rest of the way against the rushing air.

Two marines jumped through followed by Jassen then Celia and her team with the last two marines right behind them.

When they released the hatch from the other side it slammed shut and one of the marines sealed it.

Before anyone could say anything Celia took off down the corridor at a dead run and Jassen took off after her. By the time the rest of her team tried to follow the marines had their weapons trained on them, and they surrendered.

Jassen ran after Celia as she rounded corners and jumped through hatches. She continued to run until she rounded a corner only to find it came to a dead end.

She quickly spun around and brought her rifle to bear pointing it towards Jassen as he rounded the corner after her. As soon as she saw him she pulled the trigger and three rounds flew through the air at him.

Instinctively Jassen dodged to the right evading two of the rounds. The third struck him in his right shoulder a second before he hit the deck on his right side.

Less than a second after he landed his left arm was trained on Celia and two rounds erupted from the twin thirty caliber barrels on his implant striking her in the chest.

Celia collapsed to the deck as Jassen forced himself up onto his feet and walked over to her.

"I'm sorry." He said quietly as he stood over her.

A few seconds later she was dead.

Dark Avenger, C.A.C.
26:30 Abydos Standard Time
Day 24, Fifth Cycle, Egyptian Year 3201

"Report." Taymen said.

"All Tray fighters have been destroyed and the cruiser has gone silent." Titus reported.

"Damage assessment." Taymen said.

"Minor damage to the armor plating, hull breach on deck twenty-nine, frame twelve, the section is sealed off and we've got some minor damage to the power grid." The damage control officer reported.

"Deploy damage control parties to seal that breach and conduct repairs." Avril said.

"Sir." Sairon started. "We've got a report from one of the marine fire teams on deck twenty-nine. They say that they have fourteen of the intruders in custody, the rest are dead including the leader."

"Have the prisoners brought to the brig and sweep decks twenty-nine through thirty-one, let's be sure there are no others left aboard." Taymen ordered as he glanced at the main sensor display.

The mark indicating the Tray cruiser remained stationary on the display with no power emissions or transmissions coming from it.

Avril quietly moved up beside him.

"What are you thinking Sir?" She asked.

Taymen remained silent for a moment before answering.

"Titus have the prowlers prepped for launch."

"How many Sir?" Titus asked.

"All of them." Taymen replied.

"Sir, are you planning to board that cruiser?" Avril asked.

"I want one hundred marines ready to go in thirty minutes and a team of protostream techs to go with them. That cruiser has a more advanced stream system than we do; I want to know how it works."

Chapter Ten

Tray Light Cruiser at Ancient Station
01:40 Abydos Standard Time
Day 25, Fifth Cycle, Egyptian Year 3201

Arkeal waited at the corner while his fire team partner advanced to his position with the techs.

The corridors were almost pitch black and the majority of the ship was depressurized because of all the hull breaches.

The air in his pressure suit would last him another four hours, plenty of time to sweep the primary sections of the ship and get back to the prowler for a new tank.

He had one hundred marines moving through the ship trying to map it out. There was no power throughout most of the sections and they hadn't come across any live Tray yet. They've counted over two hundred bodies so far and they've only gone through about half of the ship.

The corridors were narrower than those on the Avenger and the bulkheads looked like they were double re-enforced. The deck plates were steel grates over what looked like air conduits.

The lighting was in the floor at the corners of the deck plates and the bulkheads, the hatches were manually locked and there were lifts used for moving between decks.

From what Arkeal saw the ship itself was relatively primitive in comparison to their own, proving the only real advantage the Tray seemed to have was their seemingly endless number of ships.

Once Arkeal was satisfied the deck was clear he stood up and began to walk down the corridor keeping an eye out for any movement.

"This is Mentz, deck clear we're advancing towards the engine room, I think." Arkeal said into his ear piece.

"Roger that Sir." His second in command replied. *"I think we found their command deck, some of the systems are still functioning so the techs think they may be able to get some information from the computers."*

"Good, get what you can and move on." Arkeal ordered before closing the channel.

"I think it's just down here." One of the techs said as he passed by a bulkhead that had been blown out.

"How do you know?" Arkeal asked.

"These look like the superconductors used to transmit energy from the protostream generators to the lenses, we're heading towards the center of the ship so if we follow these they should lead us to the generator."

Arkeal looked at his team mate who simply shrugged.

"Sounds good." Arkeal finally replied.

When they got to the end of the corridor there was a single hatch left open.

Arkeal went in first and moved to the left while his partner moved to the right.

The room wasn't very big, about five meters by four meters with a large cylindrical core in the center.

Arkeal and his partner worked their way around the room and called the techs in when it was cleared.

When they walked in they immediately recognized the core as the protostream generator.

"This is it." One of them said in excitement.

"And it's still functioning?" The other one said in confusion.

"Let's get to work." Arkeal said. "I don't want to stay here any longer than we need to."

Cairo Museum
02:30 Abydos Standard Time
Day 25, Fifth Cycle, Egyptian Year 3201

The halls echoed with the sounds of footsteps getting closer to the lab. John swiped his key card and entered his code on the keypad when he got to the door. When the light turned green and the door unlocked he quickly opened it and walked in setting a large black case on the nearest desk.

"John, I thought you were taking the night off?" A man said from the desk on the far side of the room.

"I was but this just came in and I wanted you to get it catalogued before the weekend." John said.

"Sure."

The man replied as he stood up and walked across the room.

"I'll start it right now." He said as he opened the case.

"Thanks Russ." John said as he left.

Russ opened the lid to the case and pulled a small silver colored medallion from the wrapping inside. It had already been cleaned so all the inscriptions were fairly easy to read.

The body was made of silver and was oval shaped with a large oval ruby in the center. Surrounding the ruby were six sapphires and inscribed on the outer edges of the body were gold hieratic characters laid into the silver.

When he looked at the back Russ almost dropped the medallion. He immediately recognized the eight symbols inscribed on the back. He didn't know what they meant and couldn't even begin to translate them but they were definitely Egyptian, and Russ distinctly remembered seeing those symbols several times while he was on board the Dark Avenger.

The question is what did they mean?

Dark Avenger Briefing Room
5:30 Abydos Standard Time
Day 25, Fifth Cycle, Egyptian Year 3201

Taymen sat at the head of the conference table with Jassen and Seahla to his left. To his right was Captain Mentz and beside him was the engine room chief, Lieutenant-Commander Marsae.

"So." Taymen started. "We have fourteen of your people in our custody, I don't have the time to deal with them right now so I'm content to release them into your custody and allow you to deal with them as you see fit." He said.

Jassen turned to Seahla who nodded.

"Very well." She said in her raspy voice.

"We will take them into custody and try them for treason against the royal family." Jassen added.

"On one condition." Taymen started. "The penalty for treason is death, I want no executions to be carried out if found guilty."

"Fine." Jassen said.

"Now then Captain." Taymen turned to Arkeal. "Casualty report."

"Three of my men are in sick bay, one with serious injuries and two are dead." Arkeal said.

Taymen sighed. More of his crew dying was obviously the last thing he wanted. As unfortunate as it was however, what Seahla said after the memorial helped Taymen to realize that he did his best to protect them, and some things are just beyond his control.

"I'll leave you to arrange the memorial services." He said.

"Commander Marsae your report."

Marsae shifted in his seat briefly before speaking.

"We've completed our evaluation of the Tray stream system." He started. "It's definitely compatible with our own. We'll need to refit the rad-exchangers on the outer hull and overhaul the main power source for the generator itself though."

"So you can enhance our own stream system to match?" Taymen asked.

"It won't be an exact match." Marsae replied.

"The Tray technology uses a more direct power feed from the PT engines and a more efficient rad-exchanger design. We can retrofit our own system with these improvements and it'll be a close match. Bottom line Sir, if our calculations are anywhere near correct we could reach the outlying colonies in a little less than a month."

Taymen didn't say anything. It sounded all too good to be true. If they could adapt the Tray technology to their own they could avoid all the Tray between them and their home so as to avoid using any more of their armament unnecessarily.

"How long would it take to refit the ship?" He asked.

"We'll need almost two weeks to complete the refit, that includes all the repairs we'll need to conduct to get the system online and we won't be able to use the stream system or PT generator two until the refit is complete."

Taymen thought for a moment. If they couldn't stream out they'd be sitting ducks and they had to assume the Tray knew where they were. Still, the gains far outweighed the potential risks.

"Get started, use whatever manpower you need." Taymen finally said. "Jassen I think you should return to your station and address your people about the incident, from now on any vessels approaching the Avenger without authorization will be intercepted." He continued.

"I understand." Jassen replied before standing up to leave.

Taymen spent the night sitting up in his cabin.

He couldn't seem to fall asleep no matter how tired he was. His mind kept on jumping between everything that's happened and everything that may happen.

If the stream system upgrades actually worked they would reach the outer colonies in about a month and they would have a clearer view of their situation.

In reality they didn't know what they were up against. They didn't know how many ships the Tray had or how they were positioned.

They didn't know what state their people were in or even where most of them were now.

Taymen's thoughts kept on jumping back to Torri.

Was she alive? Was she one of the ones who escaped and is hiding? Or was she a prisoner in a Tray slave camp?

Any one of those ideas scared Taymen, he didn't really worry about his parents so much but Torri he always felt a little responsible for, and not knowing what has become of her was killing him.

Releena sat next to Ourik looking out the window of the shuttle. They were flying over one of the cities that Ourik informed her was being rebuilt by the Tray. When she saw the city for herself she noticed that he really meant it was being rebuilt by Egyptians for the Tray.

"Isn't it wonderful when two cultures can come together to rebuild something so magnificent." Ourik said smugly.

"I don't know." Releena replied. "All I see here is slave labor."

Ourik's expression turned to disappointment.

"Now now Princess, is that all you can see here?" He asked.

Releena didn't respond.

"I see two peoples working together to rebuild a world that was shattered by war. While it is true that some of the workers are of a lower standing in this new society we are all working together none the less."

Releena was losing her patience.

"Why don't we stop with these games Ourik, just tell me what it is you want?" She snapped.

Ourik took a moment to answer.

"I've already told you." He replied.

"You've told me nothing." Releena said. "Why travel so far to conquer a people who have never heard of you much less done anything to you? And why try to rebuild what you destroyed under the guess of mutual cooperation?" She asked.

Ourik was surprised by how direct Releena's questions were. Up until now she had gone along with almost everything he had told her. Now however something changed, she was becoming more assertive and difficult to control, he didn't like it.

"I understand your people have a rather interesting history." Ourik started, diverting Releena's attention.

"I'm not fully familiar with it yet but from what I understand you aren't indigenous to this galaxy." He continued. "I've read that your people actually evolved on a planet far from here, and were taken early on in their development only to be dropped on your home planet of Abydos, nobody really knows why. I find that quite remarkable."

Releena wondered when Ourik would be getting to his point. He often told long winded stories when he was getting at something he thought was important.

"In later years your people continued to evolve and develop more advanced technologies until a single discovery changed the course of your civilization, do you recall what that discovery was?" He asked.

Releena sighed. She learned it was better to answer his questions if she wanted him to get to his point faster.

"A temple built by an ancient race that inhabited Abydos long before we were there."

"Yes, and what was the significance of this temple?" Ourik asked, knowing full well what her answer would be.

"Nobody really knows, some think it's the remnants of an ancient civilization, some think it was an ancient outpost."

She paused for a moment.

"The most disputed theory is that it's an archive left behind for us to find, to help expedite our technological development."

Ourik smiled as he did so often when he believed he had accomplished something significant.

"I think that last theory is the closest don't you?"

Releena didn't answer.

"An entire wealth of knowledge most of it militaristic in nature, things like the protostream technology, ship designs, weapons schematics, the list goes on and on Princess."

"What's your point Fleet Marshal?" Releena said.

"We found several temples just like this one on planets all over this galaxy, some with more advanced knowledge than that found in the one on your planet but not a single temple was found on our home world, any theory as to why?"

"Maybe they never got around to it." Releena said sarcastically.

Ourik ignored her.

"My people have an interesting history as well. You see we are one of the oldest races in this part of the galaxy. Only one other was said to rival us in terms of age though we vastly outnumbered them.

"After a war that lasted for centuries our victory was finally assured until the last of that ancient fleet scattered and disappeared never to be seen again, leaving us to advance through the galaxy claiming an endless number of abandoned planets including yours."

Releena wasn't sure she liked where this was going.

"Alas, with so much territory even our vast fleet was spread thin so we fell back to a more manageable perimeter until five thousand years later we discovered that several of our once barren planets had been populated by a number of different races, so we set out to once again claim what was ours."

Ourik paused for a moment.

"Imagine our surprise when we actually found remnants of our ancient enemies on almost every single one of these planets."

Ourik took another moment to pause.

Releena sometimes thought he just did it for dramatic effect.

"So Princess." He continued. "Now that you know our history as well as the history of your own people, why do you think your ancestors were abducted only to be left alone on an alien world in an alien galaxy?"

Chapter Eleven

Dark Avenger, Captain's Cabin
16:20 Abydos Standard Time
Day 7, Sixth Cycle, Egyptian Year 3201

Taymen sat at his desk reading over the latest progress report of the stream system upgrades. From what he read it seemed they were a little ahead of schedule so they'd be ready to leave in a few days.

There have been no further incidents with the Tray or any of the station's inhabitants for that matter.

Taymen was beginning to relax a little but he still found himself on edge. As he continued on through the technical details of the report, most of which made no sense to him, the door buzzer sounded.

"Come in." He said.

The hatch opened and Avril walked in.

Taymen was surprised to see her, she rarely arrived unannounced or without a data pad in her hands.

"Do you have a moment Sir?" She asked quietly.

"Of course." Taymen said. "Come in."

Avril gently closed the hatch as Taymen stood up from his desk and moved to sit on the couch. Avril took up a seat across from him.

"What's on your mind Captain?" He asked.

Avril spoke in an unusually soft tone.

"Sir, I was wondering if it would be possible to speak off the record."

Again Taymen was taken by surprise.

"Alright, what is it?" He finally asked.

Avril hooked a lock of her long dark hair behind her ear before she began.

"Sir, I think I owe you an apology."

Taymen didn't say anything.

"I know I can be a bit trying at times and it's no secret that there has been more than one occasion where I haven't agreed with your orders so I just wanted to say I'm sorry for that."

Taymen knew most of the situations she was referring to. More recently when the initial attack on their home started he ordered the ship to jump to the Princess' home world of Netara instead of Abydos like they were ordered to.

It was true that Avril was a little more outspoken than he would like an Ex O to be at times, but she was very passionate and only had the welfare of the ship and crew in mind.

"I also wanted to say." She continued. "I don't think we would have made it this far alone had I been in command and I know I wouldn't be able to attempt what you're planning on doing now."

"Avril." Taymen started cutting her off. "You have nothing to apologize for. I don't expect everyone on this ship to agree with my orders, least of all you. I do however expect that they follow my orders so long as they don't unduly jeopardize the ship and you have done that despite your objections."

He paused for a moment.

"Don't be so quick to sell yourself short. I wouldn't say you're trying at times. More like a pain in the ass most of the time." He joked.

Avril smiled a little once she realized he was joking.

"If I had any doubts about your ability to command this ship in my absence you wouldn't be my Ex O. You're a clever and strong leader who will do well in her own command one day, your only failing is that you need to learn to put your trust in others, that means both your superiors and your subordinates."

Avril simply nodded.

"I understand you moved through a few foster homes as a child, must have been difficult."

Avril didn't say anything. She was surprised that Taymen remembered such details about her.

"You worked hard to get into the Defense Force academy, it's really no surprise that you're not used to trusting the people around you, but that is something you're going to have to overcome and I'd prefer you do it sooner rather than later."

Avril nodded.

"Yes Sir." She said.

"Is there anything else?" Taymen asked.

"No Sir." Avril replied.

"Alright then, carry on." Taymen said.

Avril made her way back to her cabin after speaking with Taymen. She walked without paying any attention to where she was going. She knew the ship well enough that she didn't need to pay attention. She could find her way from her quarters to C.A.C., to the hangar deck and back again in her sleep.

As she walked through the corridor passing crewmen along the way her mind wondered back to her family. She pulled a small locket out of her pocket and gazed at the photo inside. She remembered the day it was taken.

Her foster parents stood on either side of her on the day she graduated from the Defense Force officer's academy. She was happy they were there with her and they kept saying how proud they were of her but something was still missing.

She had not seen her biological parents since she was seven years old. She tried to find them several times as a teenager but to no avail which wasn't really surprising.

She had often wondered what happened to them. When she was young she used to imagine that she would find them one day and she would be able to take care of them so they would never have to leave her again. Unfortunately she quickly learned that such fantasies were a waste of time and did her best to become self sufficient so that she didn't need anybody.

Taymen told her that she had to learn to trust the people around her. She never realized how big an impact her child hood had on her until now. It's true that she was a strong independent person, but now it seemed she was incapable of trusting others. She suddenly found herself thinking about everything Taymen had just said to her. If she could just learn to listen to him and learn from him, she just may turn out to be as good a Commander as he was.

Dark Avenger, C.A.C.
23:30 Abydos Standard Time
Day 9, Sixth Cycle, Egyptian Year 3201

Taymen stood just behind Titus' station as the diagnostics for the protostream upgrades were displayed.

Everything checked out for the third time in a row. With all the modifications that were made to the system he wanted to be absolutely sure that everything was working properly.

"All systems are operating within normal parameters Sir." Titus reported.

"Alright then, bring PT generator two back online and power up the system Titus." Taymen said.

Avril entered C.A.C. a few seconds later and made her way over to the command console.

"Where are we?" She asked.

"We're just about to power up the new system" Taymen said.

"The protostream system is powered up, all systems normal Sir." Titus reported a moment later.

"Alright then." Taymen said.

"Sairon contact the station, advise Jassen and the council that we're about to get underway." He ordered.

"Aye Sir." Sairon replied.

"Titus plot us an eight hour stream towards home and prepare the ship for departure."

"Sir I have Jassen on the line requesting a closed channel to you." Sairon said.

"Patch him through." Taymen said as he tapped the control on his earpiece.

"This is Taymen, go ahead." He said a second later.

"Colonel we've transmitted a list of supply stations that hadn't fallen under Tray control when we left." Jassen said.

"Thank you Jassen, with any luck we'll be able to send a ship back to assist you in a few months, until then good luck." Taymen said.

"Thank you Colonel, same to you."

The channel went silent a second later.

Taymen took a brief look at the sensor display focusing on the disabled Tray cruiser that was still adrift. Taymen had intended to destroy it but Jassen wanted him to leave it intact so that they might salvage anything they could use from it. It went against his better judgment but Taymen agreed to leave it.

"Stream system is charged Sir." Titus reported.

"Very well then, Aurin stream us out." Taymen ordered.

"Aye Sir." Aurin replied. "Streaming in five...four...three...two...one."

Taymen suddenly felt the familiar tingling sensation flood over his body just before everything went dark, then back to normal again. He waited at the command console for Titus's report.

"Stream complete Sir." Aurin reported.

"All systems seem to be functioning normally, outer hull radiation is nominal." Titus reported after double checking his readings. "It looks like we could have stayed in the stream for another eight hours."

Taymen couldn't believe it, the new stream system proved to be not only faster but the new radiation exchangers were almost twice as efficient as the old ones. Taymen shook off his astonishment and refocused his thoughts.

"Anything on sensors?" He asked as he glanced at the sensor display.

"Nothing Sir." Titus reported.

"Alright." Taymen said. "Have engineering do a complete inspection of the stream system, if everything checks out plot a fourteen hour stream out of here."

"Aye Sir." Titus replied as he turned back to his console.

"You don't seem to be too excited about this Sir." Avril said quietly.

"I don't want to get our hopes up just yet." Taymen replied. "The first stream went well but we don't know what kind of toll it took on the overall system. If everything checks out after the inspection then I'll get excited, until then let's just play it safe."

Avril couldn't help getting excited. This was the first real break they've had since the Tray first attacked. Even if it didn't work past the first stream, they just cut two jumps off their trip in just eight hours."

"Sensor contact, two Tray cruisers bearing down on top of us!" Titus reported.

Taymen checked the display to see the two enemy marks right on top of them.

"They're launching fighters."

"Launch sword breakers." Avril ordered.

"Incoming ordnance!" Titus snapped.

"Deploy armor!" Taymen snapped. "Bring the ship to battle mode, all even number batteries to enemy suppression fire, odd direct fire at those cruisers." He ordered as the ship shuttered from the impact of the Tray ordnance.

"Carrey launch two salvos of saber missiles down those cruisers throats, see if you can get them to back off a little." Taymen glanced at the sensor display again to get his bearings.

"Helm, bring our bow to bear on the cruisers and back us off full reverse." He said.

"Full reverse aye Sir." Aurin replied.

Taymen could here himself giving orders almost instinctively without having to think about them. He had always been quick to give his orders but never like this. He wondered when he got so good at combat? It actually frightened him. It felt like he was becoming exactly what his father and Jassen accused him of being.

"All missiles away Sir." The missile officer reported.

"The cruisers are backing off Sir but their fighters are right on top of us." Titus said.

"Have the sword breakers set up a perimeter a half a light second off our hull, don't let anything get through." Avril said.

"Radiological alarm!" Titus snapped. "Four nukes inbound, impact in twelve seconds."

"Recall the fighters, all batteries suppressive fire on those nukes and launch a salvo of counter measures." Taymen ordered.

"Helm, prepare to stream us out of here." Avril said.

"Impact in eight seconds." Titus reported.

"Ready Sir." Aurin said.

"Sword breakers are still landing Sir." One of the flight controllers reported.

"Two nukes still inbound impact in four seconds."

"We're out of time, helm stream us out now!" Taymen ordered.

Without hesitation, the stream officer activated the stream system and the Avenger flashed a split second before disappearing into a bolt of dark lightning leaving the missiles to detonate on empty space.

Taymen shook off the dizziness from the stream and checked the sensor display. The entire area was one massive debris field so it was difficult to tell if there were any other ships around.

"Report." Taymen said.

"Stream complete, no enemy contacts that we can see Sir." Titus replied.

"What about our sword breakers?" Avril asked.

"We only managed to get thirty-two back before we streamed out." One of the flight controllers reported.

It was times like this Taymen was glad that sword breakers were unmanned drones, but still, thirty-two of sixty sword breakers made Taymen sick to his stomach.

"No casualties reported, moderate damage to the hull armor, other than that we seem to be okay." Titus said.

Taymen nodded.

"Deploy damage control teams to begin repairs, we'll stay here until they're completed." He said.

"Sensor contact." Titus said a second later.

"Now what?" Avril asked.

"I'm not sure Ma'am but it's definitely not Tray." Titus started.

"Then what is it?" Taymen asked.

"It's a prowler." Titus replied.

"Sir it's transmitting a general distress call on Egyptian emergency channels." Sairon said.

Taymen turned to Avril who said nothing. She knew what Taymen was thinking because she was thinking the same thing, that it could be a trap, but if they were wrong then there were Egyptians onboard that prowler that needed their help.

"Sairon, hail them." Taymen finally said.

"No response Sir." Sairon reported.

Taymen thought it over for a moment. If it was a trap they would be defenseless against it if the prowler was loaded with explosives. If it was carrying a boarding party then there could only be fifteen or so people aboard so they wouldn't get very far against his marines on the hangar deck.

"What do you think?" He asked Avril, who wasn't sure what to think.

"Could be a trap." She started. "But if it's genuine, than those are our people and they need our help."

"Launch a pair of sword breakers." Taymen ordered. "Get me a visual on the inside of that prowler."

When the sword breakers got close enough to the shuttle for a visual check on the inside, they found several Egyptian marines onboard along with General Raise, one of the princess' council of Generals.

Taymen ordered a SAR prowler to launch and bring them aboard immediately.

Taymen and Avril walked into sick bay where General Raise and his men were being treated for oxygen deprivation. The General and a few of his marines were already awake, while four others were still unconscious.

Taymen stopped in front of Raise and saluted sharply. Raise quickly returned the salute as he pulled himself to his feet.

"At ease Colonel." He said.

"Welcome aboard General." Taymen said.

"Thank you, I hate to think of what would have happened if you hadn't come along." Raise replied.

"Sir if I may ask, how did you get all the way out here?" Taymen asked.

General Raise smiled a little.

"Straight to business I see." He said. "Well, we'd been planning to escape for some time now." Raise started. "Ever since the Princess returned with the news that your ship had escaped the Tray and was on its way back, I got a small team together and we refit the prowler with a Tray protostream system so we could reach you."

Raise sat back down on the bed behind him.

"We were going to wait a few more days before launching but our plan was discovered and we had to get away before the Tray attempted to arrest us. We took the prowler and left but we took some damage in our attempt to escape, our life support system began to fail and the stream system gave out leaving us stranded here. We had no choice but to wait and hope someone would come along to pick us up, I just thank the gods it was you Colonel."

"You say your plan was discovered, how?" Taymen asked.

"It seems that there is a traitor working for the Tray, an Egyptian who has been reporting our plans back to the Tray leadership, we don't know who it is?" Raise explained.

"But why did you come to find us if you knew we were coming home?" Avril asked.

"To help you of course." Raise replied.

"Help us?" Taymen asked.

"That's right Colonel I have information and orders from Princess Releena to launch a strike against the Tray leadership that will effectively cripple the rest of their fleet in our space. Colonel, if we pull this off we can take back our home with minimal casualties and the Dark Avenger is the only ship that can do it."

"Well whatever it is your planning it'll have to wait." The Doctor said. "I'm not ready to discharge you just yet General."

"I'm fine Doctor." Raise replied.

"I'm sure you think so, but let me be the Doctor."

Taymen didn't say anything.

"I'm sorry Colonel but they need to rest." The Doctor said.

Taymen nodded.

"Of course, we'll talk in the morning Sir." Taymen said before leaving sick bay.

Taymen closed the hatch behind Avril and led her down the corridor. Something didn't add up but Taymen wasn't sure what. He led Avril to the briefing room and sealed the hatch behind them.

"What do you think Sir?" Avril asked.

Taymen didn't say anything yet. Instead, he walked over to the computer console mounted on the back wall and accessed the ship's security system with his implant. He sorted through the system until he found the briefing room and disabled the security monitors before turning to Avril.

The look in his eyes told Avril that he was really worried about something and whatever it was, it was about to make things more complicated for both of them.

Finally, after a long and awkward silence Taymen spoke.

"Do you trust me Avril?"

Part III
Betrayal

'Treachery is in our nature. We remain loyal to ourselves and to our friends, but eventually we will come across a situation in which we must betray someone to save those we care for. Treason is inevitable, all we can do is hope we don't betray the wrong person.'

Cairon University Professor Tagass

Chapter Twelve

"Incoming ordnance!"

Titus shouted a few seconds before the ship shuttered against the impact of the Tray missiles.

"All batteries switch to suppressive fire, recall the sword breakers." Taymen ordered. "Carrey ready all missile tubes with full salvos of saber missiles at all targets." He continued.

"Sir that's the rest of our missile payload." Carrey said from the weapons stations.

"I'm aware of that Commander." Taymen replied.

"Tubes ready Sir." The missile officer said a second later.

"Fire!" Taymen snapped.

"All sword breakers are aboard Sir." Elisha reported from the flight control station.

"Incoming ordnance!" Avril snapped.

Before Taymen could say anything the ship shuttered and he and Avril lost their footing.

A few of the consoles in C.A.C. overloaded and blew out along with several of the bulkheads.

"Direct hit to the upper heat exchanger." The damage control officer reported. "Systems are starting to overheat and we've lost lateral thrusters." He said.

"Carrey prep two nukes, target them at the heavy cruisers." Taymen said as he got back to his feet. "Helm prepare to stream us out as soon as the nukes are away."

"Aye Sir." Aurin said from the helm stations.

"Colonel!" General Raise protested.

"We can't stand against these cruisers alone, we have to get out before we lose the protostream system too!" Taymen snapped.

He didn't care what rank Raise was, this was Taymen's ship and crew and he wasn't going to sit there and sacrifice their lives foolishly.

"Ready Sir." The stream officer reported.

"Missiles locked Sir." Carrey said.

"Fire!" Taymen ordered.

"Missiles away, impact in fifteen seconds."

"Helm stream us out now!" Taymen snapped.

Within seconds the hull of the Dark Avenger began to glow just before it vanished into the protostream leaving the missiles in its wake.

"Stream complete Sir." Aurin reported.

"What are you doing Colonel?" General Raise shouted.

Taymen ignored him for a moment as he checked the sensor display to make sure there were no other contacts in the area.

"Answer me Colonel." Raise said.

"We can't stand in the open against seven heavy cruisers, we'd be obliterated." Taymen replied. "If we're going to retake Abydos we're going to need this ship intact."

Raise didn't say anything.

"Your intelligence was wrong Sir." Avril said from behind the command console.

"I don't recall asking you Captain." Raise snapped.

"She's right Sir." Taymen said. "There were only supposed to be three light cruisers guarding the supply station." He continued. "Now, instead of replenishing our supplies we've used up our remaining missile payload and we barely have enough plasma rounds to take on a light cruiser!"

Taymen forgot himself for a moment as he spoke to the General but he didn't care. Ever since Raise came aboard and started giving Taymen mission orders things had gone from bad to worse.

The ship had taken some major damage and the Tray seemed to be closing in on them at every turn. Now they were almost out of ammunition, almost half their sword breakers were gone and their supplies were running dangerously low.

"We've lost the element of surprise." Taymen said. "The Tray know we're looking to re-supply and will redeploy accordingly."

Taymen turned to Titus.

"Bring the ship to stealth mode." He said.

"Aye Sir." Titus replied.

"Launch sensor drones and have them maintain a five light minute perimeter."

"Aye Sir."

"Captain you have command." Taymen said as he left C.A.C. followed closely by General Raise.

Taymen walked down the corridor to the ladder and climbed up to the next deck.

"Colonel we have a problem." Raise said.

"I agree Sir." Taymen replied as he stepped off the ladder and onto the deck.

"What makes you think you can disobey my orders." Raise asked in a deceptively calm voice.

"The fact that this is my ship and crew, and your orders would have led to their destruction." Taymen said. "I know I don't need to remind the General of the responsibility of every Captain, to ensure the survival of their ship in a questionable situation."

"Questionable!" Raise snapped. "Are you implying you can't trust my orders Colonel?" He asked.

"Not at all General." Taymen replied without hesitating.

"I'm saying that I don't think we can trust your intelligence anymore. We've been engaged by Tray fleets on three separate occasions since we've reached the outer colonies when there was no way they should have known we were here." Taymen explained. "I think it's safe to say that your informant has been compromised."

"Reliable or not my intel is all we have right now Colonel." Raise argued.

"Then it's time to gather our own intel." Taymen said. "We have the location of several data beacons, one of them should provide us with some more reliable information."

Cairon Residential District
16:45 Abydos Standard Time
Day 1, Ninth Cycle, Egyptian Year 3201

Torri made her way through the crowded streets towards her tent. Her brown hair was drenched by the rain that had lasted for the last few days all over Cairon.

She kept her bag close to her trying to keep its contents dry so they would not have to endure another night of soggy bread in their cold damp tent.

Ever since the Tray had taken over Cairon and decided to rebuild the major cities all the Egyptian families had been relocated to groups of small tents scattered throughout the cities while the Tray officers took up residence in their former homes. Torri was forced out with her husband almost four months ago.

He was a noted archeologist at the Cairon University before the occupation, now he was a general laborer at one of the restoration projects in the residential district.

119

Torri was forced to work the farms along with almost all of the other women in the city, day after day growing food for their Tray masters as they all reminisced about the lives they once had. She often cried herself to sleep at night thinking about her family.

Her parents were forced to work at one of the food processing stations as they were getting too old for manual labor, while her younger brother Alban worked at a mining facility on one of the outer colonies. Torri saw her parents almost every night and she received transmissions from Alban every week.

The one that made her cry most often was the memory of her youngest brother. He was the Captain of a ship in the Egyptian Defense force and she hadn't heard from him in years. He occasionally sent her some money to help her and her husband get by which was a great help to them. Since the Tray attack however she hadn't heard anything about him.

She didn't even know the name of his ship or what group he belonged to so there was no way for her to find out what has become of him. The only thing that Torri knew was that most of the Egyptian ships had been either captured or destroyed. There were rumors of a few ships surviving, one in particular was causing the Tray a great deal of trouble.

Torri wasn't sure she believed such a thing. She figured it was some story the Tray came up with to give the Egyptian people a false sense of hope so they would work better. Even if it was true it didn't make much difference. The ship was one small vessel against a fleet that overtook the entire Defense Force, there was no way it could beat the Tray alone.

She swept the tent flap aside and walked in letting the flap fall closed behind her.

Her husband looked up from his book and smiled.

Torri knew that when he smiled at her like that it meant he heard some wild rumor about someone coming to save them. She may not have believed such things but her husband practically planned his days around them.

"What is it this time?" She asked knowing he was going to tell her weather she wanted to know or not.

Koran marked his book before closing it and set it down on the table.

"What makes you think there's anything at all?" He asked, trying to contain his excitement.

"Are you going to sit there and tell me that you haven't heard anything about this mysterious savior of ours?" Torri replied as she took off her jacket and hung it off of a line that ran over the heater.

Koran ignored her sarcasm.

"No, I did actually." He started.

Torri rolled her eyes as she placed her bag on the table.

"Apparently that ship that the Tray have been trying to capture has been seen near the outer colonies. They're here and they're making their way towards Abydos." He said.

Torri couldn't help but smile at his excitement, it almost reminded her of a child on his birthday.

"What difference would it make anyways?" She said. "Even if it was coming here do you really think that one ship could stand against the entire Tray fleet?"

Koran's excitement faded into disappointment.

"I think it makes all the difference, especially now." He said. "Why else would the Tray be so concerned with it."

Torri didn't have an answer for that. She wasn't sure why she was so pessimistic about the whole idea, after all if there was a chance that someone was coming to rescue them, shouldn't she at least hope that they succeed.

Dark Avenger C.A.C.
19:00 Abydos Standard Time
Day 1, Ninth Cycle, Egyptian Year 3201

Taymen stared at the main screen at the head of C.A.C.

The image was haunting. It was almost like looking into a mirror and seeing yourself as a ghost.

The damage was extensive. There were hull breeches on most of the primary decks, the starboard landing deck was barely intact and the gun batteries were almost completely destroyed.

Aside from all the damage however there was no mistaking it, it was an avenger class battleship, or at least what was left of one.

It was adrift with no detectable electromagnetic signatures emanating from it and there were no Defense Force markings on the hull.

It was by pure chance they found it at all. When the Dark Avenger streamed into the system the ship almost drifted right into them. It had almost no sensor profile, they had to use the external camera to identify it.

"No response to hails Sir." Sairon reported from the communications station.

Taymen wasn't surprised.

"Can you link up to its data relay?" He asked.

"Trying to now Sir." Sairon said.

Every Egyptian ship had an encrypted data relay that could only be accessed by other Egyptian ships. The relay transmitted the ship's name and registry for identification and military ships could access class, crew compliment and even data logs through the relay.

"I've got it Sir." Sairon said a moment later.

"The ship's called the Shadow Venturer but it's unregistered." She continued. "There aren't a lot of log entries but it looks like it's some sort of experimental platform for some major system upgrades."

Avril moved closer to Taymen.

"I've never heard of this ship." She said quietly. "And no hull markings, I don't think this ship is one of ours." She continued.

"If it's an experimental platform it has to operate out of a shipyard somewhere." Taymen said. "See if you can access its navigation logs."

"Looks like they've been deleted." Sairon replied.

"There's a surprise." Avril said sarcastically.

Suddenly an alarm on the main operations station went off.

"What in the name of Anubis?" Titus said.

"Report Commander."

"Something's entered the computer network through the data stream Sir." Titus explained.

"Cut the stream and isolate the affected systems." Taymen ordered.

"Data stream severed Sir." Sairon reported.

"I can't isolate it Sir, it's already moved into the secondary protocols." Titus said.

"What is it?" Avril asked.

"Looks like some sort of virus." Titus replied. "It's penetrating our firewalls as if they aren't there and moving throughout the network."

"Can you cut the network connections to the remaining systems?" Taymen asked.

"There's not enough time, it's spreading too fast." Titus said with a hint of panic in his voice.

"Sir I just lost helm control." The maneuvering officer reported.

Taymen turned to the command console and tried to access the computer with his implant.

As the nanites interfaced with the computer system, they were unable to access the system directly, leaving Taymen and the rest of the crew locked out.

"Sir." Sairon said. "I just lost control of my console."

"Me too Sir." The stream officer said.

"The virus has accessed our primary systems." Titus said.

"I noticed Commander." Taymen said sarcastically.

"Sir it's set a course for a protostream hub." Aurin reported from the helm station.

"Shut down power to the main drive system, shut down the entire PT generator if you have to." Taymen ordered.

"I can't Sir, power distribution systems are locked out."

"Sairon contact the engine room and tell them to cut power to the main systems."

"I have no control over the communications system Sir." Sairon said.

Taymen had no idea what else to try.

In less than a minute the virus managed to infiltrate their entire network and assume control of the ship.

"Sir protostream generators are powering up, we're streaming out in ten seconds." The stream officer reported.

Taymen couldn't do anything but watch the main sensor display as his ship took them to gods know where.

"Three...two...one...streaming!"

"Stream complete Sir." Aurin said.

"Do we have control of any systems?" Avril asked.

"No Ma'am." Titus replied. "The virus is still in control of all primary systems." He continued.

"Sir it's just programmed a flight path and is powering up the main drive thrusters." The maneuvering officer reported.

"Do we know where we are?" Taymen asked.

"Looks like we're just outside of the Tri-star plasma fields." Aurin said.

"Sir." The maneuvering officer started. "This flight path takes us right into the plasma fields, at current velocity we'll enter the event horizon in three minutes."

"Can we get the armor deployed?" He asked.

"Negative Sir the system is completely locked out." Titus replied.

Taymen wasn't sure what to do. If they cut power to the thrusters while they were in the plasma fields they would drift through the plasma charges and be destroyed for sure, that's assuming that this virus wasn't trying to simply destroy them itself.

"Can we manually purge the computer systems to regain control?" Avril asked.

Taymen turned to Titus.

"Well, yes we could but we'd come back online with only the basic operating systems and it's going to take at least an hour to setup."

"Make it sooner Titus." Taymen ordered.

"Aye Sir." Titus said as he left C.A.C.

He made his way down to the main computer room along with two of the network technicians.

The room was small and cramped with fiber-optic lines coming in through conduits on every wall. In the center of the room was a set of computer processors all linked to the memory core.

"We need to isolate the unaffected systems before the virus spreads to them too, at least that way we'll be able to save some computer data." Titus said.

One of the techs pulled out a small diagnostic pad and switched it on as he made his way over to one of the wire bundles leading to the secondary systems. One by one he disconnected the cables from the core and connected it to his pad to see if the system was infected, if it was he plugged it back in, otherwise he left it unplugged to keep the virus from traveling to the system.

"This damn thing is everywhere." One of the techs said.

"That's strange." The other started.

"What?" Titus asked.

"The virus hasn't touched the weapons or defensive systems." The tech explained.

"Are you sure?" Titus asked.

"Yes Sir there's no sign of the virus, actually the only thing it seems to be actively infecting are the propulsion systems and anything that we could potentially use to stop it, it's just closing the door on everything else."

Titus double checked the diagnostic pads to see for himself. The only systems the virus took direct control of were the propulsion and power systems. It was like this virus didn't want to destroy them so much as it wanted to lead them somewhere.

"Keep working, I'll be back." Titus said as he left the room and headed back to C.A.C.

When he got there Taymen was still at the command console watching their course.

So far the flight path had led them around all the plasma clouds avoiding any significant danger.

"Sir." Titus said. "I think there's more to this than we're getting."

"What are you talking about?" Taymen asked.

"The virus has only locked out most of our systems and taken control of the propulsion and power systems, I think it was programmed to bring us somewhere."

"That would seem obvious Commander." Taymen said.

"Yes Sir but there was no sign of the virus in the weapons system, or life support for that matter. If it was going to destroy us there are far more effective ways to do it than steering us into a plasma field."

Taymen thought it over for a moment.

"Well if it was trying to steer us into the plasma fields it's doing a terrible job." He said. "Look at this."

Titus looked at the flight path on the main display screen.

"It's steering us around the plasma fields, not into them." Taymen said. "So what do you suggest?" He asked.

"I think we should make the preparations for the purge and wait to see where this virus takes us. If it looks like it's taking us into the plasma fields, then we purge it and regain control."

"Do you really think that's a good idea?" Taymen asked.

"I don't think we have anything to lose at this point." Titus said.

Taymen sighed.

Titus was right, as long as they were flying around the plasma fields they had nothing to lose by waiting.

"Finish your preparations Titus and wait for my orders."

"Aye Sir." Titus said.

Almost two hours later the ship slowly emerged from the plasma fields into a void that was occupied by three small stars.

The gravity and radiation in the area made the sensors almost completely useless, it was impossible for sensors to see anything in the system.

"Sir we've left the plasma fields and are holding position." Aurin reported.

"Anything on sensors?" Taymen asked.

"No Sir, but our range is extremely limited." Titus said.

"Titus, I want you to…"

"Sir the virus is doing something." Titus said, cutting Taymen off.

"Anything more descriptive Commander?" Taymen asked.

"It's withdrawing from all the primary systems and…standby Sir."

Titus checked his console again just to be certain.

"It's just purged itself from the system, we're back in control." He said.

"Confirmed Sir, I have helm control." The maneuvering officer said.

Taymen placed his right hand on the command console interface and tried to link to the system again. This time his nanites accessed the system with no interference.

"Okay, any idea why it brought us here?" Avril asked.

"Sir." Sairon said. "We're being hailed."

"Source?" Taymen asked.

"I can't trace it but it's close, the transmission is in real time." Sairon reported.

"Patch it through." Taymen said.

The speakers came online with the sound of a man's raspy voice.

"Battleship Dark Avenger, we're transmitting a flight plan that will bring you between the stars to our coordinates, follow the route exactly, we will provide further instructions when you arrive."

The voice went silent and the channel closed a second later.

Taymen looked at Avril and Titus who just looked back at him blankly.

"Well then, helm do you have the flight plan?" Taymen asked.

"Yes Sir." Aurin replied.

"Why not." Taymen said. "Set course and speed to take us there."

Cairon Residential District
16:35 Abydos Standard Time
Day 2, Ninth Cycle, Egyptian Year 3201

Releena made her way through the people crowding the streets. She was both surprised and relieved that nobody recognized her as she wandered around the city, her hood obviously kept her face sufficiently concealed.

Fleet Marshal Ourik finally seemed to get bored with her, either that or she became more trouble than he was willing to deal with. In any case he stripped her of her title and sent her to one of the holding facilities on Netara. Luckily however some of her soldiers managed to infiltrate the Tray command structure and were able to get her out after a few days.

Once free, Releena cut her hair to shoulder length and changed its color to a dark red before she managed to arrange passage to the planet Cairon where several of her Imperial Guard officers had been moved to. Colonel Sharr Vaye was the first officer Releena found when she got to Cairon.

Sharr was the CO of a pulsar class cruiser before her ship was destroyed by the Tray during the initial attack. She managed to escape its destruction along with most of her crew only to be captured by the Tray and relocated to Cairon to work as laborers.

"Princess." Sharr said as she approached Releena from a narrow side street.

"I've told you before Sharr, you can't call me that in public." Releena said as she looked around to make sure nobody heard her.

"Sorry." Sharr said. "I found her." She continued.

Releena sighed with relief.

"Where?" She asked.

126

"Their tent is just up this street." Sharr replied as she moved to lead Releena back up the narrow side street.

They stopped outside of a tent at the end of the street and Sharr pulled the flap aside to let Releena in.

Inside they found a man and woman sitting at a small table in the center of the tent, both of whom stood at the sight of Releena and Sharr.

"Can I help you?" The man asked.

Releena removed her hood and was about to speak when the man gasped.

"Oh my gods." He said. "Princess Releena, you're alive."

Sharr didn't say anything, neither did the other woman.

"I'm looking for Torri Orelle." Releena said softly.

The man didn't say anything.

"I'm Torri Princess." The woman said as she stepped forward.

Releena smiled in relief.

"I have news of your brother."

Dark Avenger at the Tri-Star Plasma Fields
17:50 Abydos Standard Time
Day 2, Ninth Cycle, Egyptian Year 3201

The ship shuttered as they passed between the gravity fields of the nearby stars.

"Steady as she goes." Taymen said. "Ahead dead slow."

"Dead slow Aye Sir." Aurin replied.

They had been maneuvering through the gravity fields for almost an hour and were nearing the very center between the three stars where the gravity fields cancelled each other out, that's where the flight plan was leading them.

"Sir we've reached the final waypoint." Aurin reported.

"All stop." Taymen ordered.

"Sensor contact!" Titus said. "Looks like some sort of station Sir." He reported.

"They're hailing us Sir." Sairon said.

"Patch it through." Taymen ordered.

A voice came over the speaker a second later.

"Battleship Dark Avenger proceed to docking pylon three, someone will meet you there to escort you to our briefing room."

The speaker went silent once again.

"Helm move us in for docking." Taymen ordered. "Avril, Titus, you're with me." He said as he led them out of C.A.C.

The main airlock was at the forward end of the ship five decks up from C.A.C. The corridors leading to the airlock were the most heavily armored and had the heaviest pressure doors between each section since it was a likely boarding point.

"Sir." Avril started. "What exactly are we doing here?" She asked.

"With any luck, finding out what we're doing here Captain." Taymen answered.

He realized only after he said it that it sounded like a sarcastic answer, but Taymen meant exactly what he said. He had no idea what they were doing there, the only reason he had gone along with everything up to this point was to find out what was going on.

As they reached the airlock Taymen felt the dull shutter of the outer hull contacting the docking port. He looked on the pad next to the heavy airlock door and saw that it read hard lock. He waited a moment as the airlock pressurized before opening the hatch.

Taymen hesitated a moment before stepping out into the airlock. As he crossed over onto the station Taymen felt slightly disoriented. He felt it every time he stepped off of his ship, it may have been his body adjusting to the change in gravity.

The gravity on military ships was kept a little heavier than Abydos' standard.

Taymen always felt a little strange when he left the Avenger. The ship was his home. It protected him and his crew and kept them together. Whenever he stepped off of it he felt like he was leaving that security behind.

When the station's airlock door opened there was a young man in civilian clothing standing in the corridor waiting. He didn't look like he was any more than twenty years old and he seemed almost startled at the sight of the three of them walking out of the airlock.

"Colonel Orelle." The young man said in greeting. "I'm Ashen, I'm Doctor Rayez's assistant, if you'll follow me I'll take you to meet with her."

Taymen simply nodded and fell in behind Ashen who led them down the corridor to a lift.

Looking around Taymen could see that the station was clearly civilian.

The corridors were brightly lit and very wide. The bulkheads were made from a light plastic material unlike the armored bulkheads on the Avenger and the deck was covered with a soft gray carpet. Mounted on the bulkheads were several signs indicating the way to different rooms making it easier for anyone to get around.

"What is this place?" Avril asked.

"Callon facility 377, it's a secret research and development facility used for experimental military systems." Ashen said.

"Callon?" Titus asked.

"Callon is a civilian contractor that specializes in the construction of medium to large size battleships. They build ships and specialized systems for the Defense Force." Taymen said.

"The avenger class is the smallest ship we produce for the Defense Force." Ashen said.

"Here we are." He said as he led them into a small briefing room.

Inside sitting at the head of a long table was a young dark haired woman in a white lab coat. Her hair was long and tied back and her brown eyes were fixed on Taymen as they entered the room. She stood up and waited for the door to close.

"Welcome." She said. "I'm Elia Rayez, I'm the manager and chief researcher of this facility."

"Colonel Taymen Orelle of the Dark Avenger." Taymen said in introduction. "This is my executive officer Captain Avril Raquel and my operations officer Lieutenant-Commander Titus Daverro."

Elia gestured for them to sit down before she took her seat again.

"Well, shall we get started then." She said.

"Why did you bring us here?" Taymen asked.

Elia smiled a little, not at all surprised that they had some questions.

"We programmed a virus that was specially designed to take over an avenger class ship's propulsion system and bring them here."

"Yes we noticed." Taymen said.

"But why?" Titus asked.

"This facility has been developing a number of new systems and upgrades specifically designed for the avenger class battle ship, we needed a ship to implement them on."

"Our ship has already had several upgrades." Avril said, as though she was insulted at the implication that they would need these new systems.

"I know all about the Dark Avenger's upgrades Captain, they were carried out at this facility." Celia replied.

"A lot has happened since then and we've been especially busy since you've been gone. These new systems are unlike anything implemented in the fleet right now." She continued.

"What kind of systems?" Taymen asked.

Elia moved to a large display screen on the wall and brought up a schematic of an avenger class ship. The diagram highlighted several of the upgraded systems.

"There are only two completely new systems that we want to install on your ship, the rest are replacements or upgrades." She started.

"We want to install six heavy rail cannons and six large missile silos on the Dark Avenger. These weapon systems alone will give the ship a combat capability that has never been conceived for a ship this size. As for the other systems, we will upgrade the stealth and communications systems, the targeting array and replace your current armor resin with a new hyper-dense compound. We'll also replace your prowlers and sword breakers with the latest models."

"And how long would all that take?" Taymen asked.

Elia turned off the display and walked back over to her seat.

"Well if it's just a matter of these upgrades than we can have your ship ready in a little more than a week." She replied.

"Sir we don't have much time." Avril said.

"I'm aware of that Captain." Taymen replied.

"Unfortunately Doctor, it's not just a matter of the upgrades. We need several major repairs and our ammunition stores are almost completely depleted, our protostream system has been modified to Tray specifications and we have no idea how long it'll last."

"Wait, you have a Tray stream generator?" Elia asked.

"Yes but it's in rough shape." Titus said.

"You have to let us examine it Colonel, it may be the thing we need to take the Tray's only advantage away from them." Elia said in excitement.

Taymen shook his head.

"We don't have the time." He started. "We have a rendezvous to make in six days and we still need to reach an ammunition depot to re-supply before then."

"What if we could get the repairs done to your ship while we examined the stream system, would you allow it then?" Elia asked.

Taymen thought it over for a moment. They could really use the repairs and the upgrades would certainly give them an edge in combat but something just didn't sit right with him and it wasn't just this station.

Ever since General Raise had been providing them with intelligence it seemed like the Tray have been one step ahead of them. He didn't trust the General or his men but he had no way to prove his suspicions, at least not until now. Something just occurred to Taymen that he never would have considered before.

"If we could somehow get you the time to do what you needed, to make the upgrades and repairs as well as examine the stream system, how fast could you get it done?" Taymen asked.

"We'd need a detailed damage assessment of you ship to know for certain, but how would you do that?" Elia replied.

"Your ship, the Shadow Venturer, do you have something that could tow it back here for repairs." Taymen asked.

"Sir that ship's scrap." Titus said.

"I know that Commander, but just for argument sake." Taymen said.

"Yes, we have a small recovery ship that could get it here in a day or so, but as Commander Daverro said the ship is scrap, and trying to repair it would take workers away from your ship, the upgrades would take much longer." Elia said.

"Sir you know that ship would never survive combat." Avril pointed out. Taymen nodded.

"Exactly."

Princess' Residence, Netara
18:42 Abydos Standard Time
Day 4, Ninth Cycle, Egyptian Year 3201

Ourik sat down behind what was once Princess Releena's desk and accessed the communications unit. He opened the channel to the incoming transmission.

"This is Fleet Marshal Ourik, go ahead." He said.

"We're on schedule." A voice said over the com. unit.

"How long until I can greet our heroes in person?" Ourik asked.

"I'll have them at your location in a little more than a week." The voice replied.

"Good, I'm taking a group of ships to investigate these rumors of a hidden ship yard near the outer reaches of the galaxy, I should be back by then." Ourik closed the channel and left the office.

He made his way to the outer court yard where his shuttle was waiting to take him to his ship in orbit.

There had been several rumors about a secret facility constructing a fleet of ships for a counter attack against them, Ourik was sure that they weren't true but he wasn't going to risk being wrong.

Chapter Thirteen

Taymen stood staring out the window overlooking the Dark Avenger. The ship was docked in one of the construction bays while it underwent the upgrades and repairs. They were ahead of schedule but it would still be another few days before they were finished.

The Shadow Venturer was a different story however. The propulsion systems were back online along with life support, but that was it. The ship couldn't stream and it certainly couldn't fight. Still, it was one more ship that they didn't have before.

"Quite the sight isn't it?" Taymen heard Elia say as she walked up behind him.

"I never did like seeing her like this, docked in some construction scaffold, it's like seeing a child on life support." Taymen said.

Elia smiled. She always noticed that a ship's commander saw their ship as something more than 'just a ship.' She never understood it herself. She's worked with hundreds of ships and never saw them as anything more than a collection of computers and mechanical systems. She figured that was the difference between serving on a ship and just working on one.

"I can see how you could feel like that." She finally said.

"How are we doing?" Taymen asked.

"Very well." Elia replied. "The repairs are nearly finished but you weren't exaggerating about your stream generator. We had to replace several major components, luckily we were able to rebuild the system to the Tray specifications." She said.

"As for your upgrades, the heavy rail guns have been installed and will be online by the end of the day. Tomorrow we'll start cutting into the hull to install the heavy missile silos. They should only take two or three days."

Taymen nodded as he stood silently for only a moment.

"Why are you doing all this?" He asked. "Why go through all this trouble for one ship when you can simply take everything you know and escape this place?"

"I thought that would be obvious." Elia said. "The same reason you and your crew came back. This is our home, we're not going to simply surrender it to the first group of bullies that come our way.

"We know all about your ship, what you've gone through to get here and how much trouble you've given the Tray. You can't travel to a single planet in the Empire without hearing the rumors about the phantom ship that dares defy them."

Taymen figured that she was exaggerating. He assumed that the Tray would do anything in their power to conceal the existence of a ship defeating them.

"You and your crew are already heroes Colonel. Win lose or die you'll be remembered as heroes, that's what it is to be the last hope for someone. We want to make sure that our people get the chance to see that hope alive."

"There's something I want you to do." Taymen started. "A modification I need you to make to the Shadow Venturer."

Dark Avenger Rendezvous Point
03:23 Abydos Standard Time
Day 12, Ninth Cycle, Egyptian Year 3201

General Raise watched the sensor contact on the prowlers' aft compartment monitor as it slowly moved closer.

"Sir I have a positive ID from its data relay, it's the Dark Avenger." The pilot reported.

"Get us cleared for landing." Raise ordered.

"Aye Sir." The pilot replied as he opened a channel to the Avenger's flight controllers.

"Dark Avenger flight this is prowler seven-niner-two requesting landing clearance." He said.

There was a brief silence before one of the controllers came over the speaker.

"Roger that prowler, you are clear for landing on port landing platform two."

"Confirmed." The pilot replied before closing the channel.

"We're cleared for landing Sir."

"Very well, take us in Captain." Raise said.

As they flew by the Avenger, Raise looked out the window to see the hull badly damaged by weapons fire. There were a few breaches and several scorch marks indicating the ship had recently been through a brutal battle.

As the prowler landed and was brought down to the hangar deck Raise noticed that more than half the sword breakers were missing along with most of the deck crew.

"You!" Raise shouted to one of the deck crew as he stepped out of the prowler.

"Yes Sir." The young man replied as he snapped to attention.

"What happened here, where is everyone?" Raise asked.

"We were attacked, the starboard deck took a direct hit and there was an ordnance explosion on this side, most of our crew is either dead or injured." The crewman explained.

Raise took a brief look around before leaving the hangar deck and heading for C.A.C.

As he moved through the corridors he noticed severe damage on the bulkheads. Scorch marks, missing panels and bullet holes all over the place. It was obvious that the ship had been boarded, how the Tray got this deep into the ship however was a mystery.

As he got closer to C.A.C. Raise also noticed that he didn't see a single crew member in any corridor. With the amount of damage throughout the ship he expected to see at least one damage control team conducting repairs, but there was nothing.

As he entered C.A.C. he immediately noticed Taymen standing by the damage control station.

"Officer on deck!" One of the officers called.

"Carry on." Raise said as he made his way over to Taymen.

"Report Colonel, what in the name of Anubis happened here?" He asked.

"We were ambushed." Taymen replied.

"Ambushed?"

"Yes Sir, we were heading for an ammunition depot when a Tray battle group streamed into the system. They had us surrounded before we could fire a shot off." Taymen explained. "We lost over half our sword breakers and most of the deck crew. The starboard deck took a direct hit almost instantly, nobody survived.

"Whatever ammunition we had left has been depleted and most of our gun batteries are down, armor was breached and we were boarded. We managed to stream out and get here but the modifications we made to the stream system finally gave out, we should have conventional stream capability in a few hours." Taymen continued.

"My gods." Raise said. "I can't leave you alone can I Colonel." Taymen didn't know what to say.

"So what's our status?" Raise asked.

"We know of a place where we can conduct repairs but we need the stream system to get there, and until we can get there we're sitting ducks." Raise sighed.

"Very well, tell your crew to get that stream system up and running as soon as possible, I'll be in my quarters." Raise said.

"I'm afraid your quarters are in a breached section of the ship, we had to assign you new quarters for the time being." Taymen said.

"Lieutenant Shell here will show you to them." Raise glanced at the lieutenant before he turned to leave.

"Fine then, let's go." He said.

After Raise left C.A.C. Taymen turned back to the sensor display.

"Status on the repairs." He said.

"Stream system will be ready within the hour and stealth capability is back online." The damage control officer reported.

"Very well bring the ship to stealth mode." Taymen ordered.

Raise walked into his new quarters and sealed the hatch behind him. The lights in the room were barely working and the entire room was flooded with the smell of scorched metal.

Raise rolled his eyes as he made his way to the bunk in the wall and through the blanket aside before laying down. His head was pounding and the smell of the room just made it worse.

As he lay on the bunk staring at the ceiling, Raise's mind wandered to the thought of his daughter.

She was a teacher on a station near the outer reaches of their territory, which meant she was probably among the first to be attacked.

He didn't even know if she was still alive and there was no way for him to find out. Sometimes Raise wondered what she would think of him now, of the man he had become since the Tray first arrived. Would she be proud of him for what he was trying to do for their people? Or would she simply see him as a traitor?

In truth it didn't matter now, the things he had done couldn't be undone, he was in far too deep to back out now.

Raise pulled a small transmitter out of his uniform pocket and held it up to the light for a moment as he examined it. The sleek metallic body and the markings along its length felt so alien to Raise as he pushed the button on the end to activate the device.

'There.' He thought to himself. 'It's done.'

Callon Facility 377
10:40 Abydos Standard Time
Day 12, Ninth Cycle, Egyptian Year 3201

Taymen made his way through the station's corridors to the briefing room with General Raise following close behind.

135

The station's technicians began repairs on the ship as soon as they docked but it was going to be a while before they were combat ready again.

As they entered the briefing room Elia was waiting for them at the head of the table.

"Doctor." Taymen said as he walked in. "This is General Raise."

Elia simply nodded.

"Welcome General, unfortunately we don't have a lot of time." She said.

"One of our satellites has detected a large Tray battle group on route for this facility. By now they should be just outside of the plasma fields."

"Any idea if they know we're here?" Taymen asked.

"It's hard to say what they know Colonel, but I don't think a fleet this size came out here to follow-up on a rumor." Elia replied.

"Then what would you suggest Doctor?" Raise asked.

"We've begun evacuating already, all our data has been deleted and hard copies destroyed. Your ship Colonel is the only evidence of what was done here."

"How long until they arrive?" Taymen asked.

"Who knows, it could be hours or it could be days before they locate us, but we're making use of whatever time we have." Elia said. "We've already begun repairs on your ship and what little armaments we have are being loaded on board as we speak." She continued.

"But when they do find us, we'll have no chance against a fleet that size, so the station will be destroyed and with any luck the Tray fleet with it."

"Now wait a minute Doctor." Raise protested. "Is that really wise, this facility can build a new fleet for us, let's not be so quick to destroy it."

"She's right General." Taymen said. "If it can be used to build ships for us it can be used to build ships for the Tray and given the advanced technology they would gain access to here we can't let that happen."

Raise didn't say anything, there was obviously no way for him to convince them otherwise.

"Then we'll continue with the evacuation as planned." Taymen said. "When everyone is clear and the Tray are in position we'll remote detonate the station, hopefully the blast will destroy most of them giving us a clean escape." He continued.

"How long until evacuation is completed?" Raise asked.

"Most of our staff is already gone aboard the shuttles, we have a transport vessel that will take the rest of us just before the Tray arrive." Elia said.

"Very well then." Raise said. "Colonel have Commander Daverro report to my quarters, I have an assignment for him."

"Commander Daverro is not aboard the ship Sir." Taymen said.

"Where is he?" Raise snapped.

"He's on a scouting mission along with Captain Raquel and several other crewmen searching for re-supply stations." Taymen replied. "Should I send you someone else?" He asked.

"No." Raise said. "I'll take care of it myself."

As Raise left the room Taymen waited silently with Elia until the hatch was sealed again.

"Doctor, are there any nukes left on the station?" Taymen asked.

"Just one." Elia replied. "We were going to use it to enhance the stations self destruct system."

"Have it loaded onto my ship instead, I think it'll be better utilized from there." Taymen said.

"Of course Colonel."

"When you leave the station I want you to set a course for these coordinates." Taymen explained as he entered the coordinates onto a blank data pad on the desk.

"It's a small station about four months journey by conventional stream, and they could definitely benefit from you and your staffs' help. The man in charge is an acquaintance of mine, his name is Jassen Pitt, tell him that Colonel Orelle sent you."

Taymen handed Elia the data pad who quickly looked it over committing the coordinates to memory.

"One other thing." Taymen said. "Don't tell General Raise about any of this."

Titan at the Tri-Star Plasma Fields
13:27 Abydos Standard Time
Day 12, Ninth Cycle, Egyptian Year 3201

Ourik sat in his chair on the bridge of his flagship, the 'Titan' staring at the sensor display on the front bulkhead.

"Status." He said.

"We're emerging from the plasma clouds now Sir, our scout ships have detected some sort of facility." His first officer reported. "No other ships in the area." He continued.

"Have a boarding party sent to the station to investigate it." Ourik ordered.

"Sir I'm detecting something off of our aft quarter." One of the operations officers reported.

"What is it?" Ourik asked.

"It looks like one of our transponders, it's originating about three units off of our hull."

Ourik couldn't believe how close they were. A ship managing to get that close to them undetected was practically unheard of. Ourik figured it was because of the interference from all the radiation in the area.

"Hold position here and..." Suddenly the entire ship shuttered and Ourik was nearly thrown out of his chair.

"Report." He said.

"A ship on our aft quarter has opened fire, engines are off-line." The operations officer reported.

Ourik smiled slightly.

"Bold Colonel, very bold." He said to himself.

Dark Avenger C.A.C.
13:32 Abydos Standard Time
Day 12, Ninth Cycle, Egyptian Year 3201

"All gun batteries direct fire on the flag ship and ready all available missile tubes." Taymen ordered.

"Sir they're launching fighters." The operations officer reported.

"Batteries one through five switch to enemy suppression fire, missile tubes one through four fire at will." Taymen replied.

"Sir we're being hailed by the flagship."

"Put it through." Taymen said.

"Colonel Orelle, how nice to see you again." Ourik said over the C.A.C. speakers.

"Fleet Marshal Ourik, I suggest you move your ships out of here while you can." Taymen said.

"Now now Colonel there's no need for threats, I'm calling to inform you that I am willing to accept your surrender. Turn your ship over to me and I will spare your crew." Ourik said. *"You have five minutes to decide."*

When the channel closed Taymen turned to his weapons officer.

"Lieutenant how many missiles do we have left?" He asked.

"Forty-seven Sir." The Lieutenant replied. "Communicate our desire to surrender." Taymen said.

The Lieutenant smiled slightly.

"Aye Sir, firing all missiles." He reported.

Within seconds all forty-seven missiles had left the launch tubes and sped towards the Titan. A second later forty of them detonated against the Titan's hull.

"That's it Sir, missile stores are depleted and our gun batteries are ..."

Taymen was suddenly thrown to the deck as six missiles impacted the ship.

"Direct hit to the upper heat exchanger, armor's been breached and PT generator two is off line." The damage control officer reported.

"Helm prepare to stream us out of here." Taymen ordered.

"We can't leave yet Colonel." Raise protested. "The station is still intact." He said.

"Transmit the self destruct signal." Taymen ordered.

"Aye Sir." The operations officer reported as the ship shuttered again.

"Sir the stream system is off-line." Aurin reported.

"Sir the signal's not working." The operations officer said.

"What?" Taymen asked.

"I've transmitted the signal three times and the station is still there." He reported.

"Colonel, what's going on?" Raise snapped.

Taymen ignored him as he moved over to the missile officer.

"Is our last package ready?" He asked.

The missile officer nodded.

"Awaiting your order Sir." He said.

"Fine." Taymen said as he made his way back to the command console. "Hail the flagship." He said.

"Channel open Sir."

Taymen tapped the control on his earpiece.

"Fleet Marshal Ourik this is Colonel Orelle." Taymen said.

"Calling to surrender Colonel?" Ourik asked.

"I was just wondering if your men have boarded the station yet."

There was a long silence as Raise looked at Taymen with an expression of both confusion and impatience.

"Yes they have Colonel, was there something you would like us to take care of for you?" Ourik said smugly.

Taymen simply smiled slightly at the General.

"As a matter of fact there is." He said.

He nodded once to the missile officer who simply hit the launch control on his console.

An instant later a single missile was speeding towards the station.

Raise watched it on the sensor display as the missile got closer to its target, suddenly realizing what it was.

"Colonel!" Raise snapped.

A second later the missile detonated against the station enveloping it and the surrounding ships in a massive explosion.

"Status on the station." Raise said.

"It's gone Sir." The operations officer reported.

Taymen sighed.

"Why didn't you tell me you had a nuke onboard Colonel?" Raise asked, but before Taymen could answer the ship shuttered again.

This time several consoles in C.A.C. exploded sending white hot metal fragments flying through the air.

"The Tray flagship has resumed firing." The operations officer reported.

"You think." Taymen said sarcastically.

"PT generator one is failing." The damage control officer reported. "Primary systems are failing, we have multiple hull breaches and life support is off line."

"Colonel we have to get out of here." Raise said.

Taymen watched the main display for a moment. He always knew that giving the order to evacuate was something he had to be prepared for, he just never thought he'd actually have to do it.

"Abandon ship!" He ordered. "All hands to the escape pods and prowlers, we're done here."

A moment later the entire ship echoed with the evacuation signal. Taymen opened the hatch leading out of C.A.C. and waited until everyone was out before following the General into the corridor.

"We have to get to the hangar deck!" Raise said as he bolted down the corridor.

The ship continued to shutter as more and more missiles impacted the outer hull.

Taymen followed Raise down the corridor to the hangar deck where a single prowler was waiting for them with a pilot and a few other crew members.

Raise jumped aboard with Taymen close behind who sealed the hatch and strapped in.

"That's it, let's go." Raise ordered.

"Aye Sir." The pilot said as he engaged the lift that carried the ship up to the launch deck.

Once the lift stopped the pilot disengaged the magnetic locks allowing the ship to float off of the deck a few inches before he engaged the main thrusters. The ship accelerated out of the flight deck and into open space.

Taymen looked out the window to see a group of missiles speeding towards the Avenger.

As the prowler came around Taymen watched as his ship drifted lifelessly through space surrounded by the remaining Tray ships.

Suddenly a group of missiles impacted her hull and the ship erupted into a violent explosion which sent debris and burning atmosphere shooting through space. Some of the debris impacted the hulls of a few Tray ships that got too close, the rest simply drifted off into the void leaving nothing where the ship was a moment ago.

Taymen continued to watch as the Tray flagship moved closer to them, and yet all he could think about was his lost ship. He saw several escape pods and a few other prowlers clear the explosion but it didn't make him feel any better.

"Sir." The pilot said as the flagship moved closer and closer to them.

"Stream us out of here Lieutenant." Taymen ordered.

"Belay that!" Raise snapped as he stood up.

"General?" Taymen said.

Before anyone could do anything Raise pulled his side arm and pointed it at Taymen. As soon as he did the other two crewmen on the prowler drew their side arms and had them trained on the General.

"We're not going anywhere Colonel." Raise said. "Lieutenant hold your course." He continued.

"Sir?" The Pilot said in confusion.

"Do as he says Lieutenant." Taymen said. "Lower your weapons guys." He said to his crewmen, who simply looked at each other.

"I'd do as the Colonel says." Raise said.

Taymen nodded at each of them before they finally lowered their weapons and handed them to Raise.

"Now everybody just sit down and relax." He said as he accessed the communications system in the rear compartment.

"This is Fleet Marshal Ourik." A voice said over the speakers.

"Fleet Marshal this is General Raise, I have Colonel Orelle."

"Well done General, I look forward to seeing him." Ourik said before Raise closed the channel.

Taymen watched as they approached the flagships' landing deck and the pilot set the prowler down on a landing pad.

As the ship was brought into the Tray hangar deck a security team opened the hatch and trained their weapons on Taymen and his crewmen.

Raise stepped out of the prowler and replaced his side arm.

"Bring the Colonel to the bridge, take the others to the brig." He said.

As Taymen stood from his seat two Tray guards grabbed his arms and escorted him off of the prowler.

Once he was on the hangar deck Taymen wrenched his arms free of the guards who backed off a step but remained ready to grab him. As if Taymen had anywhere to go.

"If you'll follow me Colonel." Raise said.

Taymen looked at his crewmen briefly before following Raise into the corridor.

Cairon Residential District
14:25 Abydos Standard Time
Day 12, Ninth Cycle, Egyptian Year 3201

Torri felt the tears well up in her green eyes, she just couldn't hold them back anymore.

"Taymen is the Captain of the Dark Avenger?" She asked.

She was having a hard time believing that her little brother was the last hope for them all. She couldn't imagine that kind of burden on his shoulders.

"You should be very proud of your brother." Sharr said.

"I just can't believe it." Torri said.

"It's true Torri." Releena started. "Taymen was lost to us for awhile, we're still not sure how but it's not important. What is important is that he's returned with a ship still capable of fighting the Tray but I have to be honest with you, the odds are not in his favor. I am trying to help him and his crew as much as I can from here but there is not a lot I can do."

"What do you need me to do?" Torri asked.

"Nothing Torri, I've been rallying those who served in the Imperial Guard to try and form a resistance and perhaps to locate the surviving ships to help your brother. I was hoping you would inform me if he contacts you."

"Of course." Torri replied as she wiped the tears from her face.

As Releena stood up to leave Koran shot to his feet.

"Princess!" He said.

"In the old industrial district there's a large number of soldiers working there as laborers, I think some of them are from the Imperial guard." Releena smiled.

"Thank you Koran." She said. "I'm afraid I have to ask you not to mention my being here to anyone, the Tray have spies mixed into the population and I can't risk being exposed."

"We understand." Torri said as Releena and Sharr left the tent.

"So it's true then." Koran said a moment later. "At least now you know he's alright."

Ourik watched the sensor display as what was left of his fleet regrouped.

The station was gone along with the Dark Avenger and more than half of his ships and there was no sign of any other survivors in the area.

"Helm how long until we can get underway?" Ourik asked.

"Damage control reports thirty minutes Sir." The helmsman reported.

"Fleet Marshal."

Ourik spun his chair around to see General Raise standing in front of him with Taymen standing just behind him.

"General Raise, welcome back." Ourik said. "And Colonel Orelle, good to see you again, shame about your ship."

Taymen didn't say anything as Ourik stood up.

"Your little rebellion is over Colonel." Ourik said.

"You were the last hope for your people and now your ship is gone and your crew scattered with nowhere to go, you failed Colonel." Taymen smiled slightly.

"If you think destroying one ship ensures your victory over my people, than you've already lost this war." He said.

Ourik glanced at Raise briefly who struck Taymen across the back of the head with the handle of his side arm.

Taymen fell to the deck nearly unconscious from the blow.

"Look at yourself." Ourik said as he took a few steps towards him.

"The great hero of the Egyptian people kneeling before their conqueror."

Taymen waited for his vision to clear before standing up again.

Ourik was surprised to see Taymen back on his feet so quickly.

"You have me and three other members of my crew, which only leaves about eleven hundred for you to find, victory is within your grasp isn't it Fleet Marshal." Taymen said smugly.

Raise was about to hit him again when Ourik raised his hand indicating for him to stop.

"Colonel I don't need your crew, all I need is you and the image of your ship's destruction to convince your people of their defeat and I have that."

Taymen didn't say anything.

"We'll talk again later about what I have planned for you, for now however I suspect you're tired."

Ourik looked at Raise.

"Take the Colonel to the brig but keep him separated from his crewmen."

Raise led Taymen through the corridor towards the brig.

"So what was the price General?" Taymen asked. "What was the price that turned you against your own people?"

Raise thought for a moment, he had been trying to remember that himself.

"We lost this war even before the Tray got here." Raise said. "They have a vast number of ships at their disposal, all our projections showed that we couldn't sustain a defensive line of any size against them for long, we would eventually have fallen to them anyways." He explained.

"You mean to tell me that you knew they were coming?" Taymen asked.

"Of course, we knew they were coming months before they arrived but there was still nothing we could do. We took the option that kept the number of casualties to a minimum." Raise said.

"I suppose we should be grateful for that." Taymen said sarcastically.

"I don't care about your gratitude Colonel, all I cared about was saving as many of my people as possible." Raise said.

"Is that why you betrayed us, why you handed us over to the Tray."

Raise didn't say anything.

"If you wanted to save your people then you should have let us complete our mission!" Taymen snapped.

Raise entered a small room lined with several holding cells and directed Taymen into one of them closing the door behind him.

"They have no interest in us Colonel." He said. "They're looking for something left behind by the ancients on some backwater planet. They don't care about us it's the ruins they want, they need them to complete a map to find the planet the artifact is on."

Taymen remained silent as Raise made his way back to the door.

"Ourik was right about one thing though Colonel." Raise started. "You are the last hope for our people."

Part IV
Into The Breach

'It's easy to plan a mission against impossible odds and even easier to execute such a mission. The hardest part is convincing the people you're trying to save that what you did was in their best interest as they stand in the ashes that was once their home.'

Defense Force advanced operations and tactics lesson 11-22

Chapter Fourteen

Arthur's gray eyes widened at the sight of Russ standing on the front step of his house.

"Russ." He said in surprise.

"Hey, is my sister home?" Russ asked.

"Yeah, come on in." Arthur said as he moved aside to let Russ in.

As Russ walked through the kitchen his younger sister Kaleigh came out of the bedroom.

She was a short girl with a slightly heavier build than Russ had but was by no means overweight, which was strange given Russ' naturally slim build.

"Hey." Russ said awkwardly.

"Hey you." Kaleigh said.

"What's with this?" Russ asked referring to her new hair style.

It was normally brown like Russ', but she had it cut down to shoulder length and dyed it black with dark blue streaks in the front.

"Oh my friend's a hair dresser and she wanted to try something on me." Kaleigh replied. "What are you doing here?"

"I had the day off so I figured I'd come by to see how you guys were doing." Russ said.

"Have you eaten yet?" Arthur asked from the kitchen.

"Yeah I'm fine thanks." Russ said as he sat down on the couch in the living room.

A moment later Arthur walked in and sat down next to Kaleigh placing a glass of water on the table in front of her.

"So how have you been?" Kaleigh asked.

Russ sighed.

"Alright." He said. "I had a date tonight but I didn't really feel like going out." He continued.

"Why not?" Kaleigh asked.

Russ didn't say anything as Kaleigh sighed and shook her head.

"Are you still crying over Elisha?" She asked realizing only after she said it how cold it sounded.

147

"Honestly Russ she's been dead for nine months now, she'd want you to move on."

Russ remained silent. If she really had died in the so called meteor strike like he had told everyone then he may have been able to move on by now but it wasn't that simple.

"So how's work been?" Russ asked, changing the subject.

Kaleigh was about to answer when her glass slid off of the table and shattered on the floor.

"What the hell?" Arthur said as he stood up.

A second later the entire house had begun to shake and there was a deep rumble coming from somewhere outside as all three of them ran out to see what was going on. At first they didn't see anything but then Arthur noticed a massive shadow cast itself over the entire street. When he looked up he couldn't believe what he saw. As he stared up at the sky Russ and Kaleigh turned to see what he was staring at.

Kaleigh nearly fell over as her blue eyes remained fixed on the sky.

Russ simply gasped at the sight of the object.

"Oh my god." He said.

"What is that?" Arthur asked.

Russ and Kaleigh simply stared at the massive ship floating above their city. It was unlike anything any of them had ever seen.

They couldn't tell how high up the ship was but it was massive by any scale, its shadow covered the entire street around Arthur and Kaleigh's house blocking out the sun.

The design didn't seem human at all to Russ. It was clearly significantly larger than the Dark Avenger and it had completely different hull markings.

As the ship settled into position over the center of the city a large group of smaller shuttles emerge from it and began to descend to the ground.

A few minutes later one of the shuttles landed nearby and a group of armed soldiers poured out into the street forcing people back into their houses along the way.

When they got to Russ and the others one of the soldiers grabbed Kaleigh and shoved her back towards the door.

"Get back in your homes!" The man growled.

Arthur moved to stop the soldier but before he could reach him another struck him across the back pushing him to the ground while a third forced Russ back to the house with Kaleigh.

As Arthur got back to his feet he was pushed again towards the door.

"Move it, inside!" The man said.

"What the hell is going on!" Arthur snapped.

"This planet is under Tray occupation now, stay in your homes or I'll have you arrested." The soldier said.

"Who the hell are the Tray?" Arthur asked.

The soldier didn't say anything.

Russ grabbed Arthur's arm and pulled him into the house while Kaleigh closed the door behind them a moment later.

"What's going on?" She asked as she followed Russ and Arthur back into the living room.

Arthur grabbed the phone while Russ moved over to the window to see what was happening.

"The line's dead." Arthur said slamming the phone back down.

Russ watched as groups of soldiers moved through the streets forcing people back into their homes and taking those who resisted into their ships.

Kaleigh sat down on the couch crying with terror.

Arthur sat down and wrapped his arms around her trying to calm her down. Tears ran down her face as Arthur ran his fingers through her dark hair.

Russ finally moved away from the window and sat down in the chair across from them.

"What's happening out there?" Arthur asked.

"The soldiers are taking people who don't cooperate, everyone else is being forced back into their homes." Russ replied. "But I think it's safe to say they're occupying Earth."

"Who are they?" Kaleigh asked.

"They're called the Tray." Russ explained. "They're aliens from another galaxy."

Russ realized how ridiculous it sounded after he said it aloud.

"What are you talking about?" Arthur asked as he brushed the bangs of his short brown hair to the side.

"Aliens?" Kaleigh asked skeptically.

"I know it sounds crazy but it's true." Russ said.

Kaleigh straightened herself in her seat.

"How do you know?" She asked as she wiped the tears from her face.

Russ sighed.

"Well this isn't the first time I've seen them." He replied.

Arthur and Kaleigh sat silently waiting for an explanation.

"See the meteor strike was actually an attack by the Tray. Elisha and I were helping some people get home when the Tray attacked." Russ explained.

"That's when Elisha died?" Arthur asked.

"Yeah, about that." Russ started.

149

Torri and Releena watched in horror at the image on one of the screens in the central square.

The Tray setup several small sections of the residential district to serve as 'recreational centers' for everyone. In truth they were simply a large tent with a spire in the middle. Mounted on the spire were four large display screens used for public announcements from the Tray leaders. Everyone knew it was just away for them to spread Tray propaganda.

For the last few hours now the screens displayed the horrifying image of a ship being destroyed by the Tray. The caption at the bottom of the screen read *'Dark Avenger Destroyed, Tray Heroes Welcomed Home.'*

The video was being looped over and over again and each time Torri found it more and more difficult to hide her emotions.

Releena's expression remained unaffected as she saw her last surviving ship and crew destroyed.

"How could this happen, it has to be a lie." Torri said about to break down in tears.

"Perhaps we should go." Releena said as she took Torri's arm and led her out of the tent.

They moved slowly through the crowded streets towards Torri's tent on the far side of the residential district. As they moved past another one of the recreation tents Sharr joined them, her expression almost identical to Releena's.

"I take it you've heard." She said quietly.

Releena simply nodded.

"It's a lie!" Torri snapped. "The Tray are just trying to convince us that there's no hope left." She said.

"That may be true." Releena said. "But we have to be prepared to accept the fact that the Dark Avenger is gone."

Torri was almost ready to slap Releena but drawing that kind of attention to the Princess was not something she wanted to do. Besides, she knew Releena was right.

"That's not to say that Taymen is dead." Sharr said. "The video showed several prowlers and escape pods made it out, there's a very good chance that he's alive somewhere." She said optimistically.

"Yes but our last free ship is gone and with it our best chance to fight the Tray." Releena said.

"None of my informants have been able to tell me the location of our captured ships yet." Sharr said quietly. "But if we can locate even one of them we should be able to seize control of it and that would give us our edge back."

Releena didn't say anything and Torri remained silent in thought.

"What about the survivors from the Dark Avenger?" Torri finally asked.

"There's nothing we can do for them right now." Releena said.

"If they were captured by the Tray most of them will be released into the population to expand the labor force." Sharr added.

"In any case." Releena started. "We need to start locating the rest of your crew Sharr, we need their help now more than ever."

Cairo Egypt
12:00 Abydos Standard Time
Day 14, Tenth Cycle, Egyptian Year 3201

Arthur watched the image on the screen as Kaleigh sat close beside him.

Russ was taken by the Tray almost three days ago and they hadn't heard from him since.

Kaleigh was sick with worry and Arthur was starting to worry about her.

She all but stopped eating and hadn't slept in a few days now. The last time he saw her like this was when her parents were killed in the meteor strike eight months ago, which they now know was actually a missile attack by the Tray. Russ told them that the meteor strike was just an international cover up to keep the general population from rioting about alien invasions.

"As a reminder to all civilians there is a strict curfew in effect." The man on the screen said. *"Any civilians found outside of their homes after nineteen hundred hours, or seven pm will be arrested."* Arthur turned off the TV.

It was the same announcement they've heard three times today.

Ever since the Tray arrived out of nowhere they've been flooding the city with announcements of their total control over the planet and their new rules.

From what Arthur heard the only country who put up any real fight against the Tray was China, but even they were defeated swiftly.

No military on Earth stood a real chance against them, every government had surrendered to the Tray within three days.

The Americans were the first to fall though they didn't really surrender. The Tray destroyed most of their defenses with the first salvo and wiped out their leaders leaving the military in chaos.

151

The Russians and Canadians were the next to fall along with a bunch of smaller countries that Arthur never even heard of, then the rest of Europe and Asia was hit last.

The Chinese managed to damage one of the Tray ships with some sort of EMP missile but the Tray had too many ships and a single missile wasn't effective enough to bring even one of them down.

China finally surrendered after the second day giving the Tray almost complete control of Earth except for a few other smaller countries, but they eventually surrendered too.

Arthur stood up and moved over to the window.

Kaleigh recognized the look on his face. It was the look he got when he was angry about something.

It was obvious what he was angry about. What worried Kaleigh was what he was going to do. Arthur wasn't known for doing the most intelligent thing when he was angry, Kaleigh was afraid he would do something to get himself arrested by the Tray. She just lost her brother to them, she couldn't lose her husband too.

"What are you thinking about?" She asked softly.

Arthur shook his head.

"Just wondering how long this is going to go on for?" He said. "What they want? Why they're doing this? Where they took Russ?"

Kaleigh didn't say anything. She was wondering the same things herself but there was nobody they could ask. The only thing she knew was that they're entire world had been turned upside down and they had to be willing to help turn it back somehow.

Chapter Fifteen

Taymen woke up from a dreamless sleep to hear the door to the cell block slam shut.

He didn't know how long it had been since one of Ourik's interrogators came to question him. On occasion Ourik himself would come to talk to him, but that was becoming less frequent.

Taymen told them nothing of course. Sometimes the interrogators simply laughed at him, maybe they found his stubbornness entertaining. Other times they found it trying and tried to 'persuade' him into talking.

He wasn't sure but Taymen figured they cracked two of his ribs the last time. His own blood was becoming a familiar taste in his mouth and the constant sting when water passed over the split in his lip was little more than a nuisance now.

The entire cell block wreaked of mold and bodily waste. Taymen didn't remember the cell block being so disgusting before. Obviously the Tray haven't been as fastidious about its cleanliness as the Egyptians had been.

There were at least thirty separate cells in the block. Taymen wasn't sure how many of them were actually occupied but he figured more than half.

He listened as the footsteps grew louder until they finally stopped and there was bang on his cell door.

Taymen looked up to see the grinning face of Captain Roaan looking back at him.

"Captain, I was starting to wonder what happened to you." Taymen said smugly.

"Let's go Orelle the Fleet Marshal wants to talk to you." Roaan said.

"He doesn't take no for an answer does he." Taymen said as he stood up.

The sharp pain in his ribs nagged at him as he moved towards the cell door.

Taymen winced at the bright light as he stepped out of the dark cell and started to move towards the door that led to the corridor. He had been taken for questioning so many times now he knew the way without having to have someone lead him around.

Roaan followed Taymen closely with one hand on his side arm in case he tried to escape.

Taymen turned down the corridor and followed it up a few meters before turning into a small room where Ourik was standing next to a window waiting for him.

"Ah Colonel, did you sleep well?" Ourik asked mockingly. "Please, sit down." He said gesturing to a single chair behind a small table.

On the table was a large plate of assorted meats and bread, obviously there to tempt Taymen.

"You must be hungry." Ourik said.

Taymen didn't give him the satisfaction of an answer. He knew full well what Ourik was looking for. He may have been arrogant but he wasn't stupid.

If Taymen admitted to being hungry it wouldn't mean much. They had been practically starving him since he was captured but if he gave in and ate in front of Ourik, than Ourik could take it as a sign that Taymen was beginning to break.

Anything that Taymen did no matter how subtle would give some sort of indication to Ourik. Something as simple as licking his lips could give Ourik the idea that he was winning and Taymen didn't want to do that.

The best thing he could do was to simply keep his composure and don't try to ignore the food but don't focus on it either.

"So what'll it be today?" Taymen asked as he took a seat.

Ourik smiled as he brushed a lock of his short blonde hair to the side.

"Well I thought we'd start with the location of your surviving ships." He said.

Taymen shook his head.

"I already told you I don't know." He said.

"And I told you I think you're lying." Ourik replied.

"Well think of it this way." Taymen started. "If I had more ships at my disposal, don't you think I would have used them to defend that station instead of destroying it and allowing you to destroy my ship."

Ourik didn't say anything as he turned to Roaan.

"You can leave Captain." He said.

Roaan hesitated a moment before leaving Taymen and Ourik alone in the room.

"Listen Colonel, this can be very easy for you." Ourik started. "All I want is some information, and in exchange I would be willing to release you to live amongst your people in our grand new alliance."

Taymen chuckled a little as he leaned back in his seat. He realized that Ourik genuinely believed that this occupation was an alliance between their two peoples, a forced alliance but an alliance none the less.

"You may have been able to convince General Raise to help you but I'm a little more stubborn."

Ourik moved away from the window and stopped just in front of Taymen.

"Come now Colonel what do you hope to accomplish by this?" He asked.

Taymen leaned forward again.

"Well since you asked so nicely." He started as he took a small piece of bread from the plate and slowly placed it in his mouth.

He took a moment to chew the bread but didn't take his eyes off Ourik or change his expression as he swallowed and sat back in his chair again.

"I hoped to draw these interrogations out long enough for you to do something foolish like send your only protection out of the room."

Ourik suddenly tried to pull back a step but Taymen was surprisingly fast. He struck Ourik across the face as he stood up.

While Ourik regained his footing Taymen hit him again throwing all his weight behind the punch knocking Ourik to the floor and himself into the wall.

Ourik struggled to roll to his side so he could grab his side arm only to realize Taymen had already taken it somewhere between the first strike and him hitting the floor.

He looked up to see Taymen pointing the weapon at his head.

Ourik was surprised that Taymen was still able to move so quickly let alone strike him that hard after being in a detention cell for over a month, most people barely have the strength to walk let alone put up any kind of a fight.

"Now then Fleet Marshal." Taymen started. "I think it's my turn to ask a few questions if you would be so willing. Where are you keeping our captured ships?"

"I have no idea what you're talking about." Ourik replied.

Taymen shifted the weapon down and left before pulling the trigger and sending a white hot cobalt round into Ourik's thigh.

Ourik yelled in pain as the round buried itself in his flesh.

A second later Captain Roaan came charging into the room with his weapon at the ready.

Taymen quickly turned and fired two rounds into his chest before training the weapon back onto Ourik.

"That's it, you've raised an alarm more guards will be on their way here now." Ourik said.

"Then I guess I have no further use for you." Taymen said.

He took aim and pulled the trigger but nothing happened.

Ourik instinctively recoiled into the fetal position for a second but looked up again when he didn't hear anything. He looked around the room briefly but Taymen was gone and he was left alone bleeding on the floor.

Taymen checked the chamber of his weapon as he ran through the corridor and pulled out the defective round.

"Stupid Tray piece of junk." He growled to himself.

Tray hand weapons used a primitive chemical reaction to propel a metallic round through the air. They weren't as reliable as the Egyptian weapons which used a magnetically accelerated ceramic composite round.

Taymen continued to run through the corridor towards the closest exit. He didn't know for sure but he figured he was in the detention center of the Imperial Command complex.

If he was where he thought he was, then there should be a door leading to the back compound around the next corner.

As he rounded the corner Taymen ran into a pair of Tray guards.

He quickly fired a round at the first guard's abdomen but before he could shift his aim the second guard grabbed his wrist and flung the weapon out of Taymen's hand.

Taymen wrenched his hand free and swung with the other striking the guard across the head.

The guard tumbled into the wall next to him as Taymen charged and struck him twice more before he fell to the ground.

Without wasting any time Taymen took off down the corridor again towards the exit. His ribs were screaming for him to stop but Taymen ignored the searing pain and pushed himself on. He was suddenly very grateful for the extra food their operatives had been slipping him while he was in his cell.

A few seconds later he burst out the door and jumped down the stairs into the back compound. Again his ribs screamed with pain.

Taymen took a moment to get his bearings and catch his breath. His ribs ached and he was beginning to remember that he had barely slept in the time he was there, however long it was.

As he looked around Taymen started to realize where he was. From what he could remember there were six buildings in the compound.

He was outside of the detention block, directly across the compound was a storage building. Beyond that there was the main command building and the communications building beside that.

Behind the communications building was a maintenance building and that's where Taymen wanted to go. If he could get there he could get unto the utility tunnels and take them out of the compound and into the city.

Taymen looked around for anyone before he darted across the compound to the storage building.

It was only about twenty meters or so but twenty meters in open ground during broad daylight when everyone was looking for you felt like a hundred.

He ran up against the building hard and moved into the shade where he was less likely to be seen.

The main door into the building was locked and the alarm system kept him from breaking in.

As he looked around Taymen saw a small window to his left.

The window itself would have a magnetic sensor on it so if he opened it and broke the circuit while the alarm system was armed it would alert the Tray to a break in.

As he stood there thinking Taymen noticed four guards moving towards the building. He quickly ducked into a recess in the wall and held himself as flat as he could to avoid being seen. Luckily they didn't seem to be looking for him.

As they moved closer Taymen got an idea.

If the Tray were going into the building they would deactivate the alarm and he could open the window and slip in.

He waited silently as the Tray entered the building. He counted to thirty since most alarms in military buildings went off if it wasn't disabled within thirty seconds.

Taymen peaked in through the window briefly before climbing through.

There was nobody in sight but Taymen could hear the Tray in the back of the building.

He pulled himself up on the window frame and slipped inside. The pain in his ribs shot up his side and down his right arm to his finger tips as he tried to lower himself down to the floor.

He held his breath to try and ignore the pain but it was getting to be too much and his right arm gave out sending Taymen crashing to the floor.

"What was that?"

He heard one of the guards say.

Taymen quickly got to his feet ignoring the pain that was now in his entire right side and ducked behind a group of large boxes.

Just as he peaked out from behind the stack of boxes one of the guards came into view.

Taymen ducked down and waited silently.

"It was nothing." The guard said.

Taymen wasn't sure how long it was until the guards left but it felt like an eternity.

When he heard the main doors close and lock again Taymen exhaled in relief causing the pain in his ribs to shoot up his side again.

As long as he could remain hidden he would be okay but the Tray were looking for him, so he wouldn't be able to remain hidden for long.

A quick look around revealed that most of the boxes contained blank data pads and computer components. One set of boxes in the corner was unmarked however. When Taymen opened one of them he found a set of maintenance uniforms.

'Perfect.' He thought to himself as he pulled the tattered remains of his uniform off.

Taymen quickly pulled on the gray coveralls and did up the zipper. Next he grabbed a set of black boots and put them on followed by a black tool belt and a cap pulling the front of it down to help hide his face. Lastly he grabbed a set of black maintenance gloves and slipped them on to hide the implant on his hand.

Now all he had to do was get to the maintenance building, it would be a lot easier if he knew where the Tray were focusing their search.

Suddenly Taymen got another idea.

The Tray armed the alarm again when they left the storage building, before he didn't want them to know he was there but now he could make them think he was after he left. All he had to do was walk out the front door.

The alarm doesn't distinguish between someone entering or exiting the building, they would simply think it was Taymen trying to get in.

Taymen unlocked the main door from the inside and opened it just enough to take a look around.

Once he was sure nobody had seen him and the way was clear he ran a few paces away from the building before turning around and walking past it towards the maintenance building to make it seem like he was coming from somewhere else.

The maintenance building was about thirty meters ahead of him when Taymen noticed more and more guards moving around the compound. He passed by one group who were rushing to the storage building which meant he still had a little time.

Taymen adjusted his cap pulling the front down a little further as he looked down to the ground.

The building was now just a few steps away when he heard someone call out behind him.

"You!" Taymen stopped and turned but kept his head down.

"What are you doing there." The man asked.

Taymen said the first thing that came to his mind.

"Checking the breakers for the complex, there's been some power outages in the detention block."

Taymen wasn't sure why he said that, all that came to his mind was the flickering lights outside of his cell.

"Who ordered it?" The man asked.

"Captain Roaan." Taymen replied instantly.

The man looked at Taymen for a moment as if he were trying to read him somehow.

"Alright then." He finally said. "I'll go check with the Captain, you wait here."

"Right." Taymen said as the man turned to head for the detention block leaving a guard behind to watch Taymen.

When the man was out of sight Taymen turned to open the door to the maintenance building.

"Hold it." The guard said.

Taymen released the door handle and turned to the guard.

"Look I need to check these breakers and I don't have time to stand around waiting for your friend I have a lot of work to do, I can check them while he's checking with the Captain so when he gets back I'll be done. There's no other door to this building so I'm not going anywhere." Taymen said. "You can even watch me if you like." He continued.

"Fine check your breakers." The guard said. "But be quick about it." Taymen nodded before he walked into the building with the guard close behind him.

He couldn't believe he had gotten this far. Now all he had to do was 'ditch the babysitter'.

He quickly looked around and found a piece of a small steel conduit on the floor next to him.

'Convenient.' He thought to himself.

There were circuit breaker panels all over the building but none of them were close enough to the conduit for him to grab it before the guard reacted.

Taymen sighed.

"Get to work." The guard said.

Taymen took a step towards one of the breaker panels picking up the conduit as he walked past.

"What's this doing here?" He asked.

"Drop it!" The guard snapped as he brought his weapon up, but before he could seat the butt of his rifle into his shoulder Taymen spun around and struck the guard across the head knocking him unconscious.

Taymen quickly moved back to the door and slid the conduit through the handle jamming the door closed.

The utility tunnels ran into a crawl space under a steel panel in the floor beside the door.

Taymen lifted the panel and jumped in collapsing to the ground with the pain in his ribs. He took a moment to steady his breathing before he stood up and closed the panel behind him and began to move down the tunnel. The stench of mold filled his nostrils reminding him of that cold dark cell as Taymen walked deeper into the tunnels beneath the city.

Chapter Sixteen

There was nobody around that Taymen could see. The dark alleys were almost completely abandoned from what he could tell.

The Imperial Command complex was almost ten kilometers away but the Tray would no doubt have expanded their search by now and Taymen needed a way to get off of Netara.

He was exhausted and the pain in his ribs was worse than ever. His arms and legs felt as if they were about to fall off. He had spent most of the day wondering the utility tunnels waiting for nightfall before coming up to the surface.

As he tried to ignore the pain and press on Taymen felt himself begin to tilt a little more with each step until finally he fell to the ground. He tried to regain his footing to no avail. His legs had finally given out and his vision was beginning to blur.

Taymen looked around at the sound of footsteps but with his failing vision he couldn't see anyone.

"Who is that?" He heard a voice say, but Taymen couldn't bring himself to answer.

Instead his arms collapsed and his head hit the ground hard. When he looked up Taymen could only see the silhouette of a person looking down at him before he slipped into unconsciousness.

"Are you sure this is a good idea?" Taymen heard a man ask. "The Tray are broadcasting his image all over the planet, if they find him here we'll all be arrested for treason." He continued.

"How can they try you for treason when you never pledged your loyalty?" A young woman asked.

It was a valid question but Taymen knew it wouldn't stop the Tray.

He opened his eyes and waited for his vision to clear.

"He's waking up." The young woman said.

Taymen found himself staring up at the roof of a large tent but he didn't remember how he got there or who found him.

"Easy there." The man said as Taymen tried to sit up.

He winced with the pain in his side. It wasn't as bad as before but it still hurt. It took a minute for Taymen to realize that his ribs had been wrapped.

"How are you feeling?" The young woman asked.

Taymen looked around for a second before answering.

"Fine." He said. "How long have I been out?" He asked.

"About a day." The man answered.

"We found you unconscious in the street." The young woman added.

"Who are you? Where am I?" Taymen asked.

"You're in the south residential sector of the Netara capital." The man answered. "My name is Piotre Kulove, this is my daughter Talia."

Taymen glanced over at the young woman sitting next to him.

He could see a hint of blue in her piercing green eyes as she looked Taymen over hooking a lock of her long hair behind her ear. The majority of her straight hair was a very light brown except for the very front where there were a few streaks of blond.

"And who might you be Sir?" Piotre asked.

"Taymen." He replied. "Taymen Orelle."

"What, Taymen Orelle!" Talia said in excitement. "Thee Colonel Taymen Orelle?" She asked.

Taymen straightened a little.

"I guess so." He said.

"Oh my gods." Talia replied. "It's you."

"What is it?" Piotre asked.

"This is the one I was telling you about Dad." She said. "He's the one that's been kicking the Tray's asses all over the galaxy." She explained.

The way Talia spoke about Taymen made him sound like some sort of celebrity.

"But what are you doing here?" She asked, her tone finally coming down to a normal level.

Taymen sighed.

"I was captured by the Tray and I escaped from the detention block in Imperial Command the day you found me. I'm not sure how long I was there for." He said.

"Four weeks." Piotre said.

Taymen and Talia looked at him strangely.

162

"The Tray have been broadcasting the destruction of your ship for the past four weeks. I assume that they captured you while you were trying to escape." He said.

"You said they've been broadcasting my ships destruction?" Taymen asked.

Piotre simply nodded.

"All over the Empire apparently." Talia added.

Taymen tried to stand up but quickly fell back to the ground.

"Careful." Talia said.

"From what we can tell you have two or three cracked ribs, a sprained wrist and more than a few good bruises." Piotre said. "You need time to heal."

"I don't have time, I have to get to Cairon." Taymen said.

"How?" Talia asked. "The Tray are looking for you, your picture is being broadcast everywhere. You won't be able to go anywhere without someone knowing who you are."

Taymen thought it over for a moment. If that was true then it would be difficult to get off-world unnoticed but there were ways he could do it.

"How often do the Tray allow off-world travel?" Taymen asked.

"Anyone can go almost anywhere provided they have a reason." Piotre explained. "You submit a travel request to the Tray transport authority which will either approve or deny your request.

"If approved you get a message with your travel authorization. There's a shuttle schedule at the docking terminal that tells you when transport to the other colonies is available."

"I assume that the terminal is under heavy security." Taymen said.

"I'm afraid so?" Piotre replied.

Taymen nodded as he thought it over.

"Can you find out when the next transport to Cairon leaves?" He asked.

"Sure." Talia replied. "But how are you going to get on it?" She asked.

"I'm still working on that part." Taymen said.

It was several hours before Taymen actually managed to get up and dressed. The pressure from the bandages on his ribs actually felt good and after a light meal and a lot of water he was starting to feel well enough to leave the tent.

Piotre was kind enough to lend Taymen a set of clothes so he didn't look so conspicuous in his gray coveralls.

"Do you think anybody will recognize you?" Piotre asked.

"Not if I keep my hat on and my head down." Taymen replied.

"I wouldn't be too concerned about any Egyptians turning you in, nobody here is in a hurry to help the Tray."

163

Suddenly Talia walked in.

"You're up." She said in surprise.

"What did you find?" Taymen asked.

"The next transport to Cairon leaves tomorrow morning." She replied.

"I have to be on that transport." Taymen said. "I should be able to sneak into the cargo bay easily enough." He continued.

"Great, so we'll be ready to go tomorrow morning." Talia said.

"We?" Taymen asked.

"You can't go by yourself, you're going to need my help." She said.

"Talia." Piotre started.

"Thank you Talia but I can't risk it. If you're caught helping me you'll be arrested and I can't be responsible for that." Taymen said.

"But…" She tried to protest but Taymen wouldn't let her.

"No, I've already allowed you to risk too much for me which is why I have to leave." He continued.

"Piotre, thank you for everything."

Piotre nodded.

"Of course, good luck Colonel." He said.

"With any luck all of this will be over soon." Taymen said before putting on his cap and leaving the tent.

Talia scramble out to catch him.

"Wait a minute!" She shouted. "Why can't I come with you?" She asked.

"I already told you it's too dangerous." Taymen said.

"I don't care, you need my help." Talia argued.

"You're right I do." Taymen said.

Talia was a little surprised to hear him agree with her.

"But I'll have to get along without your help. I can't risk your life for my benefit no matter the circumstances."

"You're not, I'm risking my own life." Talia said.

"And I can't let you." Taymen replied. "I'm grateful but I have to go alone."

Before Talia could say anything Taymen turned and walked away disappearing into the crowd leaving her alone in the street.

Valley of the Kings, Egypt
14:25 Abydos Standard Time
Day 23, Tenth Cycle, Egyptian Year 3201

Russ rubbed his temples as he tried to clear his mind. He knew what the symbols meant, he had translated them hundreds of times but he was so exhausted that he couldn't concentrate anymore.

The Tray had been forcing him to work with almost no sleep for a week now and he still had no idea what he was looking for.

He had been moved through almost every known temple and pyramid in Egypt as well as a few the Tray themselves discovered to translate countless texts none of which made any sense to Russ. He had been working on this particular text for a few days now and was getting nowhere fast.

All he managed to figure out so far was that it was some sort of instruction to find a map that led to a hidden chamber somewhere in Egypt. What was supposed to be in that chamber was still a mystery to him.

"You!" One of the guards shouted from just outside the chamber. "Come here." He said.

Russ closed his notebook and walked down the narrow passageway to the guard.

"The Commander's on his way, he wants to talk to you."

Russ nodded and made his way towards the temple entrance almost a kilometer away. They had discovered several secret rooms and passageways in the last few days but the temple was still relatively unexplored. It was discovered only four months before the Tray arrived on Earth so there was still a lot they didn't know about it.

Russ wasn't even sure the temple was really Egyptian. Most of the language was the same but in the hidden chambers there were symbols he had never seen before. One wall in particular was carved with a completely alien set of symbols. It wasn't Egyptian or any one of the other five scripts that Russ knew.

He had just entered a large chamber about half way to the main entrance when he noticed Commander Sourin waiting for him with a couple of guards.

"Ah Doctor Egler." He said. "How is your work progressing?"

Russ tried to hide his hostility towards the Commander.

"Slowly." He said.

Sourin simply smiled.

"Well there's no hurry, take all the time you need." He replied as he started to walk down the corridor towards the chamber where Russ had been working.

"What have you discovered so far?" He asked.

Russ fell in beside the Commander while he gathered his thoughts.

"This temple was built as a sort of instruction manual to tell us how to locate a map." Russ started. "The map is supposed to lead us to some sort of sacred chamber somewhere on Earth that holds what these texts refer to as the guiding light.

"The problem is that the instructions to find the map aren't exactly clear. They reference things that may have been commonly known at the time they were written, but the world has changed drastically since then, civilizations came and went, territory was divided and countless temples and relics destroyed. I'm not really sure where to begin."

Sourin nodded as he listened.

"Well keep at it Doctor." He said. "We need to find that chamber and for the sake of your people you'd better hope we do."

Netara Capital, South Docking Terminal
06:20 Abydos Standard Time
Day 24, Tenth Cycle, Egyptian Year 3201

Taymen crouched down behind one of the cargo haulers near the back of the cargo hangar. He managed to slip through the service gate during the shift change when one of the guards left it unlocked without realizing it.

The transport to Cairon was scheduled to leave in twenty minutes and he had to be on it.

The ground crew was almost finished loading the cargo pallets into the ships' cargo bay which meant Taymen was running out of time.

The ship was just outside of the cargo hangar about twenty meters across the tarmac. There weren't any guards, just the crew but they would surely raise an alarm if they saw him.

Taymen almost had the pattern worked out. All of the cargo and passenger baggage was loaded onto pallets or into containers that the loader picked up and loaded into the ships' cargo bay. The loader was gone for only about four minutes or so and then it was back to pick-up the next load.

Taymen had four minutes to get into one of the containers or onto one of the larger pallets where he could hide.

He watched as the loader picked-up one of the pallets and drove off with it. As soon as it was out of the hangar Taymen stood up to jump onto a large pallet loaded with several heavy cargo containers. He figured there was just enough room for him to squeeze between a few of the larger containers where he wouldn't be seen.

As Taymen took his first step towards the pallet something caught his eye and he ducked behind the hauler again. He peeked out looking towards a group of pallets near the entrance. There, amongst the cargo containers loaded onto the pallets Taymen could see someone hiding. He couldn't see their face, all he could see was the back of their head. As they turned Taymen suddenly realized who it was. The blonde locks amongst the long brown hair were unmistakable.

166

Taymen quickly darted across the hangar to the pallet just avoiding the loader. He ducked behind the containers causing Talia to jump.

"What are you doing here?" He asked.

"Following you." Talia replied casually.

"I told you it's…"

"Too dangerous." Talia cut him off. "And I told you I don't care I'm not going to sit here and let you risk your life for us while I sit back and wait for you to do everything."

Taymen didn't have time to argue.

The loader drove past with another pallet and there were only two more marked for Cairon.

He had no choice, he couldn't leave her to get caught by the Tray.

Taymen grabbed her hand and stood up.

"Come on." He said in a huff as he took off back across the hangar to the large pallet.

As he shoved Talia into the space between the containers Taymen turned to see the loader on its way back. He quickly forced his way into the space just in time to avoid being seen.

The space was tight with two people. When the loader drove up to the pallet to pick it up there was a violent shutter as the lift contacted the bottom and began to lift it.

Talia stumbled back grabbing onto Taymen who was taken by surprise. She fell hard against another container and Taymen fell up against her for a second before they regained their balance.

As they straightened Taymen noticed a gleam in Talia's green eyes. They stood silent and still for only a second before Taymen backed up a half pace realizing that Talia had her hands on his waist.

She realized it a second later and quickly removed them.

"Sorry." Taymen said clearing his throat.

A few minutes later the loader set the pallet down in the cargo bay with a shutter and drove off.

When the loader finished with the last pallet the cargo bay doors were sealed and Taymen quickly backed out of the space with Talia close behind him.

"Now what?" She asked.

"Now we need to find something we can secure ourselves to until we break orbit." Taymen answered as he looked around the cargo bay.

There wasn't much aside for the large cargo pallets. At the head of the bay there was a heavy pressure door that lead to the crew cabin and at the other end was an access panel leading to a crawl space used for maintenance. Next to the panel was a large support bar that was secured to the bulkhead.

"There." Taymen said as he moved to one of the smaller cargo pallets. "We can use that."

Taymen removed two cargo straps from the pallet and moved over to the bulkhead with Talia.

"Turn around." He said.

Talia simply looked at him curiously.

"Come on we don't have much time." Taymen said.

Talia slowly turned and faced the bulkhead. A second later she felt Taymen wrap the cargo strap around her waist then cross it over her back and bring it over her shoulders before pushing her forward a step.

He wrapped the free ends of the strap around the support bar and then back around her waist before tying it off.

"Hold onto this." He said as he placed Talia's hands onto the section of strap between her shoulders and the bar.

Next Taymen did the same thing with the other strap to himself but ran the free ends on either side of Talia before wrapping it around the bar and tying it off.

Talia turned her head to see Taymen standing directly behind her. She was about to ask what was going on when the ship shuttered and knocked her back into his chest.

Taymen winced with the pain in his ribs as he caught her and put her back on her feet.

"Hang on." He said.

Talia could feel the ship starting to accelerate as the nose pitched up on a steeper angle until their weight was being supported by the cargo straps.

As the ship continued to accelerate Talia could feel herself getting heavier and heavier until the ship was shaking violently.

"What's going on?" Talia had to shout over all the noise.

"We're passing through the outer atmosphere." Taymen replied.

Talia could barely hear him and her stomach felt like it was in her feet. Suddenly she noticed her vision starting to fade into a narrow tunnel until she finally blacked out.

Talia woke up to see Taymen kneeling beside her.

"You alright?" He asked.

Talia quickly sat up to see the entire bay spinning.

"Easy now." Taymen said.

168

She looked around and realized that she wasn't strapped to the bar anymore.

"What happened?" She asked as she rubber her eyes trying to clear her vision.

"You blacked out." Taymen said. "It's not unusual for someone who's not used to it to black out from excessive G-forces." He explained.

Talia took a moment to let her head clear and her stomach settle.

"So what do we do now?" She asked.

"Now we enjoy the ride." Taymen replied. "Most of these containers are carrying food so the bay will remain pressurized and somewhat heated. When we land on Cairon there will likely be a crew to inspect the cargo before they start unloading it. Before they get in we'll make our way into the crew cabin and disembark with the rest of the passengers."

Talia nodded as she thought about the plan.

"Sounds easy enough." She said. "How long until we get there?" She asked.

"Cairon is two stream jumps from Netara so it's going to be at least eight hours for the bleed off." Taymen said.

As he stood up Taymen suddenly felt his body tingle just before his vision went dark then back to normal.

"What was that?" Talia asked.

"You've never left Netara before have you?"

"No why?"

Taymen smiled slightly.

"That was a protostream jump." He explained. "We're half way to Cairon, in eight hours or so you'll feel another one which will put us just outside of orbit."

Taymen walked over to one of the larger pallets and sat down leaning against one of the cargo containers. He winced at the slight pain in his ribs before he settled into a comfortable position.

Talia looked around for a moment before moving over to sit with him.

"So." She started. "What's on Cairon?"

Taymen sighed.

"Some people I'm looking for." He said.

"Like who?" Talia asked.

"My sister to start with." He said. "I've also been told that most of the officers from the Imperial Guard have been relocated there."

"Why do you need to see them?" Talia asked.

"We still have a job to do." Taymen replied. "As for my sister, I just want to know if she's still alive."

Taymen sighed.

"Why are you here Talia?" He asked, as if he were trying to take his mind off of his sister.

"You needed help." Talia replied. "You can't go anywhere without somebody recognizing you now, don't you think you could use someone who could move around freely." She said.

Taymen nodded.

"I know I could but something tells me there's something more personal to it." He said.

Talia didn't say anything right away.

"You don't have to tell me." Taymen said.

"No, it's alright." Talia started.

"When we first got word of the Tray attack nobody was really worried. I mean, of course we were all afraid but in the end I guess we thought it was going to be like the separatist war, that it was happening far away and that the military would protect us.

"My mother was an officer on a ship that was destroyed in the attack with no survivors."

"I'm sorry." Taymen said sympathetically.

"We all just sat back and watched as the Tray destroyed our defenses and took over our planet without any real resistance. It was then I decided that it was our own fault the Tray managed to take over so completely." Talia continued.

"We may be civilians but that doesn't mean we can just sit back and let the military try and solve all our problems for us. We're responsible for our own freedom and we need to do whatever we can to help if we ever want our home back, we all have to fight in one way or another."

Taymen understood what Talia was saying and in the end he really didn't have the right to stop her from doing what she thought was right. At the same time however it was his duty to protect her along with all Egyptian citizens, even if it was from themselves.

"So when you find these officers of yours what are you going to do?" Talia asked.

Taymen shook himself out of his own thoughts for a moment.

"Try to find the surviving ships the Tray have captured and build up a fleet for a counter attack." He said.

Talia nodded slightly as a smile came across her face.

"What is it?" Taymen asked.

"You just seem too young to be a Colonel." She said.

"Really." Taymen replied. "I've been hearing that a lot lately."

"How old are you?" Talia asked.

"Twenty-four." Taymen replied.

"How are you a Colonel already?"

"Well." Taymen started. "I was a Major when the Tray invasion began. Princess Releena granted me a battlefield promotion in light of the situation."

"I think your young even for a Major." Talia said.

Taymen smiled.

"Before I was a Major I was a weapons officer aboard a light cruiser during the separatist war." He explained.

"What happened?" Talia asked.

"We had a mission to delay a separatist strike force on a civilian colony until re-enforcements arrived."

Taymen sighed as the memories of that day flooded his mind.

"We were hopelessly outnumbered but we had a good Captain and crew. We took a direct hit to one of the power transfer junctions and it sent a surge through the power system to C.A.C. and overloaded several of the main consoles. My Captain and Ex O were standing next to the main operations console when it exploded.

"The Ex O was killed instantly and the Captain was knocked unconscious, I couldn't wake her up. Everyone was confused and scrambling around waiting for orders so I started to give them some."

There was a long silence before Talia spoke again.

"Is that when you got that scar?" She asked, pointing to the scar running between Taymen's eyes.

"Actually that came from an earlier battle." He said.

"It was my first mission as a lieutenant. I was on my way to C.A.C. during an attack when we were boarded and I ran into one of the separatists. I don't know what he was doing alone but I managed to knock the rifle from his hands before he could fire, unfortunately he managed to draw his knife and took a swing. The tip of the blade cut just deep enough to leave a scar."

The room was suddenly filled with an awkward silence again.

Talia found her gaze shifting from Taymen's scar to his icy blue eyes. She had never seen eyes like his before, they were so young but something about them made him seem older, she couldn't stop staring at them.

"You should get some rest." Taymen finally said. "We have a long ride ahead."

Cairon Residential District
17:40 Abydos Standard Time
Day 24, Tenth Cycle, Egyptian Year 3201

Torri sat at the table in silence. The image of the Dark Avengers' destruction played over and over in her mind until she was brought to tears with the memory of Taymen. The last few knights she spent lying awake thinking about him and about the reaction her parents had when she told them.

Her mother fought so hard to hide her feelings but Torri could see that she was on the verge of crying as well. Her father didn't say anything. As far as he was concerned Taymen had been dead since he joined the Defense Force. She hadn't even told her brother Alban yet but she knew he felt the same way as their father.

Koran walked into the tent surprising Torri. She hadn't realized how late it was.

"Torri, you have to stop this." He said. "We don't know what happened to him. All we saw was his ship destroyed he very well could have escaped."

Torri was about to say something when someone else entered the tent.

"Actually he did." The man said as he stepped inside.

As the tent flap slid closed blocking the light behind him Torri fell into utter shock at the sight of her little brother standing in front of her.

She shot to her feet and flew across the tent almost knocking Taymen to the ground as she wrapped her arms around him.

"Taymen!" She said in relief as tears poured down her face.

"It's okay Torri." Taymen said.

"I knew you were alive but I was starting to worry that …"

"It's okay Torri I'm okay." He said reassuringly.

After a few minutes Torri finally managed to pull herself away from Taymen and wipe the tears from her face not noticing the young woman who had entered the tent behind him.

"Koran." She finally said. "This is my little brother, Taymen."

Taymen nodded in greeting.

"So you're the lost son." Koran said.

Taymen smiled slightly.

"I guess that's one way to put it." He replied. "Oh." Taymen said as he remembered Talia standing there behind him. "Torri this is Talia Kulove, she's been helping me since I got back." He said.

"Helping you?" Torri asked.

"Yeah there are a few things I need to tell you." Taymen started. "After my ship was destroyed I was captured by the Tray, I managed to escape but they were broadcasting my image all over Netara." He said.

"They haven't been here, at least not yet." Koran said.

"Taymen Princess Releena is here." Torri said.

"What?" Taymen said in surprise.

"She came to see us a few weeks ago, we still see her from time to time." Koran replied.

"If she's here she may be trying to do the same thing I came here to do." Taymen said. "I need to find her, can you get in contact with her?" He asked.

"If you can find Sharr Vaye she'll know where she is." Torri said.

"Sharr's here with her?" Taymen asked.

Koran nodded.

"Someone you know?" Talia asked.

"Sharr was in command of the Dying Star in the Imperial Guard, I've only met her a few times in person but we got along pretty well and she's a brilliant Captain." Taymen said. "We have to find her she may still have her ship."

Cairo Egypt
18:00 Abydos Standard Time
Day 24, Tenth Cycle, Egyptian Year 3201

Arthur winced as Kaleigh pressed the alcohol soaked cloth to the cut on his forehead. His injuries weren't serious but he had a fair few cuts and bruises.

The Tray security guards didn't take kindly to Arthur's questions and decided to remind him to keep his place.

The Tray were acting like little more than bullies. They detained anybody without good reason and if someone crossed them even in the slightest they were arrested, beaten or shot.

"Do you have any idea how lucky you are?" Kaleigh started. "They could have killed you Arthur!" She said.

"I just asked where they were taking everyone." Arthur said trying to defend his actions.

"You shouldn't have said anything, just stay away from them." Kaleigh replied.

Arthur knew she was terrified of the Tray. Honestly he was too but what could they do about it. They had no access to weapons, every military on the planet was gone and they didn't even know what the Tray wanted.

"There." Kaleigh said as she put the cap on the alcohol bottle. "All done."

As she stood up to put the bottle away Kaleigh froze in place at the sight of Russ walking through the door.

"Russ." Arthur said in surprise.

Kaleigh rushed over to Russ to give him a hug.

"What happened, what did they do to you?" She asked.

"They brought me to a bunch of temples in the desert along with some other archeologists."

"Why?" Arthur asked as Russ sat down across from him.

"They're looking for something, some sort of ancient map." Russ replied. "I was translating some ancient texts in the temples but they didn't make much sense." He continued.

"One of the larger texts that we found kept referring to humanity's children. It spoke of how they would grow and learn isolated from the rest of their kind. That they would grow to be the saviors of our world and the worlds of countless others."

Russ sighed as he tried to remember the entire text.

"It spoke about divine knowledge from something called the Star's Eye, I think that's what they're looking for but I have no idea what it is or where it could be."

"What about humanity's children, who do you think that could be?" Kaleigh asked.

"I'm not sure." Russ replied. "But I think I have an idea. In any case we need help and I know someone who could do it but we have no way of contacting them." He continued.

"Who, the one's you told us about?" Arthur asked.

Russ simply nodded.

"They're going back home and I have no way of contacting them." He said.

"Okay but what if you could get a message to them, could they really help?" Kaleigh asked.

"I think so, why?" Russ asked.

"What if we sent a message to them from the satellite control station." Kaleigh said.

Russ didn't even think of that.

Kaleigh worked at the satellite control station that Elisha worked at as a computer network administrator.

That gave her access to one of the private communications satellites in orbit, she could access it and send a message into deep space.

"Can we get to the station unnoticed?" Russ asked.

"If we're careful." Kaleigh replied.

"I would only need to know where they were heading and we could send a message to them through the laser transceiver, it would take a while to get to them but we could tell them what's going on."

Russ smiled slightly.

"Alright then we'll sneak in tomorrow night." He said as he turned to Arthur.

"What the hell happened to you?"

Chapter Seventeen

Taymen sat to the left of Releena while Sharr sat to her right. He still couldn't believe how much they both changed since he last saw them.

Sharr always had long hair whenever Taymen saw her. Now however her dark hair was cut to shoulder length and brushed back behind her ears except for her long bangs which were simply brushed to one side. Her brown eyes were just as Taymen remembered though. Sharr was very good at keeping a straight face, but he could read what she was thinking in her eyes and she hated Taymen for that.

Sitting around the rest of the table was a group of several former commanding officers most of which were in the Imperial Guard at one point or another.

Releena and Taymen had spent over a month locating enough people to carry out their plans while Sharr and her informants gathered as much intelligence as they could.

"Colonel Vaye, your report please." Releena said.

Sharr stood from her seat and looked around the table briefly.

"From what little intel we could gather we've discovered that the Tray are holding three of our ships in the Orion Ship Yards. From what I'm told they are the Phantom Wraith, the Silver Phoenix and the Night Huntress."

She paused for a moment to make sure everyone was paying attention.

"The Phantom Wraith and Night Huntress are an avenger class battle ship and a drone carrier respectively, while the Silver Phoenix is a heavy carrier. According to our operatives at the ship yard none of them are armed but they all still have their support ships in the hangars."

A few of the officers shifted in their seats. This was the first bit of good news they had in a while.

"How many operatives do we have in that facility?" One of the men asked.

"Five." Sharr replied. "They can disable the sensors for us but only for a few minutes, we have to board the ships, disengage them from their docking scaffolds and stream them out before the sensors go back up. If the Tray detect the ships trying to escape they'll destroy them."

There was a long pause while Sharr looked around the table.

"Thank you Sharr." Releena said. "As it stands now we have sufficient crew members to man all three vessels. The problem lies in us getting that many people onto those ships unnoticed." Releena continued.

"I don't think we should even try Princess." Colonel Dravin said from across the table.

Dravin was in command of an avenger class ship before the Tray attacked. He was known for being very precise with his tactics.

"Our best bet is to get enough people on the ships to fly them out, we can transport the rest of the crews to them when they're in a safe location." He explained.

"I agree Princess." Taymen said. "The fewer people going into the ship yard the easier it will be for us."

"Very well." Releena said. "Colonel Dravin you will take command of the Phantom Wraith, Colonel Vaye the Silver Phoenix, and Colonel Atlaa the Night Huntress is yours. I want you each to gather a team to board your ships and pilot it out of the Orion Ship Yard. Colonel Orelle I want you to put together a mission briefing to get those ships back, we will meet here again tomorrow night to go over the plan."

As Releena stood from her seat everyone else did the same giving a sharp salute before filing out of the tent into the night air.

Taymen and Sharr waited until everyone else had left.

"Something else?" Releena asked.

"Yes Princess." Taymen said. "Another matter I didn't want to bring up in front of the others."

"What is it?" Releena asked.

"General Raise has been working for the Tray since before the attack."

"What!" Sharr snapped.

Releena looked just as surprised as Sharr did.

"Are you sure about this Colonel?" She asked.

"I'm afraid so Princess, he sold us out to the Tray. That's how they knew exactly where to strike and that's how they managed to find my ship." Taymen said.

"That son of a bitch." Sharr growled. "He sold us out, then he set up the Dark Avenger so the Tray could destroy it!"

"Well not exactly." Taymen said.

Taymen entered the tent just as Torri and Talia sat down at the table with Koran who was reading his book.

"Taymen." Talia said.

Taymen smiled slightly.

"How'd it go?" She asked.

"I have some work to do." Taymen said.

He didn't like discussing the meetings with them in case the Tray ever decided to start randomly interrogating people.

"I guess you can't tell us what's going on then?" Koran asked.

Taymen simply shook his head.

"Afraid not." He replied. "In any case I won't be imposing on you guys for much longer." He said.

"When do we leave?" Talia asked.

"I'm afraid you're going back to Netara." Taymen said.

"What?" Talia snapped.

"This time it really is too dangerous for you to come, we're going into combat." Taymen replied.

He almost regretted telling her that much.

"But I thought..." Taymen cut her off.

"Talia you're a civilian." He started. "Yes you're right everyone has to do what they can to help free our people but we can't bring you into combat, we're responsible to keep you safe. I'm sorry but I can't take you this time."

Talia was about to argue when a voice outside of the tent interrupted.

"Torri are you guys home."

Torri shot to her feet in a panic and Koran dropped his book on the table.

Taymen just looked at Torri. He recognized the voice but wasn't sure it could actually be them.

Suddenly the tent flap was pulled aside and an older couple walked in.

"Torri are you guys..."

The woman trailed off when she looked up.

"Taymen." She said.

"Taymen!" The man repeated.

They both looked as if they had just seen a ghost.

"You're alive." The woman said.

"Hi mom."

He looked to his father who simply stared back at him with cold unfeeling eyes. Nobody moved and there was a long awkward silence.

"What are you doing here?" His father finally asked.

"Visiting." Taymen replied.

"So you survived the attack." His mother said.

"Unfortunately it would seem so." Taymen replied sarcastically.

"Who do you think you're talking too!" His father snapped, taking obvious offense to Taymen's tone.

"Don't you dare think you deserve any kind of respect from me!" Taymen snapped back. "I remember every word you said to me when I told you I joined the Defense Force and it was nothing a parent would ever say to their child!"

Taymen could hear his voice echo in the tent.

"That's enough all of you!" Torri said.

"You think you're some kind of hero don't you." His father said. "You think it's heroic fighting, wasting your life dying for us!" His father snapped. "Nobody asked you too. Nobody asked you to fight, all you soldiers do is take any excuse you can to go off and kill anyone who doesn't agree with the government. You're nothing more than an attack dog dressed up in a uniform to please his masters. It's your fault our people have fallen to what they are now."

Taymen sighed. His father had said something similar to him before.

"You're absolutely right Dad." He said quietly. "It is our fault for thinking that fighting for your freedom was the right thing to do. It's our fault the Tray came and enslaved our people."

Taymen pushed his way past his father towards the tent flap.

"And you're right, all those people in the military, all my friends shouldn't have wasted their lives fighting and dying for people like you." He said before leaving the tent with Talia close behind.

Cairo Satellite Control Station
03:27 Abydos Standard Time
Day 21, Eleventh Cycle, Egyptian Year 3201

Russ waited for Kaleigh to give the all clear before he crossed the empty parking lot and made his way up to the doors of the satellite control station.

Kaleigh was able to use her access card to unlock the doors and disarm the alarm system before it went off.

"Looks like the building's empty." She said as they walked in.

"Good, where can we send a message from?" Russ asked.

"This way." Kaleigh said as she led Russ down the corridor to a small room on the right.

Her access card unlocked the door allowing them to enter.

"It'll take a few minutes for the system to boot up." She said as she switched on one of the computers.

"Do you know what you want to send?"

Russ nodded.

"Yeah, how long will it take to reach them?" He asked.

"Depends on how far away they are." Kaleigh said. "You said they were heading for the hydra constellation right?"

"That's what Elisha said." Russ replied.

"Boot up that computer there." Kaleigh said.

Russ moved over to a computer station near the back of the room and turned the power on.

"We have a complete database of the known galaxies and constellations, we just point the satellite towards hydra and transmit the message. If they're listening they'll get it." She continued.

Kaleigh moved to the computer in the back and accessed the main database. She typed the word 'Hydra' in the search field and brought up the hydra constellation coordinates.

"Here it is." She said. "The closest galaxy along the path to hydra is NGC-3109, it's four and a half million light years from us." Russ didn't like the sound of that.

"How long would it take a message to get that far?" He asked.

"I have no idea." Kaleigh said.

"Are you serious!" Russ asked.

"I'm afraid so."

Kaleigh took down the coordinates to hydra and moved over to the other computer. She accessed the satellite control system and typed in the coordinates to redirect the satellite.

"Here." She said as she handed Russ the keyboard.

"Type your message."

Russ took the keyboard and quickly typed out a message to Taymen and his crew.

It took him almost five minutes but when he was done he passed the keyboard back to Kaleigh who instructed the satellite to send the message.

As they waited for confirmation from the satellite that it was sent they heard footsteps in the corridor. They quickly ducked behind the desk and peeked out to see who it could have been.

They could hear faint voices in the building but couldn't tell what they were saying. They waited as the footsteps grew louder as they got closer. Suddenly two Tray guards came into view.

"This building is supposed to be secure." One of the guards said. "But the alarm was deactivated using an authorized code." He continued.

"What would anyone be doing in here anyways, it's not like they could do anything." The other said.

"Yeah well they told us to check it out, let's start upstairs and work our way down." The other said.

As the two guards moved further away Russ slowly moved out from behind the desk and checked the corridor. When he was sure they were gone he signaled to Kaleigh who made her way out to the door.

As she checked back she saw the confirmation message on the monitor. She rushed back to the computers and turned them off quickly before she and Russ made their way out into the corridor and out of the building. They had sent their call for help, now all they could do was wait and hope someone answered.

Cairon Residential District
22:42 Abydos Standard Time
Day 21, Eleventh Cycle, Egyptian Year 3201

"Colonel Orelle, your mission briefing please." Releena said from the head of the table.

Taymen stood up and looked around briefly.

"As you all know." He started. "Our intel indicates three ships being held at the Orion Shipyard, an avenger class, a carrier and a drone carrier. We know the Tray have fully manned the facility in an attempt to gain access to our technology and have so far been unsuccessful. We also know that there are two heavy cruisers at extreme range ready to respond to any distress signals from the facility itself.

"We hope to get into the shipyard undetected and have three teams board the facility. Once onboard they will move to their respective ships and simultaneously take over the C.A.C.'s of each ship.

"Once in control each team will depressurize the remaining sections of their ship killing any Tray left aboard just before departure. Once the ships are clear of the shipyard you'll stream out to the rendezvous point."

Taymen paused a moment to ensure there weren't any questions so far. His briefing didn't take very long, he thought the plan was fairly straight forward.

Taymen would create a distraction so that their operatives could disable the security and external sensors without anyone noticing. That meant they would only have a couple of minutes to launch and stream out before they were detected by the heavy cruisers.

The hardest part was getting to the shipyard unnoticed.

They had a stolen Tray shuttle they could use to get there but they would need clearance to dock and that would be hard to get without good reason. They could fake an accident of some sort and request emergency clearance. That gave them the best chance.

"Is everyone clear on their assignments?" Taymen asked.

Once he was satisfied that everyone understood the plan Taymen sat back down and Releena stood from her seat.

"Thank you Taymen." She said. "I don't have to tell you what is at stake here." She started. "Our ships are more advanced and more powerful than the Tray's. The only advantage they had over us was surprise and their vast numbers."

There was a small pause.

"They no longer have surprise on their side and their numbers will be meaningless if we can rally enough ships. The Dark Avenger has proven that we can win this war without a vast fleet on our side. These three ships will help us turn the tide for our people.

"The Tray are arrogant by nature, we can use that to our advantage for a while but they won't underestimate us again after this mission."

There were several nods of agreement around the table.

"We leave at zero three hundred hours tomorrow morning, we'll arrive at the Orion Shipyard three hours later. The rendezvous point is a six hour stream from there, I want to see each of you there when this is over. Any questions?"

Releena looked around the room to ensure there was none.

"Very well, get some rest and I'll see you in the morning."

As the others got up and left Taymen stayed behind.

Releena recognized the look of concern on his face.

"What is it Taymen?" She asked.

"Princess are you sure it's a good idea for you to come on this mission with us?" Taymen asked.

Releena knew he was going to ask that at one point or another.

"I understand your concern Taymen but this is my mission. Too many have already died while I stood by. I'm not going to ask another one of my soldiers to risk their life while I sit back and wait for the reports to come in."

Taymen couldn't help but smile a little.

"Funny, Talia said the same thing." He said.

"Which is why she'll be accompanying us." Releena replied.

"What?" Taymen said in shock.

"She raised that very point with me and I couldn't bring myself to leave her behind." Releena explained.

Taymen took a moment to gather his thoughts.

"With all due respect Princess is it really right to risk Talia's life over a moral issue?" Releena smiled.

"You care about her don't you?" She asked.

Taymen could feel himself blush a little.

Releena's smile widened.

"I just thought that in the interest of her safety she should stay here." Taymen said.

"It's okay Taymen, being a Colonel doesn't mean you don't have any feelings anymore." Releena said.

"But what could she do if she came with us?" Taymen asked.

"She will be guiding the teams from the shuttle while I watch the sensors."

Taymen nodded. He really had no argument for Talia to stay. Truthfully he just didn't want to see her in danger.

"Alright then." He said with a sigh.

"Taymen do you ever wonder why I wanted you in the Imperial Guard in the first place?" Releena asked.

The question caught Taymen off guard.

"Always." He said.

Releena smiled.

"When I looked over your service record I saw a fairly average young officer, but when I read over the reports from your battle over the Sahara colony I saw a very unique, courageous and intelligent young commander in the most unlikely of places."

Taymen tried not to take it personally.

"That's why I think Talia should be on this mission, for the same reason I knew I wanted you as a commander in the Imperial Guard."

Taymen wasn't quite sure what she was getting at.

"Why exactly is that?" He asked.

"Because the greatest heroes turn out to be the most unlikely of people."

Chapter Eighteen

Forest outside of Cairon Capital
03:15 Abydos Standard Time
Day 22, Eleventh Cycle, Egyptian Year 3201

Taymen waited next to the hatch of the shuttle as the last of Colonel Atlaa's team climbed aboard. It was three fifteen hours and they were finally ready to leave.

Taymen climbed into the shuttle and sealed the hatch before taking his seat in the rear compartment.

There were twenty two of them onboard, three six man teams would board the ships while Releena and Talia would remain on the shuttle with the pilot.

Taymen would leave briefly to create some sort of distraction and then return. Once everyone was aboard their ships they would launch again.

The shuttle shuttered as they broke free of Cairon's atmosphere and flew into open space.

"Stand-by for protostream." The pilot said as he powered up the stream system.

A few moments later Taymen could feel the ship pass through the protostream hub as his vision went dark for an instant and then cleared again.

"Stream complete, we're coming up on the station." The pilot reported again.

"Begin venting the atmosphere bottles and take main engines off-line." Taymen ordered.

"Aye Sir." The pilot said.

Taymen had ordered the shuttle to be fitted with oxygen storage tanks and had them filled with the oxygen-nitrogen mixture used on the Tray shuttle so they could simulate a hull breach.

"The station is hailing us." The pilot said a few minutes later.

"Patch it through." Releena said.

Suddenly a woman's voice came over the shuttle speakers.

"Unidentified shuttle this is Orion Shipyard you are in secure space, transmit your identification code immediately." The woman said.

Releena nodded to the pilot who transmitted their stolen identification code before replying.

"Confirmed Orion, code transmitted." He said. "We have been attacked by an Egyptian battleship and have taken heavy damage, our engines are failing and we are venting atmosphere request emergency docking clearance." He continued.

There was a moment of silence before the woman responded.

"Confirmed shuttle you are clear for landing in bay three, a security and engineering team will meet you there, follow their instructions."

"Roger that Orion." The pilot replied before closing the channel.

Everyone in the shuttle let out a breath of relief.

"We'll be landing in two minutes." The pilot said.

"Alright." Sharr started. "Here we go."

Orion Shipyard
06:40 Abydos Standard Time
Day 22, Eleventh Cycle, Egyptian Year 3201

Taymen walked through the corridor towards the operations center of the station. The feeling of Tray bindings around his wrists was becoming all too familiar along with his two guard escort.

He walked into the operations center where he was almost immediately greeted by a young woman.

"Colonel Orelle." She said as she made her way over to him. "How nice to finally meet you in person." She said smugly.

"You have me at a disadvantage." Taymen replied.

The young woman smiled.

"Commander Torinna." She replied. "CO of the Orion shipyard." Taymen smirked a little.

"Funny, last time I was here General Ossay was in command of Orion."

Torinna ignored his sarcasm.

"So what brings you all the way out here?" She asked.

"We found him near one of the main power junctions on level thirteen." One of the guards replied.

"Well Colonel, trying to sabotage my station." Torinna said.

"Just planning a little surprise party." Taymen said sarcastically.

"Well in that case, allow me to invite you to a little gathering of our own, we already have your friends in our brig perhaps you'd like to join them." Torinna said as she gestured to the guards to take him away.

Taymen turned and left the operations center and made his way down the corridor to the lift that took them down to the base level. Another few hundred meters down the corridor and there was the hatch leading to the brig.

Taymen walked in first followed by the first guard and noticed that all the cells were empty. As he made his way to the cell along the back bulkhead Taymen herd two dull thuds.

When he turned around he noticed the two guards unconscious on the floor with Sharr and a few members of her crew standing over them.

"Well that was fast." Taymen said.

Sharr smiled.

"Well I know how impatient you can be." She said as she handed Taymen his com. device and a side arm.

"Remove their com. units and weapons and get them in the cell." Sharr ordered.

"Our informants managed to get us out a little ahead of schedule, they're waiting for our signal before disabling the sensors.

"How are the others doing?" Taymen asked.

"Colonel Atlaa's team is already in position and Colonel Dravin's team will be shortly. Half my team is already aboard the Silver Phoenix." Sharr explained.

"Well then let's not keep them waiting." Taymen said before taking off down the corridor with Sharr close behind.

The Silver Phoenix was docked on the same side of the station as the brig which was why Sharr's team stayed behind to get Taymen.

"Dravin to Orelle."

Taymen tapped his earpiece as he continued to run down the corridor.

"Go ahead." He said.

"We're in position and the shuttle is safely away what's your status?" Dravin said.

"We're on route to our position, standby for my signal." Taymen replied before closing the channel.

As they rounded the corner Taymen and the others came to a sudden halt.

"You have got to be kidding me!" Taymen said.

Standing in the middle of the corridor ahead was Commander Torinna along with eight armed guards.

"Did you really think your little plan would work?" She asked.

"Kinda." Taymen replied.

"Enough of these games Colonel, return to the brig and you won't be harmed." Taymen shook his head.

"I remember what happened the last time a Tray officer said I wouldn't be harmed."

As the guards began to move towards them the station suddenly shuttered knocking almost all of them too the deck.

"What was that!" Torinna shouted.

"Surprise!" Taymen said as he drew his weapon and fired.

The rest of his team did the same before most of the guards could get to their feet.

One after another they fell to the deck dead until two finally managed to get a few shots off.

One of Sharr's officers hit the deck with a wound in his head just before the Tray that shot him fell.

A second later Taymen fell to the deck with a wound in his chest.

Sharr fired two rounds into the last standing guard who fell dead instantly leaving Commander Torinna alone and unarmed. She took off down the corridor but fell to the deck when the station shuttered again.

As she tried to stand she felt a round bury itself into her back an instant before a second round penetrated her skull leaving her dead on the deck.

"Pick them up." Sharr ordered pointing to Taymen and the other dead officer. "Let's get out of here."

They managed to reach the ship without any further interference from the Tray. The only thing that slowed them down was the shuttering effect from the station's emergency oxygen storage tanks exploding.

Taymen managed to program the life support system to think that the tanks were empty. Once he disabled the safety sensors the life support system began filling the already full tanks to twice their normal capacity.

When they finally exploded there was enough force to give the station a significant nudge without causing any major damage.

It wasn't at all subtle but it was enough to keep the Tray occupied while the sensors were disabled.

Sharr opened the hatch to C.A.C. and walked in to find all the Tray already gone.

"We're ready to go Colonel." One of the officers reported.

"Colonel Atlaa and Dravin?" Sharr asked.

"Waiting on us Ma'am."

Sharr nodded.

"Send the signal to get under way." She ordered. "Seal the airlock and depressurize the remainder of the ship."

Only a moment past before her orders were carried out.

"Disengaged from the scaffold." The helmsman reported.

"All ahead full get us clear of the station and power up the stream system." Sharr said.

"Aye Ma'am" The helmsman replied.

"Colonel." She heard the medic call from behind her.

"What is it?" She asked.

"We need to get him to sickbay." The medic replied.

Sharr turned to her operations officer.

"Pressurize the route to sickbay." She said. "You two go with them." She continued.

"Colonel the two Tray cruisers are bearing down on us."

"Incoming ordnance!" The operations officer called.

"Deploy armor!" Sharr snapped.

The ship shuttered as two missiles impacted the outer hull armor which managed to deploy a split second before the missiles hit.

"Direct hit to the armor plating." The damage control officer reported.

"We're clear of the station." The helmsman said.

"Get us out of here." Sharr ordered.

"Colonel the Night Huntress is reporting a problem with their stream system." The operations officer reported. "They report the Tray removed several components while they were examining the ship, they can't stream out."

Sharr looked at the sensor display to see the Night Huntress maneuvering between them and the two Tray cruisers.

"Put me through to Atlaa." She ordered.

"Channel open."

"Atlaa what are you doing?" Sharr asked.

"Buying you some time." Atlaa replied. *"We can't stream out but we can at least keep these cruisers off your back for a little while, get those ships to the rendezvous point and tell the Princess I'm sorry."*

Sharr was about to object but Atlaa closed the channel.

She watched the sensor display as several missiles impacted the Huntress over and over again until it finally exploded leaving a cloud of debris.

"Helm get us out of here now!" She ordered.

"Streaming." The helmsman replied.

"Stream complete, we're at the rendezvous coordinates." The helmsman reported.

"No Tray contacts." The operations officer said. "I've got the shuttle and the Phantom Wraith dead ahead."

"Shuttle is requesting permission to land."

Sharr sighed.

"Permission granted, advise the Princess to meet me in sickbay and pressurize the rest of the ship." Sharr said as she left C.A.C.

When she got to sick bay Releena was just rounding the corner.

"Colonel what happened?" She asked.

Sharr sighed and shook her head a little as she opened the hatch.

"The Night Huntress' stream system was inoperative, it was destroyed trying to buy us time to escape." Sharr explained.

Releena didn't say anything as she walked into sickbay stopping dead in her tracks once she was through the hatch.

In front of her and to the left, lying on the first bed was Taymen unconscious with a life support monitor hooked up to him.

She slowly made her way past the medic who was checking his vitals and stood on the far side of the bed near Taymen's head.

"What happened?" She asked.

"We ran into Tray security on the station." Sharr replied.

"How is he?" She asked.

"Well in short not good." The medic started. "The bullet punctured one of his lungs and he's bleeding internally."

"Can you treat him?" Releena asked.

"Not here." The medic replied. "He needs an injection of medical nanites to stop the bleeding and repair the lung and there isn't a single one on this ship."

"Can his own nanites handle the repairs?" Releena asked.

The medic shook his head.

"No the injuries are too severe, he'll bleed to death before they can repair the damage. I can slow the bleeding and buy him some time but not enough for his nanites to repair the damage."

Sharr tapped the control on her earpiece to activate the internal com. channel to C.A.C.

"Lieutenant Arris contact the Phantom Wraith and find out if they have any medical nanites aboard." She said before closing the channel.

"What if we can't find any?" Releena asked.

The medic sighed.

"If we can't get the nanites than he's going to need major surgery and I can't do it with the supplies we have on board, he needs a hospital Princess."

Releena looked at Taymen lying on the bed as she considered the options.

"Arris to Colonel Vaye."

Sharr hit the control on her earpiece.

"Go ahead Lieutenant." She said.

"I've contacted the Phantom Wraith, they have no medical supplies aboard, sorry Colonel." Arris reported.

"Very well." Sharr replied before closing the channel.

"What do you want to do Princess?" The medic asked.

Suddenly Taymen's life was in her hands and Releena didn't know what to do. The fate of her entire people was resting on her shoulders and now the only thing she could think about was saving this one life.

She'd be lying if she said she didn't favor Taymen over the rest of her officers at least a little bit but could she really jeopardize the rest of the mission for him.

"Princess." Sharr whispered.

Releena shook herself out of her train of thought.

"Colonel contact the Phantom Wraith, tell them we are proceeding to the supply cache according to plan." Releena said.

"Yes Princess." Sharr replied.

"Have a prowler and a pilot ready for launch in ten minutes." Releena continued.

"Princess?" Sharr asked.

"They're going to find Taymen the help he needs."

Imperial Command, Netara
12:45 Abydos Standard Time
Day 22, Eleventh Cycle, Egyptian Year 3201

General Raise walked into the briefing room to find Fleet Marshal Ourik already waiting for him along with a few of his most trusted Commanders.

"General, please sit down." Ourik said.

Raise hesitantly took a seat at the table opposite Ourik.

"Now I'm guessing by your hesitation that you have nothing to report on the whereabouts of Colonel Orelle or Princess Releena." Ourik said.

"I'm afraid not." Raise replied quietly.

It had been over a month since Taymen managed to escape and Ourik was not particularly happy about it. His leg still wasn't fully healed from the incident and to make matters worse his superiors were holding him personally responsible for Taymen's escape.

"Well." Ourik continued. "We know how the Colonel managed to escape us, any information on how the Princess managed it. I find it hard to believe she overpowered her guards."

"No she didn't have to." Raise replied. "The guards were identified as former Egyptian marines. We believe they orchestrated her escape and got her off the planet."

Ourik nodded.

"And what are we doing with these guards?" One of the Commanders asked.

"They've already been executed for treason." Raise replied.

"Very good." Ourik said. "I want all of you to begin screening all personnel working at this facility. I want everyone identified and a full search for them to be conducted in both our own and the Egyptian databases. If they are found to be traitors I want them arrested and held for questioning before they're executed. Once you have completed with this facility I want you to expand the search to all other high level areas including the shipyards."

Raise thought about saying something but he didn't want to give them reason to doubt his loyalty. Instead he stood up and nodded.

"Was that all?" He asked.

"For now." Ourik replied.

Silver Phoenix at Outer Colony Supply Cache
20:13 Abydos Standard Time
Day 22, Eleventh Cycle, Egyptian Year 3201

"Colonel Vaye." The operations officer said as he walked into C.A.C. "Whatever ammunition we managed to find has been loaded and the Phantom Wraith reports loaded as well." He reported as he handed Sharr a data pad.

She took the pad and looked over the inventory.

"Is this it?" She asked.

"I'm afraid so Ma'am." The officer replied.

Sharr sighed as she read over the list. One hundred missiles and twenty thousand plasma rounds wouldn't get them very far especially since they didn't even have any gun crews yet.

"We need to find another cache somewhere. How long until bleed off is complete?" Sharr asked.

"Two hours." The officer replied.

"Alright let's start looking for…"

"Sensor contact!" One of the crewmen interrupted.

"What is it?" Sharr asked.

"Two Tray heavy cruisers closing in on us. I'd say they know we're here." The operations officer replied when he got to his station.

"Battle mode, deploy armor!" Sharr snapped. "Bring our bow to bear and signal the Phantom to form up on our starboard."

"Incoming ordnance!" Someone called just before the ship shuttered.

191

"Colonel what's going on?" Releena asked as she entered C.A.C with Talia.

"They've found us." Sharr said as she checked the sensor display.

"Have the Phantom fire on target two we'll take target one." She continued. "Load all missile tubes with saber missiles, full salvos on my mark!"

"Incoming ordnance!" The operations officer called.

The ship shuttered and a few consoles overloaded sending white hot sparks into the air.

Talia let out a small shriek as she held onto the command console to keep her balance.

"Direct hit to the starboard landing deck, breaches on decks twelve through eighteen." The damage control officer reported.

"Colonel we just lost targeting sensors." The weapons officer said.

"The Phantom's reporting heavy damage, they've lost maneuvering and their missiles aren't getting through." The communications officer reported.

Sharr checked the display to see both cruisers still closing in on them. They were at a severe disadvantage right now. Both ships were barely armed and neither one of them had even a skeleton crew, they couldn't even launch their fighters or fire their gun batteries.

"New contact just showed up on sensors." The operations officer reported. "It's firing!"

Sharr braced for the impact of incoming ordnance only to see one of the Tray cruisers take several hits before it exploded. The other cruiser turned to fire on the new contact.

"Who is that?" Sharr asked.

"Colonel I've got manual targeting online." The weapons officer reported.

"Full salvo fire at will!" Sharr snapped.

A second later twenty missiles sped from the Silver Phoenix and impacted the cruiser which was too busy with the third ship to see them coming.

A few seconds later even more missiles from the other ship impacted the cruiser enveloping it in a ball of flame.

Sharr stood watching the sensor display as the unknown contact continued to move towards them.

"They're hailing." The communications officer said.

Sharr hesitated a moment.

"Patch them through." She finally said.

"*Silver Phoenix this is Captain Avril Raquel of the Dark Avenger, what's your status?*" Avril asked over the speakers.

Sharr sighed in relief before hitting the control on her earpiece.

"This is Colonel Sharr Vaye, it is good to see you guys." She replied. "We're okay for now but we've taken damage and we have minimal weapons and crew." She continued.

"Captain Raquel this is Princess Releena."

"Yes Princess." Avril replied hesitantly.

"We have an emergency situation, report to the Silver Phoenix with a medical team immediately and prepare to move a patient." Releena said.

"Understood we're on our way." Avril replied before the channel closed.

Silver Phoenix Port Hangar Deck
20:53 Abydos Standard Time
Day 22, Eleventh Cycle, Egyptian Year 3201

When Avril stepped out of the prowler and onto the hangar deck both Releena and Sharr were there to meet her.

"Princess, Colonel." Avril said as she saluted sharply. "Permission to come aboard." She continued.

"Granted." Sharr replied as she returned the salute.

"Well done Captain." Releena said.

"What's the emergency?" Avril asked.

"Follow us." Sharr said.

Avril and her medical team followed Sharr and Releena off of the hangar deck and into the corridor. There was no deck crew so the prowler was left on the lift in the airlock.

"We managed to retake these two ships from the Tray but it came at a price." Releena explained.

"A third ship we were trying to retake was destroyed and we have virtually no crew." Sharr added.

Avril looked around as they moved through the corridors. She had never been aboard a carrier before.

The corridors looked pretty much the same as the Avenger's only they were a little wider. The ship itself of course was significantly larger than the Avenger, it seemed to take forever before they reached sickbay.

Sharr opened the hatch and Releena walked in followed by Avril and her team.

Once inside Avril immediately noticed a young woman sitting beside one of the beds holding a patient's hand. As she looked closer Avril realized that the patient was Taymen.

The two medics immediately moved to either side of the bed and began checking Taymen's vitals as Sharr's medic moved closer to explain Taymen's condition to them.

"Avril this is Talia Kulove." Releena said.

Talia simply nodded but didn't say anything.

Avril could clearly see from the expression on her face that she was worried.

"What happened?" Avril asked.

"He was shot while we were trying to retake the ship." Sharr explained. "When we got here there were minimal medical supplies and no nanites. We managed to get some from the supply cache here but the damage was too extensive by then. Our medic thinks he may need surgery at this point."

Avril nodded.

"Get ready to move him to the Avenger immediately, have the doctor standing by to receive him." She ordered.

"Yes Ma'am." One of the medics replied.

"I'm going with him." Talia said as she stood up.

The medics looked over at Avril who simply nodded once.

They quickly moved Taymen onto a stretcher and began to move him through the corridor to the hangar deck with Avril and the others close behind.

"We still have almost two hours of bleed off time before we can stream out." Sharr started. "After which we need to re-supply and re-arm as well as get the rest of the crew aboard."

Avril sighed.

"There's a supply station about a six hour stream from here. Our scout ships report no Tray activity in the area." She said.

"We were only four hours away when your prowler found us so we can stream out as soon as you're ready. As for your crew, that's going to take some time." She continued.

"Not really." Sharr said. "We only brought the minimum number of people we needed to take the ships but there are two full crew compliments waiting for us on Cairon, we just have to move them."

"What's the compliment of a carrier?" Avril asked.

"Twenty-eight hundred." Sharr replied.

"And an avenger class cruiser has about twelve hundred, so we need to move about four thousand crewmen and all we have to move them with are prowlers." Avril said as she did the math in her head.

A prowler with only one pilot could only move fifteen people at a time, so their best bet was to retrieve all the other pilots first so they could use the rest of the prowlers from the Silver Phoenix and the Phantom Wraith.

"Then we'll launch our prowlers to start retrieving your crew."

"Thank you Captain." Releena said.

Avril looked over the report from the ship's doctor.

Taymen was recovering quickly from his injuries. The nanites managed to repair the damage to his lung but he had to have surgery to stop the bleeding.

The Doctor was keeping him unconscious for another day or so until he fully recovered so Avril was in command for a little longer.

The ship had been patrolling the area around the supply station for the entire day while the Silver Phoenix and Phantom Wraith re-supplied and re-armed.

They managed to find everything they needed. Medical supplies and food as well as enough ammunition and fuel to completely re-supply both ships.

Avril was a little nervous with the two ships docked at the same time. It left them virtually defenseless if they were attacked and she found the idea of having to defend two ships, one of which was carrying Princess Releena a little overwhelming.

She hadn't realized how unprepared she was for full out command of a ship. She had been left in command before but the ship's Captain was never far away and it was only for a few days at the longest. She had been in command of the Avenger for almost three months and until now she wasn't sure that Taymen was going to recover.

"Captain." One of the operations officers called.

"What is it Ensign?" Avril asked as she walked over.

"One of our sensor drones has just picked up a prowler streaming into the system."

The prowlers had been moving crew members from Cairon to their new ships for two days now and they were almost fully manned.

"More crew arriving?" Avril asked.

"No Ma'am the prowler is identified as belonging to the Demon's Light." The Ensign replied.

"Launch the alert fighters!" Avril snapped.

"Have them secure that prowler but to hold fire." She ordered.

"Aye Ma'am." Elisha replied from the flight controller's station.

"Captain the prowler is transmitting a general hail, they're looking for us." The Ensign reported.

Avril sighed.

The Demon's Light was General Eazak's ship. He took it with him to the separatists during the war and has been branded a traitor ever since.

Still, he was the one who warned Taymen about the Tray attack but that didn't mean Avril had to trust him or his crew.

"Open a channel." Avril said.

"Dark Avenger this is Demon's Light prowler seven seven two, please respond." A voice said over the speaker.

"This is Captain Raquel of the Dark Avenger." Avril replied.

"I have a passenger carrying a message for Colonel Orelle." The man said.

"Colonel Orelle is not here, I'm in command you may pass any messages for the Colonel along to me." Avril said.

There was a long silence before the man spoke again.

"Permission to come aboard." The man finally said.

Avril looked at the communications officer who simply shrugged. Her training was screaming at her not to let them board but her instincts told her otherwise and she remembered Taymen telling her that she had to learn to trust her instincts.

Either way she new Taymen well enough to know that he would follow his instincts so that's just what she was going to do.

"Very well." Avril finally replied. "You are clear to land, our sword breakers will escort you to our location, Avenger out." Avril nodded to the communications officer who closed the channel.

"I want two teams of marines on the hangar deck. Have them escort everyone aboard that ship to the briefing room." Avril said.

"Yes Ma'am." The communications officer replied as Avril left C.A.C.

Elisha watched the prowler as it made its approach towards the ship. She opened the flight controller channel to the prowler and waited for a response.

"Avenger flight this is prowler seven seven two inbound." The pilot said.

"Roger prowler you are clear to land on starboard landing deck, set down on pad four and await recovery." Elisha replied.

"Roger that Avenger flight, coming in for final approach." The pilot said before closing the channel.

Elisha continued to watch as the prowler made its approach to land and opened the channel to the hangar deck.

"Attention starboard deck crews, prowler seven seven two inbound alert status one." She said indicating to the deck crew that the prowler coming in was a potential security risk.

A moment later the prowler had landed and Elisha activated the lift to bring it down to the hangar deck. All she had to do now was land the alert fighters which was not a difficult task just a tedious one.

There were twelve sword breakers in flight, she just had to make sure she landed six on both landing decks and she didn't direct two of them to the same pad.

She planned out the landing pattern before opening the channel to the fighters.

"Alert wing this is Avenger flight break formation and prepare for landing sequence." She instructed.

The fighters were unmanned drones and these new sword breakers were even smarter than the last generation they had so they rarely missed a landing but it wasn't a big deal even if they did. She would just order them to abort and they would fly through the flight deck back into space, come around and try again.

Once she got the confirmation signals from all twelve sword breakers she opened the channel again and began to direct the landings.

Chapter Nineteen

Avril hooked a lock of her long dark hair behind her left ear before opening the hatch and walking into the briefing room.

Sitting at the table were three men who all stood up when the hatch opened.

To the left of the table head sat General Eazak from the separatist fleet. Avril would have been surprise to see him there if it wasn't for who was sitting across from him.

His green eyes and glasses made it hard for Avril to mistake Jassen Pitt for anyone else.

To Jassen's left was a young man in his mid twenties. His dark hair was long in the back and his blue eyes remained fixed on Avril as she moved around the room to the far end of the table, she assumed he was their pilot.

"Captain." Jassen said in greeting.

"Gentlemen." Avril replied as she sat down. "I understand you have a message for Colonel Orelle." She started.

"That's right." Eazak replied.

"Unfortunately Colonel Orelle is not available but I will take the message if you like."

Jassen cleared his throat before speaking.

"What do you mean he's not available? Where is he?" He asked.

Avril hesitated a moment.

"He's been away on a mission for some time now." She finally replied.

Eazak smiled a little.

"Care to elaborate?" He asked.

"Not really." Avril replied with a hint of hostility in her voice.

It was no secret that Avril had no love for separatists but she figured she'd keep her disdain for them in check for now.

"Maybe we should explain." Jassen started.

"Maybe you should." Avril replied.

"We received a transmission from an unknown and seemingly primitive source some time ago." Eazak started. "We traced its origin but it was too far out for us to get an exact fix. The message was clearly meant for Colonel Orelle."

"Does the message say who it's from?" Avril asked.

"The sender is one Russ Egler."

Avril's expression turned to surprise.

"You've got to be kidding me." She said.

"Someone you know?" Jassen asked.

"Sort of. What's the message say?" Avril asked.

Eazak held up a data pad but didn't hand it to her.

"As I said the message is for Colonel Orelle and since you say he's on a mission perhaps we'll simply wait for his return." He said smugly.

Avril sighed as she continued to hold back her temper.

"You want to know what's going on, fine." She started, realizing she wasn't going to get the message any other way. "Colonel Orelle was seriously injured during a recent mission, he's recovering in our sick bay but he's still unconscious."

"What!" Jassen snapped.

"How interesting." Eazak said. "Tell us about this mission."

Avril hesitated a moment.

"It seemed obvious that the only way to get the Tray out was to orchestrate a simultaneous strike against key installations." Eazak couldn't help but laugh a little.

"Are you serious, you can't beat the Tray there's too many of them." He said.

"Their numbers are the only advantage they have. One on one our ships are far more powerful and now we have their protostream technology." Avril said.

"Yes, we managed to obtain their stream technology from the cruiser you left behind at Jassen's station." Eazak said.

"In any case all I know is that we don't have time to play games with you. We have a war to fight and you're holding a message in your hand to Colonel Orelle that I will assume to be rather important given that you've come this far out of your way just to deliver it. So you can either hand me the pad or I'll take it from you, either way I don't care."

Jassen remained silent and expressionless while Eazak's smile returned.

"Well I see that Colonel Orelle has left his ship in good hands." He said as he slid the pad across the table to Avril.

"In fact Captain." He continued. "We haven't come just to deliver that message, we came to help." Avril looked over the pad briefly.

"Help?" She asked.

"You said yourself we need to strike several targets at once, to do that you need ships and I happen to have a fleet at my command." Eazak replied.

"And what would this fleet cost us?" Avril asked coldly.

"It won't cost you anything." Eazak replied.

"To put it simply Abydos and her surrounding systems are still home to us and we really do want to help." He explained. "There was a lot of opposition to our decision to leave when we heard the Tray were coming and now we realize that wandering space aimlessly in search of a new home untouched by the Tray was a bad decision."

Avril didn't know if she should believe him or not but he had no reason to lie to her now.

"Then why are you here Jassen?" She asked.

"We want to come home." Jassen replied. "We don't want to leave it in the hands of the Tray."

Avril nodded a little as she thought it over.

"Alright." She finally said. "Then let's talk about this message."

Dark Avenger, Sick Bay
11:13 Abydos Standard Time
Day 25, Eleventh Cycle, Egyptian Year 3201

Taymen could hear the sound of people moving around him. It was dark and warm and he felt as if he hadn't eaten in days. The smell of sickbay was all too familiar to him but he didn't remember how he got there.

He began to flex his muscles one by one trying to wake them up. The pain in his ribs was back but it wasn't nearly as bad as it had been and each breath he drew in caused a sharp pain in his chest.

Slowly he moved his fingers, then his hand until he suddenly felt something. He felt someone taking his hand in theirs and squeezing it gently.

"Doctor!" He heard a voice call.

The voice was Talia's, at least he thought it was.

Was Talia the one holding his hand?

Had she stayed with him the entire time?

Taymen suddenly realized he didn't know how long he'd been here for.

Finally, he opened his eyes wincing at the light above his bed. It took a minute for his vision to clear but when it did he found himself looking up at the Doctor and Talia standing on either side of him.

"Welcome back Colonel." The Doctor said.

"How do you feel?" Talia asked softly.

"Fantastic." Taymen replied sarcastically. "What happened?" He asked.

"You took a bullet to the chest." The Doctor replied. "It punctured your lung and caused severe internal hemorrhaging. The nanites repaired your lung but I had to operate to get the bleeding to stop."

"How long have I been out?" Taymen asked.

"Almost three days?" Talia replied.

"I've got to get to C.A.C." Taymen said as he sat up.

He winced at the pain in his chest and ribs.

"Easy." The Doctor said. "You're not going anywhere for a while yet, you need to take it easy." He continued.

Taymen sighed.

"I'm not lifting anything, I'm not running around or doing anything else strenuous." Taymen started. "I'm going to get dressed and going to C.A.C., unless you need me here for testing I'm going to take command of my ship."

The Doctor sighed as he shook his head.

"Fine." He said. "But I want you back here in six hours for an examination."

Taymen nodded as he stood up to get dressed. A few minutes later he left sickbay with Talia.

"And they say Doctors make the worst patients." The Doctor said to himself sarcastically.

As Taymen made his way to his quarters he realized how much he missed his ship. The feel of the deck plates under his boots, the smell of the air and even the feel of the gravity.

He always felt too light when he was on a planet. Even though each planet's gravity was slightly different he still liked the heavier gravity of his ship.

Taymen opened the hatch to his quarters and walked in. Everything was exactly as he left it. The data pads on his desk were still there and the bed still made. Even the glass of water on his table was still there.

He opened the closet on the wall opposite the bed and pulled out a uniform hanging it on a hook on the wall next to the closet.

He took a few minutes to take a quick shower and shaved his stubble before putting his uniform on.

The material of his black tee shirt felt soft against him unlike the civilian clothes he had been wearing that always felt rough and itchy. He slid on his pants and did up the belt after tucking his shirt in then pulled his boots on. Finally he put on his black jacket and did up the zipper.

It felt good being back in his uniform again, it was like being back in his own skin.

Taymen checked that his rank emblems were set right on his jacket collar and placed his earpiece in his right ear before leaving his quarters.

Dark Avenger C.A.C.
11:43 Abydos Standard Time
Day 25, Eleventh Cycle, Egyptian Year 3201

Titus and Avril were going over the communications log from the night watch when Talia walked into C.A.C.

"What are you doing here?" Avril asked.

"I thought you'd want to know Taymen woke up a little while ago and the Doctor's released him from sickbay." Talia said.

Avril was about to ask where Taymen was when she heard one of the officers yell.

"Captain on deck!"

Everyone snapped to attention instantly.

"Carry on." Taymen said.

Avril and the others watched as Taymen made his way down to command console.

"Titus." Taymen said as he walked by.

"Welcome back Sir." Titus replied.

"Captain." Taymen said.

"Sir." Avril replied.

"How was command?" Taymen asked.

Avril sighed.

"I think I still have a lot to learn Sir." She said.

Taymen smiled.

"Maybe not as much as you think." He said. "What's our status?" He asked.

"All systems at full capacity, the Silver Phoenix and Phantom Wraith will be fully crewed, supplied and armed in the next few hours." Avril reported.

"Very good Captain, let's go talk." Taymen said.

As they moved towards the hatch Taymen turned to the communications station.

"Sairon." He said.

"Sir." Sairon replied with a smile.

"Contact the Silver Phoenix and Phantom Wraith, request Colonels Vaye and Dravin to join us in our briefing room with the Princess." Taymen said.

"Aye Sir." Sairon replied.

"Talia, why don't you go to your quarters and get some rest, I'll come see you when we're done." Taymen said.

"Alright." Talia sighed as the three of them left C.A.C.

When they got to the briefing room Taymen moved to the head of the long table and took a seat wincing a little at the pain as Avril sat to his left.

"Now, what's been going on here Avril?" Taymen asked.

Avril took a breath before beginning her report.

"First of all I should tell you that we've been in contact with Jassen Pitt and General Eazak."

Avril could see the reaction in Taymen's eyes but he managed to keep his questions silent for the time being.

"They had a message for you and I think I should brief everyone about it once they arrive." Avril continued.

"Fair enough." Taymen said.

"For now however the new heavy rail cannons proved very effective against Tray heavy cruisers." Avril explained. "I'd say we're more than an even match for them now."

"I see." Taymen replied.

"Aside from that." Avril continued. "We managed to lay low while you were away and we have a full weapons payload again."

Taymen nodded.

"Excellent, well done Captain." He said. "How have the upgrades been holding out?"

"Very good." Avril replied. "The stream system is at full efficiency and the new stealth system allowed us to get in close range of the heavy cruisers that were attacking the Phoenix. We haven't really had a chance to see how the new armor does yet."

Suddenly the hatch opened and Releena walked in along with Sharr and Colonel Eronn Dravin.

Taymen and Avril stood up immediately at the sight of the Princess.

"Please sit down." She said as she took a seat across from Taymen.

"Colonel Orelle, I'm glad to see you up again." She said.

Taymen nodded. "Thank you Princess." He said as Sharr and Eronn sat to either side of Releena.

"So what's this about Taymen?" Sharr asked.

"I wanted to know where we're at with everything for starters." Taymen said.

"Both ships will be fully armed, supplied and crewed by the end of the day today." Sharr reported.

"Once we're ready to get underway we'll stream to the outer edges of the outer colonies until we can locate more of our ships and come up with a battle plan." Releena added.

"Captain Raquel has something she wants to brief us on." Taymen said.

"Then by all means Captain." Releena replied.

Avril took a breath as she gathered her thoughts.

"We may not have sufficient time to carry out your original plan." She started.

Everyone at the table leaned in closer listening intently.

"We were recently visited by General Eazak and a friend representing several refugees." She continued. "They were trying to deliver a message to Colonel Orelle. The message came from one Russ Egler from a planet called Earth in what they call the Milky Way galaxy, the one we call the White Spiral galaxy. We spent some time there when we were originally lost nine months ago. That's where you found us the first time Princess."

Releena nodded her understanding but remained silent.

"The message was essentially a call for help." Avril continued. "A Tray invasion force has occupied Earth in the same way they've occupied our planets."

"I'm sorry." Eronn interrupted. "But why should we put this alien world above our own right now?" He asked.

"Because of what the Tray could potentially find on Earth." Avril answered.

"My gods." Releena said.

"Princess?" Taymen asked.

"Something Ourik mentioned." She started. "He said that each planet seeded by the ancients had a temple containing information meant to help them along in their development. I later found this was only half true. Each temple also contained a piece of a map that was supposed to lead to an ancient archive."

"Russ indicated the Tray were using him to find the last piece of an ancient map on Earth." Avril said.

"If they find the map and reach the archive whatever they find there could mean the end for us." Releena said.

"Then we can't let them get to the archive." Eronn said.

"What would you suggest then?" Sharr asked.

"Well it's safe to assume that the Tray have a significantly smaller force occupying Earth, I think we should take all three ships and destroy the occupation force there." Taymen suggested.

"There's more to it Sir." Avril said. "Russ also said that he managed to decipher the inscription that gave the location of the last piece of the map. He says he found it but he hasn't let the Tray know so we can get the map piece before the Tray do."

"That still leaves the problem of the Tray on Earth." Releena said. "As long as they're there they will eventually discover the map's location as well."

"There's one other thing." Avril said.

"General Eazak has offered to commit his fleet to assist us. They want to fight the Tray and Jassen has volunteered the services of several of his citizens, they're waiting for our answer near the outer colonies."

Taymen smiled.

"Sure, now that we've done all the hard work he offers to help." He said smugly.

"Can we trust him Colonel?" Releena asked.

"Now that they're officially separate from our government I see no reason why we can't trust them as an ally. They've never had any interest in completely destroying us after all." Taymen replied.

"I agree." Sharr said. "But who's to say they aren't working for the Tray?" She asked.

"General Eazak warned us the Tray were coming before the initial attack. I doubt he would've done that if he were working for them." Taymen replied.

Releena nodded.

"Very well then." She started. "We have three ships and three locations to be at all at once, what would you suggest?" She asked.

"I think it's obvious that we should split up." Eronn said. "The Silver Phoenix and Dark Avenger should go to Earth, they should be able to take care of the Tray forces there and get the map piece all at once." He continued.

"I'll take the Phantom Wraith and meet up with General Eazak to begin coordinating our offensive here."

"In that case I'll go with you Colonel Dravin." Releena said.

"Are you sure that's a good idea Princess?" Sharr asked. "After all they are still separatists."

"I'll be fine Sharr." Releena said. "I won't be much use as a hostage to them now given the circumstances." She continued.

"Then it's settled." Taymen said.

"We'll send teams to modify your stream systems to the Tray specifications. You'll be able to travel much faster that way. Even with the modifications it'll take us about three and half months to reach Earth, so you'll be on your own until we get back." Avril added.

"I think we'll manage." Eronn said.

"Alright then." Releena said as she stood up. "Prepare your ships, we're going to war."

Part V
Humanity's Children

'One of the worst fears of a parent is that the mistakes they make in life will be revisited on their children after they're gone. When it does happen however, the children must rise above and be stronger than their parents in order to correct their mistakes.'

Queen Auria's first address.

Part V
Jumanji's Children

Chapter Twenty

Taymen took a moment to catch his breath before placing the weights back on the rack. His chest still hurt from time to time but according to the Doctor everything was normal.

He had spent a fair bit of his spare time in the ship's gym working out to try and help his recovery along. It was slow going at first but he's had plenty of time over the last few months and was actually starting to feel normal again.

The hatch to the gym opened and Taymen turned to see Kaile walking in.

"Morning Sir." Kaile said.

"Morning Chief." Taymen replied as he sat down on one of the machines.

"How are things on the hangar deck?" He asked.

"Pretty good Sir." Kaile replied as she picked up a set of weights. "Those new sword breakers are pretty impressive." She continued. "Larger weapons loads, faster and more maneuverable, better armor and they're even smarter than the last generation."

"We'll just have to see how they hold up in actual combat." Taymen said.

It had been a fairly quiet trip back to Earth. They hadn't run into the Tray the entire journey there and they were going to be making the last stream into the Earth's solar system in the next hour or so.

It took a little longer for them to get underway than Taymen originally liked when they found a large supply of deep space sensor drones on the supply station they were docked at.

They figured it was a good idea to deploy them first so they could track the Tray and communicate with the Princess back in their home galaxy.

The drones were designed to be deployed into deep space where they would use passive sensors to detect any ships in the area without being detected themselves, making them perfect for tracking the Tray's movements.

They also allowed for communications signals to be relayed over longer distances. Given the distance between the two galaxies they wouldn't be able to communicate with Releena and Eazak normally, but since they left a dozen or so drones along the way they could send messages between the two galaxies in about a week.

Taymen finished his workout and went back to his quarters for a shower before getting dressed and heading for C.A.C.

It was good seeing his crew again as he moved through the corridor. When he took command of the Shadow Venturer the corridors were completely empty except for the skeleton crew he brought with him.

Truthfully Taymen wasn't sure his plan was going to work as well as it did. They barely got the ship's engines running in time to meet General Raise but once he was aboard he had no idea it wasn't the Dark Avenger.

It was perfect, the Tray found them just as the Callon staff streamed out of the area with the Avenger. Once they began the attack Taymen gave the order to abandon ship knowing full well that if Raise was working for the Tray like he suspected, than he would turn Taymen over to Ourik the first chance he got.

"Captain on deck!" Titus shouted.

"Carry on." Taymen said as he made his way down to the command console.

"Sir." Avril said.

"How are we doing Captain?" Taymen asked.

"Bleed off is complete and the Silver Phoenix reports ready to stream out." Avril reported.

Taymen checked the main sensor display and saw that Sharr's carrier was formed up just off of their upper aft quarter on the starboard side.

"Alright." Taymen said. "Prepare to stream us out, contact the Phoenix and advise them to follow." He ordered.

"All hands prepare for protostream." Titus said over the internal com.

"Helm stream us to the outer edges of the Earth solar system." Taymen said.

"Aye Sir." Aurin replied before turning to the stream officer. "Power up the protostream generator and prepare to take us out." He said.

"All stations report ready Sir." Titus reported.

"Stream system ready Sir." Aurin said.

"Sir the Silver Phoenix reports ready to stream out." Sairon reported from the communications station.

"Very well." Taymen said. "Helm, stream us out."

"Aye Sir." The stream officer replied from his station. "Streaming in five...four...three...two...one."

Taymen stood still as everything went dark then back to normal a second later and his body tingled slightly for a few seconds.

"Stream complete Sir, we're approximately ten light minutes from the system's eighth planet." Aurin reported.

"I have the Silver Phoenix off of our starboard aft quarter." Titus said.

"Very well bring the ship to stealth mode and instruct the Phoenix to do the same." Taymen said.

"Aye Sir."

"Launch sensor drones, have them do a passive sweep of the system. I want to know what's out there." He continued.

"Aye Sir." Elisha replied from the flight controller station.

"Now let's see what we're up against." Avril said.

Cairo Egypt
05:23 Abydos Standard Time
Day 27, First Cycle, Egyptian Year 3202

Russ watched as more Tray filled the streets to enforce the curfew. People had been gathering all day to try and protest the occupation thinking that it would actually make a difference.

Russ wasn't sure what made him angrier, the Tray occupation or the sheer boundless stupidity of these people thinking that standing in the streets screaming would change anything for the better.

"Russ." Kaleigh said as she walked up behind him. "How's it looking out there?"

Russ took a step away from the window and closed the curtain.

"Pretty grim." He replied. "More soldiers just landed, I don't think this is going to end well." He continued. "I don't know what we should do."

"What can we do?" Arthur asked as he walked into the room.

"I'm afraid all we can do is wait for help." Kaleigh said.

"What help!" Arthur snapped. "It's been over three months now and nobody's come, what help are we waiting for?"

"Relax." Russ said. "We don't even know if they got the message yet."

"Or if they're going to get it at all." Arthur added.

"Arthur!" Kaleigh snapped.

Arthur didn't say anything. He knew he was being overly negative and that it wasn't helping matters, but he felt so powerless and that to Arthur was the most frustrating thing of all.

"How much longer can we wait for them?" He asked calmly. "How much more can we take before complete chaos breaks out?"

211

Neither Russ nor Kaleigh had an answer. Truthfully they had been asking the same thing themselves.

"Whether they're coming or not." Kaleigh started. "There's nothing we can do right now, we have to wait weather it's for help or for the right opportunity."

Arthur knew she was right but he really didn't like sitting around waiting.

The night went on with the screams of the protestors and eventually with the sound of weapons fire.

None of them slept that night.

The next morning when they went outside there were blood stains all over the street but nobody in sight.

"My god." Arthur said.

"What do we do now?" Kaleigh asked.

Russ and Arthur looked at each other but didn't say anything.

What could they do? They couldn't fight and there was nobody else for them to turn to. All they could do now was continue to wait.

Cairo Satellite Control Station
17:40 Abydos Standard Time
Day 27, First Cycle, Egyptian Year 3202

Kaleigh watched the satellite station intently from across the street. She knew she saw something moving inside as she walked passed but there was nobody in sight now.

It had been just over three months since she and Russ sent their message and there was no sign of a response.

Kaleigh still wasn't entirely convinced that there was somebody out there who could help them but Russ insisted there was and she saw no harm in silently hoping.

Suddenly, there just inside of the main doors was someone moving back into the building.

Kaleigh took a brief look around to ensure nobody saw her before she darted across the street and up to the building. When she peaked inside she couldn't see anything.

She opened the door and moved to the alarm panel and found it had already been disabled.

As she slowly walked towards the stairwell someone came out of one of the offices down the hall.

Kaleigh quickly moved into one of the side hallways and crouched down peaking around the corner.

The man looked like some sort of soldier, but his uniform was different than the Tray's.

He wore dark gray pants and a black armored utility vest over a dark gray shirt. His head was covered by a black helmet and a pair of clear safety glasses sat over his eyes. There were several armored pads along his arms and he wore a set of black leather gloves.

He held a strange looking rifle in his hands and Kaleigh could see some sort of side arm on his belt along with a long combat knife.

As she watched silently waiting for a chance to move, someone suddenly grabbed her from behind and put a knife to her throat. She tried to fight but her captor was too strong as he stood up and moved her forward into one of the empty offices.

"Captain!" The man yelled as he sat Kaleigh down in a chair.

A moment later another man entered the room.

He was dressed the same as the others except he carried his helmet in his hands exposing his shaved scalp. His brown eyes remained fixed on Kaleigh as he placed his helmet on the desk.

"Why do they keep finding us?" The man asked himself as he shook his head.

"Who are you?" The man asked in a harsh tone.

Kaleigh couldn't bring herself to say anything. She felt the tears running down her cheeks as the man stared at her waiting for an answer.

He finally sighed as he backed off a step.

"We won't hurt you." He said. "What's your name?" He asked again, this time in a slightly softer tone.

Kaleigh took a breath before answering.

"Kaleigh." She replied.

"Kaleigh." He repeated. "My name is Arkeal." He said. "What are you doing here Kaleigh?"

"I saw someone inside, there's not supposed to be anybody here." Kaleigh said as she wiped the tears from her face.

"You had access to this building, how?" Arkeal asked.

"I used to work here, before the Tray came."

Arkeal paused for a moment.

"Kaleigh." He started. "We received a message that was sent from this building..."

Kaleigh cut him off.

"You got our message?" She asked. "You're looking for Russ aren't you?" She said excitedly.

"You know him?" Arkeal asked, his tone becoming a little harsh again.

"He's my brother." She answered. "We sent the message you got, we were the ones who called for your help."

Arkeal could see the hope glimmering in Kaleigh's eyes.

"You are here to help us aren't you?" She asked suddenly feeling like she said too much.

"Sir." One of the other soldiers said from the door. "Tray patrols heading this way." He reported.

Arkeal turned to Kaleigh.

"Is there another way out of here?" He asked.

Kaleigh nodded.

"Yeah, through the back compound." She said.

"We're moving out." Arkeal said to the soldier.

"I think we need to see your brother." He said as he helped Kaleigh out of the chair.

Dark Avenger, C.A.C.
18:35 Abydos Standard Time
Day 27, First Cycle, Egyptian Year 3202

Taymen watched the sensor display as the last sensor drone made its final landing approach.

"That's it all drones are back onboard." The flight controller reported a moment later.

"Very well." Taymen said.

The drones indicated two heavy cruisers in orbit along with four light cruisers and a few cargo vessels. The biggest concern however was hovering over one of the deserts in the planet's atmosphere.

One of the Tray flagships maintained a position above one of the larger structures there which made Taymen nervous.

With their new upgrades and the heavy rail cannons that were installed while he was away they were only an even match for the heavy cruisers, but the flagship was significantly larger and more heavily armored.

Taymen didn't have the actual specifications but according to what Sharr learned through her various informants it was the largest class vessel the Tray had and it alone had the capability of destroying an entire planets' population.

"Doesn't look good does it?" Avril said as she looked over the sensor display.

"Nope." Taymen replied.

"Do you think we can handle that flagship?" She asked.

"Nope." He said.

"What about the zero point missiles?"

"We want the ship destroyed Captain, not the entire solar system." Taymen replied.

He was exaggerating of course but not by much.

The Avenger had six heavy missile silos installed during their upgrades and each one housed a new zero point missile. One of these missiles was powerful enough to destroy Earth and its moon and probably the next two planets over. They were by far the most powerful weapon in the Defense Force's arsenal.

"We'll have to think of something, that ship alone is enough to hold Earth." Taymen continued.

"Don't forget the Silver Phoenix is with us, that should even things up a little." Avril said.

"Yeah somehow I doubt it." Taymen replied.

"Sairon." He started. "Contact the Silver Phoenix and have Colonel Vaye meet us in our briefing room."

"Aye Sir." Sairon replied.

"Captain with me." Taymen said as he made his way to the hatch.

Chapter Twenty-One

Kaleigh burst through the front door and into the living room calling for Russ and Arthur as she entered.

It had taken her nearly twice as long to get home since her new 'friends' understandably didn't want to be seen.

"Russ, Arthur!" She called.

A second later Arthur came out of the bedroom and Russ from the kitchen.

"What is it?" Arthur asked.

Russ froze in place when he saw Arkeal standing just behind Kaleigh.

"You!" He said in shock.

"Good to see you again." Arkeal replied.

"What the hell?" Arthur asked.

"It worked!" Kaleigh said with excitement. "They got our message, they're here." She continued.

"Calm down." Arthur said.

Kaleigh took a moment to take a breath before she moved to close the door and offered a seat to Arkeal and the others.

"So you got our message." Russ said.

Arkeal nodded.

"And your ship?" Russ asked.

"The Dark Avenger is holding position just outside of the system with the Silver Phoenix." Arkeal explained.

"Silver Phoenix?" Russ asked.

"A carrier class battleship we brought with us." Arkeal said. "Our orders were to locate you and bring you back to the Avenger for an assessment of the situation here." He continued.

"Wait a minute." Arthur objected. "We can't just leave, can we?" He said. "I mean, the Tray have to be monitoring the planet, how can you get off unnoticed?" He asked.

"The same way we got on." Arkeal replied. "We have a stolen Tray shuttle that'll get us past the cruisers in orbit." He continued. "But I'm afraid we don't have much time I need you three to come with us now. I would suggest packing a few things." Arkeal said.

Arthur looked to Russ and Kaleigh who stood silent.

"You'll be coming one way or another." Arkeal added.

By the time they finally left the house it was already dark.

Arkeal and his men led the three of them through the alleys of the city to one of the newer housing developments. There were several large houses already built but most of them were empty and a fair bit of the surrounding area was cleared of brush and trees. Arthur felt like he had been walking for days.

It had in fact taken them several hours to reach the development as trying to avoid Tray patrols proved to be more difficult at night for the simple fact that they were more frequent.

"The shuttle is just past the last building and into the tree line." Arkeal whispered.

Russ looked and figured it to be about fifty meters across an open sandy field to the trees.

"We'll move in teams of three, each of you will move with two of us." Arkeal said. "Russ you're first."

Kaleigh looked around as Russ moved across the field with the first group. It only took them a few minutes to reach the trees even though they stopped every few meters to make sure nobody was around.

"You're next Kaleigh." Arkeal said as Russ' group reached the tree line.

Kaleigh slowly moved out away from the building with two of Arkeal's men. Her heart was pounding as she tried to control her heavy breathing.

It was partially excitement but mostly fear that had her heart racing in the first place.

They were about half way to the tree line when Kaleigh suddenly heard the sound of a rifle firing.

Her heart jumped into her throat as one of the soldiers forced her to the ground and took up a kneeling stance on her right side while the other hit the prone on her left.

When she turned her head Kaleigh could just make out the silhouette of four men standing in the distance.

The air was filled with the sound of weapons fire from both sides. She could hear the distinct sound of both the Egyptian's and the Tray's weapons.

The Tray weapons sounded like a normal rifle but Arkeal's and his men's weapons were very different. They didn't have the sharp explosive sound of a round being fired, but instead were a higher pitched and almost muffled sound of an object being accelerated to extremely high speeds.

Both sides continued to fire at each other until two of the Tray finally went down when they tried to advance.

As she looked closer Kaleigh could see that Arkeal and his men had managed to circle around the buildings unnoticed and opened fire at the Tray from the side.

By the time the remaining two Tray realized what had happened the two soldiers next to Kaleigh had each sighted in on their targets, switched their weapons to single shot and pulled the trigger.

Instantly two magnetically accelerated ceramic rounds flew through the cold air and buried themselves into their individual targets causing them to collapse to the ground dead leaving the night air silent once again.

When they reached the shuttle Russ was the first to climb aboard.

"Hello Russ." A familiar voice said.

Russ looked up and nearly fell backwards at the sight of Elisha standing in front of him.

"Elisha." He said.

He couldn't believe he hadn't even considered the fact that she'd be with the Dark Avenger when it arrived.

Kaleigh and Arthur boarded the shuttle a moment later and were both taken aback by the supposedly dead woman standing in front of them.

"Elisha, you're here!" Kaleigh said.

Elisha simply smiled.

"Yeah it's a long story." She said. "We'll tell you on the way."

"Everyone's aboard, let's get out of here." Arkeal said as he sealed the hatch and moved up to the flight compartment.

Arthur and Kaleigh couldn't be pulled away from the windows as they cleared the atmosphere and flew past the Tray cruisers in orbit.

"Oh my god." Arthur said as he saw their planet practically surrounded by the Tray ships.

"We'll be landing aboard the Avenger in about ten minutes." The pilot said.

Russ sat silently as Elisha took the time to briefly explain how she ended up aboard the Dark Avenger and what she had been doing since they left Earth.

Arthur still couldn't believe it and Kaleigh was so excited about the entire concept that she didn't know what to think.

Suddenly she heard the pilot in the flight compartment hailing the Avenger's flight controller.

"We're coming up on them." He called out.

Kaleigh and Arthur moved back to the windows along with Russ.

There, ahead of them they could see two immense ships.

Russ immediately recognized the Dark Avenger on the starboard side. The sleek upper hull section, the landing bays and the launch tubes just under them. He could even see the missile tubes and gun batteries as they moved closer.

The other ship however, which Russ assumed was the Silver Phoenix was significantly larger.

There was one large landing deck on the upper hull and several launch tubes along the side as well as what looked like a smaller landing deck on either side of the hull a few decks below the main one.

He couldn't count the number of gun batteries or missile tubes along the hull as they passed by but he figured the ship's command center was in the large oval domed structure that sat on top of the main landing deck.

"Amazing!" Kaleigh said.

Her eyes remaining fixed on the two massive ships.

"Is this even possible?" Arthur asked still not believing what he was seeing.

Nobody answered.

"We're on final approach." The pilot said.

When they landed the shuttle was towed onto the hangar deck where Kaleigh and Arthur remained mesmerized by all the alien ships around them.

"This is unbelievable." Arthur said as he looked around.

"I'll give you guys the tour later." Elisha said. "Right now Taymen's waiting for you in the briefing room."

As they moved through the corridor Russ deliberately kept himself a few steps behind Elisha. For some reason he felt awkward around her.

When they walked into the briefing room Taymen and Sharr stood from their seats.

"Welcome back Russ." Taymen said. "Who are your friends?" He asked as he moved around the table towards the group.

"My sister Kaleigh and her husband Arthur Lewis." Russ said hesitantly.

Taymen greeted them both.

"Welcome aboard, I'm Colonel Taymen Orelle and this is Colonel Sharr Vaye." He said.

"Thanks for coming." Russ said quietly.

"Yes thank you." Kaleigh said.

Taymen smiled slightly.

"Don't thank us yet." He said as he moved back around the table to his seat. "We still have a lot of work to do. Please, sit down."

Taymen sat down at the head of the table with Sharr to his right. Russ sat down to his left with Kaleigh and Arthur next to him while Elisha sat to Sharr's right.

"From what we understand you found the last piece of the map the Tray are looking for correct?" Sharr asked.

Russ nodded.

"The map leads to something called the Star's Eye." He explained. "I'm not sure what it is though."

"We believe it's an ancient archive containing the knowledge of an ancient race that went extinct long before our people came along." Taymen said.

"The information the Tray could find in that archive could mean the end for all of us." Sharr said. "We have to find it before they do." She continued.

"Well we have the last bit of the map." Russ said.

"But it's only a small piece of a much larger whole." Taymen said.

"Yes but it's the last piece." Russ said.

"What does that have to do with anything?" Sharr asked.

Russ sighed before answering.

"The map pieces are in some sort of sequence." He explained. "Each one outlines only the next step leading to the next piece of the map and eventually the Star's Eye. Since we have the last piece of the map we have the last step, it should lead us directly to it."

"Wait a minute." Sharr said. "Why would the ancients setup the maps to be used like that?" She asked.

"My guess is that it's to allow you to find the Star's Eye from any point without having to find the entire map." Russ explained.

"From what I've learned these ancients wanted someone to find the Star's Eye, just not the Tray so they left clues on several planets. Each planet was meant to be a marker along the way to finding the Star's Eye so it didn't matter what planet you were from, that was the start of your journey to find it."

"So with this last piece we can find the Star's Eye?" Taymen asked.

Russ nodded.

Sharr turned to Taymen.

"You know what this means." She said.

Taymen nodded.

"I know." He said. "But I don't think it needs to come to that." He continued.

"What?" Elisha asked.

"We can't let the Tray find the Star's Eye no matter the cost." Taymen answered. "Now that we have the means to get their first logically we should take advantage of that." He said.

"But you never did like to be logical did you Taymen." Sharr said sarcastically.

Taymen smiled a little.

"There's a Tray fleet in this system and I'd rather not leave them here to learn what we already know about this map." He said.

"You can beat them can't you?" Kaleigh asked quietly.

"I won't lie to you." Taymen said. "We're outnumbered almost four to one here. The ships in orbit should be easy enough to destroy but they have a flagship just above the surface and it alone can outmatch both our ships."

"We need time to work out a battle plan." Sharr said.

"In the mean time." Taymen said. "It's too risky to send you back to your planet now. It's best that you stay aboard the Avenger. Elisha will show you to your quarters." He said as he stood from his seat.

Elisha led them out of the room and down the corridor to the ladder where they climbed up to the next deck.

Arthur and Kaleigh were in one of the larger cabins while Russ' was just down the corridor in one of the vacant junior officer cabins.

Russ opened the hatch and walked in with Elisha who closed the hatch behind them.

"So." She said awkwardly. "How have you been?"

Russ shrugged.

"Fine." He replied coldly.

Elisha nodded.

"How are your parents?" She asked after a long silence.

"Dead." He said.

Elisha suddenly felt even more awkward.

"I'm sorry Russ I didn't realize."

"No, you wouldn't would you." He snapped.

"What's that supposed to mean?" Elisha asked.

"You were so caught up in this little adventure of yours that you completely forgot about the people back home, our friends and families, everyone who died in the attack!" Russ was starting to yell.

"What did you want me to do Russ?" Elisha snapped back. "My family's been dead for years, you were the only thing I had in my life that meant anything." She said.

"Well I guess that wasn't enough for you then." Russ replied.

Elisha scoffed.

"You could have come with me." She argued. "But you chose to stay behind." Elisha suddenly realized she was trying to defend her actions for some reason.

"You could have stayed, this wasn't our fight!" Russ said.

"Not our fight! Have you seen what's going on Russ? The Tray are in control of Earth, weather I had stayed or not they still would have come. At least I'm trying to help stop them!"

Elisha was suddenly aware of the volume of her voice, but she didn't care.

"What the hell do you think I'm doing here!" Russ yelled, insulted at her implication. "I'm doing what I can to help get rid of the Tray. I'm sorry that it's not as grandiose as what you're doing but it's all I can do!"

Elisha took a few steps closer to Russ.

"What do you want me to say Russ, that I'm proud of you, well I am." Elisha took a moment to breath. "You want me to tell you that I've thought about you every day since I left Earth. That I sometimes wonder what it would be like if I was still with you, that I miss you and what we had."

"Maybe I would!" Russ snapped. "Maybe I want to know that you still think about me, maybe I regretted staying every day since you left and maybe I…" Russ was suddenly silenced by Elisha's lips pressing against his.

It was a feeling that he longed for forever it seemed.

He found himself unable to think. He could barely remember what they were fighting about. The only thing he knew was how good it felt to be able to hold her again.

He felt her hands running under his shirt and up his sides. As his hands ran up her back she began to force him back towards the bed.

A second later Russ fell onto the mattress with Elisha who quickly unzipped her uniform jacket and took it off.

Russ then lifted her shirt over her head and threw it to the floor beside them just before Elisha removed his shirt.

Russ' mind raced as he felt Elisha's heart pounding in her chest.

Everything about her was so familiar, so comforting and yet somehow it all felt so different from before.

Russ ran his hands up Elisha's arms before unhooking her bra, letting it slip from her shoulders.

As he looked at her in a way he had longed to see her again for almost a year something occurred to Russ. Something he didn't want to ask but something he had to know.

As she looked at him with her deep brown eyes he realized that it didn't matter. That after all that's happened to them in the last year she was still his and he was still hers.

Taymen sat at his desk reading over the tactical report from last night. They had been monitoring the Tray fleet since they arrived for any patterns in their patrols. They seemed to remain in a geosynchronous orbit around the planet and the flagship remained in the atmosphere.

Both he and Sharr were trying to work out a battle plan but each one ended the same way. They could destroy the fleet in orbit easily enough but by the time they did the flagship would be in a position to attack them and Taymen wasn't sure they could handle that.

They needed a way to take out the flagship first while its defenses were down.

He thought about having both ships make a straight run for the planet and try to get past the cruisers but it was far too risky.

Sword breakers were no match for it and any missiles they launched would likely be intercepted by the cruisers' gun batteries.

He was just about to give up when suddenly something occurred to him. It was completely reckless and he didn't even know if it was possible, but if it was they would be able to destroy the flagship before it could power up its engines.

Suddenly the sound of the door buzzer filled the room.

"Come in." Taymen said.

The hatch opened and Talia slowly walked in.

"Hey." She said quietly.

"Hey." Taymen replied as he stood up. "Come in."

Talia closed the hatch behind her while Taymen made his way over to the couch and offered her a seat before sitting down himself.

"Everything okay?" He asked.

Talia nodded.

"Yeah." She said. "I just couldn't sleep."

Taymen nodded.

"Missing home?" He asked.

Talia shrugged.

"Not really, just worried about it." She replied. "For the first time since it started I've realized just how real this whole thing is." She explained.

223

Taymen simply looked at her silently.

"I know it wouldn't make any sense to someone like you." She said.

"No." Taymen interrupted. "People don't realize what's going on around them until it's right in front of them. Three months aboard a battle ship going up against the Tray has no doubt made you aware of how serious this all is."

Talia nodded slightly.

"You and your crew, you have to deal with this every day. You're not blind to the horrible realities around us like everyone else. How do you do it?" She asked.

Taymen shrugged. He really didn't know how, he never thought about it he just did it.

"I really don't know." He said. "I guess most people simply think about what has to be done and figures that someone has to do it. We just realize if we don't do it who will?"

It was really the only answer Taymen could come up with.

Talia simply nodded a little. She knew what Taymen meant. She herself was guilty of thinking that someone should do something about one thing or another. She never until recently started thinking that maybe she should be the one to do something.

Suddenly the harsh buzz of the internal com. filled the room.

"All hands to battle stations." Avril said over the com. system.

"Excuse me." Taymen said as he stood up.

He rushed to C.A.C. where everyone was at their stations awaiting orders.

"Report." Taymen said.

"One of the light cruisers is on an intercept course." Avril reported.

"Any sign they've detected us?" Taymen asked.

"None yet Sir." Titus said.

"The cruiser received a transmission from the flagship and then set its course." Sairon added.

"Time till intercept?" Avril asked.

"Six minutes." Titus answered.

"Order the Phoenix to stream out one hour outside of the system and power up the stream system." Taymen ordered.

"Sir?" Avril said.

"I don't want them to know we're here yet." Taymen explained.

"Sir the cruiser has just streamed out." Titus reported.

Taymen checked the sensor display and saw the cruiser was gone.

"Belay my last." He said. "Maintain position and have Colonel Vaye meet me in the briefing room with her Ex O. Avril come with me." He said as he left C.A.C.

Taymen and Avril made their way through the corridor.

"Sir can I ask you something?" Avril asked.

"Of course." Taymen replied.

"I've been concerned with the way things have been going lately." Avril started. "We've been spreading our limited resources rather thin and the Tray seem to be everywhere now."

Taymen simply nodded.

"I assume there's a point to this." He said.

"Don't you think we're at a major disadvantage right now?" Avril asked.

"We've been at a disadvantage from the start Avril." Taymen replied.

"I know but now we could potentially secure a position that would allow us to regroup and rebuild our fleet for a counter attack."

Taymen knew what Avril was getting at. He had been thinking the same thing but he had to wonder if their people could afford for them to retreat now.

Dark Avenger, Briefing Room
12:30 Abydos Standard Time
Day 28, First Cycle, Egyptian Year 3202

"Are you crazy?" Sharr protested.

Taymen figured her reaction would be something like that.

"It's the only way we could make this work." He said. "A couple of nukes should destroy that flagship without significant damage to the planet."

"So fire them from orbit." Sharr said.

"The other cruisers will intercept them and you know it." Taymen replied.

"Sir we don't even know if this is possible." Avril pointed out.

"I think it is." Taymen said. "Unless someone here has a better plan." He continued as he looked at everyone sitting around the table.

Nobody said anything.

"What about the archive?" Sharr asked.

"What about it?" Taymen said.

"We have the location of the Star's Eye I think we should find it and get whatever we can out of it." Sharr replied.

Taymen sighed.

225

Sharr was right, they needed to get to the archive but they had to stop the Tray here as well. Either way somebody wasn't going to be happy.

"You're right Sharr." He finally said. "We need that archive but we need to stop the Tray here as well."

Sharr nodded.

"What are you suggesting Sir?" Avril asked.

"The Silver Phoenix will remain here and monitor the Tray. The Dark Avenger will proceed to the Star's Eye and destroy it if we have to."

"Are you sure we should split the two ships up?" Sharr asked.

"I don't want to leave the Tray here unchecked in case they find what they came here for and decide they no longer need this planet." Taymen replied.

"Alright." Sharr said. "We'll keep an eye on them for you then."

Taymen smiled.

"We'll stream out in the next hour and hopefully we'll be back in a few days." He said.

Tray Flagship in Earth's Atmosphere
13:00 Abydos Standard Time
Day 28, First Cycle, Egyptian Year 3202

Commander Soulin sat behind the desk in his quarters. His brown eyes skimmed the report in front of him as he ran his fingers through his short red hair.

His first officer stood in front of the desk waiting for him to say something.

"We still haven't found our missing archeologist yet?" He asked.

"I'm afraid not Sir, he was released during one of the work rotations, we haven't been able to locate him since." The young officer replied.

Soulin growled a little.

"Well I suppose it's of no consequence now we have what we need." He said. "Has a ship been dispatched yet?" He asked.

"Yes Sir one of the cruisers in orbit left an hour ago carrying the data to the outer relay station, it should be back tomorrow evening with orders from Fleet Marshal Ourik."

Soulin nodded.

"Very well, in the mean time we'll hold this planet as a field command base until we've secured the archive, you're dismissed." He said before the officer turned and left.

"All batteries fire at will!" Colonel Dravin ordered. "Ready all missile tubes for a full salvo on target two." He continued.

"Incoming ordnance!" Lieutenant Reyon called from the operations station.

The ship shuttered a few seconds later as two missiles impacted the outer hull.

"Fighters incoming!" His Ex O called.

"Launch all sword breakers to intercept!" Dravin ordered.

Releena stood at the command console watching as everything went on around her. She was in command of the Imperial Guard but she had no experience as a ship commander.

"Target two is closing in on us." Reyon said.

"All missile tubes fire!" Dravin ordered.

A few seconds later, twenty-four missiles sped towards the Tray cruiser.

"Sir two more cruisers have just streamed into the system." Reyon reported.

"Power up the stream system, get us out of here." Dravin ordered.

"Stream system is down Sir." The helm officer reported.

Dravin cursed.

Suddenly the ship shuttered again but it didn't feel like a missile impact.

"We're being boarded!" Reyon called.

"Have all marines report to defensive positions." Dravin said.

"No." Releena said.

Dravin turned to face her.

"Princess?" He asked.

"We're done here Colonel." She said.

"It's time to surrender."

Releena stood silent as Ourik entered the room with a very noticeable grin on his face. He was no doubt very pleased with himself after her recapture.

"Well Princess it would seem you've been busy since your escape." Ourik said smugly.

Releena noticed Ourik had a slight limp as he walked past.

"Why don't you cut the pretenses Fleet Marshal and just tell me what it is you want." Releena said.

"I want to know everything, the locations of your little resistance cells, any operations or counter attacks you've planned, names, locations, everything, and I want to know where Colonel Orelle is hiding." Ourik demanded.

Before Releena could answer, the door opened and General Assh was marched into the room.

"Princess!" He said in surprise.

"General." Releena replied.

"You're just in time General." Ourik said. "Your Princess has been busy and she was just about to tell me what I want to know." He continued.

Releena looked at Assh briefly and smiled.

"You must be more delusional than I thought." She said. "It's a shame that all those failures and defeats at the hands of Colonel Orelle hasn't taught you anything." She said smugly.

Ourik didn't seem impressed. The very mention of Taymen's name seemed to infuriate him.

"You know I'm not going to tell you anything and even if I did it wouldn't matter. The damage is done, I've set something in motion that you can't stop now. Sooner or later Colonel Orelle will lead an offensive against you and your reign here will end." Releena continued.

Assh stood silent just behind her while Ourik simply smiled.

"Well then." He finally said. "If that's the case then I see no point in keeping you with us any longer."

Suddenly, before anyone could react Ourik had drawn his side arm and fired. The round flew across the room and buried itself in Releena's chest before the sound could travel to Assh's ears.

"No!" Assh cried, moving to catch Releena as she fell backwards.

He sat on the floor with Releena in his lap. Her blood stained his hands and clothes.

"Princess." He said as he tried to keep her awake.

Releena looked up at Assh. The life slowly drained from her blue eyes.

"I'm sorry General." She said in a weak voice.

Assh moved closer to hear her. His ear was right next to her as she spoke softly to him.

Assh nodded slightly indicating that he heard her as tears welled up in his eyes.

"You've done well." He said. "You're father would be proud of you Princess, we all are." He continued.

Releena smiled slightly as her eyelids grew heavier until they finally closed over her eyes.

Assh didn't have to check to know she was dead.

"May the gods guide you home Princess." He whispered.

"How touching." Ourik said.

Assh's gaze suddenly turned to a deathly stare.

Ourik backed off a pace and trained his weapon on Assh who gently set Releena's lifeless body on the floor and stood up.

"Now General." Ourik said. "Let's discuss your future with us."

Suddenly Assh charged across the room at Ourik who instinctively fired.

The round struck just on the outside of Assh's left arm but he was so enraged he didn't even notice as he slammed Ourik into the wall knocking the weapon from his hand. An instant later his hands were around Ourik's throat choking the life out of him.

Suddenly Assh felt a sharp pain in the back of his neck and found himself on the floor.

Ourik gasped for a moment as he regained his footing and the guards hauled Assh to his feet.

"Get him back to his cell, I'll figure out what to do with him later." Ourik said.

"And dispose of her."

Chapter Twenty-Two

Taymen entered C.A.C. with Talia close behind.

"Captain on deck!" Titus called.

"Carry on." Taymen said.

Russ, Arthur and Kaleigh all stood around the command console with Avril.

Taymen wasn't used to having so many civilians on his ship but he wasn't entirely sure what he should do with them. He figured it was best to keep them close by for now however.

His crew knew what to do if something happened but they understandably didn't so he decided to keep an eye on them himself.

"Report." Taymen said.

"We're ready to stream out at your command Sir." Avril reported.

"Sairon patch me through to the Silver Phoenix." Taymen said as he tapped the control on his earpiece.

"Go ahead Sir."

"Orelle to Colonel Vaye." Taymen said. "We're ready to stream out, keep an eye on the Tray while we're gone."

"Roger that." Sharr replied. *"Good luck Colonel."*

Taymen closed the channel and turned to Aurin at the helm.

"Commander, stream us out." He ordered.

"Aye Sir." Aurin said as he turned to the stream officer.

"Set coordinates and power up the stream system." He said.

"Aye Sir stream system powering." The stream officer replied. "Streaming in five...four...three...two... one, streaming." He said.

Russ suddenly felt sick to his stomach for a moment as he grabbed the edge of the command console to keep his balance.

Kaleigh fell back a step into Arthur who almost lost his own balance.

"Stream complete Sir." The stream officer reported a moment later.

"That's it?" Kaleigh said in disbelief.

Avril smiled slightly.

"That's it." She said.

"Well that took no time at all." Arthur said.

"Actually about fourteen hours have passed." Avril explained.

Suddenly something appeared on the sensor display.

"Sensor contact!" Titus called. "Ten Tray fighters inbound." He continued.

"Launch the alert fighters!" Taymen snapped.

As he looked at the main sensor display something didn't seem right. They could see the fighters but there was something else there that they couldn't get a clear reading on. A second later something occurred to Taymen.

"Deploy armor and ready all heavy batteries!" He ordered.

"Incoming ordnance!" Avril called a second later.

"Brace yourselves." Taymen said just as the ship shuttered with the impact of two Tray missiles.

"Batteries report ready Sir." Titus reported.

"Helm bring us about all ahead full." Taymen ordered.

"All ahead full aye Sir." Aurin said.

"Order our sword breakers to defend our aft quarter and launch sensor drones." Taymen continued.

Nobody was exactly sure what Taymen was doing but they all trusted him enough to carry out his orders without question.

Taymen knew that those missiles had to come from somewhere and it wasn't the fighters firing them, he had to find out what was.

"Drones away Sir." Elisha reported.

"Have them maintain a position five light seconds off of our bow." He said.

"More Tray fighters have appeared on sensors." Titus reported.

"Launch remaining sword breakers." Avril said.

"Ready all remaining batteries, have them prepare for enemy suppression fire." Taymen ordered.

"Drones in position." Elisha reported.

"Switch us to passive sensors." Taymen said.

The passive sensors made it impossible for the Avenger to detect anything that wasn't giving off a significant power signature or its own sensor signal, but it also made it harder for them to be detected by the Tray.

"Contact, Tray light cruiser dead ahead." Titus reported a moment later.

"Why couldn't we see it before?" Avril snapped.

"They're behind something that's blocking our sensors." Taymen said. "Heavy batteries fire at will!" He ordered.

A second later six heavy plasma rounds erupted from the Dark Avenger and charged towards the cruiser.

Since the rounds were unguided they would be harder for the Tray sensors to pick up and they couldn't intercept them before they struck the hull.

The rounds exploded into a focused stream of super charged plasma that burned through the outer hull and tore through nearly half the ship. As the first set of rounds detonated the second salvo fired.

Since these rounds were heavier than the ones used in the Avenger's valkerie cannons it took longer for the system to reload between salvos.

"Ready saber missiles, tubes one through four." Taymen said.

"Ready Sir." The weapons officer reported a few seconds later.

"Fire!"

Suddenly four missiles sped towards the cruiser and detonated against the hull just after the second salvo of heavy rounds.

The cruiser drifted lifelessly for a moment before it finally exploded.

"Sir the remaining Tray fighters have streamed out." Titus reported.

"Damn it." Avril said. "They know we're here now." She snapped.

"We have to hurry." Taymen started. "Recall the sword breakers and bring us to stealth mode." He continued. "Dispatch the sensor drones in a ten light second perimeter, have them use passive sensors only."

"Aye Sir." Elisha replied.

"How did you know the cruiser was out there Sir?" Avril asked.

"You saw that distortion that was blocking our sensors?" Taymen asked.

Avril nodded.

"If I couldn't see through something it would be the first place I would hide in case someone showed up looking for me." He explained. "That distortion is probably our archive in some sort of stealth mode."

"Helm all stop." Taymen ordered.

"All stop aye Sir." Aurin replied.

"Now, what's out there?" Avril asked.

"Good question." Taymen said. "Titus, anything?" He asked.

Titus accessed the sensor system using his implant but was unable to see anything.

Taymen and Avril did the same after a moment trying to see what was outside of the ship.

As they placed their hands on the console and logged into the sensor system they were suddenly able to see outside of the ship.

It was as if they were looking through the Avenger's eyes, seeing everything that it saw as a ghost image that overlaid anything they saw with their own eyes.

When he focused his eyes correctly Taymen could see the ghost image clearly and just allowed what he was seeing fade into a blur in the background. As he looked around he could see the stars in the distance but nothing else.

As he continued to search there was a large area of space that seemed to stand out from the rest. He could still see the stars through it but it was as if he were looking at them through a slightly curved lens. Taymen could just make out the edges of the object through the distortions as he tried to look through them.

"There's something there but we can't see it." Titus said.

"Switch us to active sensors for a moment." Taymen ordered.

After a few seconds the object went from transparent to a massive distortion. Now instead of looking through a glass lens it was like the object was shrouded in smoke.

It still prevented Taymen from seeing what it was however. He disconnected from the sensor system and turned to the main display at the head of C.A.C.

"Titus switch us back to passive sensors and bring the external camera online, patch it through to the main display." He said.

The display screen flickered from the sensor displays to a real time image of a massive station like structure that dwarfed the Avenger.

It was a massive thin spire with a bulged section in the middle. Surrounding the spire was a series of six oval shaped domes that were each connected by two small tunnel like structures.

"My gods." Titus said as he stared at the screen.

"Hail them." Taymen said.

Sairon sent a general signal to the station on all known communication channels but didn't get a response.

"Nothing Sir." She reported a moment later.

"Helm move us in closer, dead slow." Taymen said.

"Aye Sir." Aurin replied.

"Sir I think I found a docking port." Titus said.

"Can you initiate docking?" Avril asked.

Titus checked his console for a moment.

"I think I've connected to an automated docking system." He said. "It's giving us docking instructions."

Taymen looked at Avril who simply shrugged.

"Alright, take us in for docking." He finally said. "In the future Titus you may want to consult me before connecting to an unknown computer system" He continued.

"Sorry Sir." Titus said.

He wasn't sure why he didn't check with Taymen first he knew better than that. It must have been the fatigue starting to take hold of him. The entire crew was starting to feel it in one way or another with everything that's happened in the last year. It really wasn't an excuse but it was understandable why it was happening.

Taymen watched the main display as the station slowly drew closer.

There were several docking ports around the bulged section to choose from. Aurin ordered the maneuvering officer to dock at one of the ones closer to the center.

"We're in position for final approach." The maneuvering officer reported.

"All ahead, docking speed." Aurin said.

"Contact in fifteen seconds." The maneuvering officer said.

"Cut thrusters, let the inertia take us in." Aurin ordered.

"Thrusters off." The officer said.

A few seconds later the Avenger gently contacted the docking port and the magnetic docking clamps energized locking the ship in position.

"We have hard-lock Sir." Aurin reported.

"Pressurize the airlock and have three marine fire teams meet me there." Taymen ordered.

"Titus, Russ, you're with me."

"Me?" Russ asked.

"The fact that you're from Earth aside you are the only historian onboard." Taymen explained. "You know more about this facility than any of us."

"But I really don't know that much." Russ said.

"Hence how little the rest of us know about it." Taymen replied.

Russ didn't argue the point any further. He was actually a little curious to see what they would find on the station anyways.

"Avril you have command." Taymen said after a moment.

"Aye Sir." Avril replied.

As the three of them made their way towards the airlock Titus began to speak.

"Sir." He said quietly.

"What is it?" Taymen replied.

"About what happened earlier, with the computer system…."

Taymen cut him off. He already knew what he was going to say.

"Don't worry about it Titus." He started. "I know everyone is feeling the pressure and mistakes are bound to be made. Let's just be glad that this time it was a mistake we can get away with."

Titus nodded as Russ remained silent behind them.

"We don't have the luxury of learning from our mistakes in this job." Taymen continued. "If we screw up people die, especially now. I know that only adds to the pressure but it's a reality we all have to face."

Silver Phoenix at Earth
07:40 Abydos Standard Time
Day 29, First Cycle, Egyptian Year 3202

Sharr rushed into C.A.C. and moved to the command console as she hooked a few strands of her dark hair behind her right ear as she focused her brown eyes on the sensor display.

"Report." She said.

"A Tray battle group has just streamed into the system, two heavy cruisers are on an intercept course and the rest are on course for Earth." Lieutenant-Commander Rian reported from the operations station.

"Looks like they've detected us." Captain Tae, her Ex O added.

Sharr watched for a moment as the two cruisers closed in on them, her expression remaining emotionless as she ran the scenarios in her head.

Sharr naturally had a gentle look to her but she could be as cold and unforgiving as space itself when she was provoked into a fight.

"Bring the ship to battle mode." She ordered. "Helm, all ahead full."

"All ahead full aye Ma'am." The helmsman replied.

"All stations report battle mode Ma'am." Rian reported a moment later.

"Batteries one through fifteen lock onto target one, sixteen through twenty on target two. Load missile tubes one through eight with javelin anti-ship missiles and prepare to fire." Sharr said.

"Ready." The weapons officer reported.

Sharr watched as the Tray cruisers moved closer.

"Cruisers are painting us." Rian reported.

"Tubes one through four on target one, five through eight on target two." Sharr said.

She waited a moment for the cruisers to move a little closer.

"Launch javelins!" She ordered.

Almost instantly eight javelin missiles flew through space towards their respective targets.

The cruisers opened fire destroying three of the incoming missiles and the rest impacted the two ships' outer hull and detonated.

"All batteries fire at will!" Sharr ordered a second later as the Silver Phoenix moved into range.

In an instant all three ships had opened fire sending missiles and long range rounds across the void between them.

"Incoming ordnance!" Rian called.

The ship shuttered a little with the impact.

"Batteries eight through twelve switch to suppression fire." Sharr ordered. "Helm maneuver us between both cruisers all ahead full." She continued.

"Aye Ma'am." The helm officer said.

"All tubes ready saber missiles, starboard tubes on target one, port tubes on target two." Sharr continued.

Tae knew exactly what Sharr was planning and he didn't like. She was known for being bold in combat. She's been called reckless on more than one occasion but it didn't bother her.

The ship shuttered and more ordnance impacted along her hull as they continued to move closer.

The two cruisers began to decelerate as the Phoenix charged them at full speed.

After only a moment the Phoenix was beginning to move between them just as Sharr wanted.

"Helm slow to one third." She said. "All batteries switch to direct fire, starboard on target one, port on target two!"

Almost instantly ten valkerie batteries on each side of the ship fired plasma rounds directly on both targets destroying most of their gun batteries and tearing through the outer hull armor and into the inner decks.

Only a few batteries on each cruiser continued to fire on the Phoenix but since their rounds required a certain amount of time to develop enough force to do any damage, the Phoenix was too close for them to penetrate her armor.

Sharr watched the display until both cruisers were parallel with the ship's hull.

"Fire sabers!" She snapped.

Suddenly sixteen missiles launched from both sides of the Phoenix and detonated against the cruisers before they could intercept them.

"Helm all ahead full." Sharr ordered.

As a series of secondary explosions began to tear the cruisers apart the Phoenix accelerated away and both cruisers finally detonated into a large blast wave that enveloped the aft quarter of the ship for a few seconds before she managed to pull away.

"Both cruisers have been destroyed." Tae reported.

"Several ships from the battle group are changing course and are heading right for us, they'll be here in ten minutes."

"Bring the ship to stealth mode." Sharr said.

"Send a message to the Dark Avenger, advise them the Tray are rallying additional ships and that we've been compromised but are executing evasion maneuvers.

"Helm set a course for the seventh planet, keep us on the night side to avoid detection and prepare to stream out." She continued.

The Star's Eye
18:27 Abydos Standard Time
Day 29, First Cycle, Egyptian Year 3202

Taymen slowly moved through the dark corridor with two teams of marines.

Titus was off to his left with Russ and the third team of marines was about ten meters ahead of them all.

The lights throughout the station had been coming on automatically as they moved through the corridors. It was as if it was sensing their presence and waking up from a long slumber.

There was nobody on the station to speak of yet but the entire structure was massive. There were several markings on the bulkheads.

Russ recognized some of the symbols but the translations for them didn't make any sense to him.

Titus and Taymen recognized them as an ancient dialect of their written language. Some of the markings indicated the location of the central control room.

The interior of the station reminded Taymen of the station where they met Jassen and the other survivors. It was very spacious inside and the entire station looked like it was very well preserved.

"Sir." One of the marines called.

Taymen moved forward towards a set of large pressure doors.

"What is it Sergeant?" Taymen asked.

"I think this is it." The Sergeant replied.

Taymen looked at the markings on the door. Roughly translated they meant control room.

"Alright fan out." Taymen said. "Teams one and two set up a defensive perimeter here, team three let's get these doors open."

As the marines tried to pry the doors open to no avail Titus looked around for anything that might be a control panel.

Russ continued to try and read the markings on the walls. He had managed to learn a few of the symbols from Titus and was able to translate the rest based on those but it took him some time to do so.

As he looked around Russ noticed something familiar on the wall next to the doors. A small shiny black panel mounted into the wall like the ones near the hatches on the Avenger.

"What's that?" Russ asked as he pointed at the panel.

"It looks like an NDI interface." Titus said.

Taymen moved to the panel and placed his right hand flat against it. He used his implant and tried to access the system. It was slow to respond to him at first, like the system was still booting up. He focused on locating the door controls and found a security program.

Taymen thought for a moment. The program was asking for his identification. Obviously it wouldn't recognize him so he would have to try and bypass it.

After several unsuccessful tries Taymen was growing impatient. He figured he had nothing else to lose by trying. He input his name and rank into the program input and waited. After only a few seconds the program deactivated and another one took its place.

"*That's odd.*" He thought to himself.

As he looked over the new program it asked him to identify his home world.

"What in the name of Anubis?" He asked.

"Sir?" Titus asked.

"There's a security program asking for my identification."

"Not surprising." Russ said.

"But it accepted my identification." Taymen explained.

"What?" Titus asked.

"I put in my name and it let me through the first login." Taymen said.

"How would the system know who you are?" Russ asked.

"I don't know." Taymen said. "But now it's asking for my home world."

Taymen thought it was a little strange as he entered Abydos. The system rejected it right away.

Abydos was the home planet of his people but he couldn't expect this system to recognize it by the name they had given it.

Next Taymen tried to input the spatial coordinates of Abydos in relation to the current projected center of the universe but the system rejected that as well. Frustrated Taymen disconnected from the system.

"Nothing." He said.

"I can't get past the second lockout. It won't accept Abydos by name or by coordinates." He explained.

"You used the coordinates in relation to the center of the universe?" Titus asked.

Taymen nodded.

Everyone remained silent for a few moments until something occurred to Russ.

"Wait a second." He said. "How old is this station?" He asked.

Titus shrugged. "I don't know, why?" He said.

"What if the coordinates of your planet are different now than when they were input into the station's computer."

Taymen realized what he was saying.

"Because of stellar drift." He said.

"Right." Russ said. "You need to calculate the coordinates of your home world when this place was built." He explained.

"Well." Titus started. "We know that the ancients died out roughly ten thousand years ago." He said.

"Okay now who can calculate the coordinates of Abydos ten thousand years ago?" Taymen asked.

There was another few minutes of silence before Russ spoke.

"Arthur could do it." He said. "He's got a degree in astro-physics I'm sure he could do it."

Taymen hit the control on his earpiece.

"Sairon is Arthur still in C.A.C.?" He asked.

"Yes Sir." Sairon answered after a moment.

"Put me on speaker." Taymen said.

"Go ahead Sir."

"Arthur can you hear me?" He asked.

"Yes." Arthur said hesitantly.

"We need you to do something for us." Taymen explained. "We need you to calculate the coordinates of our home world in relation to the center of the universe ten thousand years ago based on the current coordinates and the rate of stellar drift."

There was a long pause before Arthur spoke again.

"That's going to take me some time." He said.

"We need it as soon as possible Arthur." Taymen said.

"Okay I'll get started." Arthur said before Taymen closed the channel.

Arthur turned to Avril who handed him a data pad.

"These are the current coordinates of Abydos." She said.

Arthur took the pad and looked over the coordinates.

"You don't happen to have the coordinates from a hundred years ago or so do you?" He asked.

"We do but we're not sure how accurate they are, space mapping was fairly primitive back then." Avril answered.

"Why do you need them?" Kaleigh asked.

"I need to know which direction the planet is drifting in and the rate of drift to calculate the coordinates." Arthur replied.

"Aurin go through the navigational database and pull up the earliest coordinates for Abydos on record." Avril said.

"You have that kind of information onboard?" Talia asked.

"The navigational computer needs the same information to calculate protostream events accurately." Avril explained.

"Got it Ma'am." Aurin said a moment later.

Avril checked Aurin's console and entered the coordinates on Arthur's data pad.

"There." She said.

Arthur looked over the numbers again and continued with his calculations.

"Ma'am." Sairon said from the communications station. "We've just picked up a message from the Silver Phoenix. Signal lag is almost twelve hours." She reported.

"What's it say?" Avril asked.

"They say that a Tray battle group has arrived in the Earth solar system, they engaged and destroyed two cruisers but their position has been compromised. They're beginning evasion maneuvers but may need to stream out of the system for a while."

Avril nodded.

"Okay I think that's it." Arthur said.

Avril checked over the data pad. She wasn't an expert but it seemed right to her.

"Sairon put me through to the Colonel." She said.

"Go ahead."

"Colonel we have the corrected coordinates I'm relaying them to your com. unit." Avril said as she connected the data pad wirelessly to the communications system and waited for Taymen's order.

"Stand by." Taymen said as he placed his hand back on the interface and accessed the system again.

He quickly got passed the first lock out and waited for the second one to come up. When he saw the request for his home planet he hit the control on his ear piece.

"Alright Avril." He said. "Relay the coordinates through my com. unit to my implant."

After a few seconds the download was complete and the coordinates were stored in his implant's temporary memory.

Taymen accessed the data and entered the coordinates into the security program. After a few seconds the program accepted the input and the doors opened. Taymen disconnected from the system and backed off a few steps.

"There's one other thing Sir." Avril said.

"What is it?" Taymen asked.

"We've received a message from the Silver Phoenix. The Tray have moved additional ships into the Earth system and they were engaged."

Taymen nodded.

"Understood." He said before closing the channel.

Taymen and the others moved into the command center as the lights slowly came on one at a time illuminating the large room.

The main doors seemed to be the only way in or out. The bulkheads were all lined with a series of control consoles and monitors but the rest of the room was empty except for a small table in the center.

Titus moved to one of the active consoles and looked it over. It was a schematic of the entire station.

"Sir look at this." He said.

As Taymen began to move towards the console he heard a voice from behind him.

"There's nothing of interest to you there." The voice said.

Taymen and the others whipped around to see an old man standing near the door.

In seconds all the marines had their weapons trained on him as he simply stood and watched them unflinchingly.

The man looked very old. His hair was gone except for a white beard. His eyes were a piercing blue and his clothes were simple but well kept.

As Taymen looked closer he realized he could see the marines behind him. It was as if it were a ghost standing in front of him.

"Stand down." Taymen said.

Hesitantly the marines lowered their rifles but remained ready to react.

"Who are you?" Taymen asked.

"I am a holographic representation of this facility's core artificial intelligence which was programmed to emulate its designer." The man spoke very clearly and very precisely, it really was like speaking with a computer.

"What do you want?" Taymen asked.

The man smiled slightly.

"To help you Colonel Orelle." He replied.

Taymen looked at Russ and Titus who simply shrugged.

"How do you know me?" He asked.

"I accessed your ship's computer database, why do you think the door computer recognized your name and rank? I know all about you Colonel." The man replied.

"Alright then." Taymen said. "You said you wanted to help us, why?"

The man took a few paces forward.

"This facility was built over ten thousand years ago in an effort to preserve our people's knowledge for the next generation." He began.

"Why?" Titus asked.

"Approximately twelve thousand years ago based on your planet's annual cycle we were exploring the last corners of the galaxy. It was there we discovered a young but promising race. They had just discovered interstellar travel and were eager to learn everything we could teach them.

"We taught them to use the protostream technology and gave them the means to defend themselves. We were so arrogant in thinking we could interfere with a cultures natural development without any serious consequence.

"One thousand years had passed and our arrogance caught up with us, for that very race we had launched into the stars launched further than we ever thought possible in so little time.

"They had expanded their territory into a vast empire enveloping every race in their path either destroying them or integrating them into their empire. It wasn't long before this galactic dominion, which evolved to call themselves the Tray made it to our galaxy.

"They attacked us without warning and we were drawn into a war that lasted over five generations ending in our defeat."

Taymen realized this was starting to make sense.

"How could they beat you, you gave them the technology they used against you." He said.

"It is true that the Tray have always been technologically inferior to us but their vast numbers soon turned the tide in their favor. During the last years of the war we could see our defeat and realized that we weren't going to stop the Tray.

"We sent the last of our ships on their final mission to seed several small planets throughout the universe with human life in the hopes that some of them would develop safe from the Tray and would eventually be able to defeat them.

"Our last ship was on its way to their assigned world when they found a small backwater planet and a race of humans that impressed them. They were still primitive but very advanced for their time. They abducted a small group of these people and relocated them to a planet in another galaxy hiding them from the Tray.

"It was their hope that with the information they left behind on the planet with them these people would be one of the races to develop into a formidable foe for the Tray and it would seem that you have."

Taymen sighed.

"So you seeded our planet hoping we would develop into a living weapon that was capable of cleaning up your mess." He said.

"It was not a burden we would wish anyone to bear but the Tray must be stopped." The man said. "They are arrogant and careless, the information they would gain from us would be disastrous."

The man sighed.

"There are things in this universe that should not be discovered by those who aren't ready for them." He said.

"What makes you think we're ready for them?" Taymen asked.

The man simply smiled.

"You are the second evolution of our race, the children of humanity who have evolved so far beyond our original expectations. You may not be ready for all the universe has to offer but you are wise enough to realize that."

There was a brief silence.

"On that console you will find a storage device, it contains a complete copy of this facility's database including all tactical data on the Tray as well as several designs that may be integrated into your ship. It is our hope that your people do not make the same mistakes ours did."

Titus walked over to the console the man pointed to and picked up a small device. It was a little bigger than the palm of his hand with a dark case and a port where it was plugged into the console.

"This?" He asked.

The man nodded.

"It is under your care now. Do not allow the Tray to find it, if they do…" The man suddenly stopped.

"The Tray are here." He said.

"Raquel to Colonel Orelle." Avril said over the com. unit.

Taymen hit the control.

"Go ahead Captain." He said.

"A Tray battle group has just streamed into the system, they're closing in on the station." She said.

"Stand by."

"You must destroy this facility." The man said.

"What?" Titus asked.

"The Tray cannot be allowed to set foot here and you cannot hold them off forever." The man said.

"How can we destroy it?" Taymen asked.

"I've gone through your ship's weapons inventory. Your nuclear weapons are not powerful enough to completely destroy the database and there is no self destruct. However your ship carries a type of missile similar to the singularity bombs used by our people, they should be sufficient."

Taymen nodded.

"You have what you need Colonel now go." The man said.

"Back to the ship." Taymen ordered.

Everyone began to move out of the room when the man suddenly spoke again.

"Colonel." He said. "Remember, you are humanity's children. You inherited our legacy and our knowledge, but with it comes a great responsibility, a responsibility the Tray chose to ignore. Do not let your people do the same thing."

"I understand." Taymen said.

"And remember Colonel." The man continued. "Some things in this universe are better left undiscovered."

Taymen nodded before he turned and took off down the corridor.

When they got back to C.A.C. the Tray were almost right on top of them.

"Have they found us yet?" Taymen asked.

"I don't think so, they're probably too fixated on the station." Avril said.

"Helm get us clear. Titus bring us to stealth mode." Taymen ordered.

"Carrey arm one of the zero point missiles and prepare to launch it at the station."

Avril's eyes widened.

"Sir." She protested.

"We have the information we need. I'm not going to let the Tray get their hands on this facility." Taymen explained.

The Avenger slowly pulled away from the station as the Tray continued to move closer.

"We're clear Sir." Aurin reported.

"All ahead full prepare to stream us back to the Earth solar system." Taymen said.

"Sir." Avril started. "The Tray have committed significant resources and time searching for all the map pieces to locate this archive."

Taymen nodded.

"Yes." He said.

"Now we got here first by following them to Earth." Avril continued.

"Yes." Taymen replied.

"And now they think they finally have it and we're about to announce the Avenger's survival to the Tray by destroying it right in front of them." Avril said.

"Yes." Taymen repeated.

"I'm guessing that they're going to be very angry about that and they'll probably have every ship in both galaxies looking for us."

Taymen nodded again.

"I hope so Captain." He said.

Avril nodded and smiled a little.

"Alright then." She said.

"Stream system ready Sir." Aurin reported.

"Missile ready." Carrey said.

"I think we've been detected, two cruisers are closing in on us." Titus reported.

Taymen checked the display briefly.

"Carrey launch zero point missile." He ordered.

"Aye Sir." Carrey said.

A second later the outer door of one of the missile silos near the bow of the ship retracted open and the large missile inside launched out into open space. Once it was clear of the hull the engine ignited and the missile sped towards its target.

"Impact in twelve seconds." Titus reported.

"Helm stream us out." Taymen said.

A second later the ship's hull began to glow just before it erupted into a bolt of dark lightning and disappeared.

A few seconds later the missile detonated enveloping the entire area in a massive tear in space.

The station and all the ships around it were torn apart and vaporized in a wave of intense energy and light before everything faded back into darkness leaving nothing, not even debris.

Chapter Twenty-Three

"Sensor contact." Rian reported.

"Identify." Sharr snapped.

A few seconds past before Rian got a positive identification.

"It's the Dark Avenger." He said.

"Patch me through to them." Sharr ordered as she tapped the control on her earpiece.

"Go ahead Ma'am." The communications officer said.

"Dark Avenger this is Colonel Vaye." She said. "Welcome back."

"Thanks Sharr." Taymen replied. *"Meet me in the Avenger briefing room in one hour, we have some things to discuss."* He continued.

"Understood." Sharr replied before closing the channel.

Dark Avenger Briefing Room
08:30 Abydos Standard Time
Day 30, First Cycle, Egyptian Year 3202

Taymen sat at the head of the table with Titus and Avril to either side.

Next to Titus sat Sharr and Captain Tae sat next to her.

"What do you mean you destroyed it?" Tae asked.

"The Tray found it shortly after we did, there was no other choice." Taymen said.

"However we obtained a data storage device containing a significant amount of tactical and historical data." Titus added.

"We've spent the last hour going over it trying to find anything pertinent. Titus your report please." Taymen said.

Titus stood up and walked over to a large screen on the wall.

"As the Colonel said we've been going over the files in the device for an hour and have barely even begun to scratch the surface." He started. "Some of the files contain scientific data on a variety of natural and unnatural phenomena as well as technical specifications for things we can't even identify. If any of this falls into Tray hands it would mean the end for anyone who tried to resist them."

Titus paused for a moment.

"The most significant thing we found was a file referencing something called the hyper-stream."

"What in the name of Anubis is that?" Tae asked.

Titus hit a few controls on the screen behind him and pulled up a diagram of a protostream hub.

"We all know that proto-space exists beneath normal space on the subatomic level. The hubs are designed to transfer matter into energy and back again as well as transmit the energy through proto-space to the next hub in the series."

Titus looked around to make sure everyone was still following him.

"Apparently the ancients discovered another way to utilize the hubs." He continued. "They managed to modify them to create a series of artificial wormholes in subspace. These wormholes somehow accelerate an object to speeds that are impossible to achieve in normal space."

"What kind of speeds are we talking about here?" Sharr asked.

"Initial calculations show that a ship could theoretically make the trip between Earth and Abydos in a little more than two weeks."

Titus saw the expressions of disbelief on everyone's face.

"That can't be right." Tae said.

"We've checked the numbers six times." Taymen replied.

"We could cross the void between our two galaxies in less than a month without having to modify our stream system." Titus continued. "It's a simple computer algorithm that we would install into the system. It instructs the hub to open a rift in normal space and proto-space that will allow the ship to enter the wormhole."

"Wait a second." Tae interrupted. "We don't even know if that aspect of the hub network is still working or if the wormholes still exist." He pointed out.

"I think they do." Titus said.

"How can you be sure?" Sharr asked.

"During the initial Tray attack we attempted to stream away from Netara to avoid a nuclear missile, only instead of streaming to the Netara evacuation point we ended up here, in the White Spiral Galaxy." Titus explained.

"We thought that the Tray missile detonated and overloaded the hub exactly as it was transmitting us to the next hub causing it to send us much farther than we thought possible. Now however I believe that the excess energy created by the nuclear detonation was enough to force open a rift into a wormhole that brought us here."

"Thank you Titus." Taymen said.

"There are a few other things that we found in the device. We have a complete map of every protostream hub throughout the universe as well as the entire hyper-stream network. But probably the most important thing we found is the location of the Tray home world." He continued.

Everyone around the table remained silent.

"We have a major advantage over the Tray now." Taymen started again. "We can stream anywhere in a fraction of the time and now we can strike the Tray in the heart of their territory. What we have to do now is decide how to utilize this knowledge."

Taymen looked at everyone around the table.

"I think we should do just what you said Sir." Avril said. "Hit the Tray in the heart, destroy their home world." She continued.

Sharr shook her head.

"I don't think that's a good idea. Who knows how many galaxies they control. If we destroy their home world they'll simply gather a larger force for a massive offensive and we don't have the ships to fight a full out war against them right now even with this new information."

Taymen nodded.

"I agree." He said.

"I think we have to prepare for the fact that we may never fully defeat the Tray and settle for simply driving them back to their own galaxy." Sharr added.

"However in the short run we have an occupied planet to liberate as well as our entire galaxy to purge." Titus pointed out.

"Yes." Taymen said.

He had been considering something for some time now, something he really didn't want to resort to.

"Clear the room." He said. "Sharr, you stay." He added as everyone stood up to leave.

Once they were all gone Sharr moved closer to Taymen at the head of the table.

"I know that look Taymen." She said with a sigh. "I'm not going to like this am I?"

Taymen shook his head.

"Even with Eazak's fleet we don't have the resources to retake our galaxy right now." He started. "We need our ships back and we can't continue to hide from the Tray in space that they control."

Sharr nodded.

"I know." She replied. "I've been thinking the same thing."

Taymen's expression remained blank.

"I think we should consider the option of retreating back to this line." He said. "We can operate out of this system until we can retake enough ships and rearm them for an effective counter attack. With the discovery of the hyper-stream it's a much more feasible option now."

Sharr knew he was right. There was no way they could take back their entire galaxy right now. She had come to grips with the reality that this war may not be over in her lifetime, but still it somehow felt like they were abandoning their home and their people for a more defendable position.

"You're right." She finally said.

Taymen nodded.

"Alright then." He said. "First things first, we have to liberate Earth."

"Do you still want to go through with that insane plan of yours?" Sharr asked.

Taymen smiled. He had briefed Sharr on his plan earlier. She of course thought it was insane which was quite the statement coming from Sharr, but it could work.

"Unless you managed to come up with something better." Taymen replied.

Sharr simply shook her head.

"Then yes." He said. "We have to take out that flagship before they know we're there. If they see us coming the fleet in orbit will intercept us and the flagship will launch before we can get a shot off." Taymen explained.

"I know." Sharr said. "But there are two more heavy cruisers in orbit now."

"We can handle them." Taymen said.

"And you know that if the flagship escapes it'll be back with more ships. We'll never retake Earth if that happens." Sharr pointed out.

"That's why we can't let it escape." Taymen replied.

"What about the Tray ground troops?" Sharr asked.

"We'll deploy all the marines from both ships to take key installations." Taymen started. "Once the Tray start losing ground they'll retreat."

Sharr seemed somewhat skeptical.

"We only have about four hundred marines between the two ships, do you really think that's going to be enough to pull this off?" Sharr asked. "Even with the flagship gone the cruisers can simply land more troops." She continued.

"That's why once we take out the flagship we have to move into position to intercept any landing craft the Tray may launch."

Sharr shook her head.

"We can't defend the entire planet with two ships when the Tray are so close." She said.

"We don't have to." Taymen started. "Your sword breakers are going to move into the upper atmosphere and target any incoming Tray landing craft. The Avenger's sword breakers will remain aboard in case the Tray launch their own fighters."

"I also have fifteen stealth assault fighters aboard." Sharr said. "They can carry saber missiles into close range undetected. They could take out a couple of the light cruisers for us."

Taymen nodded.

"Okay then, we launch in two hours." He said.

Dark Avenger C.A.C.
10:50 Abydos Standard Time
Day 30, First Cycle, Egyptian Year 3202

Taymen stood at the command console in C.A.C. Everyone was at battle stations and the ship was in stealth mode.

Russ, Arthur and Kaleigh all stood on the other side of the command console out of the way.

Taymen wanted them to stay behind in a prowler but they insisted on being there, it was there planet after all.

They knew they couldn't really do anything to help but they still wanted to be there and Taymen couldn't bring himself to refuse.

Suddenly the hatch to C.A.C. opened and Talia walked in.

"What are you doing here?" Taymen asked.

"I don't really have anywhere else to be." She replied.

Taymen shook his head as he turned to Avril.

"Well your audience is all accounted for." She said jokingly.

"There are more civilians in C.A.C. than crewmen." Taymen said with a smirk.

Arthur thought it an odd time to be joking around but didn't say anything.

"Alright." Taymen said. "Stay over there with them." He continued pointing to Russ and the others.

Talia moved around to the far side of the console and stood next to Russ.

"Sir all stations report ready." Titus reported.

"The Silver Phoenix is hailing Sir." Sairon said.

"Patch them through." Taymen replied.

"Sharr what's your status?" He asked.

"All stations report ready and the stealth fighters have been launched. They're holding position on the night side of Earth's moon." Sharr replied over the speaker.

"Alright follow our lead, you know what to do." Taymen said.

"Roger that." Sharr replied before the channel closed.

"All stations, status." Taymen started.

"Helm standing by, stream system charged." Aurin reported.

"Gun batteries and missile tubes standing by." Carrey said from the weapons station.

"All sword breakers are ready for launch and prowlers are in position on the far side of the planet, they should be landing in five minutes." Elisha reported.

Taymen took a deep breath as he made sure everything was covered.

"Titus bring us to battle mode." He started. "Load all missile tubes with javelins and prepare one nuke."

"Nukes?" Arthur asked.

"You're going to use nuclear weapons on our planet?" Kaleigh said in a panic.

"It's the only way we can take down that flagship without destroying the planet." Taymen said.

"All stations report battle mode Sir." Titus reported.

"All tubes ready Sir." Carrey said.

"Wait a second, what about the radiation?" Russ asked.

"You'll render the entire area uninhabitable." Kaleigh said.

"It's a desert." Avril pointed out.

"Relax, the radiation will dissipate after a few days." Titus explained.

"What?" Arthur asked.

"Your weapons must use a different element than ours do." Avril explained.

Once Taymen was satisfied there were no other concerns he turned to Aurin.

"Helm ready vertical thrusters and stream us out." He ordered.

A second later the Avenger flashed into a bolt of lightning and disappeared followed by the Phoenix a few seconds later. Both ships suddenly appeared five minutes later almost two kilometers directly above the Tray flagship.

Taymen felt dizzy and light headed for a few seconds as his vision cleared. The sudden jolt of the ship stopping mid air when the thrusters engaged caused his stomach to float for an instant.

"That was new." Avril said.

"Stream complete Sir, we're right were we're supposed to be, vertical thrusters stable." Aurin reported.

"All missiles fire!" Taymen snapped.

The Avenger fired twelve javelin missiles directly at the flagship while almost simultaneously the Phoenix fired sixteen more. Being so close and acting so quickly all twenty-eight missiles struck the upper hull of the ship tearing through the outer armor.

Tray Flagship
11:10 Abydos Standard Time
Day 30, First Cycle, Egyptian Year 3202

"Commander Soulin struggled to his feet as the lights on the bridge of his ship flickered and consoles exploded around him.

"What is going on?" He snapped.

"Two Egyptian battle ships have just streamed in above us and opened fire. The outer hull has been compromised, several vital systems are exposed." One of the operations officers reported.

"They streamed into an atmosphere, that's impossible." Soulin replied. "Get us out of here and ready all weapons stations. Destroy those ships!" He snapped.

"We've lost helm control." The helmsman said.

"All upper gun batteries have been destroyed." The weapons officer reported.

"Signal the fleet!" Soulin ordered.

"Communications are down!" The operations officer replied.

Dark Avenger C.A.C.
11:15 Abydos Standard Time
Day 30, First Cycle, Egyptian Year 3202

"Direct hit, all missiles." Carry reported.

"Patch me through to the Phoenix." Taymen ordered. "Sharr now." He said before closing the channel. "Launch the nuke. Aurin stream us out!"

A second later both ships fired a single nuclear missile at the flagship and disappeared in a bolt of dark lightning as quickly as they had appeared.

Both missiles detonated just above the flagship. The combined force of the explosions melted the remaining outer hull as the inner structure was ripped apart leaving nothing but a massive glass crater in the middle of the desert.

"Stream complete Sir." Aurin reported.

"The Phoenix?" Avril asked.

"They're five light seconds off our port quarter." Titus replied.

Right where they should be.' Taymen thought to himself.

"Status on the Tray?" He asked.

"They've detected us." Titus said.

"More likely that explosion." Avril said quietly.

"Five heavy cruisers are closing in on our position and three light cruisers are forming up behind them."

"Prepare a full salvo of javelins." Taymen ordered. "Heavy batteries prepare to fire on target three, all remaining batteries direct fire on target two." He continued. "Signal the stealth fighters, order them to engage the light cruisers."

Cairo Egypt
11:40 Abydos Standard Time
Day 30, First Cycle, Egyptian Year 3202

Arkeal led his team out of the prowler and into the empty streets.

Three prowlers landed at his location to clear the Tray out of a building they thought they were using for a backup command post.

He fired off a few rounds before moving to the side of the street to take cover behind a building.

The rest of his men poured out of the prowlers and took up positions along the street firing a few rounds at the guards defending the building.

The prowlers began to lift off into the air as they each fired off four smoke canisters to conceal Arkeal and his men.

Arkeal hit the control on his earpiece.

"This is Mentz." He said. "All teams move in, secure the main entrance to the building and hold position." He ordered.

A few seconds past before Arkeal fired off a few more rounds and then moved out from behind his cover and advanced up the street with his fire partner.

Everyone was moving in the same way. They moved in teams of two, one holding position to provide cover fire while the other moved forward a few paces then switching.

It wasn't long before all fifteen fire teams advanced through the street and were surrounding the building.

Arkeal hit his earpiece again.

"Teams two through ten hold position and provide cover fire, remainder follow my lead and move in." He ordered.

Arkeal ducked behind cover again while his partner continued to fire at the Tray. He hit the release button above the trigger and removed the magazine from the rifle replacing it with a full one. A second later he moved out into the open and fired his weapon hitting the first two guards near the main doors to the building.

The remaining teams followed and moved out as they opened fire. They slowly advanced on the Tray forcing them back until most of them backed themselves into the building.

"Remaining teams move in now." Arkeal ordered.

After only a short time any remaining Tray guards had retreated inside the building, allowing Arkeal and his men to advance unchecked.

Once inside it was only a matter of time before they cleared the Tray out.

Dark Avenger C.A.C.
12:17 Abydos Standard Time
Day 30, First Cycle, Egyptian Year 3202

Taymen regained his balance and checked the display again.

Two of the heavy cruisers had been destroyed and the stealth fighters destroyed one of the light cruisers and crippled another before returning to the Phoenix to rearm.

"Incoming ordnance!" Titus shouted.

The ship shuttered for a few seconds after the missiles impacted the Avenger's armor.

The armor upgrades the Avenger had done at the Callon facility proved to be invaluable. It was capable of withstanding almost twice as much force as the previous armor which made a noticeable difference with the heavy missiles being fired from the Tray heavy cruisers.

"Batteries five through ten switch to enemy suppression fire." Taymen ordered.

Within seconds the gun batteries along the center of the ship had switched from plasma rounds to heavy flak rounds to try and detonate the incoming missiles before they reached the ship.

"Heavy batteries open fire on target five." Taymen said. "Forward missile tubes ready sabers and lock onto target four." He continued.

"Tray fighters are closing in." Titus reported.

"Launch sword breakers to intercept!" Avril said.

"More landing craft are trying to enter the atmosphere." Titus said.

"Signal the Phoenix and tell them to have their sword breakers intercept them." Taymen replied. "Launch saber missiles." He ordered.

"Missiles away Sir." Carrey reported a second later.

As a salvo of saber missiles sped towards their target one of the other heavy cruisers exploded. The shock wave detonated some of the sabers before they reached their target.

"Target five is down." Avril reported.

"Direct hits on target four, they've reduced fire and are adrift." Titus said a second later.

"Heavy batteries finish off target four." Taymen said.

"Incoming ordnance!" Avril shouted just before the ship shuttered again.

"Direct hit to the upper heat exchanger." The damage control officer reported. "Fires on deck twelve frame thirty-seven." He continued.

"Fire suppression system?" Taymen asked.

"Fully discharged but we still have a few spot fires." The damage control officer replied.

"Dispatch damage control parties to put out those fires." Taymen ordered.

"The Tray fighter wing's been destroyed." Avril reported.

"Recall the sword breakers to rearm." Taymen said.

"Target four's down." Titus reported.

That was it. There was only one heavy cruiser and two light cruisers left.

"Helm bring our port side to bear. All batteries fire on target one." Taymen ordered. "Signal the Phoenix, have them engage the light cruisers." He continued.

"Ready saber missiles, tubes one through eight."

"Ready Sir." Carrey said a moment later.

"Fire!" Taymen ordered.

"Missiles away!"

Taymen checked the main sensor display.

"Helm bring our bow to bear on target one. Heavy batteries fire at will." He ordered.

It took a few seconds for the Avenger to turn but as soon as she was facing the cruiser the heavy gun batteries launched several salvos of heavy plasma rounds which tore through the outer armor and the inner decks, tearing the cruiser apart from the inside out.

"Target one is down Sir." Titus reported.

"Sir the Phoenix reports they've destroyed both light cruisers." Sairon said.

"What about our ground troops?" Avril asked.

"Last reports indicate they have seized the enemy command posts and all primary targets." Sairon reported.

"Deploy damage control parties, get that heat exchanger repaired." Taymen said.

"Sensor contact." Titus snapped. "Tray flagship has entered the system."

"Another one?" Avril shouted.

"They're opening fire!" Titus said.

Taymen checked the display.

The flagship was between the Avenger and the Phoenix.

"Helm bring our bow to bear and back us off full reverse." Taymen ordered.

"All batteries switch to enemy suppression fire, launch a salvo of countermeasures to cover us!" He continued.

Taymen watched as the gap between them and the flagship slowly grew larger.

The flag ship fired off a few missiles but they went for the countermeasures as the Avenger continued to back off.

"All missile tubes load two salvos of saber missiles and fire when ready." Taymen said. "Signal the Phoenix, order them to back off and attack from the flagships aft quarter. Heavy batteries fire at will. All forward batteries switch to direct fire."

"Sir only four of our missiles got through." Carrey reported.

"What?" Avril asked.

"Sorry Sir but they've got a lot of gun batteries to get through." Carrey explained.

Taymen thought for a moment.

Something had occurred to him, something he knew Sharr wasn't going to like but it may be their only chance. The only advantage they had right now was that the Avenger and the Phoenix were smaller and more maneuverable than the flagship, an advantage they would have to use.

"Radiological alert!" Titus said.

"Four nukes inbound!" He shouted.

"All batteries to suppression fire!" Taymen called.

"Launch alert fighters to intercept." He continued.

"Fighters away!" Elisha called.

Taymen watched as two of the missiles disappeared from sensors, than a third. The fourth managed to pass through the gun batteries' salvos and the sword breakers.

"All hands brace for impact! Sword breakers break off!" Taymen shouted just before the missile detonated just off of the upper hull.

Taymen and Avril were thrown to the deck along with Russ and the others. Several consoles overloaded and the lights flickered for several seconds.

Once the ship stopped shuttering Taymen got back to his feet.

"Report." He said.

"That hurt." Avril said sarcastically.

"Breach in the upper hull armor, hull breaches on several decks, the upper heat exchanger has failed and PT generator two is offline." The damage control officer reported.

"Seal off the breached sections and take non-essential systems off line. Switch effected systems to independent power and deploy damage control teams to get that generator back up." Taymen ordered.

"Sir the Phoenix has moved between us and the flagship, she's taking damage." Titus reported.

"Sairon put me through to Sharr." Taymen said.

"Go ahead Sir."

"Sharr report." Taymen said.

"We're taking damage but we can hold our position for a while." Sharr replied.

"I want you to stream out to the edge of the system on my order." Taymen explained.

Sharr wasn't sure what Taymen was planning but she was learning to trust his ideas.

"Standing by." Sharr said a moment later.

Taymen kept the channel open as he turned to Carrey.

"Ready missile tubes one and two and ten through twelve with nukes, the rest with saber missiles." He said.

"Aye Sir." Carrey replied.

The ship shuttered for a few seconds as they took another missile hit.

"Helm set a course that will bring us past the Tray ships' underside at close range and prepare to stream us back to the far side of Earth."

"Aye Sir." Aurin replied.

"Ready all batteries for direct fire." Taymen continued.

"All stations report ready Sir." Titus reported.

"Alright Carrey tubes one and two, set them to detonate on the Phoenix's position." Taymen said.

"Excuse me!" Sharr asked over the com.

"Fire!" Taymen ordered, ignoring Sharr.

"Nukes away." Carrey said.

"Sharr stream out now."

A second later the Silver Phoenix streamed away leaving two nukes in her wake witch detonated a half second later blinding the flag ship's sensors.

Taymen watched as the shockwave began to dissipate.

"Aurin all ahead full!" Taymen said.

"Heavy batteries fire at will!"

The Avenger sped towards the flagship as her heavy batteries fired a hail of heavy plasma rounds that burned through the outer layers of its armor.

By the time the flagship's sensors cleared the Avenger was right on top of them, or rather right below them.

"Fire all saber missile! All batteries fire at will!" Taymen said.

As the Avenger passed under the flagship she launched a barrage of missiles and plasma rounds into the underside of the flagship where Taymen hoped the armor was thinner.

As they moved to the aft end of the flagship the last of the saber missiles were fired.

Taymen waited for them to put a little more distance between the two ships.

"Carrey launch remaining nukes." He said.

"Nukes away." Carrey said.

"Aurin stream us out now!" Taymen snapped.

A second later the Avenger streamed out and the three missiles detonated into a massive wave of energy. As the shockwave enveloped the flagship its outer hull armor burned away and several sections of the inner decks were exposed.

"Stream complete Sir." Aurin reported.

"Set course all ahead full, bring us around the planet towards the flagships' last known location. Ready javelin missiles, all tubes." Taymen ordered.

The Avenger came around the planet to see the flagship still on sensors. As they charged forward two more nukes detonated and enveloped the flagship this time tearing it apart leaving a massive debris field in its wake.

"What happened?" Avril asked.

"I've got a sensor contact dead ahead." Titus reported. "It's the Silver Phoenix."

Taymen checked the display.

"All stop. Sairon patch me through." He said.

"Go ahead Sir."

"I thought I told you to stream outside of the system." He said.

"Well I couldn't let you have all the fun." Sharr said smugly.

Taymen smiled slightly.

"Well done." He said. "We'll rendezvous in orbit and launch sword breakers to provide air support for our marines." He said. "We're not quite done yet."

"Roger that." Sharr replied.

Chapter Twenty-Four

Arkeal ducked behind a low wall for cover. He and his team had managed to clear out the secondary command post and were moving to destroy one of the Tray ammunition caches when they were pinned down. He had lost several of his men and they were running low on ammunition.

"Team three can you move to flank their position?" He asked over the com. unit.

"Negative they've got us completely pinned down." One of the officers replied.

"Orelle to Captain Mentz." Taymen said over the com. unit.

Arkeal hit the control on his earpiece.

"Go ahead Sir." He replied.

"How are you guys doing down there?" Taymen asked.

"Oh you know, making friends everywhere." Arkeal said sarcastically.

"I have sword breakers on route to your location." Taymen said.

"Good we could use some fire support here. I'm throwing a beacon." Arkeal replied as he pulled out a small cylinder from his vest.

He hit the switch to activate it and threw it over the wall towards the Tray position.

"Alright, beacon's away." He said.

"Roger that." Taymen replied.

About a minute later Arkeal could see two sword breakers moving towards them. They opened fire targeting the area around the beacon.

When Arkeal peeked over the wall after the sword breakers had passed overhead the Tray were all dead and the cache was destroyed.

"Ashraa to Mentz." Major Ashraa said over the com. unit.

Arkeal hit the control on his earpiece.

"Go ahead." He replied.

"The Tray are mobilizing their armored companies at our location we were unable to neutralize their heavy fire support units, we need back up."

Ashraa was the commanding officer of the Silver Phoenix's marine detachment. He and his teams were assigned to clear the Tray out of a city Elisha called Athens where the majority of the Tray armored vehicles were along with most of their large transport ships.

"The Dark Avenger is back in orbit." Arkeal said. "Contact them and request fire support, we'll get there as soon as we can."

"Roger that." Ashraa replied.

Dark Avenger, C.A.C.
13:17 Abydos Standard Time
Day 30, First Cycle, Egyptian Year 3202

"Sir we have a request for fire support from major Ashraa." Sairon reported.

Taymen checked the command console to see if he could bring up Ashraa's position.

"Patch him through to me." He ordered as he tapped his earpiece.

"Go ahead Sir." Sairon said.

"Major what's your status?" Taymen asked.

"The Tray armored units have been mobilized. They're being loaded into their transports for planetary deployment. If they're able to deploy those heavy units we won't be able to take the planet from the ground any time soon." Ashraa reported.

"Can you paint the targets?" Taymen asked.

"Negative there's too many and they're spread out too far." Ashraa replied.

Taymen looked around C.A.C. at Avril and then to Russ.

"What can you tell me about that area?" He asked.

"Most of the population's been relocated from that area, but I can't say for sure." Russ said.

"Why would they do that?" Avril asked.

"To establish an isolated base in case of a planetary uprising." Taymen explained.

"Fall back and stand by Major." Taymen said over the com. unit.

"Aye Sir." Ashraa replied.

"Titus get me a thermo-graphic image of that area." Taymen ordered.

Titus accessed the sensor system and activated the thermal filter.

"Thermo-graphics indicate no civilian population in the area." He reported.

"Thermo graphics can't differentiate between Tray soldiers and Earth civilians." Avril pointed out.

"I know." Taymen said. "But civilians would be fairly obvious right now if the Tray are mobilizing heavy units."

Taymen's instructors at the Command Academy called this sort of thing investing in loss. You had to use the enemy's advantage against them but it means it costs you more to win than it does for them to lose.

If there were civilians in that area they would fall to friendly fire, but if Taymen didn't give the order than the Tray would deploy their heavy units around the world and they would lose the planet.

He had no choice.

"Carrey." Taymen said. "Ready a spread of banshee plasma missiles. Prepare to bombard the area."

"Aye Sir." Carrey replied.

"You're going to carpet bomb the city?" Avril asked.

Taymen nodded.

"Ironic." Russ said quietly from the command console.

"There's no other way." Taymen started, ignoring Russ' comment. "There's not enough time for our forces to paint the target locations."

"Ready Sir." Carrey reported.

Taymen hit the control on his earpiece.

"Ashraa what's your status?" He asked.

"Everyone's in the prowlers and waiting your orders Sir." Ashraa said.

"Get your men out of there now." Taymen ordered.

"Aye Sir."

Taymen watched the display until he saw Ashraa's prowlers clear the area.

"Carrey." He started. "Glass it."

"Aye Sir, missiles firing." Carrey replied.

A few seconds later seventy-five planetary missiles entered the atmosphere and blanketed Athens in a massive wave of super dense plasma similar to that used in the heavy plasma rounds that leveled every building and destroyed everything in the streets indiscriminately.

The wave enveloped the city and then dissipated almost twenty minutes later leaving nothing but a glass sheet where the city once stood.

Dark Avenger, Briefing Room
14:37 Abydos Standard Time
Day 13, Second Cycle, Egyptian Year 3202

Taymen entered the briefing room with Sharr and Avril.

Russ, Arthur and Kaleigh were all sitting at the table waiting for them.

It had been almost a week since they began the attack on the Tray and it seemed to finally be over.

"The remaining Tray have surrendered." Taymen said. "We've managed to locate and neutralize most of the larger groups across the planet but we'll be leaving a small detachment of marines, prowlers and sword breakers on the planet's surface to help deal with any other Tray soldiers we may have missed."

"We'll send a ship with more troops as soon as we can." Sharr added. "But for now at least the Tray threat here is gone."

Kaleigh held Arthur's hand tightly as tears began to well up in her eyes. She was so relieved to be going home but scared at the same time. She had no idea what their lives would be like after everything that's happened.

"Thank you so much." She said.

"There's a prowler waiting to take you all back home." Taymen said as he stood up.

He led them all to the hangar deck where Elisha and Talia were waiting next to one of the prowlers.

"So this is it then." Kaleigh said.

Taymen simply nodded.

"I'm afraid your world has a lot of work ahead of it. Governments will have to be restored and there is a lot to be rebuilt." He said.

"It could have been a lot worse." Arthur said.

"You're also going to have to come to grips with the reality that you're not alone in the universe." Sharr added.

"We'll manage, somehow." Russ said.

"Yeah we'll be okay." Elisha said as she moved up beside Russ who simply looked at her.

She was dressed in her old civilian clothes instead of her uniform and she carried a small duffle bag over her shoulder.

"Are you sure about this?" Taymen asked.

Elisha nodded.

"It's time I helped my own people rebuild their home." She said.

Taymen sighed.

"Well it was a pleasure having you aboard." He said. "We'll miss you."

"Thank you for everything Taymen." Elisha replied as she gave Taymen a hug before moving back to take Russ' hand.

"We'll be in orbit for a few more days until repairs are complete and as we said, we'll send help as soon as we can." Taymen said.

"Good luck." Sharr added.

"Taymen." Russ said as he reached out.

Taymen hesitantly reached out and took his hand unsure of what to do. Russ smiled slightly as he shook his hand.

"Thanks for coming back for us." He said.

"You're braver than you realize Russ." Taymen started. "Defying the Tray to help us and your people took courage. You should all be very proud of yourselves."

As Russ moved back a pace Kaleigh moved up and gave Taymen, Avril and Sharr a hug thanking each of them before turning to board the prowler with Russ and Arthur.

"Good luck guys, I hope you'll come back when this is all over." Elisha said before turning to board the prowler with the others.

Taymen backed off as the hatch sealed.

"Chief." He called. "Get this prowler onto the flight deck." He ordered as Kaile made her way over with a crew to tow the prowler onto the lift.

"So." Sharr started. "What about falling back to this system to rebuild our fleet?" She asked.

"Change of plans." Taymen replied. "I've been thinking about something I learned on the Star's Eye. We have a greater responsibility than we originally realized." He explained. "We're humanity's children. We've inherited a responsibility that we can't ignore now. I've decided that retreating isn't the best course in this case, there are too many people counting on us."

"So what's the plan Sir?" Avril asked.

"We're going to go back and rally Eazak's fleet. Then we're going to take back our home one system at a time."

Part VI
History Re-written

'History is written by the victors though there will always be the few that remember the truth. Truth or fiction however history always seems to want to repeat itself until someone decides to change its course.'

Defense Force history lesson 27-03

Chapter Twenty-Five

Talia's eyes shot open as she sat up in a panic gasping to catch her breath. She was covered with sweat and her heart was pounding so hard it felt like it was going to beat out of her chest.

She got out of bed and walked over to the sink in the back corner of her room. She turned on the light before taking a minute to splash cold water on her face.

She had been having the same nightmare for almost a week now, each time the Dark Avenger is destroyed and the last thing she sees is C.A.C. exploding around Taymen just before she wakes up in a panic.

Talia checked the time and realized how early it was. She found herself going to see Taymen more and more lately to talk. She wasn't sure why but being around him seemed to make her feel a little more at ease.

Talia got dressed and left her room heading down the corridor to the ladder. She climbed down two decks and made her way up the corridor towards the bow of the ship stopping outside of Taymen's quarters.

She was just about to knock when someone startled her.

"You're up early." Taymen said as he walked up behind her.

"You too." Talia replied.

Taymen smiled.

"Something tells me I would have been awake soon anyways." He said.

Talia could feel herself turn red.

"Sorry, I don't mean to bother you." She said.

"Not at all, I enjoy the company." Taymen replied as he used his implant to unlock the hatch and accessed the lighting controls before they walked in.

"So when are we leaving?" Talia asked as she took a seat on the couch.

"Later this morning." Taymen replied. "Repairs are complete and the planet seems to be secure." He continued.

"What will happen to the people on the planet?" Talia asked.

"That'll depend on them." Taymen replied. "The Tray destroyed most of the governments and their resources, and what we did probably didn't help much either." He said as he sat down on the couch beside her.

"Most of the governments have a few surviving officials to help them start rebuilding but as for my actions." Taymen sighed. "I've apologized to the countries surviving officials and offered any assistance they may need."

"And what did they say?" Talia asked.

Taymen smiled slightly.

"Well needless to say they were more than a little angry with me and pretty much threw the offer back in my face so I don't think I'll be hearing from them again."

Talia nudged Taymen's shoulder a little.

"It's not your fault you know. You did what you had to do to free them from the Tray." She said reassuringly. "So what if one government on some backwater planet can't see that."

"I know and I really don't care what they think of my decision. I'm just wondering if I would have done the same thing had it been on Abydos." Taymen said.

Talia didn't say anything.

Taymen shook himself out of his thoughts and turned in his seat.

"Have you considered staying behind on Earth Talia?" He asked, changing the subject.

Talia nodded slightly.

"I thought about it but decided not to." She said. "I want to go home and help our people rebuild. I want to see my father and my friends free again, unless you want me off your ship."

Taymen shook his head.

"Not at all." He replied. "It's just, the last time I had civilians on my ship one of them got hurt pretty badly and I don't want anything like that to happen to you."

Talia smiled as she shifted closer to Taymen.

"Well than I guess you'll just have to keep me where you can keep an eye on me." She said softly as she gazed into Taymen's icy blue eyes.

Taymen's smile faded slightly. He gazed back into her green eyes as the hints of blue shimmered in the light.

"I guess so." He finally said as he slowly moved closer to her.

"At least that way I can keep an eye on you too." Talia replied as she slowly began to move closer to him.

Taymen's smile returned for an instant as he closed his eyes and then finally pressed his lips softly against hers.

Talia's heart jumped into her throat for an instant before it began to race. The feel of Taymen's fingertips gently running up her arm gave her goose bumps.

She slowly ran her hand up his muscular arm and onto his neck as she relished the feeling of him so close to her.

Taymen's heart pounded in his chest as his hands moved seemingly by themselves across Talia's back and back down her arms.

The unfamiliar feeling of her soft skin and her lips against his was a cruel reminder of just how inexperienced Taymen was at intimacy.

Taymen slowly pulled himself away a little trying to make sense of what he was doing. When he opened his eyes Talia was smiling at him as hers opened a second later.

"What is it?" She whispered.

Taymen smiled.

"I'm..." He hesitated a moment. "I'm really not very good at this sort of thing." He said.

Talia's smile widened a little.

"You seem fine to me." She said.

Taymen smiled again.

"Well I mean I don't have a whole lot of experience in this. I've spent more time in command of a ship than I have in a relationship." He explained, embarrassed by the whole thing.

Talia continued to smile at him as she stood up taking his hand in hers.

Demon's Light, Briefing Room
08:30 Abydos Standard Time
Day 21, Second Cycle, Egyptian Year 3202

Jassen sat next to General Eazak at the table in the briefing room of the Demon's Light.

Sitting opposite to them were the commanders of the four separatist battle groups.

Jassen wasn't really sure why they called them battle groups. Each one was made up of only seven or eight ships but it was all the battle ships the separatists had.

"Gentlemen." Eazak started. "I understand your feelings in this matter but running away at this point will not accomplish anything."

"We disagree General." One of the men said. "The Tray have total control of this galaxy and we are vastly outnumbered. If we leave now we can rebuild somewhere else."

269

"How long do you think it will be before the Tray find us there and start this whole cycle over again!" Jassen snapped. "You said it yourself, they have a vast number of ships. If we leave now we simply spread our resources even thinner making it easier for the Tray to finish us off." He continued.

"We're willing to take that chance." Another one of the commanders said.

"You're willing to give up and let the Tray get away with all this?" Eazak said.

"We did not come here to debate the issue General we came to inform you in person that we're leaving."

Eazak remained silent for a moment before standing up.

"Well then since there is clearly nothing we can say that will convince you to stay, I wish you good luck." He said before leaving the briefing room with Jassen close behind.

"Are you really going to let them go?" Jassen asked as they moved down the corridor.

"It's not like I have a choice." Eazak replied. "There's nothing we can do to stop them."

Jassen scoffed.

"I thought you were their commander. Can't you order them to stay?"

Eazak smiled a little.

"That sort of mentality was the exact reason we sought independence in the first place." He replied. "To get away from the dictatorship of the military that so clearly controlled the Empire."

Jassen thought it over for a moment. It was true he had no love for the military but he never thought they were in control of the Empire, though he could see how someone could think so.

The military was in charge of the security of the Empire. There were no local police or security guards to handle domestic disputes just Defense Force soldiers.

"In any case they've made their decision and nothing we say or do is going to change that." Eazak continued.

"Still." Jassen said. "How are we supposed to tell Taymen that we lost almost thirty ships while he was gone?"

Eazak smiled.

"He'll understand. If I know Taymen he's probably got a backup plan for just such an event."

Dark Avenger at the Outer Belt
10:23 Abydos Standard Time
Day 28, Second Cycle, Egyptian Year 3202

Taymen stood in C.A.C. watching the display screen.

"We've transited back into normal space Sir." Aurin reported from the helm station.

"What's our location?" Avril asked.

"About three light minutes from the outer belt." Aurin replied.

"Amazing." Avril said.

"We just crossed the void between two galaxies in almost two weeks."

"Yes, but two weeks in a wormhole made me a little nervous." Titus said.

When they transited into the hyperstream, it felt similar to being in the protostream except there was a noticeable difference in the transit time. In protostream the transit was pretty much instantaneous. In the hyperstream however, Taymen noticed a sizeable gap in his perception of his environment. It was as if he blinked for a very long time and when he opened his eyes something in the room changed, he just couldn't tell what.

"Bring us to stealth mode." Taymen ordered. "Move us into the belt all ahead one quarter." He continued.

"Back to where it all began." Avril said quietly.

Taymen nodded.

It was here that he first spoke with Eazak and it was here that they first heard of the Tray attack.

"Titus access the sensor drone network and send an encoded message to General Eazak and Princess Releena informing them we're back." Taymen said. "And start putting together a model of current Tray deployments, I want to know where their ships are."

"Aye Sir." Titus replied.

"Sir." Sairon said. "We're receiving an automated message from the drone network. It's from General Assh."

Taymen glanced over at Avril before looking over to Sairon.

"Put it through." He said.

The speaker crackled for a moment before Assh began to speak.

"Taymen, I've programmed the drone network to transmit this message once it's detected your ship." The message started. *"I'm still a prisoner of the Tray, they're holding me on Abydos but some of our operatives managed to escape the Tray screenings allowing me to send you this message."*

There was a brief silence.

"Fleet Marshal Ourik is furious, the Phantom Wraith's been destroyed and he captured Princess Releena."

Taymen sighed.

"Taymen he killed her when she wouldn't tell him what he wanted to know."

271

There was a long silence as Taymen looked around C.A.C. at the look of shock on his crew's faces.

"Our operatives have included the locations of the last eight ships the Tray are trying to reverse engineer along with a detailed status report. I'm told that there are several of our people in place ready to take these ships at a moment's notice. Our fate falls to you now Taymen, good luck."

A second later the channel went silent.

"Oh my gods." Avril said.

"Sairon." Taymen said quietly. "Patch me through to Sharr."

"Go ahead Sir." Sairon said.

"Sharr patch me through ship wide." Taymen said. "Sairon give me ship wide here." He continued.

Once he was patched through to both ships Taymen hit the control on his earpiece.

"All hands this is Colonel Orelle." He started. "I've just received a message from General Assh informing us of the situation here. Since we left the Tray have discovered and executed most of our operatives in their midst. The few that managed to remain hidden have provided us with the locations of eight Egyptian ships still held by the Tray.

"More importantly however I've been informed that the Phantom Wraith has been destroyed and her crew captured including Princess Releena. I don't know what's happened to the crew but it saddens me to have to inform you all that Princess Releena was killed by the Tray commander Fleet Marshal Ourik."

Taymen took a moment to regain his thoughts.

"We have them now." He said. "We have a major advantage over the Tray. I intend to gather our fleet and make a full out assault on the Tray forces occupying Abydos. Keep it together a little longer people. Focus on your jobs and we'll drive the Tray from our galaxy for good."

Dark Avenger, Briefing Room
17:43 Abydos Standard Time
Day 28, Second Cycle, Egyptian Year 3202

Eazak and Jassen waited in the conference room for Taymen to arrive. Neither one of them expected the Avenger to be back so soon and Taymen's message requested they rendezvous immediately.

The hatch opened and Taymen walked into the room with Avril close behind.

"Colonel, welcome back." Eazak said.

"Thank you." Taymen replied as he sat down.

"Let's not waste any time." He started. "We found the Star's Eye and unfortunately so did the Tray."

"I assume you destroyed the facility to keep it from them." Eazak interrupted.

"Yes." Taymen replied. "Luckily we managed to get a copy of its database before doing so."

Jassen and Eazak both shifted in their seats.

"And Earth?" Jassen asked.

"The Tray on Earth have been eliminated and I left a small detail there to assist the remaining governments until we can send a proper relief group." Taymen explained.

"What about the database." Eazak asked. "Have you been able to access it?"

Yes." Taymen replied. "We've already managed to get some invaluable information though a deeper look revealed that much of the data has been corrupted." He continued.

"Corrupted?" Jassen asked.

"It's not surprising really." Avril said. "The database is ancient. It's not surprising that there was so much degradation. We have a team working to try and salvage what they can but it's a slow process." She continued.

"You said you've already found some valuable information, what exactly have you found?" Eazak asked.

"We've discovered what the ancients refer to as the 'hyperstream.'" Avril explained. "Another way of utilizing the hubs to allow us to travel even faster than we could in the protostream. We were able to travel from Earth in about two weeks."

"What?" Jassen said.

Eazak remained silent.

"It's true." Taymen said. "We've also discovered the location of the Tray home world and now with this hyperstream we have the means to get there." He continued.

Suddenly the hatch opened and Sharr walked into the room.

"Started without me I see." She said smugly.

"You haven't missed anything Sharr." Taymen said. "Now then." He continued. "We intend to begin a full out campaign against the Tray using Abydos as our staging area."

"That may be a problem." Jassen interrupted.

"Why's that?" Avril asked.

Eazak shifted forward in his seat.

"The separatist battle group commanders have decided to withdraw."

"What!" Taymen snapped.

"They figured it would be better for them to cut their losses and retreat while they could." Jassen explained.

"That's ridiculous." Sharr replied.

"We tried to convince them to stay but they wouldn't hear it." Eazak said.

Taymen sighed and shook his head.

"How many ships did we lose?" He asked.

"Twenty-eight." Eazak replied.

"And with the Phantom Wraith that makes twenty-nine." Sharr added.

Avril sighed.

"What do we do now Sir?" She asked.

Taymen thought it over for a moment.

"We need to rethink our tactics." Eazak said.

"No." Taymen replied. "We'll proceed as planned."

"You want to retake Abydos with just three ships?" Jassen asked.

"Of course not." Taymen replied. "The only thing that's changed is our timetable." Taymen explained. "I want you all to return to your ships and set a course for the outer supply station. We're going to rearm and prepare to take Abydos."

Chapter Twenty-Six

Corrin opened his eyes when he heard the main cellblock door open and then close again. He wasn't sure how long it had been since anybody came to interrogate him, a few days he figured.

The stench of the damp cell was so familiar to him now that he barely noticed it, along with the constant pain of starvation.

As a shadow cast itself across what little light there was under the door Corrin straightened himself but didn't stand. He heard the locks of his cell door release before it was pulled open.

Corrin winced at the flood of bright light as the silhouette of a man filled the doorway.

"My how the mighty have fallen." The man said.

Corrin thought he recognized the voice as he slowly made his way to his feet.

"General Assh, I understand you've been less than cooperative." The man continued as he stepped into the cell.

As Corrin's eyes focused on the man's face he suddenly recognized him. His short dark hair and gray eyes were all too familiar to Corrin.

"General Amaat Raise, I see that the Tray still haven't killed you." He said.

Raise ignored his hostility as he took a few paces forward.

"They're getting around to it." He said. "But before they do I figured I'd do something constructive."

Corrin scoffed.

"I'm not going to tell you anything," He said.

Raise smiled.

"You misunderstand me." He said. "I'm not here to interrogate you I'm here to get you out."

Corrin hesitated a moment when he noticed that there were no Tray guards with Raise.

"And why should I trust you?" He asked.

"Because I'm trusting you." Raise replied, handing Corrin a sidearm.

Corrin slowly reached out and grasped the weapon by the handle.

As Raise released it and backed off a pace Corrin darted at him grasping him by the collar and forcing him back against the wall pointing the barrel of the weapon at his head.

"I should kill you where you stand!" He growled.

Raise didn't struggle as he gasped for a breath.

"If you do you'll never escape." He said.

"Why would you turn against the Tray now, after all that you've done?" Corrin asked.

Raise coughed before speaking again.

"I'm not proud of what I've done." He said. "But you have to believe me when I say I was doing what I thought was best for the Empire."

Corrin was about to argue when Raise cut him off.

"Look we can stand here and argue about this or you can let me help you escape. Either way I've accepted my fate, at least this way you'll be free to change yours."

Corrin thought it over for a moment and then slowly released Raise.

"If you betray us again death will be a blessing compared to what I'll do to you." He said.

Corrin followed Raise down the cell block to the far end.

As they turned around the corner Corrin stopped and looked around for a moment.

"What is it?" Raise asked.

"This isn't the way out." Corrin replied.

"No it's not." Raise explained. "There's someone else we need to rescue first."

Raise continued down the cellblock to the furthest corner of the complex.

The lighting in the corridor was very dim and the passage narrowed as they approached the solid metal door at the end.

Corrin immediately recognized the cell as a solitary confinement room.

"Who's in there?" He asked.

Raise didn't answer as he placed his implant on the reader to unlock the door. He reached out and grasped the handle on the door only to find it was still locked.

"No." He said as he tried his implant again.

"What's wrong?" Corrin asked.

"They must have revoked my clearance." Raise said.

"Or you never had access to this cell." Corrin pointed out. "Who's in there?"

Raise turned to face Corrin.

"It's Queen Auria." He said.

Corrin jumped back a step.

"What!" He snapped. "That's impossible."

Raise shook his head.

"I thought so too until I saw for myself. Releena's mother is alive, now she's the last surviving member of the royal family. We have to get her out."

Corrin began looking around frantically for anything they could use to open the cell door. He considered trying his implant but he knew the Tray would have deleted his security access from the system long ago.

"How can we get that door open?" He asked.

Raise thought for a moment.

"Try your implant." He said.

"You know that won't work." Corrin replied.

"It won't work in the conventional manner." Raise said. "My security ID is still in the system so it can block me out but you've been deleted from the system completely so you're an unknown user. You can hack through the system before it realizes you shouldn't be in there and override the locks."

Corrin thought it over for a moment.

It made sense. With a valid user ID the system knows instantly where you should and shouldn't be but it takes it slightly longer to recognize an unknown user. If he was fast enough he could open the door before the system shut him out.

"Alright I'll try." Corrin said as he placed his hand on the reader.

He accessed the system and came to a user login. He managed to bypass the login with an administrator code he remembered and accessed the base operating system for the locking mechanism. It felt like he was sneaking around under the surface. A few seconds later he located the door override algorithm and accessed it.

There were a number of reasons a door could be overridden so once he was in it wasn't difficult to trick the system.

Suddenly the distinct thud of the locking mechanism retracting from the door echoed through the dark corridor and Corrin disconnected from the system.

"We need to hurry, the security center will have been alerted to the door being overridden." He said as he entered the cell.

Sitting in the darkness in the corner of the small cell was an older woman. Her clothes were filthy and torn and her face was covered in dirt.

It was clear to Corrin that she had been here for a long time when she didn't even look up when they walked into the cell.

"Your Majesty." Corrin said.

The woman looked up at him slowly. Her blue eyes looked him over as she slowly shifted away from the corner and began to stand.

"General Assh, is it really you?" She asked.

"Yes your Majesty." He said. "We've come to get you out of here."

"We?" Auria asked.

A second later Raise entered the cell.

"Traitor!" She snapped as she backed up against the wall.

"I know." Corrin said. "But like it or not he's getting us out."

Auria looked Raise over making no effort to hide her disgust.

"Come on." Raise started. "I have a shuttle waiting out in the compound and I've arranged for one of our captured ships to escape the Tray. It should be waiting for us now."

Dark Avenger at Outer Supply Station 278
07:33 Abydos Standard Time
Day 3, Third Cycle, Egyptian Year 3202

Taymen woke up to the feeling of Talia's hand running down his chest slightly. He rubbed his eyes for a moment until his vision cleared before gently moving out from under Talia's arm. He carefully pulled the blanket up to her shoulders as she rolled onto her side.

They had been docked at the outer supply station for almost a week now rearming all three ships.

Taymen ordered more of the heavy rail cannons installed on the Dark Avenger turning her into what was generally known as a heavy ship killer. Usually only pulsar class cruisers were heavy ship killers.

The term referred to a ship fitted mainly with heavy weapons designed for the sole purpose of destroying larger starships.

Since they really didn't have any pulsar class cruisers at their disposal they had to improvise.

As Taymen stepped out of the shower and dried off Talia slowly sat up in the bed.

"Morning." She said softly.

"Good morning." Taymen replied just before he moved across the room to the bedside.

He bent down and kissed Talia who place her hand softly on the side of his face.

She loved the feeling of his lips against hers. He was so gentle and she could still sense a little uncertainty in his movements that she could only describe as cute.

"Does this mean you're kicking me out?" She asked as Taymen straightened out.

"No of course not." He said. "I have to report to C.A.C. and see what our status is."

"Good." Talia said as she lay back down with a yawn. "Because I'm not moving."

She watched as Taymen got dressed and checked to make sure his rank insignias were straight. He finally placed his earpiece in his right ear before giving Talia another kiss and leaving the cabin.

The corridors were filled with people either conducting repairs or bringing supplies aboard. The Avenger had taken a lot of punishment since the Tray first attacked and Taymen was amazed she had held together this long. With all the repairs and upgrades they had made over the last few months it was barely the same ship anymore.

Taymen entered C.A.C. to the sound of Titus shouting 'Captain on deck!'

"As you were." Taymen said a second later as he made his way down to the command console.

"Sir." Avril said in greeting.

"Captain, how are we doing?" Taymen asked.

"Everything's on schedule." Avril replied. "The refitting of the forward batteries has been completed and we're fully armed. The Silver Phoenix and Demon's Light will be ready by the end of the day today." She continued.

Taymen nodded as he looked over a data pad.

"Titus." He started.

"Sir." Titus replied.

"Have our prowler pilots report to the pilot's briefing room in fifteen minutes. I have a job for them."

"Aye Sir." Titus replied.

"Sairon open a secure channel to the drone network and prepare for a long range general broadcast on all channels." Taymen ordered.

Spear of Osiris Somewhere Near Netara
07:45 Abydos Standard Time
Day 3, Third Cycle, Egyptian Year 3202

Corrin looked himself over in the mirror briefly. It had been so long since he wore a clean uniform he had almost forgotten what it felt like.

As he turned to the side he could see that he had lost quite a bit of weight. It wasn't surprising. He had spent almost a year in a prison cell with minimal food and water.

Raise kept his word.

The Spear of Osiris was a pulsar class cruiser that was stolen from the Tray a few days ago by a small group of Egyptians operating as technicians in one of the ship yards.

They had been hiding near the outer edge of their galaxy ever since they escaped while they repaired and manned the ship. Normally a pulsar class cruiser had a crew of about thirty-two hundred people so it was going to take a fair bit of time to get even half that.

As Corrin put on his uniform jacket he heard someone knocking on the hatch to his cabin.

"Come in." He said.

A second later a young lieutenant walked in.

"Excuse me Sir but Queen Auria wants you to report to C.A.C." The officer said.

"I'm on my way." Corrin replied.

When he entered C.A.C. Corrin could see Queen Auria standing at the command console with General Raise.

It had been so long since Corrin last saw her.

Her long dark hair had begun to turn gray and her face began to show signs of her age but not so much as to fully reveal how old she was. Her eyes however were the same. A deep blue color that simply penetrated anyone she looked at.

"General Assh I trust you slept well." Raise said.

"Fine thank you." Corrin replied.

The truth was it was the first full night of sleep he had gotten in almost a year.

"Good." Auria said. "We have a lot of work to do."

"Sir." The communications officer interrupted.

"What is it?" Corrin asked.

"We're receiving a transmission from the secure drone network."

"A transmission?" Auria said.

"The signal lag indicates the message is only about twenty minutes old." The officer explained.

"Let's hear it." Corrin said.

A second later the speaker crackled as the message came through.

"This is Colonel Taymen Orelle of the Egyptian battleship Dark Avenger." The message started. *"I know you've all been informed that the Dark Avenger was destroyed and her crew captured by the Tray. I'm here to tell you that is not true, we are here and we are ready to fight."*

There was a brief silence as everyone in C.A.C. listened intently.

"The Tray want you to believe there is no hope. They want you to bow down and believe that the lives you are now living are the best you're going to get.

"I want you all to look around. Look at the faces of those around you of the people you know and care about and remember how your lives were just one year ago. We haven't given up and I ask that you don't either.

"Now is the time. Now is the time for us to make a stand, it's our future and nobody's going to give it to us. We built this empire together and now we need to fight together to restore it. I call upon everyone, every Egyptian who is able and every free ship to come forward and prepare to retake what's ours. You know where to find us. On the seventeenth day of this cycle stand ready and stand with us. We are the Dark Avenger and we fight to win."

Suddenly the speakers went silent.

"Well." Raise said. "He certainly has a talent for the dramatic."

"There's a good chance the Tray heard this as well." Auria said.

"I think that's what Taymen wants." Corrin started. "He's getting them wound up to make it easier to predict their ship positions. Now he knows the Tray will be on the defensive so they'll move their fleets to defend key planets and installations."

"He's trying to herd them?" Raise asked.

"I think so." Corrin replied.

"Can we find him with this transmission?" Auria asked.

"I'm afraid not." Raise replied. "He sent the message through the drone network as a general broadcast into deep space. Anyone would hear it even if they weren't listening, there's no way to tell where it could have originated from."

Corrin sighed.

"Luckily we don't have to worry about that." He said.

"Why not?" Auria asked.

"Remember Taymen saying 'you know where to find us.'" Corrin said.

"Yes, what did he mean by that?" Auria asked.

"Defense Force standing orders." Raise explained. "There's a rendezvous point where all ships are to report to in the event they're cut off from Abydos and the field command posts." He continued.

"You think he's there?" Auria asked.

"It's the only place everyone would know of." Raise said.

"The question is do the Tray know its location?" Corrin asked, staring intently at Raise.

Raise took the not so subtle hint but smiled a little.

"I haven't revealed anything about our standing orders or procedures, or our technology for that matter." Raise said.

"Alright then." Auria said. "Take us there General."

Chapter Twenty-Seven

Taymen walked into the briefing room to the sound of the senior pilot calling the room to attention.

"At ease." Taymen said as he took up a position at the head of the room.

"We don't have much time so I'm going to get straight to the point." He started. "In a little more than three days we're going to launch a full out assault on the Tray at Abydos. I've sent a general message informing everyone of our intention to do so including the Tray."

Taymen took a moment to look around the room.

"With that in mind I have a very important mission for all of you. You're all being assigned a separate planet and your job is to land undetected and begin spreading rumors about the upcoming attack amongst its population. You are to inform people when the attack will begin and that our staging area is the outer belt that lies just outside of the Abydos system."

Taymen could hear a few people muttering to each other in confusion.

"The idea is to give people time to prepare and hopefully decide what they're going to do when the attack begins."

"Excuse me Sir." One of the pilots said. "But how can we expect the people on the planets to launch an effective attack against the Tray?"

"You'll be carrying enough weapons to arm any Defense Force soldiers you find on each planet." Taymen said.

"Sir." Another pilot started. "Won't the rumors of our staging area make its way to the Tray as well. I mean they may have operatives in the general population."

"I hope so Captain." Taymen replied.

"This is a very serious problem Fleet Marshal." The voice said over the speaker.

Ourik sat behind his desk reading over the transcript of the message they received.

"I don't see how Sir." He replied. "If they want to kill themselves by committing their last few ships to this insane attack then let them." He continued.

"Don't underestimate the Egyptians' lust for freedom, if they rise up against us now we will not be able to hold all the occupied planets." The voice said.

Ourik smiled.

"There will be no need to." He said.

"What?" The voice scoffed.

"We've already received intelligence informing us that the Egyptians are massing a fleet in the outer belt." Ourik explained. "I've already sent the bulk of our fleet around Abydos to intercept them before they can launch their little attack."

There was a moment of silence.

"That is a very foolish move Fleet Marshal." The voice finally said. *"I am sending the last of our ships to Abydos. They will arrive in just over two days from now and I will be joining them."*

Ourik didn't say anything for a moment. He knew there was no point in arguing. If the Chancellor wanted to waste resources on these silly precautions that was his business.

"Very well Chancellor." He finally said before closing the channel.

He sat quietly at his desk for several minutes thinking about the upcoming attack.

Something didn't seem right. This type of tactic was too direct for Taymen. Up until now his tactics had been far more creative. Why would he all of a sudden want to commit what little resources he has in an all or nothing assault?

Ourik opened the channel to his second in command.

"Commander." He said.

"Yes Sir." The young man answered over the speaker.

"Prepare the Titan for launch, I want to be off this planet within the hour." Ourik said before closing the channel.

'Perhaps I'll have a little surprise waiting for the Colonel.' He thought to himself.

Dark Avenger, Briefing Room
11:54 Abydos Standard Time
Day 5, Third Cycle, Egyptian Year 3202

Jassen sat in the Dark Avenger's briefing room staring at the photo he had kept in his pocket for the last year.

As he looked over his son's face he remembered the exact day the photo was taken. It was only two years ago but they had all changed so much since then.

His son had grown into such a strong young man. If anyone could have survived this whole ordeal alone it was him.

Jassen regretted never telling him how proud he was of him even though they were constantly fighting. He knew it was because his son had turned out to be just like him, stubborn.

When he heard the hatch begin to open Jassen wiped a tear from his eye and stood up as Taymen walked in and closed the hatch behind him.

"You wanted to talk to me about something Jassen?"

Jassen nodded as he took a few steps towards Taymen.

"Yes." He said.

Taymen moved towards him and stopped a few paces away but didn't sit down.

There was an awkward silence for a moment as Jassen tried to put together what he wanted to say.

"You don't have children do you Colonel?" Jassen asked.

Taymen shook his head.

"No." He replied.

Again there was silence.

"Do you still have family, I mean before the attack did you have family back home?" Jassen asked awkwardly.

Taymen nodded slowly.

"Yes." He said unsure of what Jassen was trying to get at.

"Were you close with them?" Jassen asked.

"Not really no." Taymen said.

"Why not?"

Taymen looked at Jassen for a moment trying to figure out what he really wanted. The look on his face was one Taymen had never seen on him before.

Usually when Jassen talked to Taymen there was a degree of confidence even authority in his voice and his expressions, now however there was none. The only thing Taymen could see in him was a vulnerability that made Taymen a little uncomfortable.

"When I decided to join the Defense Force." Taymen started. "My family pretty much disowned me. With the exception of my sister I wasn't welcome anymore." He said.

"But you didn't stay close with your sister?" Jassen asked.

"I didn't want her caught between me and my parents." Taymen said.

Jassen nodded.

"Do you regret not getting along with your father?" He asked.

"Sometimes but I mostly regret that my father wouldn't even try to understand my perspective." Taymen explained. "In the end though it was his decision to push me away." He continued.

"Jassen what's this all about?" Taymen finally asked.

Jassen handed the photo to Taymen who took it and looked it over.

"That's my son, Mattin." Jassen said. "I told you I didn't know what happened to him and with the way everything is going I don't know if I'll ever see him again." He continued. "I want you to do something for me Taymen."

"Alright." Taymen said.

"When this is over I want you to find Mattin and give him this." Jassen said as he handed Taymen a data chip.

"What is it?" Taymen asked.

"My last message to my son." Jassen replied.

Taymen hesitantly took the chip.

"You know I don't know what you said on this." Taymen started. "But whatever it is I'm sure it would mean a lot more if you said it in person."

"I know but I'm not sure I could say it to him even if I had the chance."

Taymen placed the chip in his pocket and handed the photo back to Jassen.

"I'll hold onto this for you until this is all over but when you have the chance you have to tell Mattin yourself." He said.

Jassen nodded before heading for the hatch.

"Taymen." He said before leaving.

Taymen turned and faced him.

"Speaking as a father." He started. "I can tell you that even though he may never say it, your father is very proud of you."

Taymen stood silent for a moment. He had never even considered the possibility that his father would have been anything but ashamed of him. Still it didn't matter now, he had come to terms with the fact that his family was ashamed of him a long time ago.

Taymen adjusted his uniform jacket and left the briefing room closing the hatch behind him.

He made his way to C.A.C. where Talia was waiting for him along with Avril and Titus.

"Report." Taymen said as he made his way to the command console.

"All stations report ready, all repairs are complete and we're fully armed and supplied." Titus said.

"Good." Taymen replied.

He took a brief look around the room before turning back to Avril.

"Prepare to stream us to the rendezvous coordinates." He ordered.

"Aye Sir." Avril said. "Sairon signal the Silver Phoenix and the Demon's Light, advise them to stream to the rendezvous coordinates."

"Aurin stream us out." Taymen said.

"Aye Sir." Aurin replied.

"Charge the protostream generator." Aurin said to the stream officer.

"Aye Sir protostream system coming online." The young officer replied.

"Sairon give me ship wide." Taymen said.

The ship echoed with the harsh buzz of the internal com. system.

"All hands prepare for protostream." Taymen said before closing the channel.

"Protostream ready Sir." Aurin said a moment later.

"All stations report ready Sir." Titus reported.

"Very well, whenever you're ready Aurin." Taymen said.

A few seconds later the ship's hull began to glow just before it disappeared into a flash of dark lightning with the Demon's Light and Silver Phoenix following a few seconds later.

When his vision cleared Taymen checked the command console.

"Stream complete Sir. We've arrived at the rendezvous coordinates." Aurin reported.

"Sensor contact." Titus said. "One ship directly ahead about two light minutes out."

"Identify." Avril said.

There was a brief silence as Titus checked his console.

"It's the Spear of Osiris." He said.

Taymen looked at Avril who simply looked blankly back at him.

"They're hailing us Sir." Sairon said.

"Patch them through."

A second later a man's voice came over the speaker.

"Colonel Orelle this is General Corrin Assh aboard the Spear of Osiris, report to our briefing room immediately." He said before the channel closed.

Taymen looked over at Titus and Avril.

"Well he's in a hurry isn't he." Avril said.

"Yes he is." Taymen replied. "Have a prowler ready for launch and I want a marine detachment to meet me on the hangar deck." He ordered.

"Aye Sir." Avril replied.

"Sairon have General Eazak and Colonel Vaye join me aboard the Spear of Osiris." Taymen said as he opened the hatch and left C.A.C.

He made his way to the starboard hangar deck where his prowler was waiting with an eight man marine detachment.

Taymen quickly boarded the ship and sealed the hatch behind him as they were towed to the airlock and the lift raised them to the flight deck. Within a few minutes they were clear to launch and the prowler sped out of the flight deck and into open space.

As he looked out the window he could see two other prowlers form up just off of their aft port quarter. It was only a few minutes before they reached the Spear of Osiris' flight deck. The pilot gently set the ship down on the first lift which immediately began to lower them down to the airlock on the hangar deck.

As the hatch opened his marine team readied their weapons and took up positions between Taymen and the hatch.

Captain Mentz had given them all strict orders to protect Taymen at all costs, and even though Taymen wasn't particularly comfortable with that order he knew exactly what Arkeal would say if he were to object.

When the hatch was fully open the marines one by one stepped out onto the hangar deck in a staggered pattern keeping an eye on everything that was happening. When the last one stepped out Taymen stood from his seat and stepped out behind him.

He looked around the deck and noticed there was nobody there to meet them. Everyone was busy going about their business. Some were still bringing in the other two prowlers with Sharr and Eazak aboard but the rest seemed too busy to notice Taymen or his marines.

The deck was clearly larger than the Avenger's and there were at least twice as many sword breakers and prowlers in addition to a few other models of ships.

The bulkheads looked to be very heavily armored and the hatches were hydraulically assisted to help compensate for the extra weight. There were also internal defense turrets mounted on the ceiling which would make boarding this ship from the hangar deck very difficult.

A few minutes later Sharr and Eazak stepped onto the hangar deck with their own marine teams.

"What's this about Colonel?" Eazak asked.

"Not sure." Taymen replied. "General Assh ordered me to report to their briefing room, he didn't say why."

"If you'll follow me the General is waiting." A voice said.

Taymen turned to see a young Lieutenant standing near the prowler.

Taymen looked to Sharr and Eazak who didn't say anything.

"Lead the way then Lieutenant." He said.

Taymen and the others followed the Lieutenant off of the hangar deck and into the corridor.

Taymen took note of every turn they made in case they needed to get back to the prowlers in a hurry. It all just seemed a little two convenient that General Assh managed to escape the Tray with a pulsar class cruiser right before Taymen was about to launch his attack.

The Lieutenant opened the hatch to the briefing room and stood aside to let them in.

Taymen walked in first followed by his marines, then Sharr and Eazak.

"Welcome aboard Colonel." Assh said as he stood from his seat near the head of the table.

"Sir." Taymen said as he saluted sharply along with Sharr.

Eazak remained silent in the background.

Assh returned the salute and offered them a seat.

"Good to see you again Atla." He said.

"You too Corrin." Eazak replied.

"How'd you escape Sir?" Taymen asked as he sat down. His marines took up positions along the bulkhead behind him.

"I had a little help actually." Assh replied.

Before he could explain the hatch opened and General Raise walked in.

Sharr and Taymen shot to their feet, both of them drew their side arms and had them trained on Raise along with all the marines in the room.

"Wait Colonel!" Assh snapped.

Raise simply froze in place with his hands up.

"Sir this man is a traitor." Taymen said keeping his eyes on Raise.

"I'm well aware of that Colonel but he was the one who helped us escape." Assh explained.

"Us?" Eazak asked.

"Sir with respect this is the second time you've shown up with our enemy." Taymen said.

"Colonel stand down. General Raise for the time being is with us." Assh said.

Taymen slowly lowered his weapon and then finally placed it back in its holster.

Sharr did the same a few seconds later.

"Stand down." Taymen said to his marines.

Raise slowly took a pace forward.

"I know there's no way you'll trust me now but I mean it when I say that everything I did, I did because I thought it was best for the Empire." He explained.

Taymen scoffed.

"You're right, I don't trust you. As far as I'm concerned you're a traitor and should be tried as one." He said.

"And he will be later, for now however we need him." Assh said.

"Am I interrupting?" A voice said from the hatch.

Taymen turned and froze in place.

"Queen Auria!" He said in shock before dropping to one knee with Sharr and Eazak.

"As you were." Auria said.

Taymen and the others slowly stood up and waited as General Assh made his way around the table to her side.

"Queen Auria, may I present Colonel Taymen Orelle and Colonel Sharr Vaye of the Imperial Guard." Assh said.

"Welcome." She said. "I've heard a great deal about you two, I understand you've given the Tray good reason to fear your ships."

Sharr smiled a little while Taymen remained expressionless.

"I've heard several of the Tray commanders refer to your ships as death's harbingers on more than one occasion." She continued before turning to see Eazak standing near the table.

"General Eazak I must say I'm surprised to see you here."

Eazak smiled.

"The Egyptians are still my people." He said.

Auria smiled a little as she moved to the head of the table. They all waited for her to sit down before taking their own seats.

"Now then." She started. "We're here in answer to your call Colonel Orelle. The Tray are likely well aware of your plan to attack as was no doubt your intention."

Taymen nodded.

"Yes Ma'am." He said. "We've started rumors that the outer belt is our staging area, hopefully the Tray will focus the bulk of their ships there. Our prowlers are also in position to provide us with a full account of their actual ship locations the moment we stream into the system."

Corrin couldn't help but smile. It was the sort of plan that he should have expected from Taymen and yet he never would have thought of it.

"How many ships are you expecting to rendezvous with us?" Raise asked.

"I'm not expecting any." Taymen said. "We're prepared to take Abydos with the three ships we have."

Nobody said anything.

"Do you really believe that's possible?" Auria asked.

"I wouldn't risk it if I didn't Ma'am." Taymen replied.

Auria smiled.

"I can see that your reputation is well earned Colonel." She said as she stood up. "Still, I do not believe that either of you are properly equipped to command this offensive." She continued as she moved around the table to the back of the room.

"General Assh, General Raise if you please." Auria said.

"Yes Ma'am." They said as they moved next to her and faced Taymen and the others.

"General Eazak join us please." Corrin said.

Eazak hesitantly moved to take up a position to Corrin's left.

"Colonel Vaye, Colonel Orelle." Raise said calling them both forward.

Assh turned briefly to Auria who simply nodded once.

"Under the authority of her majesty Queen Auria, Colonel Orelle and Colonel Vaye you are herby promoted to the rank of Major-General." Corrin said.

Both Sharr and Taymen stood silent more so because of the shock as both Corrin and Amaat stepped forward and replaced their rank insignias.

"In addition you are both granted command of the newly formed battle group Insurrection with General Orelle as the senior commanding officer. Congratulations." Corrin said.

"Thank you Sir." Both Taymen and Sharr replied almost simultaneously.

"This new battle group needs a new kind of commander." Auria started. "I think you two are the beginnings of a new generation of leaders for our Empire."

Both Taymen and Sharr stood silent not knowing what to say when suddenly the room echoed with the buzz of the internal com. system.

"All hands bring the ship to battle mode." A voice said.

"We'd better get to C.A.C.; I want the three of you to join us." Corrin said.

Taymen and the others followed Corrin to C.A.C. where everyone was already at their stations.

"Report." Corrin said.

"Two ships just streamed into the area and are closing fast." The Ex O reported.

"Any idea who they are?" Raise asked.

"Not yet." The Ex O replied.

"Sir I've got multiple protostream events. More ships are entering the area." One of the operations officers reported.

"Have our ships form up on us and prepare for battle." Raise ordered.

"Sir several ships are broadcasting hails on an open band." The communications officer said.

Raise looked to Taymen.

"Patch them through one at a time Lieutenant." Auria said.

The speakers clicked as the first channel was opened.

"This is Commander Drailen of the first Egyptian Independent battle group." The voice said.

"They're separatists." Corrin said in surprise.

"They're back." Eazak said.

"We've come in answer to Colonel Orelle's message to assist the Egyptian people." The Commander continued.

The speakers clicked as the channel switched.

"This is Colonel Anri of the Egyptian battle ship Avatar of Darkness responding to Colonel Orelle."

The channel switched again.

"This is Colonel Barak aboard the Egyptian battle ship Obelisk. I am in command of twelve Egyptian battle ships and we've come to fight alongside the Dark Avenger."

Taymen looked to Sharr and then to Corrin. Both simply smiled in excitement.

"How many ships are out there?" Raise asked.

"Forty-one Sir." The operations officer replied.

"Well it's better than four." Eazak said.

"Much better." Corrin added.

"Sir I've got another protostream event. More ships have entered the system." The Operations officer reported.

"They're Tray!" The Ex O snapped.

"Order all ships to prepare for battle." Raise snapped.

"Wait, they're hailing Sir." The communications officer said.

Raise and Assh simply looked at Taymen.

"Well General this is your battle group. What are your orders?" Corrin said.

Taymen suddenly felt like he was going to be sick. He took a moment to shake off the nausea and stepped closer to the command console.

"Order all our ships to form up on us and paint their targets but do not fire until I give the order." He ordered. "Ready all missile tubes and prepare all forward batteries for enemy suppression fire." He continued.

"All stations report ready Sir." The weapons officer reported a moment later.

"Patch the Tray through." Taymen said.

The speaker clicked as the channel opened.

"Egyptian flagship this is Fleet Marshal Phay of the Tray Republican Guard. We've come in response to a message from Colonel Taymen Orelle, please respond."

Taymen looked at Sharr.

"Tray Republican Guard?" He said in confusion.

Sharr simply shrugged.

Taymen looked at the others who gave him similar responses. After a few minutes he hit the control on his earpiece.

"This is Major-General Taymen Orelle of the Egyptian battle group Insurrection. Hold your position and explain yourself Fleet Marshal." He said.

There was brief silence before Phay spoke again.

"My apologies General. The current situation is somewhat complicated but you should know that the Tray that now occupy your territory are a renegade faction of our republic. My battle group has been hunting them for almost six years now. We followed them to your galaxy but were too late to stop the occupation of your worlds."

Again Taymen turned to Sharr who remained silent.

"Very well Fleet Marshal we will transmit docking instructions to you. You and you alone have permission to board the Dark Avenger. Tell your ships to maintain their positions. If they deviate or we detect more than one shuttle approaching you will be fired upon." He said.

"Understood General." Phay finally said before closing the channel.

Taymen turned to the communications officer.

"Order our fleet to stand-by. Do not fire unless fired upon." He said.

"Yes Sir."

"Have our prowlers prepped for departure." Taymen continued.

"General Eazak please return to your ship and coordinate with your battle group. I want a general report on the status of every one of your ships within the hour."

"Yes Sir." Eazak said somewhat sarcastically.

"General Raise if you could prepare the same reports from all of our ships."

Raise nodded.

"The rest of us will greet our 'guest' on the Avenger and try to get to the bottom of all this."

Dark Avenger, Briefing Room
18:23 Abydos Standard Time
Day 5, Third Cycle, Egyptian Year 3202

Taymen waited in the conference room with Sharr, Corrin and Queen Auria.

"What are you thinking Taymen?" Sharr asked quietly.

"It might be worth listening to what this Fleet Marshal has to say." Taymen replied.

Suddenly the hatch opened and two marines walked in followed by a young woman and then two more marines.

The woman who Taymen and Sharr assumed to be Fleet Marshal Phay, seemed very young. As far as Taymen was concerned she wasn't much older than he was.

She was almost a full foot shorter than Taymen. Her long brown hair flowed down to just above the center of her back and her dark brown eyes scanned over the room and everyone in it.

She stepped towards Corrin looking up at him before speaking.

"General Orelle it's a pleasure to finally meet you in person."

Corrin smiled a little as did Sharr and Auria while Taymen remained silent and waited. It wasn't surprising that Phay assumed Corrin was Taymen. He obviously seemed old enough to be a General, Taymen however seemed too young to be a Major.

"I'm afraid you're mistaken." Corrin said.

Phay looked at him puzzled.

"Excuse me?" She said.

"I'm General Corrin Assh, aid to Queen Auria of the Egyptian Empire." Corrin gestured towards Auria who nodded once.

Phay turned to face Auria and bowed.

"Your majesty." She said in a respectful greeting.

"This is Major-General Sharr Vaye." Corrin continued.

Sharr nodded once in greeting as did Phay.

"And this is Major-General Taymen Orelle." Corrin finally said gesturing to Taymen who took a few steps forward.

Phay slowly walked up to Taymen staring up into his icy blue eyes.

"General, it's a pleasure." She said.

"Yes, I heard you the first time." Taymen said with a hint of humor in his tone.

"I'm Fleet Marshal Taneaa Phay." She said.

"Have a seat Fleet Marshal." Taymen said gesturing to the end of the table opposite Auria.

"We don't have a lot of time so let's get to the point." Taymen started. "You can start by explaining yourself Fleet Marshal." He continued.

Taneaa sighed.

"Of course." She started. "We're from a distant corner of the universe several years travel from here." She explained.

"I'm aware of the general history of your people and your war with the ancients." Taymen said.

"Then you should know that my people have come a long way since that war." Taneaa continued. "Our technology has evolved since the ancients left. Unfortunately there were several people on our planet who thought we should pursue the ancient's knowledge elsewhere and expand our empire once again. This caused a major conflict on our planet but eventually those who wanted to expand our territory were overruled by the majority government."

"But that wasn't the end of it was it?" Corrin asked.

"No." Taneaa replied. "Several factions banded together under the command of one man and left our world to search for the ancient's knowledge. Our government of course tried to stop them but it was too late. By the time they realized what was happening these rebels had taken what resources they could and left our planet. My battle group was dispatched to hunt them down and bring them back or if necessary destroy them." She explained.

"Well you've done a great job so far." Sharr said sarcastically.

"Ourik is the one in command of these renegades?" Taymen asked.

"No." Raise said. "He's just the field commander, he reports to someone else."

"Fleet Marshal Ourik was a very prominent figure during the original dispute." Taneaa explained. "He's a brilliant commander but he's also a bit of a coward. He reports to Chancellor Crowell and we have no idea where to find him."

"He isn't our problem right now." Taymen said. "Ourik is and we know where to find him."

"I'm afraid it may not be that simple." Taneaa said. "Ourik's ship has been outfitted with ancient technology that he's discovered during his campaign making it much more powerful than anything you've faced so far."

Taymen sighed.

"Leave the Titan to us." He said. "If you want to help end this and go home, commit your fleet to our campaign and follow my orders."

Taneaa sighed.

"My fleet won't submit to an alien commander." She said.

"Well I'm not about to allow you to go roaming around our territory while we try and launch a major offensive." Taymen said.

"With all due respect General my fleet outnumbers yours at least four to one. What makes you think you can stop us?" Taneaa asked.

Taymen sighed.

"Fleet Marshal I'm about to put my fleet against a Tray force that outnumbers us at least twelve to one." He said. "Do you really think your little fleet worries me?"

Taneaa didn't say anything.

Sharr smiled a little to herself as Taymen waited for a reaction.

"I see your point General." Taneaa finally said.

"I'm not asking any of you to submit to us." Taymen continued. "I'm asking you to fight with us."

Taneaa thought it over for a moment.

"Very well General." She replied. "We will join you in the interest of stopping Ourik."

"Good." Taymen started. "Ready your ships for battle. I want a detailed report of all your ships in one hour. We leave tomorrow morning." He continued.

"How do I know I can trust you?" Taneaa asked.

Taymen tapped the control on his earpiece.

"Sairon." He started. "Advise the fleet to stand down." He ordered.

Taneaa simply smiled as Taymen left the briefing room.

He made his way back to C.A.C. after escorting Auria, Sharr and Corrin back to their prowlers on the starboard hangar deck.

Fleet Marshal Phay's shuttle was on the port deck.

"Captain on deck!" Titus shouted as Taymen closed the hatch.

"Carry on." Taymen said as he made his way down to the command console.

"Report." He said.

"The fleet's stood down and the Tray ships haven't moved." Avril reported.

"Colonel." Titus said as he brought a data pad over to him.

His eyes widened at the sight of the new rank insignias on Taymen's jacket.

"Excuse me, General." He corrected himself.

Avril took a second look at the rank insignias and realized what she had missed a moment ago.

"What is it Commander?" Taymen asked as he took the data pad.

"A report from General Raise aboard the Spear of Osiris." Titus said.

"What!" Avril snapped. "Raise is here?" She asked.

"Yes." Taymen said. "It seems that there are a few things that need explaining." He continued. "I want all senior ship captains in the briefing room in two hours."

"Aye Sir." Avril said.

"I'll be in my cabin until then." Taymen said as he turned to leave.

Chapter Twenty-Eight

Taymen sat at the head of the table in the briefing room.

Sharr sat to his left and Corrin to his right. Next to Corrin sat General Eazak and the other senior captains surrounded the table along with Fleet Marshal Phay.

"Alright let's not waste time." Taymen started. "You all know why you're here."

He looked around the table once.

"Including the Tray ships from their Republican Guard we have ninety-six ships ready for battle though some are in need of experienced Captains. I will be assigning senior officers from other ships to fill those roles for the time being." Taymen said.

"Now the Tray know we're coming for Abydos and thanks to our prowler pilots they think we'll be coming from the outer belt."

He took another look around.

"We have a significant advantage over them and now with the additional ships we can attack several targets at once."

"What did you have in mind?" Eazak asked.

"We will take Abydos as planned as most of the Tray forces will likely be concentrated there. However now we will also launch attacks to retake Netara, Cairon and Nilea as well."

"That's quite ambitious." Eazak said.

"The bulk of the Tray ships will be at Abydos, they won't be expecting us to have the resources to launch such a wide spread campaign." Sharr said.

"We will deploy fleets made up of ships from all three groups and launch a simultaneous attack against these locations. With any luck we'll hit the Tray hard enough that they won't be able to recover." Taymen explained.

"That's a good plan." Taneaa said. "Knowing Ourik, if he feels that he's losing too much ground he'll withdraw his forces to a more defendable position. If we can keep them off balance long enough we can hunt them down as they're trying to regroup and destroy them before they can make a final stand." She continued.

"Which is why it's important that we maintain communications between each location." Taymen said. "The drone network will allow us to coordinate our attack and advise each other of our progress. As the Tray retreat from one location we'll hopefully be able to intercept them at another."

He looked around the room at everyone's face and saw nods of approval from them all.

"Now, here are the ship assignments."

Dark Avenger, C.A.C.
21:54 Abydos Standard Time
Day 5, Third Cycle, Egyptian Year 3202

Taymen walked into C.A.C. and found Avril and Titus at the command console going over their systems checks.

"How are we doing Captain?" He asked.

"All sections report ready, we're just doing our final checks now Sir." Avril reported.

"Good." Taymen said.

He looked around C.A.C. briefly before turning to Avril again.

"All hands." He started.

Everyone looked up from their stations at Taymen.

"As you know there are ninety-six ships out there ready for combat. What you may not know is that there are twelve in need of experienced captains. I've assigned senior officers from several ships including this one to fill those positions."

Taymen pulled a small box out of his pocket and opened it.

"Captain Avril Raquel." He started. "Effective immediately you are promoted to the rank of Major and assigned command of the Chaos Breaker."

He removed Avril's rank insignias and replaced them with his old Major insignias.

"Congratulations Major." He said.

Avril smiled.

"Thank you General." She said.

"You'd better get your things. You're crew is expecting you shortly."

297

Avril nodded before leaving C.A.C.

"Commander Daverro you're my new Ex-O."

Titus smiled.

"Aye Sir." He said.

Taymen went back to his cabin to find Talia waiting for him. By the look on her face he figured he knew what was on her mind.

"What's this I hear about you sending me to another ship?" She asked.

Taymen closed the hatch before answering.

"We're about to go into battle Talia, I don't want to put you in harms' way anymore." He said. "You'll be aboard the Starry Venture with Queen Auria. You'll both be safe there."

Talia sighed.

"I don't want to be safe." She said. "I want to be with you."

Taymen smiled.

"I want nothing more than to have you with me but this is too dangerous. I need to know that if something happens at least you'll be safe." He explained.

"And who's going to look after you?" Talia asked.

"Don't worry about me." Taymen said. "This is something I need to do, there's too much at stake."

Talia sighed again as she wrapped her arms around Taymen placing her head on his chest.

"Promise me you'll come back." She said.

Taymen wrapped his arms around her and kissed her head.

"I promise." He said softly.

Titan. Bridge
22:00 Abydos Standard Time
Day 5, Third Cycle, Egyptian Year 3202

Ourik watched the display screen to ensure everyone was in position. He had sent the bulk of his ships to the outer belt to intercept the Egyptians but kept a sizeable fleet in reserve on the far side of Abydos just in case.

"We're in a low orbit now Sir." The helmsman reported.

"Good, maintain our position." Ourik said.

"Have all ships remain on high alert. Fire on the Egyptians on sight, do not let them near the planet." He ordered.

"Sir, what about the rumors of the rebellion that's been massing on the surface?" The operations officer asked.

Ourik scoffed.

"Without any kind of heavy weapons support from a ship or fighter squadron they won't be very effective against our armored units on the ground." He said.

"Leave them be for now. We'll deal with Colonel Orelle and his ship first."

Dark Avenger, Briefing Room
22:25 Abydos Standard Time
Day 5, Third Cycle, Egyptian Year 3202

Taymen sat at the head of the table in the Dark Avenger's briefing room.

To his left was General Eazak with General Raise sitting next to him and to Taymen's right sat General Assh.

"Taymen we called you here for an informal session before the attack begins." Corrin started.

"The fact is Taymen." Eazak started. "The promotion from Colonel to General is different from any other and being put in command of an entire battle group is intimidating in itself no matter who you are or how experienced you may be."

"I understand Sir." Taymen said.

"In truth we called you here because it is tradition that a new General be given the opportunity to ask the advice of an experienced General before their first assignment." Raise explained.

Taymen felt a wave of relief pass over him. It was as if they had just given him permission to tell them how overwhelmed he was feeling.

"Sir." He started. "Wouldn't one of you be a more appropriate choice to lead the battle group?" He asked.

Corrin smiled.

"No." He said.

"Taymen this is your fight." Eazak said. "It's been your fight from the very beginning. Nobody knows the Tray like you do and you have the most experience fighting them."

"But Sir an entire battle group, I'm in way over my head." Taymen argued.

"Look at it this way." Eazak started. "You're relying on the fleet more than they're relying on you. You're responsible for seeing the situation from a wider angle and putting each ship in its place. Just concentrate on where you want them and what you want them to accomplish they'll take care of the rest." Corrin said.

Taymen nodded his head as he thought it over. When he heard it put that way it made things sound much simpler. It wasn't all that different from commanding a ship.

"In that case Sir I have a favor to ask." He finally said.

"Of course." Corrin replied.

"I want you and General Raise aboard the Starry Venture during the attack."

Raise smiled.

"Don't want the two of us looking over your shoulder?" He said.

Taymen sighed at the joke.

"Regardless of the outcome our people are going to need leaders, experienced people who can guide them to rebuild our homes. Queen Auria is a political ruler but not a military strategist, she will need guidance to help defend our people again."

Corrin and Raise smiled.

"Thought this through have you." Corrin said.

Taymen didn't say anything.

"Alright Taymen, we'll stay with the Queen."

"I'll leave three ships behind with the Starry Venture in case the Tray show up." Taymen said.

"Now then." Raise started. "Surely we could all do with a little sleep before the attack."

"Yes." Corrin said as he stood up. "Unless there was something else Taymen."

"Actually there was Sir." Taymen replied.

Corrin sat back down.

Taymen sighed as he pieced together the question he had been afraid to ask.

"Sir did you know the Tray were coming?"

Corrin and the others remained silent for a moment.

"What would make you think that?" He asked.

"General Raise." Taymen said.

Corrin and Eazak looked at Raise who remained silent.

"You told him?" Eazak said.

Raise nodded.

"I didn't see the harm at the time." He replied.

Corrin sighed as he shook his head.

"Yes Taymen we did." He replied.

"Then how could this have happened?" Taymen snapped.

"You have to understand." Corrin started. "We were in no position to fight a war on two fronts. Not when the Tray was on one of those fronts."

"Just how long have you known?" Taymen asked.

Eazak looked at Corrin briefly before answering.

"We found out towards the last few months of the war." He said.

"Right about the time you left to join the separatists." Taymen said.

Eazak nodded slightly.

"A Tray advance force entered our territory with an ultimatum for surrender several months before the initial attack." Corrin explained.

"We refused of course." Raise added.

"But we didn't have sufficient time to build an effective defense. Nobody expected the Tray fleet to be so vast or to arrive so soon."

Taymen nodded slightly.

"Did you know what they wanted?" He asked.

"Not at first but it wouldn't have mattered." Corrin said. "We didn't have what they wanted nor did we know where to find it."

There was a long and awkward silence before Corrin finally stood up.

"I think that's enough for now." He said.

"Yes, we'll get off your ship and leave you to your battle group." Raise said.

"I'll be just a minute." Eazak said. "I want to talk to Taymen privately."

Once the hatch closed Eazak moved closer to Taymen.

"Listen I have a favor to ask." He said.

"Alright." Taymen said with a slight hesitation.

"I've left Jassen in command of one of my ships, the Dragon's Claw." He explained.

"Jassen's a civilian." Taymen said. "Are you sure that's a good idea?"

"I trust him." Eazak said. "The fact that he's a civilian aside he's a natural leader and we need experienced leaders to command our ships but there's no denying the fact that he has limited experience in combat, so I want you to look after him."

Taymen nodded.

"Of course." He said.

Eazak smiled.

"I meant what I said." He continued. "This has been your fight from the very beginning and I think I knew that from the first time I met you. You should be very proud of yourself Taymen. I can tell you that every Egyptian who knows your name is."

Dark Avenger, C.A.C.
02:40 Abydos Standard Time
Day 6, Third Cycle, Egyptian Year 3202

Taymen stood at the command console in C.A.C. anxiously waiting. He had declared the attack would begin at zero-six-hundred hours that morning.

Prior to that the fleets would depart for their various staging areas so that they were all the same distance from their respective targets. He checked the display screen and saw all ninety-six ships waiting for his order.

Taymen felt terrified at the thought of all those people waiting for his order. It was almost like the feeling he had his first day in command of the Dark Avenger. There were so many people depending on him to make the right choices at the right time even when he had no clue what the right choice was.

Now there were far more people depending on him for the same thing, except now he would have to look at a much wider view of everything.

He had divided the battle group into four fleets each with a different target but their orders were the same. Retake the target and destroy the Tray. Failure was not an option.

Taymen of course would lead the fleet going to Abydos while he left Sharr in charge of the fleet going to Netara.

General Assh and General Raise remained behind with Queen Auria and Talia on the Starry Venture.

General Eazak was in charge of the fleet heading for Cairon while Fleet Marshal Phay insisted on going with Taymen to Abydos to ensure Ourik didn't escape.

Taymen assigned ships from the Tray, Egyptian and separatist fleets to all four groups making it a true joint effort between them all.

"Sir." Sairon said. "The Starry Venture is hailing us." She reported.

"Patch them through." Taymen said as he hit the control on his earpiece.

"General Orelle this is General Assh."

"Go ahead Sir." Taymen said.

"You are clear for departure. Good luck." Corrin said.

"Understood Sir we'll see you soon." Taymen said before closing the channel.

He took one last look at the display screen and took a deep breath.

'Here we go.' He said quietly to himself.

"Sairon." He started. "Patch me through to the battle group."

"Aye Sir." Sairon said.

Taymen took a moment before hitting the control on his earpiece.

"All ships this is General Orelle of the Dark Avenger." He started.

The word General before his name still sounded so strange to him.

"We are clear for departure. You all have your targets and you know your orders. I don't have to tell you what's at stake here. Our people, all our peoples are counting on us. They're waiting for us to give them the signal to fight back.

"We are their last hope and I will not allow hope to be lost again not as long as I command this fleet. The Tray hold our planets and our people hostage but that gives us a reason to fight. The Tray are no match for us now, they are arrogant cowards and today they will rue the day they ever crossed the Egyptian people."

Taymen's tone became more aggressive as if his own words were giving him the confidence to lead the fleet.

"Stay alert and stand fast. We will win the day, not just for our people but for all those that the Tray have oppressed and all those that they will oppress if they're not stopped. Today is the day we make our stand! Today is the day of insurrection!"

Suddenly the crews throughout the fleet on every ship including the Dark Avenger let out a cheer. None of them were willing to surrender, they all had someone they hoped to see again and that was enough to give them all the courage they needed.

As Taymen looked at the faces of his crew in C.A.C. the images of Talia, Auria and Corrin flashed through his mind. He didn't know why but that made him feel a little more at ease. The memory of everyone he had left behind and everyone he was fighting for made Taymen feel like any decision he made today would be the right one.

All the lessons he learned over the last year echoed in his mind. The images of his lost crewmen and the things Seahla said to him stood out now. He understood what she was trying to say now more than ever before. He couldn't focus on what might be, he had to focus on what is and try to mold it to what he wants it to be.

Taymen suddenly felt like no matter what he did his crew and his fleet would make it a victory for them all. They would bend this imperfect universe to their will and turn the dark reality that is into the bright future they all longed for.

"All ships." He started. "Prepare to stream out!"

Part VII
Insurrection

'The greatest offensives in history were only made possible by those who fought from the inside. Without them we would have been doomed to failure and the lives of thousands would have been lost.'

Defense Force history lesson 27-02

Chapter Twenty-Nine

Dark Avenger at Abydos Staging Area
05:45 Abydos Standard Time
Day 6, Third Cycle, Egyptian Year 3202

The vast darkness would seem endless if it weren't for the brilliant stars shinning in the distance.

The Abydos sun was the closest star. Just under a hundred light minutes away it was less than a thirty minute trip through the protostream.

As the light from Abydos continued to radiate through the darkness the empty void was suddenly filled with a group of dark lightning bolts that flashed and dissipated leaving a group of thirty-five ships in their wake.

Taymen checked the sensor display briefly before turning to the operations stations.

"Report." He said.

"Stream complete we've arrived at our staging area Sir." The operations officer reported.

"Time till zero hour?" Taymen asked.

"Zero hour in thirty minutes Sir." Titus said.

Taymen nodded.

"Advise the fleet to go to stealth mode and to prepare for battle."

Silver Phoenix at Netara Staging Area
05:47 Abydos Standard Time
Day 6, Third Cycle, Egyptian Year 3202

Sharr watched the countdown on the display screen at the head of C.A.C. anxiously waiting for it to reach zero. She could feel how tense her crew was and was feeling rather tense herself. She had seventeen ships with her waiting for her order to attack.

Taymen had left her in charge of the fleet going to retake Netara and she promised him she wouldn't fail.

She didn't know why but she felt like she owed Taymen so much she couldn't bear the thought of failing him now, not after everything he had done for all of them.

Sharr continued to watch the display screen ensuring everyone was in position as the counter reached ten minutes.

When the counter reached zero all four fleets would stream from their respective staging areas to their targets arriving at the same time to launch a simultaneous attack against the Tray cutting them off from any major support and throwing them off balance.

"General." The operations officer started. "The drone at Netara is reading six sensor contacts entering a low orbit."

"How many Tray vessels are in the system now?" Sharr asked.

"Thirty-seven." The operations officer replied.

Sharr sighed.

"We're outnumbered two to one, this is going to be interesting." She said.

Demon's Light at Cairon Staging Area
05:51 Abydos Standard Time
Day 6, Third Cycle, Egyptian Year 3202

"How long?" Eazak asked.

"Nine minutes." The operations officer said.

Eazak sighed. They had been waiting for almost an hour for zero hour and he was getting impatient.

As a General in the Defense Force and then in the separatist fleet he had fought dozens of battles and led several missions and each time he felt the same anxiety he was feeling now.

He trusted Taymen and thought him a brilliant commander for his age but he couldn't help but wonder about this plan. It was ambitious for certain but Eazak also found it to be more than a little reckless. Still there was a lot riding on this plan and they couldn't afford to fail.

Dragon's Claw at Abydos Staging Area
05:53 Abydos Standard Time
Day 6, Third Cycle, Egyptian Year 3202

Jassen slowly moved from station to station impatiently waiting for the order to stream out. He was used to being in charge but he had never been in command of a ship before, let alone a warship about to go into combat. He was terrified to say the least.

Eazak had given him a crash course in battle ship command tactics but it was all happening so fast that Jassen didn't have time to assimilate anything.

308

There were nine hundred people depending on him now to do the right thing and to make the right choices but Jassen had no idea what the right thing was. Is he supposed to simply safeguard his crew or was he supposed to sacrifice everything to ensure the success of the mission? He really didn't know.

He had asked Eazak that very question and his words still echoed in his mind.

'Sometimes it's one and sometimes it's the other. And sometimes it's both but in the end you'll know when the time comes which is right.'

For some reason that didn't make Jassen feel at ease about it.

Dark Avenger, C.A.C.
05:58 Abydos Standard Time
Day 6, Third Cycle, Egyptian Year 3202

"Sir two minutes to zero hour." Titus said.

Taymen took a deep breath before straightening his uniform jacket.

"Alright." He said. "Sairon patch me through to the fleet."

"Go ahead Sir." Sairon said.

"All ships this is General Orelle. You all have your orders, lead group stream to your designated coordinates, main group form up on us and stream out to your assigned coordinates on our lead. Follow up group stream out on my order. Good luck to us all."

Taymen closed the channel and watched the display screen. A moment later six ships disappeared as they streamed out.

"The lead group is away Sir." The operations officer reported.

"Alright helm charge the stream system and prepare to stream us out." Taymen ordered.

"Aye Sir stream system charging." Aurin replied.

"I'm linked to the drones at Abydos and the outer belt Sir." The operations officer said a moment later. "Lead group has arrived at the outer belt and the Tray fleet has detected them. They're moving ships towards the outer belt." He continued.

"How many?" Titus asked.

"Looks like forty Sir." The operations officer said.

"That leaves us with twenty-five around Abydos." Titus said.

Taymen didn't say anything. He figured there would be more ships guarding Abydos, but they only saw about half of what they predicted.

"Alright." He said. "How far out are those forty ships?"

"They've just streamed to the edge of the outer belt." The operations officer said.

"Well they're not wasting any time." Titus said.

"Tell me when they've entered the belt." Taymen ordered. "Sairon advise the main group to prepare to stream out and have the Dragon's Claw remain on our port flank."

"Sir the Tray ships have entered the outer belt but fifteen are holding position just outside of it." The operations officer said a few minutes later.

"That'll have to do." Taymen said. "Advise the lead group to launch their nukes and get out of there. Have the main group stream to Abydos. Aurin stream us out." He continued.

"Aye Sir." Aurin said.

A few seconds later Taymen's vision went dark and then cleared again.

"Stream complete Sir, we're between the Tray fleet and the planet." Aurin reported.

"The fleet has formed up on us and the Tray are moving to engage." Titus said.

"What's the status on the lead group?" Taymen asked.

"The lead group has streamed to the Tray's starboard flank and are closing in." The operations officer reported.

"What about those forty ships?" Titus asked.

"The drone is showing only twenty-seven Tray ships of the original forty. Looks like they're getting ready to stream back." The operations officer said.

"Bring the fleet to battle mode." Taymen said. "Deploy armor, launch all initial salvos and have the fleet break formation to engage their targets but keep the Dragon's Claw on our flank." He continued.

A few seconds later every ship in Taymen's fleet fired a full salvo of assorted missiles at every target in range.

Taymen watched the display screen as the Tray fleet broke formation in response to the attack.

"Tray fighters are inbound." Titus said.

"Launch all sword breakers. Have them engage any target within five light seconds of us." Taymen ordered. "All odd number batteries prepare for enemy suppression fire, remaining batteries direct fire on any targets in range." He continued.

"Helm set an intercept course for heavy cruisers five and six all ahead full. Carrey prepare all heavy batteries and missile tubes."

"Incoming ordnance!" The operations officer said.

The deck shuttered for a few seconds as Taymen checked the displays at the head of C.A.C. to see where the fleet was.

"Switch the left display screen to show the firing solutions of all weapons in relation to all available targets." He said.

"Aye Sir." The operations officer replied.

A few seconds later the left display screen flashed to a three dimensional image of the Dark Avenger surrounded by a series of colored sections to show the firing arcs of all the gun batteries.

Another second later the screen displayed all of the Tray targets in range and any Egyptian ships within the firing arcs. The two cruisers Taymen specified were each marked with a red diamond.

Taymen scanned the image on the screen focusing on the two cruisers directly ahead of them as they entered the heavy batteries' arcs.

"All heavy batteries fire at will!" Taymen said. "Batteries one, seven and nine switch to direct fire, four, ten and twelve switch to suppression fire." He continued as more cruisers passed through their arcs.

"Sir I'm detecting more Tray ships approaching from the planet's surface." Titus said.

"What?" Taymen snapped.

"I'm reading almost fifty Tray ships closing in on us from the planet's night side." The operations officer continued.

"A trap!" Titus snapped.

"They have us flanked from the planet side." The operations officer said.

"Damn it." Taymen cursed. "I walked right into that one."

Silver Phoenix, C.A.C.
06:47 Abydos Standard Time
Day 6, Third Cycle, Egyptian Year 3202

Sharr scrambled to her feet and checked the display.

"All missile tubes fire!" She snapped.

"Two more cruisers are bearing down on us!" The operations officer reported.

"Bring our bow to bear on the two cruisers to our starboard." She said. "Launch all remaining fighters and drones and ready another salvo from all missile tubes."

"Fighters are away." One of the flight controllers said a moment later.

"Missile tubes ready." The weapons officer reported.

"All missiles target the two cruisers on our aft. All gun batteries switch to direct fire on the two cruisers off our bow." Sharr continued.

"Missiles locked."

"Fire!" She snapped.

A few seconds later two of the targets on the display screen disappeared while the other two continued to close in on the Silver Phoenix.

"Two cruisers have been destroyed." The Ex O reported.

311

"Helm hard to port. Bring our starboard side to bear on those cruisers. All starboard batteries fire at will and ready all starboard missile tubes for another salvo." Sharr ordered.

"Ma'am we're receiving a transmission from General Eazak via the drone network." The communications officer reported.

"The message says the Tray forces have retreated from Cairon and he is sending reinforcements to assist us. They will be arriving in the next thirty minutes." The communications officer said.

"That was fast." The Ex O said.

"Let's see if we can finish this before those reinforcements of his arrive." Sharr replied.

Dragon's Claw, C.A.C.
07:12 Abydos Standard Time
Day 6, Third Cycle, Egyptian Year 3202

Jassen stood near the helm station watching the display screen. They had been intercepting a lot of ordnance that was probably meant for the Dark Avenger but they managed to hold their own.

The ship was seriously under manned. There were no experienced leaders aboard which made Jassen the only one with any kind of real leadership experience.

"Sir two light cruisers are closing in on us and another wing of fighters is heading for the Avenger." The operations officer said.

"Launch a full salvo of missiles at those cruisers and have all gun batteries target those fighters." Jassen ordered.

It took a little while before he was comfortable giving combat orders, but given the circumstances he had to learn quickly.

"Incoming ordnance!" The operations officer called out just before the deck shuttered.

"Sir more Tray ships are closing in on us."

Jassen checked the screen briefly.

"They're boxing us in." He said to himself.

"If they manage to surround us we won't have a chance." The operations officer pointed out.

Titan at Abydos
07:25 Abydos Standard Time
Day 6, Third Cycle, Egyptian Year 3202

Ourik sat in his seat watching the display screen at the head of the bridge. They had been watching the battle from a low orbit near the planet's North Pole so that the Egyptian ships wouldn't be able to detect them.

"Sir should we break orbit?" The helmsman asked.

Ourik smirked.

"No the fleet is doing just fine without us." He said. "We have the Egyptians surrounded and outnumbered. There's no way they'll be able to fight their way out of this."

Dark Avenger, C.A.C.
07:32 Abydos Standard Time
Day 6, Third Cycle, Egyptian Year 3202

"That's it Sir the Tray have us boxed in. We're taking fire on all sides." Titus said.

"Sir we're receiving a report from our operatives on the planet. They're calling for supporting fire against Tray installations and armored units." Sairon said.

Taymen sighed.

"Great timing." He said sarcastically. "Sairon order the fleet to form up on us and ready all forward firing weapons." He said. "Helm bring our bow to bear on the planet and hold our position but prepare for full thrust." He continued.

"Aye Sir." Aurin replied.

"The fleet's in position Sir." Titus said a moment later.

"Sairon open a channel for a general broadcast." Taymen said.

"Channel open Sir." Sairon replied.

"General Orelle to all prowlers, execute." Taymen said before closing the channel.

A few seconds later all of the Avenger's prowlers streamed into the system just a few light seconds from the Tray's rear flank. Each one fired off a single missile before streaming away again.

"What in the name of Anubis?" Titus started.

Before anyone could say anything else all of the prowler's missiles detonated almost simultaneously enveloping the Tray ships in a massive wave of radiation tearing several of them apart immediately leaving a large gap in their line.

"You gave those prowlers nukes?" Titus asked.

"Well I had to do something with all those extra missiles we found on the supply station." Taymen said.

"Alright Aurin all ahead full. All forward weapons prepare to fire at my command. Sairon inform the follow up group to execute their secondary orders." He continued.

A moment later eight ships streamed away from the main fleet and appeared inside the atmosphere where they launched all of their fighters while the Avenger and the rest of the fleet charged towards the remaining Tray ships ahead of them.

More and more missiles detonated around them as they continued to charge forward.

Taymen watched as a few of their ships disappeared from sensors as they were destroyed by the flanking Tray ships. He continued to watch as the first of the Tray ships entered their firing range.

"All forward weapons fire at will!" He snapped. "Aurin charge us straight through that gap then come about and slow to one half."

Before the Tray could recover from the prowler's attack a seemingly endless stream of missiles and heavy plasma rounds poured into their lines destroying several of the already damaged ships.

As Taymen's fleet continued to charge forward more and more missiles and heavy rounds erupted from their batteries tearing through the Tray ships leaving them with no time to move out of their arcs.

"Sir the Tray line is crumbling." Titus reported.

"The Tray to our port and starboard flanks are closing in on us Sir." The operations officer said with a hint of panic in his voice.

"They're too far out. We'll have cleared the gap by the time they reach us." Aurin said.

"All the same, all lateral batteries switch to direct fire at will." Taymen said.

A few seconds later the Avenger charged through the gap and cleared the Tray line with the rest of the fleet close behind.

"We're clear Sir, coming about." Aurin said.

"Sir the Tray are regrouping." Titus reported.

"How many Tray ships are left?" Taymen asked.

"I'm showing forty Tray ships regrouping directly ahead of us Sir?" The operations officer said.

"Status on the fleet?" Titus asked.

"We have twenty-one ships formed up on us awaiting orders Sir and the eight ships from the follow up group have streamed back to the far side of the planet." The operations officer said.

"Time to finish this." Taymen said. "All ships prepare for…"

The operations officer cut him off.

"Sir there's another ship coming out of low orbit." He said.

"It's the Titan!" Titus snapped.

Taymen checked the display screen to see the massive ship emerge from the planet's atmosphere and take up a position just behind the rest of the Tray fleet.

"Sir Fleet Marshal Phay is hailing." Sairon said.

"Put her through." Taymen replied.

"General, Ourik won't risk his ship unless he's sure he can win. If he feels his fleet is being overrun he will flee. He can't be allowed to escape." She said.

"We're well aware of that Fleet Marshal." Taymen said before closing the channel.

"Signal the fleet." He ordered. "All ahead full and fire at will."

"Aye Sir." Sairon said.

"Carrey ready all missile tubes for multiple salvos and have all gun batteries switch to direct fire at any targets in range." Taymen continued.

"Aye Sir." Carrey said.

"Sir may I suggest we load nukes?" Titus said.

"We're not firing nukes this close to the planet." Taymen replied.

"Missile tubes ready Sir." The weapons officer said.

"Lock onto the six closest cruisers and fire a full salvo at each." Taymen ordered.

It took a moment for all the missiles to clear the tubes and show up on the sensor display.

Taymen watched as they closed in on their targets. Some were shot down and some were intercepted by enemy fighters while the rest hit their targets causing massive damage.

"Two cruisers destroyed Sir. The other four have taken moderate damage." The operations officer reported.

"All heavy batteries cycle between the remaining four cruisers and fire at will." Taymen said.

"Incoming ordnance!" Titus shouted.

The deck shuttered for a moment nearly knocking Taymen from his feet.

"Sir several Tray shuttles have landed in the starboard hangar." The operations officer said.

"They're boarding us." Titus snapped.

Taymen hit the control on his earpiece activating the internal com. system.

"All hands enemy boarding parties in starboard hangar. All marine teams secure the area and repel all boarders." He said.

"Sir three of the four cruisers have been destroyed and the fourth has stopped firing." The operations officer reported.

"All batteries switch to any target that presents itself." Taymen said.

"What's the fleet status?" Titus asked.

"Two more of our ships have been destroyed Sir but the rest of them are holding their own." The operations officer said.

"What about the forces on the planet?" Taymen asked.

"No word yet Sir." Sairon reported.

The deck shuttered again as one of the consoles overloaded and sparked.

"Direct hit to the upper heat exchanger. Hull breach on deck six, frames eight through eleven." The damage control officer said.

"Seal off those frames." Titus ordered.

"Sir marines report all enemy boarders are contained just outside of the hangar." Sairon said.

"We're receiving a transmission from the Titan."

"Patch it through." Taymen said.

A moment later the speakers crackled and Ourik's voice filled C.A.C.

"What are you doing here Taymen?" He asked. *"You're little rabble can't take this planet. Face it, you're losing. Your ship has been boarded, your fleet is failing and I have more ships on the way."* He continued.

"Don't be so confident Ourik." Taymen said. "My fleet is beginning to overrun your position. Your boarding parties are contained and right now most of your reinforcements are busy dealing with the three other fleets I've sent to retake other key planets from you. Face it Fleet Marshal, you're the one who's losing."

Taymen closed the channel before Ourik could respond.

"Sir the Titan is making a run for it. They're heading away from the planet and they're in a hurry." Titus said.

"Helm pursuit course all ahead full!" Taymen snapped.

"Sir we're being hailed by Fleet Marshal Phay." Sairon said.

"Put her through."

"General, Ourik's making a run for it. He can't be allowed to escape." Phay said.

"We're in pursuit. Take command of the fleet here and retake that planet at all costs." Taymen said. "Leave Ourik to me."

"Sairon signal the Dragon's Claw, tell Jassen to…"

Titus cut him off.

"Radiological alert!" He snapped.

"The Titan's fired nukes at the planet." The operations officer reported.

"All batteries switch to enemy suppression fire take out those missiles!" Taymen ordered.

"Sir if we move to destroy those missiles we'll lose the Titan." The operations officer said.

"Sir the Dragon's Claw is moving away from us." Titus said.

"What?" Taymen snapped.

"Sir they're moving to intercept the nukes."

"What is he doing? Put me through to Jassen." Taymen said.

"Jassen what are you doing?" Taymen asked once the channel was open.

"You have to go after the Titan, we'll take care of those missiles." Jassen replied.

"Two missiles down but six are still inbound for the planet. They're moving beyond the effective range of our batteries." Titus said.

"Go after the Titan you're too far out to do any good now."

Taymen glanced up at the display.

"Those missiles will reach the atmosphere in forty seconds." The operations officer said.

"Jassen those missiles are going to detonate on your hull in less than thirty seconds if you don't move out of there." Taymen said.

"Three missiles still inbound." Titus reported.

"It's the only way we can be sure they don't hit the planet's surface." Jassen said. *"Remember your promise Taymen, I'm counting on you."*

Taymen was about to speak when the channel suddenly went to static then silence.

"Nuclear detonation." Titus said.

Taymen looked at the display just in time to see the Dragon's Claw disappear.

"The missiles didn't reach the atmosphere Sir." The operations officer reported.

"But the Dragon's Claw didn't survive." Titus added.

Taymen sighed.

"Sir we'll overtake the Titan in one minute." Aurin reported.

"Let's finish this then." Taymen said.

Chapter Thirty

Talia sat in the conference room drumming her fingers on the table as she waited for any kind of news.

Queen Auria sat quietly across from her reading a data pad. She looked up at Talia briefly and smiled slightly.

"Try not to think about it." She said.

"What?" Talia asked.

"You're worried about Taymen aren't you?" Auria said.

Talia nodded.

Auria put down her data pad and glanced out the window briefly.

"There's nothing you can really do for him right now." She started. "And I'm afraid worrying about him is only going to make you paranoid."

Talia sighed.

"Then what am I supposed to do?" She asked.

"The only thing you can do is trust that he'll come back to you. Until then try to keep your mind occupied."

Talia took a moment and glanced out the window wishing the Dark Avenger would suddenly appear.

"What's that you're reading there?" Talia asked referring to the data pad on the table.

Auria smiled as she picked up the pad.

"It's a copy of the first Pharaoh's address to our people." She said.

"I've been trying to find some sort of inspiration from it. Anything that may help me prepare for what's to come." She explained.

Talia was familiar with the first address. In fact most Egyptians were, it was taught to them in their first few years of school.

"What do you mean?" She asked.

"I can't imagine what it must have been like to try and build an entire civilization on an alien planet and I certainly can't imagine how we're going to rebuild what we had after the Tray are gone." Auria explained.

Talia knew what she meant, at least to some degree. It was hard for her to imagine how their lives could ever be normal again but Auria was the last survivor of the royal family. She would be the one to lead them all into the future.

"So is it helping?" Talia asked.

"I'm afraid not." Auria said.

Talia was about to say something when the hatch opened and Corrin walked in.

"General." Auria said.

"We've just received a message from Sharr." Corrin said as he closed the hatch.

"The Tray have fallen back from Netara and Cairon but we still haven't heard anything from Taymen. Sharr is taking some of her ships to Abydos to assist him."

Auria looked over at Talia briefly as she stood up.

"Then I think it's time we checked up on the young General." She said. "General Assh take us to Abydos."

Dark Avenger, C.A.C.
09:35 Abydos Standard Time
Day 6, Third Cycle, Egyptian Year 3202

Taymen braced himself just before four missiles detonated against the outer hull armor.

"Batteries seven through ten switch to suppressive fire." Taymen ordered. "Helm come about. Bring our bow to bear on the Titan."

"All heavy batteries fire at will as soon as the Titan's in range." Titus said.

"Incoming ordnance!" The operations officer shouted.

The deck shuttered for a moment as three more missiles hit the outer armor.

"All forward missile tubes fire a full salvo at the target." Taymen said.

"Sir the Titan is turning. It looks like they're trying to slingshot around one of the moons." Aurin reported.

"Back us off then Aurin." Taymen said.

"Aye Sir." Aurin replied.

Taymen watched as the Titan continued to pull away from them.

"Sir if they get around the moon we'll lose them." Titus said.

"I'm aware of that Titus." Taymen said as he continued to watch the Titan move away.

"Almost there." He whispered.

"That's enough." He said a moment later. "Aurin hard to port all ahead full sling shot us around the other side of the moon." He ordered.

"Aye Sir." Aurin replied.

"All heavy batteries ready to fire on my mark." Taymen continued.

Only a few seconds past before the Avenger made its way around the moon.

"Titan coming into sensor range again Sir." The operations offices said.

Taymen watched as the Titan entered their forward firing arc.

"All heavy batteries to continuous fire!" He snapped. "Ready a salvo of countermeasures to cover us."

A few seconds later a dozen heavy plasma rounds tore into the Titan's outer armor and burned through the hull before she managed to pull up out of the Avenger's firing arcs.

"Sir they've escape our effective arc of fire." Carrey reported.

"Looks like they were ready for that." Titus said.

"All batteries switch to direct fire." Taymen ordered.

"Sir the Titan's powering up her protostream generators." The operations officer reported.

"If they get away it'll all be over." Titus said.

"Damn it." Taymen muttered. "Engines all ahead full bring us right on top of them." He ordered.

"Sir if we get much closer and they stream away we could be pulled into the protostream with them." Aurin said.

"Good." Taymen replied. "All forward missile tubes ready a full salvo of javelins for point blank range." He continued. "Titus prepare all…"

The operations officer cut him off.

"Sir the Titan is streaming."

Taymen checked the display just to see the Titan disappear from sensors an instant before his vision went dark.

Titan, Bridge
11:27 Abydos Standard Time
Day 6, Third Cycle, Egyptian Year 3202

"We've arrived at the rendezvous coordinates Sir." The helmsman reported.

"Hold our position here." Ourik ordered. "We'll rendezvous with the rest of the fleet and bring them back to Abydos to finish off the Egyptians." He said.

"Sir another ship has entered the system with us." The operations officer said.

"Identify." Ourik snapped.

"It's the Dark Avenger Sir." The operations officer replied.

"They must have slipped into the protostream behind us just before it closed." The helmsman said.

"It looks like it's running in stealth mode." The operations officer added. Ourik smirked.

"They probably think we can't detect them." He said smugly. "Well, I think it's time we burst General Orelle's bubble." He continued.

Dark Avenger, C.A.C.
11:40 Abydos Standard Time
Day 6, Third Cycle, Egyptian Year 3202

"It worked Sir. We entered the protostream right behind the Titan." Titus said.

"We're five light seconds off her starboard quarter." The operations officer said.

"All batteries prepare to fire on my mark." Taymen said.

"Radiological alert!" Titus snapped.

"Nuke inbound." The operations officer said.

"Deploy armor!" Taymen snapped. "All batteries to suppressive fire..."

Before he could actually give the order to fire Taymen was thrown from his feet and he hit the deck hard as the ship shuttered.

The lights in C.A.C. flickered as several consoles exploded along with a few of the bulkheads. A fire erupted near the damage control station and Taymen could hear the entire deck shifting as if the ship were being twisted and compressed.

He scrambled to his feet trying to regain his balance. His head was spinning and there was a ringing in his ears that made it difficult for him to concentrate.

"Report." He managed to mutter.

"Direct hit to our aft port section." The operations officer said.

"The armor was only partially deployed." Titus said.

"Helm back us off from the Titan. Launch a salvo of countermeasures to cover us and bring the ship to battle mode." Taymen ordered.

"Damage assessment." Titus said.

"The upper heat exchanger's been completely destroyed, breaches on all decks between frames forty-two and forty-eight and we have fires all over the ship." The damage control officer said.

"Protostream generator is off line and we have limited maneuverability." Aurin added.

"Deploy damage control teams to get the protostream back online." Taymen ordered.

"Sir we're receiving a hail from the Titan." Sairon said.

"Patch them through."

"Taymen I do hope you're still alive." Ourik said over the speakers.

"It'll take more than that to finish me off." Taymen said.

"Good." Ourik replied. *"As you can see my ship's sensors are far more advanced than yours. They've been upgraded with ancient technology that allows me to see your ship even with its enhanced stealth systems."*

Taymen couldn't help but notice that Ourik sounded rather proud of that fact.

"Face it General, you've lost. Your ship is heavily damaged and now you're all alone." Ourik continued.

Taymen was about to speak when more sensor contacts appeared on the screen.

"Oh and it would appear the rest of my fleet has arrived as well." Ourik said.

"Good. I was starting to worry that I'd have to go looking for them." Taymen said before closing the channel.

"Status on the protostream system." He said.

"Damage control teams report it'll be at least twenty minutes." Titus said.

"Tell them they've got ten." Taymen replied.

"Sir we're being hailed again." Sairon said.

"The Titan?" Taymen asked.

"No Sir." Sairon replied. "It's another flagship that just entered the system." She explained.

Taymen glanced to Titus.

"Could buy us some time." Titus said.

"Put them through." Taymen replied.

"General Orelle this is Chancellor Crowell of the Tray empire." A voice started. *"I believe you have something I've been looking for and wish to make you an offer."*

Taymen turned to Titus who simply shrugged.

"Go ahead." Taymen said.

"Surrender the Star's Eye database to us and we'll let you and your crew go free." Crowell said.

Taymen hesitated a moment.

"And what makes you think I have the database?" He said as he reached around the side of the command console for a blank data pad.

"Let's not play this game General we know you have the database onboard your ship." Crowell said.

"Well it's a rather large database Chancellor, was there something specific you'd like me to find for you." Taymen said dividing his attention between Crowell and the message he was writing on the data pad.

"Stop stalling General. Whatever it is you're planning it won't work I know your ship's specifications. I know what kind of payload you are capable of carrying you can't beat us." Crowell said.

"Well Chancellor I'm actually curious to know what it is that would make you so interested in this database that you would travel clear across the universe for it."

Taymen handed the data pad to Titus.

Titus looked at the screen and saw the words *'Ready PSM for armed launch.'*

Titus looked at Taymen who simply nodded.

Titus nodded back and moved to the weapons control station.

"Ready a point singularity missile for an armed launch." He said quietly to the missile officer.

"Sir you know without the protostream we won't be able to escape the blast." Carrey said.

"I know just do it."

"Very well General since you're so curious." Crowell started. *"The database contains information about something the ancients discovered shortly before they were wiped out. A biological weapon of some sort created by a race that predated even the ancients.*

"These 'creatures' as it were flew through space like ships but were artificially created organisms more powerful than anything the ancients had ever seen before."

"I see." Taymen said. "And you want to try and create these weapons to use against the rest of the Tray people?" Taymen asked.

"I was thinking on a much larger scale but the point is I need that information General. Hand it over and you can go free."

Taymen looked over at Aurin who simply shook his head indicating the protostream system still wasn't ready. As he glanced over at the weapons stations Titus nodded indicating the missile was ready for launch.

"What makes you think you can control these creatures Chancellor?" Taymen asked.

"I don't need to control them General I just need to unleash them." Crowell replied.

Taymen sighed.

"Chancellor if you want that database you're going to have to take it from us." He said before closing the channel.

"Sir the stream system is still offline." Aurin reported.

Taymen nodded.

"This ends here." He said quietly. "Launch!"

"Fleet Marshal the Dark Avenger has launched a heavy missile." The operations officer reported.

"What!" Ourik snapped. "They don't have that kind of payload." He said.

"Apparently they do Sir." The weapons officer said.

"Sir transmission from the Chancellor." The communications officer said.

"All ships stream away now!" Crowell ordered.

"Stream system charging Sir." The helmsman said.

"General broadcast from the Dark Avenger." The communications officer said as Taymen's voice suddenly came over the speakers.

"You're ship's not the only one that's been upgraded Fleet Marshal." He said.

Taymen watched as the missile approached its detonation point.

"Sir protostream is still down." Aurin reported.

Taymen sighed.

"This is it then." He said.

"Six seconds to detonation." Carrey reported.

"Sir we have hyper-stream available!" Aurin said.

"Charge the system and take us out!" Taymen snapped.

"Get us out of here!" Ourik snapped.

"Streaming in ten seconds." The helmsman said.

Ourik watched the display as the missile suddenly detonated releasing a massive shockwave that enveloped the entire region tearing apart every ship in its wake.

Sharr stared at the sensor display waiting for anything to show up. They had been in orbit around Abydos for almost an hour now.

Fleet Marshal Phay informed them that the Dark Avenger streamed out after the Titan over four hours ago just before the Starry Venture arrived.

By the time Sharr arrived most of the Tray ships had been destroyed and the few that remained surrendered without much incident when more Egyptian ships entered the system.

"Anything?" Sharr asked.

"Nothing yet Ma'am." The operations officer replied.

"I think we have to assume that if the Avenger made it they'd be back by now." The Ex O said quietly.

Sharr didn't want to think about it. The very idea that the Dark Avenger may have been destroyed made her stomach turn.

"Ma'am we're receiving a transmission from General Assh." The communications officer said.

"Patch him through."

"General Vaye, any word?" Assh asked.

"Nothing yet Sir I was just about to dispatch my prowlers to go look for the Avenger." Sharr replied.

"Negative General." Corrin said.

"But Sir I …" Corrin cut her off.

"I think it's time we cut our losses Sharr." He said softly.

Suddenly something appeared on the sensor display.

"Sensor contact!" The operations officer snapped.

"Stand by Sir." Sharr said as she put the channel on hold.

"A ship has streamed into the system."

Sharr looked up at the screen.

"Identify." She ordered.

A few seconds passed which felt like an eternity to Sharr until she saw a large grin come over the operations officer's face.

"It's the Dark Avenger."

Epilogue

Taymen sat at his desk reading over the new repair schedule for the Dark Avenger.

The damage was extensive after catching part of the blast wave from the point singularity missile, it was a wonder they were able to land the ship when they returned to Abydos.

It had been three weeks since they retook Abydos, Cairon and Netara and there were still some ships from Ourik's fleet scattered throughout the Egyptian territory.

The Avenger was still on Abydos' surface and the Silver Phoenix maintained a high orbit with half the battle group while the rest hunted the remainder of Ourik's fleet with Fleet Marshal Phay's help.

Queen Auria and General Assh worked out of the Defense Force Command building trying to organize the former members of the Defense Force and get them back to their posts. There was a lot of work to be done but Taymen figured his people were up to the challenge.

Suddenly the sound of the door buzzer filled the quiet cabin.

"Come in." Taymen said.

The hatch opened and Sharr walked in.

"Am I disturbing you?" She asked.

"Not at all, come in." Taymen said.

Sharr closed the hatch behind her and took a seat on the couch as Taymen stood up and made his way to the chair next to her.

"What brings you planet side?" He asked.

Sharr sighed.

"I just came from the Command building." She started. "I figured I'd check into the ancient database research and see if they found anything yet."

Taymen nodded.

"Something tells me you didn't find what you were expecting." He said.

"I didn't find anything at all." Sharr replied.

Taymen simply looked at her silently. He had turned the database they salvaged from the Star's Eye over to General Assh who was supposed to pass it on to a research team so they could try and find anything related to what Chancellor Crowell described.

Taymen had checked in a few days ago and was told that they hadn't found anything.

"What do you mean?" Taymen asked.

"When I tried accessing the research files the computer locked me out and when I asked a couple of the researchers they insisted they didn't know anything about it." Sharr explained.

Taymen didn't like these implications. If the researchers were insisting that the database didn't exist it meant they were ordered to cover it up.

As it was now there were only a few people who could override Taymen's and Sharr's orders in this matter.

"Taymen something's going on here. Why would we suddenly be cut out of the loop?"

Taymen thought it over. If someone was trying to cut them out of the loop it was because they found something they didn't want to risk being made public.

"I think we should have another look at that database." Taymen said.

"How?" Sharr asked. "All the records pertaining to it have been sealed."

Taymen smiled.

"Then it's a good thing I kept a copy." He said.

Sharr simply looked at him for a moment.

"Does anyone know?" She asked quietly.

Taymen shook his head.

"I've recently learned that it's better to keep some things to yourself." He said.

Sharr smiled.

"I doubt that General Assh would approve of that." She said.

"General Assh is the one I learned that from." Taymen replied.

Defense Force Command Building, Abydos
16:46 Abydos Standard Time
Day 27, Third Cycle, Egyptian Year 3202

Corrin walked next to Queen Auria through the hall of the Command Building's archive level.

"All information pertaining to the ancient database has been removed from the network." He said.

"And what about the research team?" Auria asked.

"They've all been briefed." Corrin replied.

"Good." Auria said.

"However that still leaves us with Taymen and Sharr." Corrin added.

"I don't think we'll have to worry about them." Auria said. "I doubt they would have given this a second thought with everything that's been going on."

Corrin shook his head.

"I don't know." He said. "Those two can be quite relentless at times. I'd be surprised if they let this go so easily."

"It doesn't matter." Auria said. "There's nothing they can do about it. Besides, as it stands now we are simply researching the ancient knowledge. Surely they won't be able to fault us for that."

Corrin didn't say anything.

They turned the corner and entered one of the data libraries.

"Now how are the preparations for tomorrow night going?" Auria asked.

"Everything's been taken care of." Corrin replied.

"Good." Auria said. "It's about time we held a celebration in honour of our heroes."

Corrin nodded. They had all been so busy trying to get everything into some working order that they hadn't had time to just stop and celebrate. After all, the Tray occupation was over and they had Sharr and Taymen to thank for that. It was about time they were honoured for their heroism.

"What's to become of General Raise?" Corrin asked.

"His hearing is scheduled for two weeks from tomorrow. He'll be found guilty of treason." Auria said coldly.

Corrin sighed.

"Something wrong General?" Auria asked.

"Not at all." Corrin said. "About Taymen and Sharr..."

Auria cut him off.

"You worry too much General." She said.

"I'd simply hate for something to go wrong because we overlooked them." Corrin explained.

"Oh?' Auria asked.

Corrin sighed again.

"If they ever found out about what we were trying to do they would never forgive us."

"That's why they won't find out." Auria said.

"I hope you're right." Corrin said. "Those two alone could plunge us into another civil war."

Raise heard the distinct sound of the cell block door opening followed by the sound of footsteps making their way towards his cell. A moment of silence passed before the dull thud of the door unlocking echoed in the cell and the door opened.

There, standing amongst the flood of white light was a figure Raise knew all too well.

"Well General Orelle." Raise said. "To what do I owe this visit?" He asked smugly.

Taymen took a few paces into the cell.

"Come to gloat have we?" Raise asked.

"Not really." Taymen started.

"Then what?"

"Something's been bothering me and I thought maybe you could shed some light on the situation." Taymen said.

Raise sat staring at Taymen for a moment. Something about him seemed different all of a sudden. It was as if his eyes were suddenly opened and he was no longer ignorant of the things happening around him.

"Well I'll do what I can." Raise said. "On one condition."

Taymen saw that coming. He figured he already knew what the condition was.

"I'll tell you what I know if you agree to get me out of here." Raise said.

Taymen sighed as he held up a small data pad.

"What's that?" Raise asked.

"A full pardon and an order of exile from Queen Auria." Taymen explained. "She's willing to drop the charges of treason against you and settle for your banishment from all Egyptian colonies in exchange for your help."

Raise sat silent for a moment thinking it over.

Taymen figured that exile would be preferable to execution but he never did understand Raise's way of thinking.

"Very well." Raise said. "What is it you want to know?" He asked.

"First of all how much did you know about the Tray before the attack?" Taymen asked.

"I didn't know anymore than the rest of the council." Raise replied.

"Then why did the council keep the information about the Tray from us, and what else are they keeping?"

Raise hesitated a moment. Something didn't make sense to him. Assh was on the council and he knew everything Raise knew. Why would Auria or Taymen need that information, unless it wasn't Auria asking the questions.

Raise finally sighed.

"We knew all about the Star's Eye and the information left behind by the ancients." He started. "We knew that there was a lot more to what we were seeing here on Abydos we just didn't know what until you found the Star's Eye."

"And now?" Taymen asked.

"When you handed the database over to Corrin we looked it over briefly before I was finally arrested." Raise continued. "The ancients weren't losing the war to the Tray. They were losing because they were fighting a war on two fronts against two different enemies."

Taymen listened intently.

"The Tray were no match for the ancients. The only advantage they had was their numbers but the ancients had their hands full with something else."

"Something else?" Taymen asked.

"We still don't know where they came from or what they really were. The ancients described them as biological entities more powerful than any battleship they ever created and they were beating the ancients at every turn until finally there were only a handful of ships left."

This was starting to sound somewhat familiar to Taymen.

"All we know is that the ancients sealed these creatures in the hyperstream cutting them off from our galaxy."

"Why didn't you say anything before?" Taymen asked.

Raise shrugged.

"I didn't think it mattered at this point." He said. "You had already used the hyperstream and broken the ancient's seal. The odds of these creatures still being in existence now are remote at best."

"And if they do exist and they come back?" Taymen asked.

Raise didn't say anything.

Taymen turned and left the cell again.

"That pardon." Raise started. "It isn't legal is it?" He asked.

Taymen sighed.

"Who's to say what's legal and what's not right now." He said before walking away leaving the cell open.

Raise slowly made his way out of the cell looking around for any sign of the guards. He crept out of the cell block to the main corridor where he noticed the guard unconscious on the floor. Raise looked around briefly before taking off down the corridor to the door that led him out of the building and into the compound where there were two prowlers waiting.

As he looked closer he could see Taymen climbing onto one prowler.

Taymen looked back at Raise for a moment with a cold expression before glancing over to the second prowler. Raise looked at the second prowler then back to Taymen who simply nodded once before climbing aboard and closing the hatch.

Raise darted for the second prowler and climbed aboard sealing the hatch behind him. He looked briefly out the window at Taymen's prowler as it slowly lifted off of the ground.

'Thank-you Taymen.' He thought to himself.

Defense Force Command Complex, Abydos
20:35 Abydos Standard Time
Day 28, Third Cycle, Egyptian Year 3202

Sharr led Taymen through the halls of the Command building as they made their way to the main courtyard. She practically had to drag him off of the Dark Avenger to get him to go to the celebration, even though General Assh had practically ordered them both to attend.

"So I guess you've heard about General Raise." Taymen said.

Sharr nodded.

"Still don't see how he could have escaped so easily?" She asked sarcastically.

Taymen smiled.

"The report said the guard was hit with a tranquilizer round. He didn't see who fired it." He said.

"Did you find out anything?" Sharr asked.

"Only that we should keep a close eye on our superiors." Taymen replied.

"What do you think they're up to?" Sharr asked.

"I have no idea, but it would seem that we underestimated what they're capable of." Taymen explained.

Sharr sighed.

"This isn't over is it?" She asked.

"Not by a long shot." Taymen replied as he opened the door leading to the courtyard where everyone was gathered.

There must have been a few thousand people gathered for the Queen's celebration including the entire crew of the Dark Avenger.

As they made their way into the crowd Sharr immediately noticed Queen Auria and General Assh moving towards them.

"Here comes trouble." She said quietly to Taymen who didn't say anything.

"Well I'm glad to see you both here." Assh said.

"Didn't really leave us much choice Sir." Taymen replied.

Auria giggled a little.

"Well I have to admit I never thought I'd stand on Abydos again." Assh said.

"Yes, we have you both to thank for that." Auria added.

Taymen shook his head.

"The crews of those ships are the real heroes here." He said.

"Yes and they will all be recognized for their heroism."

"So how's the research of the ancient database coming along?" Sharr asked.

Assh looked at Auria who remained silent.

"Slowly." Assh finally said. "I'm afraid a good portion of the information was corrupted and our researches were unable to reconstruct it."

Taymen nodded.

"Maybe it's for the better." He said. "Some things are better left undiscovered."

"Perhaps." Assh said.

Taymen remained silent as he looked at both Assh and Auria with cold eyes. Assh could see something in Taymen he hadn't seen before, something that scared him.

"Well." Auria finally said. "If you'll excuse us."

"Of course." Taymen said as he and Sharr moved aside to let them pass.

After they were a few meters away Sharr turned to Taymen.

"What do you think?" She asked.

Taymen shook his head.

"Well we know they're lying." He said.

Sharr sighed.

"Time to save the Empire again." She said as she turned to see General Assh glance back at them briefly.

Corrin smiled slightly at Sharr before focusing his attention back in front of him. He continued to walk silently through the crowd next to Auria, his eyes remained fixed on the ground in front of him.

"What is it General?" Auria asked.

"He knows."